Conflicts of Interest

Susan Staneslow Olesen

To MJF
With grateful thanks for
creating the avalanche

Also by Susan Olesen

Kerasi Caste System under Emperor Nághtas

Caste controls Kerasím: it dictates who you touch, where you live, who you marry, your employment, who can do what to you. The higher your caste, the more power you have. It is hereditary and does not change, though on rare occasion a high court may move someone upward one level for a political purpose. The Emperor can also grant "privilege" above a caste, granting the male many of the rights of that caste without becoming it.

Thósikh – The Emperor, his wives, and his eldest son only.

Bhísroti – includes all other relatives of the Emperor.

Fáhganid – traditionally in charge of military and civilian justice.

Dáhneg – lowest of the upper castes.

Díhnarwharl – "Honorable *Nhásarwharl*" Sometimes considered lowest upper caste, but officially the highest of the middle castes.

Nhásarwharl – once the top middle caste, they often bully the lower castes.

Whátaral – the average common citizen and largest caste; lowest acceptable caste for *aghát.*

Rhibáni – Lowest acceptable caste for *bhantim* (brownshirt) officers in the military. Lowest of the middle castes.

Tághinet – "The casteless caste," equally sought after by all other castes: artists, actors, librarians, musicians, entertainers, writers, nurses.

Tápahtin – Highest of the lower castes.

Soláhrin – In ancient times, the caste of slaves.

Ghinadín – originally the slaves of slaves, used and abused by all other classes.

Union Delegation Sent to the Kerasi Accord

Against diplomatic relations
In favor of diplomatic relations
Presently undecided

Ori Kel, (m) Centauri; Union Secretary of State
Wodu Mosi (m), Earth, Commissioner for Non-Union Populations
Vanora Aikerman (f), Earth; Union Security Council, emerita.
Hawet Quin (f), Noor, Union Ambassador at Large
Vee M'para (f), Ashaan; Council for Union Women
Chedna Kerek (f) Mensara, Union Council on Education
Raju (m), Morpu; representative at large
Marisi Belenn,(m) Cygni, Union Council on Economic Affairs
Davion Foote (m), Alshain; Union Space Fleet, Alpha Sector
Aila Perrin (f); Earth; Union Council for Kerasi Affairs
Altair Huum (m), Arcturus, Commissioner for Galactic Science
G'ong fay Lep (m) Mensara, Union Council on Health, Medicine, and Welfare
N'ua (f) Demu El; Council for Non-Union Populations
Reqi Posht (m) Kye; Planetary Prime Minister
Melli Vergara (f) Mars, Commission on Space Exploration
De'a Moann (f) Koos; Planetary Prime Minister
Kuu Taam Fi Aal (f) Capella, Galactic Commission on Justice
Yoma Calti (f) Fornax; Planetary Prime Minister
Vis Na Wa Din (m); Naborine; Union Council on Kerasi Affairs
John St. John (m); Earth, Council at Large
Li Shissi (m); Mensara, Council at Large
Tandi-Ba Loor (f) Capella, Council at Large
Halden Kane (m), Centauri, Council at Large
Kuana Raveset (f) Vega; Council at Large

One

No matter how ultra-lightspeed or expensive the technology, the ridiculous distances between solar systems always resulted in some type of pause while messages were sent, then responded to. One was never quite sure if there would be a response. The signal might have been lost in either direction, or the other person may have clicked End. Satellites and relays could be taken out by even low-velocity space debris. Depending on the distance and the level of equipment, the pause could be almost imperceptible or as long as a minute or more each way, leaving the speakers in a permanent sort of limbo. By the time the speaker sent out a question or comment, the next reply they received was not to the last question but the one before it, always a statement behind. When the message was considered to be in the utmost secrecy, on privately funded alien equipment, it made waiting for the response twice as intolerable. This pause wasn't nearly as long as it should have been for the distance; the signal had to be coming from somewhere inside Union space. Risky, but no longer so illegal.

Patience came naturally to Mr. Friend. He was a man of importance, and he'd fought long and hard to get where he was. He liked politics when politics were easy. Listening to complaints and patting people on the back, making them feel good about themselves, their worlds, their place in the universe, had a certain kind of joy to it. People were grateful to be remembered. Thirty-five worlds had agreed to a common set of values despite the huge disparities in races, beliefs, wealth, and technologies. Every so many years a new world on the fringes of space or a colony demanding emancipation would apply to become a new member. Sometimes one was accepted, sometimes it wasn't. Everything hinged on whether or not they could accept the common set of values.

Never had Mr. Friend been so dead-set against a world joining up with his.

1

He'd been briefed on the proposals, sat in meetings upon meetings upon meetings, listened to their delegates speak for weeks. He'd met with their envoys, a handful of men surgically altered to appear less threatening, looking and speaking and dressing with the same precision as clones. They were nice enough men, unfailingly polite and attentive and patient, but it didn't change Mr. Friend's opinion. It couldn't erase the fact their homeworld was built on a core of violence, a rigid caste system where rape and murder were legal, where women had no more rights than draft animals, where the military was the arm of the government that controlled the information, technology, and justice of an entire world ruled by a single man whose leadership had been passed down father to son within the current dynasty for more than 1500 years without a single break.

For a hundred years the governments had kept to themselves, agreeing that they would never agree, and that staying away from each other was in both of their best interests. Four years ago their treaties were blown to hell when both sides realized the other had developed an ability to travel through time – and the unknown potential of annihilating each other – and an immediate moratorium was called until new treaties could be written, information shared, new scientific understandings forged. In the process came the push to open the path for an alliance, if the planet was willing to make the changes necessary to bring their values into the common line. Emperor Nághtas was willing to do that.

And Mr. Friend just couldn't allow it.

Thankfully, he wasn't the only one.

He sat in the most spartan of office spaces, a bare-walled industrial cubby rented by a sympathizer, in a cluster of rented cubbies. It contained exactly three items: a desk, a chair, and the transmitter/receiver that was hidden away inside the desk when not in use. The cubby had no windows, not even on the door.

"How many?" said the voice on the speaker. Both sides had agreed to voice feed only, no visuals. Safer that way. The sound was staticky, with a lot of 'space wind' whistling through the feed.

"Twenty-four invitations have been sent. Six will be separatists who must be given immunity to all action. I will send those files the morning they depart. Of the remainder, there are three who must be considered prime targets. They must not return."

2

The voice on the speaker was thickly accented but understandable. There was little doubt it was the voice of a translator; the elite in any culture didn't bother doing things for themselves. They hired others to do it. Few people on either side of the speaker spoke the other's language; both were still learning basic words, let alone nuances. Mr. Friend himself knew no more than perhaps five words of Mr. Red's native tongue. "And the *fiveteen* remaining?"

"That is your choice. There is collateral damage in every conflict, Mr. Red."

"Please explain *'kholatterahl dahmij.'* Please make words small."

"Deaths, Mr. Red. There are accidental victims in every conflict. Their life or death is your decision, but I suggest leaving some survivors to tell a story of fear."

"Ten?"

"That will be enough. Wait!" Mr. Friend realized a way to up the stakes in his favor just a little more. Dead people faded away into memories in data bases or statues people forgot about. Wounded people, however, could be rolled out year after year, ripping sympathy out of the populace over and over each time. Every cause needed a martyr. "There is a young female delegate with much sympathy inside the Union. She is a loud supporter of the Emperor. I would like an example made of her."

"Ex ample?"

"Give her to your men for an hour or so. That is what the Union fears most. Damaged is expected, but I need her returned alive, to prove my opinion. There could be a problem, however."

"Problem?"

"She has friends of your kind. It is possible they will be with her. Those of your kind that wear blue."

There was a longer pause. *"Aghát?"*

"Yes."

This pause was long. Mr. Friend was certain it was due to private conversation, but worried the word 'problem' might cause the transmission to be ended. Mr. Red was of a type that put the fuss in fussy.

"That will change the price. *Aghát* swear to the Emperor. They do not break honor; it is too dangerous to try. *Aghát* have military strength behind them. That will require extra support."

3

"How much support?"

"Five million interstellar."

"Hah!" It wasn't professional, but Friend's supporters had paid out enough to fund the economic power of a small country. More was an insult. "I can access two million more, paid after events are concluded, if and only if the other conditions are met. That should be far more than you need."

Pause.

"That is agreed."

"Excellent. I will contact you again before I leave. Friend out."

Two

Aila Perrin slipped the special-delivery envelope under her shirt and snuck down the hall to her room, locking the door. She took it out again and removed the paper from inside, reading it over and over, her smile widening farther each time until it consumed her face.

Mom's going to mess herself.

At eighteen, she was currently in limbo; her diploma just a month old, she hadn't begun any university-level courses yet, and she'd just begun her fourth year working for the galactic government. When she became adult, she'd been allowed to drop the *Special Assistant to* from her title, and became a full member of the Planetary Union Council on Kerasi Affairs. Being the youngest member by fifteen years was no spacewalk, but the government couldn't exclude her. Youth aside, she had more experience and more understanding of the violent Kerasi race than anyone else, and almost no one in the Union could speak Emperor's Tongue better than she could. It wasn't that Aila was anything special when it came to ambition or study; she'd never cared much for school at all. Five years before, in an attempt to force open a dialogue with the Union, the Kerasi Emperor had ordered eleven Union citizens kidnapped and held for "educational purposes," and she'd been caught in their net by mistake. Aila was the only one to survive more or less unscathed, spending more than a year under the control and tutelage of five Kerasi diplomats and their General. It wasn't until her rescue – and the incarceration of her captors – that Aila truly understood what the point of her kidnapping was about, saw how the isolationist tactics of her own people were hurting so many – especially women – on Kerasím. She fought hard to get the Union to listen to Kerasím's demands, got the governments to start talking to each other, and now, after four years' work educating the two cultures about each other, things were actually coming together.

The paper in her hand was a dream come true.

She clicked her viewscreen on, turned the volume low, and sent a live feed to the Union Embassy on Calenna, where her former *aghát* mentor was teaching classes in Kerasi language and protocol to politicians and military officers. "I'm sorry to bother you off schedule," Aila said. "Can you talk, or do you want to call me back when you're free?"

Masákh's face didn't change, but Aila swore it softened just a bit when he saw the speaker. The tightness around his mouth eased, and his eyes seemed to brighten. Masákh was full-blooded Kerasi, a former grand enemy of the planetary Union, and one of her former captors. He'd been subject to extensive cosmetic surgery on his homeworld to make him more familiar-looking to humans, cutting back the heavy Kerasi brow-bone, creating two eyebrows from the infamous characteristic unibrow, and bleaching his skin from copper to an almost human yellow-tan. His traditional hank of chin hairs, the symbol of virility and manhood across Kerasím, was trimmed back into a tight goatee, mimicking Human chins. Aila was never sure if his lack of expression was his own personal stoicism or a result of all that surgery. All *aghát* diplomats underwent such surgery, but some *aghát* were certainly more expressive than others.

"I am at my meal break. I can speak now. I will move somewhere more private." The scenery in the background of his com unit changed as he walked. "What did you wish to discuss?"

Aila glanced sideways at the camera pickup with an impish sparkle in her eye. Her eyes were hazel, a lighter shade of brown than most Kerasi. Blue eyes confounded the hell out of them; they weren't used to the color, didn't know how to read them. "Know that conference we were talking about last time?" She held the formal-looking paper before the camera. "Guess who got an invitation! I'm going to Kerasím!"

Masákh's dark eyes narrowed. "Aila, I do not recommend you accept."

"Why? I get to meet the Emperor! You've never even done that! Am I not the Emperor's brainchild? Am I not the one person in the entire galaxy who was able to open peaceful relations between our two worlds? Do I not still sit on the Union Council for Kerasi Affairs? Who the hell better to send? Do you know what this will do to my résumé?"

He frowned, the black eyebrows trying to crawl back together where they belonged. "It has never been attempted. It is better to wait and observe how the first meeting is handled. Then you will have information to make the second meeting more productive."

"That's a really lame excuse. History loves the second time around."

His mouth pinched as if he wanted to say something but for some reason wasn't supposed to. Kerasi – at least every one Aila had ever met – gave information by the teaspoon. Every thought, every fact was examined on all sides, turned inside out, held up to the light, and probably tasted to make sure no more information was given than necessary, lest one be held accountable for giving away too much.

"I will say it direct. I do not like the idea of you going to Kerasím. It is not safe for you there."

"You're not being overprotective of me like my mother, are you? Or are you jealous?"

Masákh sighed. "Did you ever consider why you were held on Kye and not Kerasím? There is more involved than that. The delegates will most likely be housed at the palace. You would be under the Emperor's guard. Your movements would be limited but you would be safe from most random violence. You debate the political question in your Union whether to increase open relations with Kerasím or to keep us separated. The same debate goes on in the councils on Kerasím, but our politics are not as democratic as yours. The Emperor makes all laws; that is indisputable. His is the final word. But his council is made up strictly of the *bhísroti* and *fáhganid* castes, feeding him information as they see fit. There is no democracy to it; less than one percent of the population has any say at all in government. There are those that see economic opportunity in trading with the Union. They favor increased relations as a gateway to even more wealth. But there is just as vocal a contingent who stand to lose wealth from the move. They present a danger."

"How can they be a danger? You just said combined they represent less than one percent of the population. You're talking a handful of people spread out over an entire planet."

"I am speaking of regional presidents, governors, leaders of industry, heads of the branches of the military – what you would call a presidential cabinet – those who control every aspect of Kerasi economy and law. The *bhísroti* control the *fáhganids*, and the *fáhganids* control the military, including what you call law enforcement. The *fáhganids* carry out the orders of the *bhísroti*. If the *bhísroti* think there is too much support for reforms that may hurt them, they will order the *fáhganids* to raze the offending towns, and it will be done. Worse, if the Emperor feels too many *bhísroti* are not supporting him, he may demote them, possibly even execute them. You do not wish to be caught in the middle of Emperor Nághtas cleansing his council. It has happened before."

"It wouldn't be my first choice." Aila turned her head to give him the coy sideways look once more. "Masákh? If I file a request and get you freed from your instructional duties, would you come with me as my bodyguard? You're a trained Kerasi diplomat. You've been my teacher of all things Kerasi for the last five years. You'll be able to point things out to me that I would miss. You taught me to speak Kerasi better than almost anyone in the Union – Ross Halian's the only one that probably even comes close – but I would do better with you as my translator. Please? I would feel much safer if you were there with me. You know my mother's going to have a total freakout when I tell her. Maybe if she knows you're there to watch my back, she won't go as crazy."

Masákh looked away from his interface, but not before the flicker of disgust could be seen. "To speak politely, your mother does not approve of me. Telling her of my presence may be exactly what makes her 'go crazy.'"

"Well, there is that whole kidnapping thing there. I got over it, but she hasn't. You kept me safe then; I trust you to keep me safe now. Please, accompany me?"

"I will request leave immediately," he agreed. "I am certain General Tokh will agree. I can learn particulars you will not have access to. I forbid you to go without me. You know of Kerasím, but you do not know Kerasím. You will need my experience."

Aila broke into a huge grin. "I knew you'd see my way."

Three

Aila knew exactly where her stubbornness came from. Her bravery she chalked up right or wrong to her father, but no matter where you knew her from, Leila Perrin was a woman who would not be ignored. As an idealistic young lawyer, she made strong cases and argued to the last contingency. As a background lawyer for the galactic government, she was used to researching laws and motions and precedents, making sure all loopholes were closed before presenting her information. As the wife of a retired spacefleet Admiral whose last ten years of service were spent mostly in space, she made damned sure that her husband never forgot just who he was married to, the children he was missing, and where his ass belonged. When her daughter was kidnapped by Kerasi nationals during a visit to the Union embassy on Fornax, Leila Perrin called the President's office daily for more than two months, demanding to know what progress had been made. When the President assigned a special investigator, Leila's calls dropped to once a week, but she never let up, not once, some weeks more polite, some weeks rude and desperate. When, after eleven months, Aila managed to escape long enough to send them a message and give her location, Leila went right back to daily calls. And when her daughter was returned to her, mostly unharmed, Leila never, ever, backed down on her hatred and distrust of the Kerasi, no matter what praise her daughter gave them, no matter how much her husband came to support them, no matter how polite and respectful they were when they addressed her. Kerasi were, and always would be, evil incarnate in Leila's playbook, and no amount of evidence to the contrary could persuade her. Leila would never, ever, let them harm her daughter again, not while she had breath to fight with.

Aila hadn't forgotten all the tears she herself shed during her kidnapping, the fear and pain and longing for home, and she understood how hard it must have been for her parents, wishing the same. She just wished sometimes her mother would run out of breath once in a while.

"Absolutely not. I forbid it! Fourteen months! Fourteen months those bastards held you prisoner, fourteen months of your life stolen from you, or have you forgotten that? You go there and no one will find you alive, ever! You know what they do to women!" Leila Perrin all but frothed at the mouth. She tried ripping the invitation from Aila's hand, but Aila was too quick.

"Motherrrrrrr." Aila waited until she had eye-contact. Her words were deliberate and over-enunciated, trying to force rational thought into a woman who'd become so overprotective she stood outside the door while Aila showered. Aila hadn't had much choice when she was younger, but she was an adult now, and her mother couldn't force her to do anything anymore.

"That was four years ago. It's a different world now. We've had open negotiations with the Kerasi for three years. They are no longer mysterious hostile strangers. I have been serving on the Council for Kerasi Affairs for *four years*. Ross Halian's been to Kerasím half a dozen times – he's come back without incident *every single time*. He's over there right now, making sure things are safe. We have treaties now, we have protocols now, we have honest to goodness *progress* coming out of this. I played a historic role in that progress! It's only fitting that I be invited on the first official diplomatic mission to Kerasím. I would be insulted if I wasn't. Masákh said…"

"How did he say anything when I've asked you repeatedly NOT to speak to him? It's not right the way he stays in contact with you, Aila! Victims do not stay in touch with the people who kidnapped them. I thought they got that through to you in all those therapy sessions? Maybe you should go back. If I find his number on our comm system, I will have it blocked."

Aila rolled her eyes. The argument never ended. Any word that didn't implicate the entire Kerasi race as spawn of evil meant that Aila was permanently damaged by her ordeal and made her sanity questionable, but only to Leila. Her mother working for the State Department didn't help, either – every outrage wound up with a legal threat attached to it. Even Aila's brother Ramie was on her side. At fifteen, he felt every one of his mother's limitations worse than Aila, so much so he threatened to have his father sign him up for a military school, just to get away.

"*He did not kidnap me!* He was only my liaison! I will *never* go back to that therapy nonsense, Mother. I got over my kidnapping. I saw the bigger picture. I know my kidnappers were not nice people and they were murderous and treacherous and dangerous men, but they weren't to *me*. They were gentle and honorable and stuck to their promises, Masákh above everyone else. All the times he could have hurt me – all the times he probably *wanted* to hit me – he never did. Not once. He was my teacher, and still is my teacher. Whenever I have questions, I call him and he tells me what I want to know. That's all, Mom. There's no secret mental conspiracy agenda like you've convinced yourself of. We are *strictly colleagues*. With very boring technical conversations. Do you want to listen in on one?"

Leila glared hard. She'd married late in life, had children late in life. At fifty-five, she could easily pass for ten years less than her age, but fury brought out the worst tones and angles on her face. "I don't care what specie he is or what planet he's from, there's only one thing a man that age wants out of a young girl, but you're determined not to see it until it's too late."

Aila twisted her face into a mocking oily smile in perfect imitation of Masákh. "Even if he did, I am eighteen, a perfect legal adult in both the Union and on Kerasím, and that would be my business, not yours. And let's not speak of how old he is, Mother – let's remember you're still old enough to be his mother, too."

The barb hurt. Leila's breath caught. Her mouth clamped shut, her face turned red, and she looked about to cry. For a second Aila felt bad for saying it. But only for a second.

She waved the page in the air, out of reach. "This is galactic history in the making, Mother. I am going to Kerasím as part of the first major diplomatic group to visit. I am going to meet Emperor Nághtas himself, which I've wanted to do for years. Not even General Tokh had that privilege. And Masákh is going to accompany me as translator and bodyguard whether you approve or not, because of any Kerasi outside of maybe General Tokh, I trust him to get me back out in one piece."

Leila Perrin's face went from red to an exceptional shade of merlot. Her eyes gave off a murderous glare of their own. "We'll just see about that. I'm sure your father knows someone who can get you pulled off that list, so I wouldn't get my suitcase ready just yet, young lady."

Aila stormed off to her room. She slid the invitation deep under her mattress, just in case Mom came looking for it. It didn't matter; her name was on the roster, that's what counted, but it was a beautiful, formal-looking invitation, and certainly something Aila wanted to save for a scrapbook. Hell, at this rate, she'd have a better resume by twenty-one than half the old folks who'd been in politics for thirty years! Not that she'd recommend kidnapping as the way to start a career, but it sure gave her a lot of experience with top-secret information rather quickly.

She sat at her desk and activated her comm, calling up Thayer. Thayer had been fifteen when she was inadvertently brought forward through time with Aila while trying to escape a Kerasi fighter ship. Thayer was never supposed to be aboard the Union ship and they couldn't take her back; she was trapped in the future just as Aila had been trapped in the past, but Aila had always had hope she would go home. Thayer never could.

Thayer's homelife had been tempestuous. She was everything Aila wasn't: streetwise, aggressive, sarcastic, and antisocial. Shoplifting, cigarettes, and alcohol had been only a few of Thayer's vices by the time she'd come to live with Aila. Thayer tried. She really did try to toe Leila Perrin's lines, but the last thing Thayer wanted was someone else telling her what to do. She no longer had parental controls and no social services system telling her what to do. While Leila was tearing her hair out trying to settle Aila back in, Thayer used the distraction to stay out late and get into trouble. Aila's tantrums with her mother were downright civil to those of Leila and Thayer, and as soon as Thayer was old enough, the Perrins sent Thayer back to Earth to attend a university while Aila was still a captive in her parents' apartment on Centauri Major, where her dad, Fleet Admiral Ramden Perrin, held a position on the Galactic Defense Council. Aila and Thayer's friendship had waned over the last three years, but Aila still considered Thayer her best friend, and Thayer considered Aila a socially inhibited and slightly misdirected younger sister.

"Hey," Thayer said on the screen.

"Hey."

"You look pissy. Your mom on you again?"

"When isn't she? Actually, I'm really really excited. I got an invitation to participate in the first diplomatic mission to Kerasím. Is that not the most awesome thing ever? We get a week's tour of the major sights, a meeting with the Emperor and his council, and a formal banquet! Can you believe it? And I have a guest pass, I have a guest pass!" Aila sang and bounced in her seat.

"That is so totally fuckin' awesome!" Thayer said. "And your mom had a fit about it, I guarantee. Weren't you afraid of ever goin' to Kerasím? I thought you said even that General you knew wouldn't have been able to keep you from being killed if you ever went there."

"That was back then. Things are much friendlier now. I talked to Masákh; he says the offer is completely honest. This is Emperor Naghtas's first major effort to show good will about the reforms he plans on implementing."

"Ha! Does your mother know you talked to him? Is that why she's pissed?"

Aila choked and rolled her eyes, Thayer's favorite behavior. "It didn't help matters. Of course, she only thinks I talked to him once; I didn't tell her I talked to him seven times in the last month. He's got Monday nights off. He makes me converse in Kerasi to stay in practice. I think he just likes correcting me, like always. He sent me a little book of Kerasi mythology. I think it might have been his. It smells like him."

"Every week, huh?" Thayer teased. "Sounds like more than just casual conversation to me. Gifts and all."

"You're the one that's been through three major boyfriends in the past year," Aila said dryly. "Kind of hard to date anyone, Kerasi or Human, with my mother sitting between us. If it was the least bit romantic, I wouldn't be speaking in Kerasi. He has this thing about perfection; he was my teacher and the more correct everything he can get into me, the better he thinks it will reflect on him, especially if I get to Kerasím, even though he's not technically my teacher anymore. He worked really hard to get where he is; he thinks everyone should work just as hard. He works too hard at everything."

"So how are you goin' to get your mother to let you go?"

"Wait until my dad gets home and show it to him. I'll ask him to find out all the specifics on our side, make sure security is adequate, he'll think I'm being really responsible and smart, so he'll agree, and in the end he'll win my mom over. You'll see. It's the fact I told her Masákh was going with me to be my bodyguard that was the final straw, I think."

Thayer squealed. "Ooohoo! All alone, no parents – yeah, guardin' isn't what he's gonna be doin' to your body. Nice move, Toots! You're finally growin' up. About time."

Aila made a sour face. "Yeah, I'm going to be rolling someone with all those diplomats around me, most of whom know my parents and will no doubt be reporting to them every hour exactly what I'm doing, including photos. I don't know what the sleeping arrangements are going to be; I'll probably get paired with the highest, bitchiest diplomat going to make sure I behave. I'll bet half the people on the list are there just for recon."

"Yeah, yeah, so you say. You better tell me every single sordid detail. And if there really aren't any, make somethin' up so I'll wish I'd gone with you."

"Sure. There's always one dumb diplomat that gets drunker than a monkey and starts dancing naked on a table somewhere. And no, not me."

Thayer frowned, incredulous. To Thayer, Aila was someone incredibly famous, someone whose name showed up in news columns, someone who sometimes brought Thayer to banquets and gatherings with the government-elect, a fact Thayer still marveled over years later. All those events were foreign and frightening and stuffy to Thayer; to think that uppity people like ambassadors could get caught in bad public behavior made them seem no better than herself. In Thayer's eyes, uppity people *needed* to be taken down to normal size. "Seriously? Why didn't you ever tell me that before?"

"Because I was underage and not allowed in the bars, that's why. I only heard about things by accident. You still stuck on those astrography assignments? Maybe I could have Masákh explain the problems to you. Then he could shake his head at you and call you 'stupid female' as well. Since those words seem to be soooo romantic in your imagination." Aila crossed her hands over her heart, tossed her head back, and rolled her eyes again. She giggled. Kerasi were the least romantic creatures in the universe. *You, female, come here, remove your clothing or I will beat you* didn't come close.

"Hmph. We didn't have astrography back in my time. We'd barely made it to the moon. I'll pass. I got one professor bangin' their head, I don't need two of'm mad at me. Lemme know what happens."

"Will do."

Aila had three weeks to get everything ready, which amounted to three weeks of listening to a constant barrage of misgivings from her parents, and trying to find clothing that would be appropriate not only for streetwear but for meeting an Emperor. She sent dozens of photos of outfits to Masákh for approval, changing things around as he thought fit. There were identification documents that needed to be filed, medical certificates to be signed, new inoculations, and several dozen forms that had to be read and signed and registered for the State Department. The only document she didn't like filling out was the one in case of death or disability. Yes, it was standard for any state-sponsored activity, but Aila was eighteen; death and disability were at least seventy years away. As fast as she could, she signed off that her parents were to be notified and could take care of any arrangements. Picking out funerary details was not something she was wasting a minute of her time on at this point in her life. Aila knew the Emperor's plans. Killing her wasn't among them.

Leila Perrin tried. The night before Aila left she had a small dinner party for their closest friends, allegedly to see Aila off. Aila knew better; it was her mother's way of saying, "You're going to die, so please say goodbye to everyone." Aila knew she'd figured out the truth when Leila burst into tears while cutting the dessert and had to leave the room. Ramden Perrin said nothing, but Aila caught his eyes accusing her.

See what you're doing to your mother?

I'm going, she mouthed at him.

The argument resumed the next day on the way to the spaceport, and Aila's patience wore thin. Galactic travel was a pain in the ass. Yes, a fast ship could do hyperspeed, but it still took days to get anywhere, and then you had to wait to dock. Saying goodbye on Centauri wasn't good enough; her parents were seeing her all the way to Lacaille Space Station, where the Union cruiser *Solar Breeze* was docked waiting for the voyage to Kerasím. The commuter flight meant thirty-eight extra hours of listening to arguments, with nowhere to escape.

"Please, Aila. There are twenty-three other delegates, most of them seasoned members of various councils," Leila said. "No one's denying you've done your part for Union-Kerasi relations, and you're only eighteen. Give someone else a shot at it. I swear, if it goes well and they make a second accord, I will let you go without making a sound. Just please, not this time."

"Mom, what difference does it make if I'm eighteen, twenty-eight, or forty-eight? I'd be doing the exact same thing, and the risks would be exactly the same. How can you support me going into politics like this if you're going to freak out every time I leave the house? I'm sorry I was kidnapped; I know that was my stupidity for being where I wasn't supposed to be, but I'm not going into this blind. I know what I'm doing and I have excellent support people around me to steer me straight if I get off track. How the hell did you ever deal with Dad away on missions for months at a time if me going away for just ten days is giving you a nervous breakdown? Did you think I was never going to leave home?"

"Maybe it's because of all his time away!" Leila snapped viciously. "Maybe I know what dangers lurk in space, more than you ever thought of! Maybe I don't like being so damned far away!"

"Easy, easy, Leila." Ramden pulled her into a hard embrace. "I've been home more than six years; that's not a concern anymore. Aila will be fine. I know exactly which ships are being deployed into that sector. There are two heavy armors staying with the ship all the way to orbit. I know the commanders, I know the crews, I know their records, I spoke with Secretary Kel. I couldn't keep her safer myself. At this point I think we need to be positive, wish Aila luck on her first formal mission, and hope it's the kickoff to a wonderful career. She's in good hands."

Aila hugged him from the other side. "Thank you, Daddy. I'll be fine. I promise."

Ramden put an arm around her and pulled her in tight. "I trust you more than I trust the others to know what's right and what's wrong. You understand the language, you understand how they think; you'll hear what they don't want you to know. You get one hint of something wrong, one bad feeling, you blast me a message and I'll have half the sector in there to pull you out. They're going to have a small fleet waiting near Fornax, just in case. You got that?"

Aila gave him her best smile. "I know you will, Daddy. I'm counting on it."

Four

Nadigh drove the open transport cart across the grounds; his father could not walk such a distance, at least not where the public could see him so slow and breathless. An Emperor needed to be invincible in the eyes of the people or they would lose faith, despite his age, despite his infirmaries, despite his immense girth, an affliction all too common among the older emperors. Nadigh was already fifty-six, and although he was no longer as toned as a foot soldier, he made sure his strength and fitness were still something to be reckoned with. Should anyone doubt his father they would know who waited in his shadow, and think twice.

He sped them across the huge lawns to a secluded fountain by a tall gold-leafed *gahlmaar* hedge, where the splashing water made a background noise that made hearing on spy equipment difficult. A quick scan of the area with the field identifier on Nadigh's handcom revealed no signs of hidden electronic surveillance. They could speak freely; a rare treat. His father climbed off the cart on his own and they sat on a polished stone bench near the fountain. The day was overcast, rolling gray clouds covering the sky with occasional breaks. Nadigh couldn't tell if it was a sign that bad things were to come, that the future was merely uncertain and hidden from Fate, or a blessing of the weather that would keep people from wandering this far onto the grounds. Anywhere his father was spotted spawned an immediate crowd of people seeking his favor.

Emperor Nághtas stared off into the fountain. He wore simple, soft clothing that did not call attention like his official uniforms did, though he wore the emblems of his office on a ribbon around his neck. His white hair was shoulder-length and fluffy as a cloud, blown about by the soft breezes that flowed across the expanse of lawns. It framed his face in stark contrast to the dark shirt below, making the deep copper color of his face look leathery and worn. His chin hank was just as

18

white, today held tight by a platinum clasp decorated with his seal of office. Nadigh had been attending to duties all morning and still wore the blue and silver attire of his station.

"We did it, Nadigh. Twenty years of utmost secrecy and planning, and it comes to a head at last. The Union delegates have departed for Kerasím and should arrive in three days. They are bringing General Tokh's Little Wonder, the female child he trained. I don't know if I should give more honor to Tokh for finding and training her, or to her for finally breaking open negotiations. I want to sit down with both her and Tokh and discuss his method, so we may repeat his success. Rimas should be there as well."

Nadigh shook his head. "I don't recommend it, my Father-Emperor. They will turn it into something foul. Tokh's head is still wanted by the Union, as recently as a few weeks ago. The last exchange made a specific request for him, as well as a subsequent request that they be allowed to hold him on board a Union ship as collateral while the delegates are here, to ensure the safety of the female. I denied both requests."

"As well you should. Their continued ignorance is folly. If it wouldn't run the risk of antagonizing the Union, I would have him at my side during the accord. It is almost as much his victory as mine. I made the request; he is the one who succeeded."

"It is a regret that cannot be avoided. Tokh understands. He has volunteered his entire unit of men for our use during the visit. All of his *aghát* will be in the city. Two will be guarding the envoy, *tansohr Keralihn*. One is assigned to the other delegates. Your negotiator will be embedded among the senators as a personal assistant to us, a familiar bridge to the guests. The other two are running background support as needed. General Rhigandir is keeping a clamp on the disruptions to the south; General Ondahar has fifty thousand troops stationed in Kanok Sohr until the delegation leaves, a fright tactic more than anything. They are under orders not to engage. General Whareg is controlling the *tápatihn* conflicts in Vendrighon. Planetary news agencies have been warned what to highlight and what to ignore, should issues arise."

"And the locations for the official tours?"

"Local Governors have been offered large incentives to make sure those areas of their cities are beyond reproach. One thousand troops will be stationed along each of the routes dressed in civilian clothing to keep security tight, as well as rescue transports waiting no more than ten *fasim* from any location. Arch-General Trannor and I have gone over almost every possible scenario. With their own security personnel and camera crew they number thirty-nine; two of those are our plants, and with the guides, that leaves a seven to one ratio, less than five to one if you count only the dignitaries. Not bad. Add in our discretion troops, and the only way to keep them safer is to cover them with a laser-proof bubble as they move."

Nághtas sighed heavily, sinking forward as if his great stomach was going to pull him off the bench. His back heaved upward with the next breath. "And at the palace?"

Nadigh shrugged, out of ideas. "What more can we do? All non-military space flight will be grounded from the time the Union enters orbit until they depart. All satellites and orbiting military ships will remain on highest alert status, monitoring all transmissions. As courtesy, we did not place surveillance in the dignitaries' apartments, but we did place them directly outside the doors. We will know who enters and who leaves at all times. If they choose to enter the halls to avoid being overheard in their rooms, they will have gambled poorly. The *aghát* will serve any foods requested from the kitchens, allowing them to examine anything entering the rooms for safety. All excursions beyond the assigned apartments will be with *aghát* escort. They are free to request to visit any of the public areas at any time. Obviously, the family apartments and the basement levels are off-limits, but we are trying to convey an atmosphere of openness and trust, so we are granting more access than normal. Sixty *aghát* will be stationed at the palace and in the city, qualified speakers in six different Union tongues. Add in the Union Representative Ross Halian and Tokh's envoy, both of whom can converse in our language, and it will be almost impossible to run out of qualified translators short of a direct asteroid impact on the capital."

Nághtas smiled. He clapped a hand on Nadigh's shoulder and shook it. "Excellent, my son. I could not do better. While they are here, I would like to meet with Tokh's envoy, in private chambers. Arrange it for me, Nadigh."

Nadigh eyed his father with a frown. "You are not thinking of using your authority to bed her, are you, your Majesty?"

The Emperor chuckled, a wheezy gasping that shook his whole middle. "*Gah.* Wishful thinking, at my age. It took me how many months and pills to fill Lassehne with a child? Perhaps ten years ago, but I don't have that kind of energy anymore. That's her name, isn't it? Lassehne's the young one? Twelve wives is folly. At one a night, I see them every two weeks. If it's for a week, it's months before I see the same one again. I can't keep them straight. For all I know I have fifty and I never see the same one twice. I'd be happy with just Lassehne."

Nadigh smiled in reply. Lassehne wasn't very bright, but he wouldn't mind seeing her every night, either. Wives were limited by caste; below *whátaral* were limited to one, all they could afford. *Whátaral* through *díhnarwharl* were allowed two if desired, *dáhneg* three, *fáhganid* four, *bhísroti* up to six, and *thósikh*, which constituted only the Emperor and his heir, unlimited, which Nadigh thought ridiculous. "That's why I stopped myself at six. If a female offers herself to me, I am happy to indulge her as many times as she likes, but I will not have more than six married to me. I can remember six, at three a day."

"No, I just want to speak to her," Nághtas said. "She has acted on our behalf, defended me to her people, and I will pick her mind before I talk with the higher Union officials. I will know where I stand and how to approach them. By Tokh's report she is well-acquainted with our needs; I trust her opinion over that of Union officials."

"An excellent idea, my Father-Emperor." Nághtas tried to stand from the bench; Nadigh let him try several times before offering an arm for leverage.

Nághtas hauled himself to his feet. He straightened himself up against the pull of gravity, a regal pose falling on him that befit an Emperor, and for a private moment he did indeed look invincible, if rather round. He surveyed the expanse of property, the monstrous castle-fortress looming huge and white in the distance. "Our time has come, Nadigh. Our names will be written large in history, right or wrong. We are about to change a world."

Five

Aila waited in the main corridor after receiving her room assignment. It was a decent ship, not luxurious but not bare, with most of the infrastructure hidden behind smooth cream-colored walls that made it feel more like a hotel than a spaceship. She sat on her carry-on, impatient. Maybe it wasn't professional, sitting in a hallway like a kid waiting for their parent, but this was personal.

She messaged him twice, but it still took fifteen minutes for Masákh to appear, most unlike him. It had been months since she'd last seen him in person, but Masákh never changed. He was impeccable as always, his black hair and goatee trimmed to perfection, his blue *aghát* uniform pressed exactly as the day it was made. He wore low black boots that never showed a fingerprint, let alone a speck of dirt or scuffmark. Aila's first instinct was to greet him with a hug as an old friend, but she knew better than to touch a Kerasi male – bare handshakes pushed the limits of personal contact – and resorted to a bow and an excited grin.

"You made it! I worried we were going to leave without you. Where were you? What took so long? My mother didn't see you, did she?"

Masákh's heels didn't quite click as he bowed in reply, formal and crisp. His face had that faint relaxed look, and he forced a small social smile. "No. I was careful to avoid her. It was your father this time, waiting by the entry to speak with me. I understand that within the Union he is a Fleet Admiral and a Defense Councilman and deserves honor, but that should not give him the right to threaten me when I have made no move against him."

"He *threatened* you? He's been one of your supporters for years! What did he say?"

"Perhaps that's why I find his action so unexpected. He acknowledges neither he nor your mother approve of your place on this voyage but they cannot stop you. He admitted that while you trust me, neither he nor your mother does. He made me swear an oath to return you home unharmed, or he will, quote, 'Do the Kerasi thing and remove my head from my shoulders and then defecate on my neck.' Beheadings are a part of Kerasi culture, but I am most disturbed by the remainder of his statement. I did not know that was common practice among Human males."

Aila winced. *That* made sense. She could hear the words being said. "Rip your head off and shit down your neck. Yeah, that's my dad. I'm sorry. It's a phrase, that's all. No one actually does that. It's supposed to mean an insult beyond the action. They're just really worried."

"You are worried?"

"Not with you here. Did you see this?" She showed him her rooming assignment on her pocket interface. "Look at my roommate. I told you! I was so hoping they were going to put me with Vee M'para of Ashaan. She's fairly young, she's on the council for women, so there'd be *sooo* much we could be talking about, but no. They put me with *Vanora Aikerman*. She's like a hundred and fifty! She's so old she's actually retired! She's old Defense Council. What the hell am I going to talk to her about? She's going to pick on everything I say, do, or wear. She probably knows my dad and will report back if I so much as burp. I am not looking forward to that."

"I will find out what I can. I have already scanned your room; they have placed me in the next cabin to you. I found nothing to signal that there are cameras or spybugs planted. Unless Miss Aikerman has placed them, the room should be secure. I will check again tomorrow."

"You're really taking this seriously, aren't you."

Masákh bowed his head. "You hired me as a bodyguard; I serve as a bodyguard. You are long aware I take all duty quite seriously." He paused. "And I strongly wish to avoid your father's feces."

Aila burst out laughing. Masákh was not one for humor; too much laughter got in the way of duty. She didn't know if he was serious or attempting to make a joke, but it was funny. "Let's hope none of the other translators get caught up by phrases like that, or we'll have one big galactic mess. Come on. Let's go get this over with."

23

Aila swiped her ID at the door and it opened. Mrs. Aikerman was already in the room. Aila entered, Masákh in tow. Her luggage sat waiting in the empty half of the room.

She held her hand out. "Hi. I think I'm your roommate. Aila Perrin, Council for Kerasi Affairs."

Mrs. Aikerman rose from her seat to shake the hand. She was several inches taller than Aila without her shoes, thin, but gave off an aura of steely strength. Her white hair was close-cropped, but the makeup she wore said it was by choice, and she hadn't given in to her age yet. "Vanora Aikerman, Union Defense Council, emerita. Pleased to meet you. Is this your Kerasi affair? He's not staying with us, is he?"

"What?" Aila caught her meaning. Her eyes grew large and she blushed so hard she missed a breath. "No! He's not – I'm not – He's only – . This is my translator and bodyguard, Masákh gha Lil. He's got his own quarters. Next door. I figured, for something this important, go to the source. I'm happy to share – he can scan your things too, if you'd like. Ask him questions. Anything."

Technically, she'd committed a major breach of etiquette – Kerasi used only first names during address. Family names were invoked as a form of intimidation, such as in disciplinary action, threats, or belittlement where the intent was to shame the family as well, or for something grand, where the family was to be honored, or for official reasons. A family name was supposed to be protected. Masákh had gotten used to the Union demand to use all names, but Aila knew better than to commit such a blatant *faux pas*. How could everything go to hell this fast on a single question?

"Thank you, but I don't think that will be necessary. He's not the only personal guard on this trip, and not the only Kerasi." Mrs. Aikerman sat down on her bed. The room's walls were the same creamy ivory of the hall, but the bedcovers were a brilliant peacock blue with a profusion of green and yellow pillows, making the room bright. "I'm a bit old school. I think for myself, I investigate for myself, I take care of myself. That way, the only one who ever lets me down is myself. Nothing against you, young man. I'm sure you're quite good at what you do. Considering her age and experience, it's probably not a bad idea to have someone overseeing her."

"It is my honor," Masákh said.

Aila frowned, but ignored Aikerman's dig at her age. She didn't need to start bad blood in the first three minutes. She placed her personal interface and her lap pad on the computer desk on her side of the room, and placed the carry bag in her small closet. "There're more Kerasi on the ship? Do you know who, who they represent, where they're from?"

Masákh bowed his head. "It would be a failure of duty if I did not. Haghíde is returning to act as auxiliary staff at the Emperor's request. I was also requested, but I had been hired privately two days before."

Haghíde, another of Aila's captors-turned-educators. When gotten alone, Haghíde was the least typical *aghát* of the *aghát*. He was distractible, insatiable in his curiosity about the Union, and Aila was usually able to use that combination to keep him off task and to extract information from him Masákh would never have told her. Aila loved him just for being his naïve self. Haghíde was the gentlest of her captors, apologetic for the tiniest infraction, and never, ever hurt her in the least. "I should have known. The two most experienced Kerasi-Union diplomats. Of course they'd send you on the mission. I feel stupid now."

"You're new at this," Vanora Aikerman said. "If you stay in the field, you'll learn."

Aila turned to Masákh. How strange being the one ordering Masákh around, when all these years later she still felt herself waiting for his instruction. It wasn't right. What did one do with a bodyguard when they weren't needed? Did you dismiss them, or did they wait outside the door night and day, in case you called? Were they allowed to sleep? "I'm going to unpack and get settled for a bit, so you might as well do whatever you need to do. I'll message you if I'm leaving the room, okay?"

"As you request." He left with a bow.

The silence grew heavy, until Aila felt compelled to speak. If she didn't break the ice, it was going to be a very long three days to Kerasím. Did they room with the same people on the return flight?

"They brought you out of retirement for this, or did you volunteer?" Aila heaved one of her travel bags on the bed and opened it. "I assume they wanted people with a lot of experience for this. I only glanced at the list of delegates, but it looked pretty high-end."

Vanora glanced up from what she was reading on her interface. "Don't fool yourself, Child. Yes, I have all the experience they were looking for. I'm not intimidated by the posturing of men with titles. I know what to look for, the right questions to ask, and I know bullshit when I hear it in any language, but most important, I'm retired. In a worst-case scenario, if the Kerasi roll out their little mind-reading machines, the information in my head is old and out of date. I can't spill secrets I don't know. I'm expendable."

Aila shook out her fancier clothing and hung it in the closet. "That's awful! No one is ever expendable."

Vanora chuckled and returned to her interface. "Here's a little lesson from an old-timer: read over the list of delegates very carefully, and you keep believing that."

The last thing Aila wanted was to start off looking stupid and ignorant. When she'd settled in to the room, she sat at the desk and called up the list of delegates onto her lap pad. The Galactic Secretary of State, one actual Ambassador willing to serve until a permanent Ambassador might be assigned; the Planetary Prime Ministers of Kye, Koos, and Fornax, the closest Union systems to Kerasím; two heads of commissions, eight persons who sat on various Union committees, including Aila herself; seven councilors-at-large, one representative at large, and the Commander of the Space Fleet, Alpha Sector, far away from Kerasím.

What's wrong with this? What am I not seeing?

She messaged Masákh, sent him the list and repeated her questions to him, using the privacy button on her interface. "Why am I not seeing anything wrong with this?"

Masákh sighed and bent his head. Aila could see the information shifting through his brain, what to say and what not to say. But Masákh was an educator by assignment, and the need to explain won out. "There is nothing unusual with the list. I understand Councilwoman Aikerman's statement, but she is wrong to worry you. I warned you not to take the first mission but wait for the second. This is why. What persons broker a major peace accord?"

"The leaders of the parties involved."

"Precisely. How many persons on this list are capable of brokering any sort of deal between planets?"

Aila skimmed the list again. "Secretary Kel. Possibly the temp ambassador, Hawet Quin. I'm not sure what Wodu Mosi is allowed to do. Possibly Wodu."

"How many people have little or no input on government treaties, just file reports?"

Aila counted down the list and grew sober. A little chill ran up her spine as she realized what he was leading her to. "About twenty out of twenty-four of us. Not counting our security guards. Most of us."

"Precisely. You never send your heads of state on the first mission; you let the little people and the diplomats start the process. If anything goes wrong, no sensitive information can be lost, no loss to governmental function will occur if the worst happens."

Aila's face paled. She had light skin to start with, a few little freckles dotting her cheeks like forgotten confetti, and her brown hair did nothing but frame the paleness. "So Vanora was right. We are expendable."

"Do not think of it that way," Masákh insisted. "It is a standard protocol. It is your first major mission between new worlds; all you did was discover truth. Your father understood that. I believe that was part of the rationale behind his threat. If this is successful and a second is arranged, that is the mission you will want to be on. That is when the powers will align."

Aila gave an unhappy smile, twisting her mouth around until she used only half of it. "Well, if my dad knew that and he still let me go, I guess I'm pretty safe."

* * *

Mission briefing began just an hour after the ship left orbit. The conference room was spartan, just a long table that sat twenty, with twenty-four squeezed into it. A monstrous eight-foot divided viewscreen hung on the wall, already split three ways into informational subroutines. None of Union delegates had ever been to Kerasím. Aila, who had lived under Kerasi thumbs at a base on the planet Kye and had worked side by side with them at different conferences across the Union, found some of the information being brought up outdated, overgeneralized, and sometimes just plain wrong.

27

Omi Kel headed the mission. Secretary of State for the Galactic Union, he had the authority and control to make decisions on the fly. The risks of sending someone so high up in government channels were incalculable; the Kerasi had ways of extracting information the Union could not duplicate, and any classified information Kel knew was at risk. As Secretary, however, the most important classified materials remained beyond his knowledge, a need-to-know basis only, which is why neither President Mijono nor Vice-President Rill would make this trip.

Kel was born on Centauri, average in height but of thick frame, with wide shoulders, hands, and powerful limbs that worked hard for the natives of the Pausan mountain region. His pale ivory face offset the faint blue mottling of the rest of his skin, and his poker-straight white hair was cut to stand on end, making him look as if he'd just come in out of the wind. He was a seasoned negotiator, a believer in planetary sovereignty, and had more than thirty years' experience in politics. Aila paid strict attention when he spoke, even if some of what he said irked her. He was someone who could make or break her career before she even had one, and her desire to impress him weighed heavily against the almost-but-not-quite misinformation he was pushing. It was so hard not to raise her hand and correct him. She was glad Masákh wasn't in the room to hear it.

"You've all been briefed to some degree on the planet, the culture, the politics at hand," Kel said before the room. "These are a violent, dangerous people. There are no allowances in the law for offworlders; any legal rights for us are directly at the whim of Emperor Nághtas, and he's as old as the planet. No one, not one of you, should be walking anywhere without one of the official guides – their title is *aghát*. We will have two native speakers with us; there are supposed to be more available when we arrive, as many as one to two, or even one to one if we request it. There is a program, one of the official downloads you're supposed to have, that has some basic Kerasi translation on it. You can scan signs, talk to it, it should give you enough phrasing to get through a simple situation. Use it. Practice it. Learn it. If you're having trouble accessing it, I want to know by today. Miss Perrin?"

Aila lowered her hand. She couldn't sit this one out. "I'm also fairly fluent in Emperor's Tongue. I can hold basic conversations when needed. My reading and writing is a bit weak, but if it's spoken, I'm pretty good."

Kel held up a finger. "Yes, but there's a problem with that, besides the fact you haven't been certified. That brings us to issue number two. Women have no rights. None at all. If for some reason you leave the group, you must, repeat *must*, have a male person with you. A coworker, one of our guards, one of the palace guards, but someone must accompany you. An unaccompanied woman is seen as a sexual opportunity and the law agrees, and yes, although we cannot reproduce together, Kerasi parts and human parts are similar enough to mate in similar fashion. You ladies take Miss Perrin aside to bargain with a street vendor, you're now both in jeopardy."

Several of the women gave loaded sighs. Aila shook her head. "It's not quite that bad. Be cautious, but no one's going to attack you at first glance."

Kel stopped and glared down the table at her. "And you've been there? You can guarantee that?" He moved his hand in a circle to indicate everyone sitting. "You want to take responsibility for all the women at this table? Because right now, they're my responsibility. And if I say wandering to the end of the hall can place them in danger, then they are in danger."

Aila bit back a longer retort. "Yes sir. The possibility does exist, but I lived with them for over a year, and even when General Tokh knew I was above the age of consent, not one person ever approached me."

"You have no special protection, Miss Perrin. I don't expect you to be wandering off under some delusion that you're safe from attack and can talk your way out of anything. We're going there with minimal staffing; I have no one to send to look for you if you disappear. Just because you brought a private guard doesn't give you any more leeway than someone who didn't. You're either part of this group or you stay on the ship."

Aila's cheeks burned red. She wasn't that stupid. And Masákh had never been to the Emperor's City, so it wasn't as if he knew his way around. "Absolutely not, sir. I'm here to learn, just like everyone else."

"Good. Now, everyone should have downloaded the itinerary to their hand units. I don't care what kind you have, but I expect you to have your personal interface with you at all times. The ship can track

29

you with it, you can send an emergency signal to the ship if needed. Always, always keep it with you, even if you're just running to the lavatory. If you call up the itinerary, you can see we will have very little free time.

"Day one we fly to the capital city of Keranihn and check in to the Emperor's palace, Derahl Nohr. There will be extensive lessons in ceremony and protocol so you will know how to address the Emperor, his wives, those of the elite *bhísroti* and *fáhganid* class and the other seven classes, or castes. They will all be present at the evening's banquet, at which we will actually meet all this royalty we've been learning about. The Emperor may or may not show for that, so be prepared. Day two we leave the palace and tour three different cities. We tour a factory, a religious facility, a boys school, and a new school for girls, one that will allow them to study until the age of fourteen. We are supposed to have enough time to walk through a marketplace, and then have dinner with several local officials. There is supposed to be a theater presentation in the evening, so expect a long, tiring day from the start. Day three is a country tour; a private charter will take us to three different regional states – we'd call them countries – to visit a major farm, have some sort of wine-tasting event in the next region, tour a coastal city, and then visit with the regional governor and dine with him.

"Day four we are back at the palace. We'll be touring a museum in the morning, I'll have a news interview over lunch, and then we finally get a break of several hours to prepare for the big hoopla. In mid-afternoon there will be the formal gathering of the governments in the throne room, which is more what we would call a senate gathering, all the top advisors from around the Kerasi globe. Following will be a banquet with the Emperor, and then the standard entertainments of music and dancing, circus acts, or whatever they call for. There will be cameras everywhere, so please, please, please, do not slip up on protocol," Kel urged. "This is live, this is being seen not only on Kerasím but across the entire Union as well. If you drink yourself stupid on Kerasi rum, everyone at home is going to know it immediately. Understood?"

"Do we get to sleep?" asked Marisi Belenn, a member of the Council on Economic Affairs.

"We're going to try to fit that in if we can, but it's not guaranteed." A twitter of laughter made its way around the table. Kel looked behind him at the wall screen, touched it with a finger and pulled an event downward one hour. "Maybe here. Day five you can sleep in, unless Emperor Nághtas decides he wishes to speak with us further. We will probably confer once more with his cabinet, then pack up and we're out of there. If all goes right, we sail through, learn everything we can, and get back out before an incident can occur. Questions?"

"Focus?" said Melli Vergara, Commission on Space Exploration. "Are we just gathering random information, or should we be paying attention to building layouts, number of security, available tech, living conditions, number of restaurants per quarter, anything like that?"

Kel spread his hands. "You all have your pet specialties. Ms. M'Para, I'm sure you'll be paying attention to the women you meet. G'ong Fay, we're still trying to arrange to tour a hospital; that would fall under Health, Medicine and Welfare. Living conditions would also be of interest to you. Make note of anything, good or bad. I'm sure they're going to try to show us only the good, so pick apart anything you do see. Question everything; the worst they're going to do is not answer. Ask the same question to different people, see if the answer changes. Vanora, you're security council. Weapons, aircraft, military presence, anything you can think of to make note on would be important."

"I do that automatically," Vanora Aikerman said in jest. "I was hoping for something I'd actually have to think on."

Kel didn't laugh. "Then think about security for the delegation – exits, coding, locks, where are their guards, where are ours, where might the dangers be, are they carrying open weapons, which they're fond of doing. That's fine, we can see them, but who might be carrying something concealed, and why? If we think an issue's brewing, I'll call for an evac and get us the hell out of there. I'm not taking chances. This is uncharted territory. It's never been done. When in doubt, be cautious. Ms. Perrin, you have something to add?"

Aila had been thinking sarcastic thoughts; she didn't realize they were showing on her face. "No. I'm set."

"You look like you had something to say."

Not that you want to hear. Aila examined her fingernails. She'd have to paint them up nice before they landed. She carried *dáhneg* status on Kerasím, fourth from the top; she had an image to uphold. Maybe little Kerasi flags on one hand, and Union flags on the other. "I just thought you were being a little harsh, that's all."

"I'm sorry, did you receive the same notes and briefings I did? Being held in a private little enclave is not the same as being on the homeworld," Kel said. There was an edge to his voice that said *enough*. "I hope you're done with the comparisons, because that kind of know-it-all attitude gets even experienced people killed. Just because you made friends with one or two progressive outliers doesn't mean you understand the other five billion of them. Are we done with that now?"

Aila folded her hands and kept her eyes on the table, as any Kerasi would do if chewed out by a superior. It also kept her from seeing any stares from her workmates. "Yes, sir."

Six

It wasn't until the evening's informal meet and greet that Aila finally ran into Haghíde. More than anything she wanted to hug him, but instead shook his hand and gripped it hard for longer than was polite. He wore his black gloves, part of his *aghát* uniform when physical contact with others could be misconstrued. On Kerasím, skin contact could mean the difference between assistance and assault.

"Haghíde! I'm so glad you're here! It's been too long since we've been able to speak in person. Are you excited?"

"Yes," he said, though his voice didn't show it. "I have not been to Kerasím in a year now. I am looking forward to it. I serve the Emperor, but I never expected to pull duty at the palace itself. I am certain it will be even more glorious than I have imagined." Haghíde was taller than Masákh, broader, but from a distance they could have been mistaken for each other, with the same uniform, same haircut, same goatee, same facial surgery. Even before Aila learned their names, when she was still giving them numbers to keep them straight, she knew Haghíde by the small scar on his chin, a reminder that swordsmanship was not his greatest skill. Now, so many hours and years later, she could tell him just by the way he walked, or the way his hand touched her shoulder. "I am most happy to see you also. It will be a pleasure working with you again. I am proud you are among the first visitors to Kerasím. I hope we have prepared you well for it."

Aila laughed. Haghíde's grasp of Union Standard was excellent, but his speech often came out textbook-choppy. It was part of his charm. "I don't think anyone could be better prepared than me. You taught me well. Will you have time to have lunch or something together, or will they hold you to duty the entire trip? I hate for you to be this near and not have time to talk. It's so strange that you're off lecturing on Earth and I'm stuck out on Centauri. I want you to tell me everything you think of it."

Haghíde bowed his head. "I have only been there for three months, but perhaps we could exchange thoughts on each other's homeworld. I will speak with the scheduler to make certain it can be arranged. Probably not on Kerasím due to time constraints, but certainly on the ships before or after."

Aila squeezed his hand. "I look forward to it. I'll see you around, I promise," and she left him to speak with Vee M'para, the head of the Council for Union Women.

Aila wandered over to an empty table and sat with her lone glass of wine. The food at the kick-off dinner was exceptional for ship food, but meet and greets were so boring and phony. It would be better if everyone could just stand up, say what they thought about the top ten most relevant points, and sit down again. She could check off the boxes, decide who she supported and who she needed to watch out for, and life would be so much simpler than smiling and shaking hands and pretending to be on everyone's side at once until you were stabbed in the back. She'd spoken at least once with everyone, introduced herself, made sure Secretary Kel had seen her acting in an appropriate capacity, never once mentioned any of her in-depth knowledge of the Kerasi, and now she was done. How long were they supposed to stand around and pretend to be interested in small talk? Many of the delegates already knew each other, and none of them was particularly interested in talking to someone still being treated as a kid. She had no spouse, no children, no previous career placement or other experience to discuss that didn't involve her captivity. She glanced around the room, but Haghíde was speaking with Wodu Mosi and Darien Foote. So much for free time.

Masákh left his observation spot by the wall. "You are well?"

"I'm fine." She patted the table across from her. "Sit. Please. Talk to me. Before someone else does. I know you've been listening to the conversations. Who do you think is trustworthy?"

Masákh hesitated. Aila knew he had more opinion than he was about to let on. He always did. "I am cautious of the one called Raju. His words seem more hostile than most of the others. Perhaps I am misinterpreting his culture."

"Raju." Aila consulted her pocket interface. "I remember him. Dignitary from Morpu; that's in the Cygna system, I think. Small-time player. They're too far away from Kerasím to have any real stake in the negotiations; they're here as fillers. I wouldn't worry too much about him."

"Small players have the most to gain. How much of this have you had?" Masákh seized her glass. He took a small case from his pocket, removed a thin metal rod with a slim cap, and dipped it briefly in the wine. The cap flashed a white light. Satisfied, he returned the glass.

"My second glass of wine in three hours. I know not to drink too much, mix too much, and never ever let my glass out of my hand. I have no idea what you just put in there, so now I can't touch the rest of that one."

Masákh gave a snort. "I tested it for narcotics. It is clean. That is part of my job as your bodyguard. I will be doing it frequently once we are on Kerasím, just to be certain."

"That's the part my mother doesn't seem to get; I'm far safer with you than with her. You're not just thinking of things, you've already taken them into account. What will we be able to drink once we're there? I mean, is the water safe, or will we get hit with some god-awful brain-eating parasite? How will we know?"

"Most things within the Emperor's palace should be safe, but requesting sterilized water, *bhink chémnagi*, is always preferable," Masákh said. His eyes continued to scan the room, always watching, always noting, always looking for the first sign of trouble. "For most Kerasi, the public water supplies, outside of *ghinadín* slums, are quite safe. If they are safe for humans – that I cannot guarantee. Fruit juices should be acceptable. I would suggest *trobe, harfa, or lipuhr*; they are the sweetest and least acidic."

"I remember *trobe* and *harfa* from before," Aila said. "Like grape and strawberry."

Masákh nodded. "There are multitudes of popular bottled drinks; anything commercially bottled and still sealed, as long as it is randomly selected, should also be safe for human consumption. Touch nothing if you doubt the seal. As for alcoholic content…" He grasped the stem of her glass and swirled the liquid that was left before putting it back down. "There are almost an infinite number of varieties, infinite qualities, and they are consumed freely at almost every occasion. That is when you will need to be careful. Some are as innocent as your wine there; others are what you would label 190-proof and could rapidly impair your senses and damage your stomach. Those are what you will need to beware of, but depending on who is doing the serving, you may not be able to refuse. It would be a major breach of protocol to refuse the Emperor."

Aila grew serious. "I don't like that. How will I know what's what?"

Masákh glanced around the room again. Most of the dignitaries were gathered around the food displays or standing around talking in clusters. "Can you leave here yet?"

Aila glanced around as well. "Yeah, probably. Why?"

"Come with me. I have samples of many Kerasi alcohols. I will teach you what you should and should not touch. You can either share the information with your allies, or laugh when they are overwhelmed. That will be your choice."

"Okay." Aila stood up. "Follow me." She stumbled on standing. Masákh caught her by her elbows. She walked over to Vanora Aikerman, fingers massaging her temple. "Hey – this wine's going right to my head. It feels a hundred degrees in here and my stomach's not great. Masákh's going to walk me around a bit until I feel a little better."

Old Mrs. Aikerman reached out and touched her face. "You're terribly flushed. Don't have another drop tonight or you'll regret it later." To Masákh she said, " Get her some cold water to drink, sit by an air vent or something. That should help. If she feels any worse, you are to come get me immediately, do you hear? That's an order."

Masákh bowed. "Exactly as you say, Lady Aikerman. Come, Miss Perrin." He held onto her until they were some distance down the hall.

"Skillfully done."

Aila smiled. "I'm not quite as dumb as I look."

Masákh looked down at her and raised one of his carefully shaped eyebrows. "Dressed in such an official manner, you look exceptionally intelligent and attractive."

Aila laughed. "Ha! Flattery will get you everywhere. If only the rest of the delegates saw me that way."

"Remember, I will not be able to touch you like that once we are on Kerasím. I am *whátaral,* you are designated *dáhneg*. I cannot touch you, except in emergency."

"I'll remember. I'll have to progress to fainting."

"Do not antagonize your mother."

Aila burst out laughing. "I do believe you just made a joke, Masákh. Excellent job. You're right. She'd hear about it before I had a chance to regain my feet."

They stopped before his cabin door, next to hers and Mrs. Aikerman's. He scanned the lock with his ID and entered.

Aila hung back at the doorway. "Is it safe for me to come in here? I'm not breaking any Kerasi rules I don't know about, am I? Entering your room as an unmarried female?"

Masákh paused, contemplating, and Aila was certain once again he was trying to make a joke in his understated intellectual way. He sighed as if annoyed. "This is a Union ship. I am under Union jurisdiction, therefore I must abide by Union laws. I will guarantee your safety if you enter. You are a Union female; you are free to leave at any time."

"Then I accept." She entered and allowed the door to close. A second later she opened it and peered out before closing it again.

Masákh rummaged through a travel case, retrieving items. His room looked untouched, his bags placed on the floor of his closet with such precision they could have been an advertisement. There wasn't even a crease from sitting on the bedcover. It was exactly as Aila would have imagined it. "You do not trust my word?"

"Let's just say when Kerasi are involved, I like checking for locks and guards. It's an old habit." The words came out far sharper than she ever meant.

Masákh nodded, unperturbed. "Understandable. Would it be considered too informal if I removed my jacket? I find the ship's temperature to be higher than my preference. The halls are cooler, but I have yet to get the room to an agreeable temperature."

"Not at all. It's your room."

Masákh removed his blue jacket and hung it from an empty clothing rack. He unfastened the shoulder holster he wore under the jacket, always at the ready even aboard ship, checking the weapon and sliding it compulsively back in as he hung it next to his jacket. Aila'd only seen him in his white shirt alone a few times. He was average in height, his weight not daring to deviate more than a single pound from some chart that told him what was ideal. He had the lean muscle of someone in peak form, not the over-worked bulk of someone who lifted weights. His shirt was tucked into his pants so precisely the tucks looked pre-creased to sit that way, and wrinkles were out of the question.

He placed several small bottles and a larger one on the room's table, and a stack of tiny plastic cups the size of her thumb. "You may sit at the table."

One did not sit on Kerasím unless instructed. Chairs were ranked by caste, and many times women sat on floors. Even though she expected it under Union custom, Aila felt honored by the invitation. Equal chairs, equal rank. He sat across from her.

He grasped the larger bottle and showed her the shimmering gold label, waiting for her to decipher the symbols.

"*Lunahl.*"

"*Lunahl,*" he confirmed, "made from fermented *trobe* fruit. It is the mildest alcohol you will encounter. It is similar to your wine, with a four percent alcohol content. Qualities and prices vary according to who will purchase it. Always ask to see the label. You are *dáhneg*; you will drink nothing that does not have a silver, gold, or purple label. If it is a lesser label, you will loudly demand a better one." Masákh wrestled the bottle open with a loud pop and poured a sample into two of the cups, barely a spoon's worth. He placed it before her. "You may treat it as you would a wine. You may swirl it, tip it, smell it, sip it. You may not swallow it all at once; that would be extremely poor manners."

"I remember *lunahl*. A proper toast?"

Masákh gave a brief chuckle of amusement. "You would consider most of them offensive. The safest would be 'to your strength.' 'To the health of Emperor Nághtas, long may he rule,' is always acceptable."

"He's been on the throne fifty years. I think he achieved that." Aila sniffed it, dipped a finger in for a taste, then sipped it down. "Very nice, actually. Light, sweet, but not overpowering."

Masákh swallowed his. He opened the first of the small bottles and poured two more tiny cups. "This is *muhr*. It is perhaps the most common, also with a low alcohol content, between six and ten percent. It is grain-based, although some may also be mixed with fruit. It is popular among the lower castes, but not out of line for the upper castes also to drink it."

Aila made a face. "Too sour. I hope I don't get stuck with that. I'm not sure I could drink an entire glass. Ew."

"The point is that it is safe." He poured a splash of a third type. "*Flehdan*. A celebratory alcohol, grain based, often mixed with flavoring. It has a higher alcohol content, twenty-five percent. Some will dare you to drink it plain and at once; do not. Ask for it mixed, and sip at it."

"With... *harfa*?" Aila remembered.

"Yes, that is common."

Flehdan, bohjis, ghor, dhurwah. Aila wasn't sure she could keep them all straight. *Ghor* tasted sweet, but the kick from just the little sip made her tongue numb, and *dhurwah* was far too bitter for her to swallow at all.

Masákh laughed as she spit it back into the tiny cup. He smiled wide enough to show his teeth, points ground flat and whitened until they looked human. "You will never be mistaken for a true Kerasi. It is fortunate that refined females do not drink *dhurwah*. Beware of any female that does."

Aila smiled. "I miss this, Masákh. I miss just conversing with you like this. I learn so much more from you than all those other airheads blowing and blowing about politics. They're missing the people aspects, the culture. Understand the culture and you'll learn the underpinnings of the politics. I haven't even made it to university yet and I get that much. I don't understand why my mother can't see that." She reached across the table and took his hand.

"You're not wearing your gloves. I always wondered what your skin felt like, locked inside those gloves all the time."

Masákh gave her a quizzical glance. Direct touch had always been off limits, but Aila was intent on his hands. He folded them around hers, and she didn't pull away. "I did not wear them off duty. I will be wearing them again once we land on Kerasím. *Whátaral* cannot..."

"I know, I know. *Whátaral* cannot touch *dáhneg*. It's all a farce. Your skin does not burn me, desecrate me, or anything else."

"You were not born *dáhneg* on Kerasím. Does my touch offend you?"

"Not in the least. I like it better than when you go out of your way not to touch me."

"Even if I touch here?" He reached up, brushed her hair back, then caressed her cheek with his fingers. "You look most attractive when you dress for official functions. Most adult. Perhaps that is what your mother fears."

Aila blushed and glanced down at the table. "My mother can jump out an airlock. I'm not thirteen anymore. Babies don't get taken seriously. I need every advantage I can for my job."

Masákh sat back with a snap. He reached for the last bottle, petite and expensive-looking. "This is what I wanted to warn you of. It is illegal within the Union. It is difficult to obtain even on Kerasím, and it is almost never tasted by anyone under *díhnarwharl* status because of the great cost. This bottle is the price of two weeks' *whátaral* salary."

Aila's eyes grew round. "You spent that much on a bottle of booze?"

"I would have, but I have connections that supplied me free of charge."

"If it's illegal in the Union, how did you get it through customs?"

The familiar smarmy smile crept over his face, sarcastic amusement at her naïveté. "Officials are the same everywhere. I started with three bottles. I made sure to choose a male customs agent. When he discovered the bottles, I pleaded personal use. I offered him two if he would ignore the first. He did not refuse."

"Very slick. Oooh! What's it doing?" Aila stared at the tiny cup. He had poured her not even the full teaspoon or so, but pink crystals were forming up the sides of the cup.

"They are vaporized sugar crystals. The vapor clings to the cup, the alcohol fumes remove the water, and the crystals form. Because of the cost, it is used to convey wealth and power. Therefore, it is quite likely to be served at palace functions. *Rhimáhdia*: the coveted Kerasi Pepper Rum. Do not, under any circumstances, drink it fast. It will make you quite impaired very quickly, and is harsh on the stomach due to the extreme alcohol content. Smallest of quantities."

Aila nodded and gave it a try. The pink crystals tasted like candy, sweet and inviting. Then the liquid hit. There was not enough in the cup to wet her entire mouth. Her tongue burned with peppery fire, the fumes went up her nose, her eyes watered, her mouth went numb, and she began to choke. The liquid ran down her throat, tearing at it with the fury of a razor blade. A miniature explosion began in her stomach, burning like a firework before dying away.

She panted. "Ooh! Ooh! Oh my gosh. My stomach! Oh hell, my head!" Aila's head spun as if she'd gulped too much air. She blinked hard and breathed deep until she felt steadier. "Holy light of the universe. And that was just a *taste*?"

Masákh gave a deep chuckle. "That is why I wanted you to know in advance. If you cannot avoid it, pretend to sip at it. I guarantee the males of your company will seek it out; they will be overcome while Kerasi nobility ridicules them. Do not fall for that."

Aila's chin rested on her fist, a sweetness in her eyes. "You are so knowledgeable about *everything*. You amaze me."

"You are still young. You are still learning. Has this tasting impaired you?"

"I don't think so. That rum twisted me for a minute, but my head feels clear now. In fact, I would like more of that *lunahl*," she said. "I liked that." Masákh scrambled to find actual glassware and poured them both a reasonable amount. Aila took down a mouthful, easing the burn of the pepper rum.

Masákh sipped at his. "What do you see as your personal goal for this mission? What do you hope to achieve?"

Aila held a finger to her mouth. "No. Let's not talk shop right now. I have to listen to twenty-three other people do that for the next ten days. My only goal is for both of us to get there and back alive, okay? Talk about something else."

"I have more training in diplomacy than you. You should be asking me questions so you are prepared for every circumstance. Do you have a preferred alternate subject?"

Aila laughed. "You are always so *serious*! You confuse the hell out of me."

Masákh sat back. He pulled his hands down into his lap, reorganizing himself lest he somehow caused offense. He seemed rather disappointed. "I was unaware I made conflicting statements. Have I misunderstood something said?"

"No," Aila said with a long sigh. "I mean I have so much affection for you, Masákh. I know that's what my mother's afraid of, deep down. But I don't know what it comes from. Is it just friendship-affection, true affection, is it loyalty going wrong, is it the kidnapper-victim thing – I don't know. I just don't know. Half of me is scared to death of you, of what you've done, of what you can do, of what you might do and never think twice. I'm afraid you're just manipulating me to some purpose I don't know. And at the same time, every minute we're apart, I feel lost, like I'm missing something. When we're apart, I live just to talk to you. It's not the same feeling I get when I can't wait to talk to Thayer, or my mom. It's different. It's as if I can't breathe unless I do it. And it confuses the living daylights out of me. I don't know what to think. I could spend the whole night just watching you work, and I'd be happy."

Masákh jumped away from the table and paced in the open space at the end of the cabin. He wiped imaginary dust from the touchplate of the overhead lights. He adjusted the tilt of the viewscreen on the wall. His breath came hard, as if her words had frightened him. She'd never, ever seen him nervous before. It was not possible. Nervous did not enter into Masákh's behavior, ever. She'd seen him threatened with weapons, chained to a chair, screamed at and beat on by his commanding officer, she'd seen terrifying anger when his prisoner slipped through his fingers. Nothing made him react like this.

Ever.

"I wish – I wish you had not confessed that until after the mission." The reply was pressured and sharp but nowhere near strong enough to be a reprimand, a balancing act between letting words out and holding them back. "Such admissions can be distracting to the proper tasks."

"I'm sorry. I just – Sitting here with you, speaking with you face to face like an adult with no one trying to listen in… Maybe it's the *lunahl*." Aila glanced at her cup. It was almost empty. *How did that happen?* "As I said – I'm really confused, so I apologize if I said too much."

"No. No. Do not apologize." He darted around the room in distress, but had yet to find an escape. Between his frantic movements and heavy breathing, he looked as if he were physically wrestling with something invisible, and the something was winning.

"Do not apologize," he repeated. "This is not the proper time and I should not speak of it at all, but after such an admission I am finding it difficult to remain silent. Please forgive me if I am inappropriate and have overstepped the limits of courtesy.

"I have suffered deep affection for you for four years. I have never mentioned it, implied it, or acted on it, because I knew that even if it was allowed in my culture, it was not in yours. It was too great a risk.

Events would upset you and I would wish very much to comfort you, but touching was forbidden. When I learned Kassán took your speech, I was most angry. I jeopardized my position and questioned Tokh on it, made him swear to set it right, and he agreed he would do so before you were freed. You fled before that could be achieved. I have appreciated every word you spoke in my behalf. I value the fact you continue to exchange words with me. I have wasted sleep thinking about you. I allow myself pride, watching you use the skills I taught you, accept the position I trained you for. With your admission, now that you are adult on your world, I cannot stay silent. I am Kerasi. I am *aghát*. We live for honor. We fear lies, because we can be forced to admit the truth. My words are my truth and I admit them freely, with no manipulation intended. I can say nothing else."

Aila's hands flew to her mouth, failing to hide her surprise. "Oh Lord of Space! I never knew! Not for an instant. You are the most patient Kerasi I've ever heard of. You are the exact reason why our worlds must fight to learn about each other, to destroy the stereotypes that prevent us from progressing."

Demon truth released, Masákh stopped moving about, once more his reserved and proper self. He didn't sit but he didn't look at her, either, his shoulder toward her, keeping a cushion of distance between them. "Do not dwell on idealism. There are many men of honor on Kerasím, but they are outnumbered by those to whom your 'stereotype' applies. Do not trust in false security."

Aila stood up. Her feet felt solid enough beneath her; what she felt was her alone, not any alcohol misleading her. She took his hand. "And in four years, you never told another soul? You kept that secret?"

"Sóghar accused me of it, as many of my decisions should have been harsher. I confessed it to my commanding officer. By admitting it to him, if I made a mistake no one could use it to threaten me. If General Tokh felt I was a risk to the mission, he could reassign me, but he did not. I was most grateful, both of his trust and his inaction."

Aila stared up into his dark eyes for a moment, looked away, then stretched upward to give him a timid kiss to his cheek. "I'm sorry you had to wait so long to tell me."

His hand tightened on hers until it started to hurt. "Do not make a game with me. Do not make such a gesture unless you mean it."

"If I didn't mean it, I wouldn't have done it."

Aila expected a nice, sweet tender little kiss in response, something that said, "Thank you, that was nice." Instead, he seized her and kissed her with more force than she ever imagined, four years of control lost in a matter of seconds. The sudden motion frightened her, and at the same time made her feel electrocuted all over. Her heart stopped beating, the blood fell from her head, and the gravity of the room seemed to shift, leaving her dizzy. She wasn't sure if she should stay or run, the scent of his exotic cologne filling her lungs, the scrape of his goatee rough against her chin, the warmth he gave off burning against her fingers, making her aware of him in a manner she'd never suspected. She returned the kiss just as hard.

For a minute. His hands moved from her shoulders to her back, pressing her to him. She slid hers against his chest and pushed him away. "No, Masákh."

He frowned at her as she took a step back. "You said you felt attraction as well. You were most clear."

"I did, and I said I was really, really confused by it. I can't rush into something like this. There are so many cultural barriers –"

"We are adult on both worlds, both unpromised. There is no barrier."

"There's the age difference for one thing – on my world, you're way too old for me."

"I am thirty-five of your years. I am still considered a young and highly desirable husband."

"But I'm eighteen – you're twice my age! We prefer our couples be close in age, especially if one is very young."

"So you reject me for my age. On Kerasím, adult is adult. There is no differentiation."

"I'm not rejecting you! Stop confusing me worse!" Aila raised her hands as if she could push the words away. "That's what my culture says, not what I said. Look – your parents didn't make you go to counseling for three years after being kidnapped. They tried everything they could to break my loyalty to you – warned me how kidnappers can seem like redeemers, how victims can get attached, that it's all very common, and to this day I don't see it that way. I knew you all had bad sides – I never lost sight of that, even as I learned to think of you as real people, trapped in the same mess I was. I saw Tokh kill, I watched him order me tortured, I know he has evil in there as much as he has good. I knew Sóghar was dangerous. Even Haghíde lost his temper with me, so I have no doubt he's probably raped and killed like everyone else. I saw you kill Sóghar, so I know you're just as capable of murder. And I don't see where that makes me a blind follower. I know you have bad sides, but I know it's your society that's fostered that. I also know how much goodness and kindness you're capable of, too. But that doesn't make my head clear, either."

"Despite your words of trust, you fear me."

Confusion wrapped itself a little tighter around Aila's head and pulled. It wasn't going to give up anytime soon. "Yes. No. That's not what I mean."

She allowed him to kiss her again, gentler, slower. His voice lowered to a whisper. "You said you feel unhappy when we are apart. I would ask you to remain happy, and not leave."

"You mean, stay here with you."

He nodded as he kissed her neck. The electrocution feeling overwhelmed her again, crinkling her spine, stealing her breath, shaking her belly. Her arms found their way around his neck, her lips to his face.

"As in, through the night?"

"It is much easier to protect you when you are lying next to me."

"Masákh, I've never... I've never even bedded a human male. I have no idea what you people do, or how you do it, or anything else. I know what you want, and it may be I want that too, but there are so many unknowns I'm not sure I can say yes right now, or that I should. There are no glowing accounts of encounters between Kerasi men and human women because none of the women lived to say anything. I told you, I'm completely confused by all of this."

Masákh rubbed two fingers over her lips. "Touching your mouth gives you fear?"

"No."

He pressed his lips over hers, far too briefly. "Then why does this frighten you?"

"It shouldn't. It's where it leads..."

His finger pressed her lips, stopping her. "So you are not afraid of any given moment. You fear only when you put too many moments together, when the moment you think you fear is still in the future. Moments should be lived one at a time."

45

Aila couldn't argue that, but it didn't help her confusion. He resumed his kissing, and all sense of time and place and propriety disappeared as the electrocution resumed and she returned his affection with more confidence. His hands moved along her back, tugged her blouse from the waist of her pants. He walked her backwards until she hit the wall, her hands untucking his shirt even as her lips never left his face, his ear, his neck. His hands slid under her blouse while she struggled clumsily with the buttons of his shirt.

He returned his attention to her throat, one hand stroking a young breast through her undergarment. His other hand guided hers toward the waist of his pants. Aila pulled back but the hand was insistent, sliding her fingers behind the fabric. Biology was something never discussed during her captivity, and had never been a topic of diplomatic concern. She had no idea what Kerasi genitalia, male or female, even looked like. Here was a moment that did frighten her, and the fear chased away the electricity.

Am I really ready for this?

Her fingers dipped behind the cloth, but not beneath whatever undergarment he wore. She forced herself to lower her hand, his privacy pressing against her through the thinnest layer of cloth. It responded to her touch. Whatever he carried there, whatever it looked like, it moved of its own accord, seeking her out.

And it was wrong.

This whole thing is wrong.

Aila snatched her hand back. She wrenched out from under him, pushed at his chest, stepped back out of reach, breathless. "Stop! Stop, Masákh! This isn't right. It's not right."

His face clouded over, eyebrows pulling inward, angry and puzzled. "I have waited years for you to reach adulthood. How is this not right?"

Aila fixed her blouse in a rush. "Because it isn't. This isn't the time. I told you I was confused, and even the least doubt in my mind makes it not right. Going even a moment further could jeopardize this mission. We should both be focused on that right now, not on each other. I cannot pay attention to what is going on around me if I'm busy making love faces at you across the room. If anyone on Kerasím senses something is between us, they can use that attachment to control either one of us. They could pry it out of us with a scanner. Kel is already on me about every little thing I'm doing wrong; he'd never let me off ship if he found out. Above everything else, we must remain absolutely professional. I'm not saying I won't be staying here with you the entire voyage home, I'm saying tonight is not the night to start. I know you're not happy, but I know you are a perfectionist when it comes to duty. My first duty is to the mission. I am discredited at every turn because of my age, no matter how correct I am. I have to work twice as hard to be heard. Like you, I cannot afford to be negligent in the least way. If I stay here any longer, my mind will never be anywhere near the mission. It will only be filled with you. Can you understand that?" She tucked her shirt in, tried to smooth her hair back into place.

Masákh grabbed her by the wrist, bending it until it hurt, and the fear soared upward again. The dark eyes flashed at her. "A female does not consent to touch and then walk away."

Aila froze, trying to read his intent. She'd seen his eyes angry before, and they frightened her no less now. Would he force her as a regular Kerasi would, or was this just a moment of cross-cultural learning? Her voice was calm, hiding her nerves, and she tried to keep it friendly. "Duty before pleasure, Masákh. I know you understand that. Loyalty, duty... What's the third one?"

"Honor to the Emperor."

"Loyalty, duty, honor to the Emperor."

His hand crumpled into a tight fist, squeezing the distant perfectionist back into place. "There is my door. Leave. You are free, as humans are. Remove yourself. Pleasant night." He turned his back and dismissed her with a wave of his hand.

"Masákh – I'm not rejecting you, I just think …"

He raised his voice to a frightening command. "I said leave me!"

Aila bowed as she left. "Good night."

Mrs. Aikerman was waiting for her next door in the stateroom. "Aila, where have you been? I didn't have your ID number or I would have messaged you. Where's your shadow?"

The distress in Aila's stomach was quite real, but from emotional cause, not physical. Simple lies were usually best. "I've been in the public restroom on B deck; there's no one up there. I sent Masákh away ages ago. I was too embarrassed to explain to a male Kerasi about – *diarrhea.*"

Mrs. Aikerman laughed out loud. "You poor thing. You're not used to the rich foods they always serve. Here, I have tablets for that. Never go on a mission without them; they'll save you every time." She retrieved one and handed it to Aila with a glass of water.

Aila took it gratefully and went straight to bed, wishing to tears it was the bed in the stateroom next door.

Seven

Masákh met her in the hall for her escort to breakfast, his blue suit crisp and sharp, shirt tucked in with such perfection it might have been sewn in place. He said good morning with a short bow, but not another word. Every movement, every gesture, every blink was pure *aghát*. Not a hair gave away anything that might have taken place the night before. In a way, Aila was mad. Here she was, ready to apologize, discuss the night rationally as adults were supposed to do, and he had retreated back behind the wall of duty. Wasn't that what she had requested? Had he lain awake most of the night, too? Did he weep silently like she did, remnants of electricity short-circuiting his heart, or did his fury curse her in the dark? Was he filled with crushing self-doubt and remorse as she was, beating himself up for everything he said and did, or was he plotting revenge? As he checked his pocket interface, Aila noticed the perpetual black *aghát* gloves were back; direct contact was off-limits, and the urge to cry over botching her first attempt at a love affair became so strong she had to look away to stop it.

You're out of your league, baby.

She touched his arm at breakfast. The dark eyes stared at her with reptilian warmth. "*Dáhneg* do not touch *whátaral*. That is a lesson you must perfect before we arrive."

She glared back and dug her fingers into his arm as hard as she could. "*Dáhneg* touch whoever the hell they damned well want, and there's nothing a *whátaral* can do about it."

There was little time to dwell on it, with morning meetings, a short break for lunch during which Aila went back to her stateroom, and a full afternoon of briefings.

"You sure you're all right?" Mrs. Aikerman asked as Aila lay on her bed with a miserable expression. "You don't look well. Everything okay? Anything you want to tell me? Don't take Omi's crassness personally; he's got a huge responsibility ahead of him. He's just trying to keep everything in control. Think of him as a teacher on a field trip to Hell."

Aila wrinkled her nose. She squirmed, then sat up. "No, my stomach's still not right. I think I'm going to head to the sickbay and see what they can give me. If Masákh's looking for me, I'll see him at this afternoon's meetings." She knew exactly what was wrong with her stomach: heartache and regret, two things Aila was pretty sure the sickbay couldn't fix.

She watched him working, checking out rooms, inspecting corridors, consulting with computers and Union security, but he never said a word to her. It was on their way to dinner – a blessed private dinner free from programmed rigmarole – that she was able to catch him alone in a lift.

She turned to him and snapped, "Stop it! Just stop it! Stop all the perfectionist *aghát* crap! I'm sorry about last night! I didn't want to stop, but I meant what I said. I can't concentrate on the mission with you mad at me like this, either. I'm trying very hard to act like a seasoned professional and you are making it exceptionally difficult for me to do my job. Can we please just call a truce for now? You want to beat me up, do it after the mission. You want to scream at me until I choke to death crying, do it after the mission. You want to screw me until sun-up, I just might say yes, but it won't be until after the mission. I'm sorry, but that's the way it's going to be."

Masákh growled. His head dropped and he wouldn't look at her. The attitude disappeared, as if he'd stepped from behind a curtain to join the world. "I am not angry. Not with you. Every word you said was truth. I lost my professionalism when you admitted affection for me. I beg forgiveness. The mission is highest priority, well beyond personal feelings, and always should have been. I would ask for opportunity to resume our discourse on the matter after the mission is completed. Until then, I am fully in charge of my duties ensuring your safety." The curtain fell down again with a snap, and he hid behind it.

Truce was truce. She placed a hand on his arm, proper or not. "I forgive you."

* * *

50

The room stood at attention as Nághtas entered. His personal guard waited by the door. He crossed the room and hauled himself up the step to the velvet-covered council chair to sit with a heavy exhalation.

"All may sit. Council will begin." The assembly of the Emperor's inner council sat with a scrape of chairs. One seat of prominence remained empty.

"Thirty of our years we have struggled for this day. We risked interstellar war, reaching out to the Planetary Union. Today our risks have paid off. A Union delegation has left for Kerasím and will arrive here in two days. If there are objections, I will hear them now. If there are difficulties that have not been overcome, I will know them now. We have two days to pull together every last bit of grandeur we can muster, hide every Union objection we can. Moragh, report."

Nághtas's second son spoke. "Sixty-three *aghát* have been recalled to the city; one remains on personal guard for a delegate, *tansohr Keralihn*, a second is embedded as a person familiar with several of the delegates. There are three thousand extra security that have been assigned to the city, three hundred for the palace itself. Twelve extra staff have been assigned to communications. All transmissions to and from the palace will be monitored, no exceptions. All other channels will be blocked. The kitchens have been provided with eight cooks trained in various Union dishes, as well as the limitations and preferences per the directives given us by the Union. Tour locations are preparing on schedule; final security checks will be made one hour before arrival of the delegates. All hosts have been cleared and instructed to prepare at imperial levels."

"That should be sufficient," Nághtas said. "Durghid, speak."

Durghid was Naghtas's brother, just two years younger. He was soft and pampered as only a high *bhísroti* could be. Should anything happen to Nághtas and all his sons, Durghid would be left as Emperor. The fact wasn't lost on Nághtas. Durghid was one of his top advisors, whether or not Nághtas listened to a word he said. Nághtas kept his enemies close, and his family closer. His younger brothers Fremas and Malegh sat at council but at lesser positions; still royal, but less of a threat.

The door to the councilroom opened and the room stood, save for the Emperor, as Heir Apparent Nadigh entered, followed by his daughter, Rimas, a surprise to almost all. The room began to buzz.

51

Females did not enter council chambers, unless they were consorts brought in for entertainment.

The pair bowed to Nághtas, then Nadigh took his empty seat by his father. All seats at the table were filled; Rimas had nowhere to sit. Tradition deemed it should be on the floor, despite her bloodline.

"Come, Smalldaughter," Nághtas said. He waved his hand. "Taral, bring her a chair. She may sit here by me."

A servant scurried to find a seat for her as the whispers and grumbles made their way around the table. She sat, silent, arrogance on her face along with a determined resolve to bear something unpleasant.

"Since when are our councils open to females?" Gindral said. The son of a cousin to the Emperor – cousin being a complicated term when Nághtas's father had forty-seven siblings by eleven mothers – he was the regional president of Padhrot Whinar, a place he saw less than four weeks a year.

"Since I gave my permission," Emperor Nághtas said. "I want her to see a council in action, and this is as good a time as any. Now show her your best, so she can sing your praises when she leaves. Durghid, you were about to speak."

"Send her here to me, and I will give her praises to sing about," said Fremas, who was Nághtas's youngest half-brother, just five years older than Heir Nadigh. He grabbed his crotch and shook it, and most of the table erupted in hard laughter. "Better than that *dinkorhat* of a husband you married her to." *Dinkorhat* were boneless sea creatures with many tentacles, and they hung limply when removed from water. Rumors circulated that Rimas's husband, a thin creature with a sour disposition, was impotent, that his children weren't his, that he was *hihven* and liked only males and that's why he tolerated Rimas wearing pants, that he was weak-stomached and could not manage discipline, and more. None were true; their marriage was never more than a political arrangement and neither of them had a say in it. They'd done their duty, produced three children, and they simply wanted nothing to do with each other.

Control the situation, Nadigh had taught his daughter. *Don't let it control you. Take the situation in hand and let them know you will not be toyed with, whatever it takes.*

Rimas jumped up faster than most of the men could follow, sliding across the wide round table on her knees. By the time she stopped, her sword was out and against the throat of her Wise-Uncle. It was no small feat; Rimas was not young, and certainly not lithe or willowy. She was built like her father, taller than average, strong of frame, and packed with two hundred pounds of rounded fat and considerable muscle underneath it. Ambition hadn't come naturally to her, she'd had to be pushed toward it until the idea became ingrained, and little by little the pieces had come together and made sense. Defense had been easier.

"At last! The female is where she belongs, backside on the table," said Indgon, a cousin of Rimas's by marriage, a *bhísroti* snot in his late thirties. "I knew there was a reason you brought her, Nadigh." He stood as if he planned to grab her.

One hand holding her sword to her Wise-uncle's throat, Rimas grabbed her knife from her belt and threw it sideways, landing it deep in Indgon's shoulder. His eyes went wide as he realized what she'd done. The table gave an audible gasp and chairs scraped backwards. Several wore swords but no one drew; for most, they were nothing but decoration.

"You *trixahg*!" Indgon shrieked. He pulled the knife free with a sklortching sound. Blood ran down his sleeve and the side of his shirt. "I'll slit those trousers back into the skirt they should be and I'll show you where this dagger belongs!"

Rimas never moved her eyes from her Wise-Uncle or her sword. "If I listened to gossip, it's not that you don't know where to put your dagger, but your ability to put it there that's the problem." A raucous buzz hummed up from the table, both shock and admiration. Nadigh's face broke out in a huge grin before he wrestled it back.

Indgon's face burned a dark brown. "Now, I kill you." He raised the dagger.

"HOXT!" Nághtas grunted. He held his hand out; his guard placed his staff in it. Nághtas banged it on the floor three times. "You threaten the royal child of my heir. When you threaten my heirs, you threaten me. She may take your head, be it one stroke or five."

Rimas turned to stare at her Wisefather. Fremas pushed the point of her sword down and away.

She bowed her head. "I would not desecrate your council room with such mess, Wisefather. I meant merely to make a point."

Vedon chuckled, jiggling his sagging copper jowls. The agricultural minister, his chin hank was long, silver, and braided with fat cords to hide how wispy it had become. "You can try all you want, Nághtas, but it will never work. She might have the strength, but she'll never have the *khatas* to rule so much as a *hyrak* farm."

Rimas glanced at her father; he gave a single slow nod.

"No?" she said. "Then you may hold him, Revered Lord Vedon Doubter, and pray to fortune my aim does not also take your *hihvat*-hand."

Vedon froze. Rimas was royalty; she could not be ignored. Indgon tried to back away, but he was in the farthest corner of the room. Every person, including the Emperor's guards, stood between him and the door, and his left arm was all but useless. The room urged Vedon to his feet with catcalls. He rose from his chair with uncertainty. Several of the men around the table stood up, blocking Indgon until Vedon could grab him. Indgon struggled violently, but Vedon kicked out his feet, shoved him over the table, and held him by his hair.

"This is outrage!" Indgon shouted. "She is a monster! You have created an unholiness, Nághtas! The people will not allow her to live! Female does not command male! My line will not forget, and they will not forgive you, Nághtas! Don't do this, Vedon! She will take you next!"

Rimas slid from the table and focused forward, blocking out the room, blocking out the eyes watching her, blocking out Indgon's shrieks and her memories of him over the years. There was no backing down. She'd never taken the head of a man, just the livestock her father had her practice on. She bent down to whisper in Indgon's ear, "And when I am done, I will take your seat, as is my right." Indgon thrashed and howled, but Vedon held him firm.

For a second Rimas looked as if she were about to walk away, and the room held its breath. Then she turned fast, and in one smooth move brought her sword down on Indgon's neck with all her strength. It wasn't the neatest of blows, too low, taking a chunk from his shoulder as well, but she'd done it on a single strike. She kicked his body so it fell to the floor, grasped the head by the chin hank and held it high for all to see, brown blood bathing her arm. She dropped the head onto the floor before Vedon's astonished eyes.

Rimas sheathed her sword without a word and sat in Indgon's chair, as was her right if she were male. She shook hard and forced her chin high, but she didn't cry or vomit or make blubbering speeches, as females often did. "My apologies, Emperor."

The guards moved to haul the body out. Knee-slapping began, at first faint, then picking up in tempo and volume; Rimas was sure it started with her father.

The *bhísroti* to her left gave a guffaw and slapped her hard on her back, as she was also *bhísroti*, then passed her his drink. Rimas downed half of it in one long swallow, never losing the hard, angry glare from her face.

"Gah, your Majesty!" said the *bhísroti*. "She does have a set of *khatas* in those pants! She's more like her father than she looks. Perhaps in time she can do the job after all. You may be right, Emperor. Time will tell, but she is off to a good start."

Eight

The Emperor's palace burned with fire in the early morning sun. No picture, no video, could do the palace justice. The white stone façade sparkled with silicates, reflecting the orange sunlight in constant shimmering waves as the transport circled, waiting for permission to land. Statistics in a database meant nothing when faced with a building six stories tall and nineteen hundred feet long. Two dozen tall spires and minarets rose higher still, each bearing a gold flag with the Emperor's crest snapping in the air. A quarter-mile of gardens and lawns made a living carpet before it, centered by a thirty-foot statue of a younger Emperor Nághtas standing amid a large fountain with a circle of jets spewing water into the air. The gardens in the back were three times as large, an entire city park, with more fountains and statues and walkways connecting them. Colorful figures in trailing robes walked about, with small children running every which way. They must have been *bhísroti*, relatives or offspring of the Emperor or his immediate cronies.

The transport circled slowly, the translator pointing out the one-story-high friezes above the top floor depicting famous scenes from Kerasi mythology and history. The sheer size of it, encircling a building of that magnitude, covered thousands of years of history. Even the seasoned dignitaries were impressed.

Their 'craft touched down on a landing pad on the roof. From the roof one could see for miles over the city, all the way to an inlet of the sea, the air sharp and clear in the morning sun. At least a dozen armed troops stood at attention, while three Kerasi in blue suits waited patiently for everyone to disembark. They looked frighteningly similar to Masákh.

"*Aghát?*" Aila whispered to him. "Do you know them?"

"There are perhaps seventy *aghát* overall. It is not unusual that three would be assigned here for such an occasion. I expect there will be more. They will speak Union tongues and be able to answer questions without difficulty. Be polite, but do not trust them blindly," Masákh cautioned. He gave a silent nod to each of them.

They entered what appeared to be a waiting room. The body scan was expected; this was not only the Emperor's living quarters, but the entire center of government as well. Masákh and Haghíde were allowed to keep their weapons, but the Union security had to surrender theirs. Expected, but Kel tried bargaining anyway. A security team photographed and confirmed everyone, and official Kerasi identification tags were distributed. They gathered together as the last few finished.

One of the *aghát* bowed. "Grand Citizens of the Planetary Union, welcome to Keranihn, the capital city of all Kerasím, and to Derahl Nohr, the hereditary home of Kerasím's grand Emperors for the past one thousand years. His Majesty Emperor Nághtas, Emperor of All Kerasím, is extremely pleased to host such honored guests and is most anxious to meet you." His speech was clear and precise with just a trace of accent, no more than Masákh or Haghíde.

Secretary of State Kel bowed back. "The honor belongs to the Union. We are most grateful for the Emperor's invitation."

"My name is Dihr. My associates Ráhnif, Ular, and I will be your head liaisons, available to you at every hour of day and night, with more assistants available if desired. You may ask us questions on any subject at any time. You may make requests of us at any time and we will do our best to serve you. If you will follow us, please, there will be a brief period of refreshment and greetings, followed by a tour of the palace, after which you will be given your guestroom assignments." His heels clicked together and he bowed once more, a perfect picture of *aghát* efficiency. He led them to two large lifts.

From the security checkpoint they were led down three floors to a reception lounge, where an array of both Union and Kerasi foods awaited them – along with the initial Union diplomatic team already ensconced in Keranihn.

Ross Halian, special operative for the Union, had worked with the Kerasi since the cessation of hostilities four years previous, after a preliminary fragile truce was established. He was the first voluntary Union representative ever to set foot on Kerasím, swapping scientific information to ensure time experiments on both sides didn't result in mutual annihilation. Halian was the current unofficial ambassador, more steeped in some aspects of Kerasi culture than even Aila. It was his fearless work that had solidified the trust and led to the accord. Six of his eleven-man team greeted the delegation.

"Welcome, welcome!" Ross said, shaking hands all around. His sandy-brown hair was the same, but he'd let his beard grow out and sculpted it into a passable Kerasi chin hank, so odd and so familiar at the same time. "It's good to see friendly faces. Welcome to Kerasím, and being a part of history in the making."

"You're the trail blazer, Captain Halian," Kel said, shaking the hand with familiarity and friendship. "We're just following your path."

"I might have paved the road, but this is our trail blazer, right here." Halian took several steps to Aila and pulled her forward with an arm around her shoulders. "Without Aila's bravery and stubborn resolve, I never would have had the chance. Our success this week is her doing. How are you, Aila?"

Aila caught the shadow falling over Omi Kel's face at the praise, but she returned Halian's warm smile, hiding her embarrassment. She hadn't meant to draw attention at all, but Ross Halian had been the one who rescued her from Kerasi captivity four years ago. Aila considered him an old and dear friend.

She squeezed his hand and gave him a peck on the cheek. "Way too excited to see this happening. It's good to see you again, Mr. Halian. I suppose it's not proper protocol to hug you."

Halian's eyes scanned the room with amusement. "Not in front of the cameras, but catch me later and I'll take you up on it." He gave her a playful wink.

Aila laughed. "I'll do that." She caught Kel's cold glare as she backed away, and dropped her gaze to the floor.

All the briefings on board the ship had been clinical, information skimmed from a text book. Having many of the same things explained by Ross and his crew, people living it first hand, seemed more real, more serious, yet less dangerous at the same time.

"You will be accompanied at all times by *aghát* officers," Ross emphasized. "They are specifically trained to be of service to you, just like those who work inside Union space. Each of them has had a month's rotation at the Embassy to ensure they know what they're doing. You can bring any concern to them at any time. If they don't know the answer themselves, they have permission for direct contact with the Embassy, and we can explain things in a way they might understand better. You already have two extra *aghát* embedded with your delegation – Major Masákh, and Captain Haghíde." Halian gestured toward the officers standing out of the way by the wall, and they bowed in return. "Some of you are familiar with them from their work inside the Union these last several years. They are available to anyone, and will accompany you throughout your stay. When in doubt, the safest greeting in any situation is to bow and say, '*Jihtar saar om seh.*' 'It's an honor to meet you.' It works for all castes. Practice that. *Jihtar saar om seh.*" A minute or two passed with the delegates murdering pronunciation to varying degrees.

"Correct, Captain Haghíde?" Halian asked.

Haghíde's head snapped up. "Yes, Captain Halian. Quite correct. It is a faultless greeting for all people."

Kel's eye fell on Aila. "I didn't see you practicing, Miss Perrin. You are not exempt."

Aila blushed again. "You asked me not to show off, sir. I already know *jihtar saar om seh,* and when to use *morae* instead." She rolled it off with better accent than Halian.

Halian waved her away with his hand. "I'm not worried about you, Miss Perrin. You're well-acquainted with the basics."

De'a Moann, the Prime Minister of Koos, raised a timid hand. Most Koos were thin with graceful, slender limbs, nothing to hold up to Kerasi violence. "We are safe on this mission, aren't we? Have you heard anything at all that raises a red flag? I mean, should we be sleeping with one eye open, just in case? Will we have any privacy at all?" Her eyes darted to the sides, where the five Kerasi *aghát* stood waiting for a need.

Halian nodded methodically. "I have met with the Emperor himself no less than six times, to go over exactly what we requested for security and safety of everyone involved. I can say that as of yesterday, my team inspected the arranged living quarters and found no evidence of surveillance plants. It is my utmost belief that Emperor Nághtas is sincere in his efforts to make this accord a success. The fact remains, if the Union really wanted to, we could overpower their empire through sheer numbers, invade their planet and lay everything waste. No one wants that. Yes, this is new and untested, but stay positive, and we'll take one day at a time. They are just as terrified about your security and how it reflects on them as you are of being here."

De'a's delicate shoulders slumped down in relief, as did many of the other delegates'. "Thank you."

The private reception lasted an hour, before several Kerasi officials arrived to begin the formalities, offer a tour of the palace, and show them to their suites. Ross Halian stepped to the side as the officials took over. He beckoned Masákh to him with a finger. His face carried a seriousness he hadn't shown in his briefing.

"Major, I saved your ass when you were a prisoner of the Planetary Union, did I not?"

Masákh took on a defensive formality. He bowed his head. "You assisted in getting us released from holding, yes."

"I did that based on Miss Perrin's testimony, and her unwavering faith that you kept her from personal harm. I know she's hired you as a personal assistant. She trusts you. She's very high-profile, both at home and here on Kerasím. By rights, she should not have been allowed on this mission because of that. I don't know if you know anything I don't, but I'm telling you, both on and off the record, if she comes to any harm during this mission, there will not be an asteroid in the universe where you can hide. I will find you, and you will wish for death a thousand times before you ever see it."

As the threat turned personal, Masákh lost his diplomatic neutrality, staring Halian in the eye with unbreakable resolve as he had the first time they had fought over Aila. "Captain Halian, not only am I sworn upon my life to protect her, I have already made that promise to Admiral Perrin. The Emperor's claim is sincere: he is most grateful for her efforts that have brought about this peace, and it is his utmost wish for that peace to continue. Even though Miss Perrin is unaware, know that no fewer than thirteen persons are personally charged with ensuring her safety while she is on Kerasím, persons of power, from the Emperor himself downward. You yourself do not have that kind of protection. Be assured: no person on Kerasím is under greater protection at the moment, not even the Emperor's wives."

Halian bowed his head in concession. "Then may this accord be the success Emperor Nághtas seeks, and the beginning of great friendship between our people."

Aila had been to consulates large and small, top of the line modern and buildings hastily renovated to functional for the various populations they served. She'd stayed in hotels, apartments, embassies, wherever Dad had been granted living quarters in his travels. Visiting landmarks and world treasures was an unavoidable part of every destination. Never had she been inside a building so ostentatious as Derahl Nohr. The oldest sections dated more than 1100 years back, a living museum, state building, and Emperor's living quarters rolled into one. The accumulation of a millennium of gold and silver leaf, artistic treasures, and styles of architecture left no rest for the eye; every turn of the head brought something fantastical into view. Yes, most of the paintings were sexually explicit or were violent battle scenes through the ages, but the style of the art itself was commendable. A three-hour tour barely made a dent in the first floor and grounds, but they did get to view the room for the evening's reception, and the council room for the accord.

Aila collapsed on the bed in her grand guest room, exhausted from walking the long hallways. The delegates were housed at the palace in two huge apartments with common areas and eight bedrooms each, one apartment for men, one for women. Masákh and most of the other security staff had a dormitory room across the hall.

The inequity didn't seem right. Aila had a room with a monstrous bed of yellow and pink naturally striped wood carved and painted with gold accents, and heavy draperies hanging from the ceiling to showcase it. The walls were encrusted with layers of trim and deep red brocaded cloth, showcasing paintings, mirrors, cabinets, white and red furniture, and a desk with Kerasi computer interfaces built into it. She was afraid to touch anything for fear of marring the magnificence with fingerprints. All that extravagance for just one person.

"You are not Kerasi," Masákh said, amused by her complaint. "I, a lowly *whátaral*, am assigned a bed in a staff dormitory in the royal palace. I would be most honored to sleep on a folded carpet in a storage closet. You do not understand the privilege just to walk freely in the halls. *Whátaral* do not dream of this. I would wait on a list for years just for the privilege of washing a floor."

Aila shrugged. It was nice, it was a special luxury treat for the delegates, but it was just a famous building. She didn't want to tell Masákh that, though. "As long as you're happy, I guess."

She sat up and changed the subject. "So, did you figure out what I'm wearing tonight?"

Nine

One by one the Union guests were announced as they entered the banquet hall, so that the Kerasi would know who they were. The hall was immobile with etiquette, people bowing, kneeling, speaking, drinking, and dozens of armed security officers prowling the walls. Some two hundred Kerasi mingled about, various *bhísroti* heads of state, advisors, *fáhganid* magisters, governors, overlords, Generals, Admirals, and several 'lowly' *dáhneg* lords, a Who's Who of Kerasím. The banquet table extended at least forty feet, with numerous personal servants ferrying food back and forth, for *bhísroti* didn't serve themselves. The Emperor's wives clustered off to the side, resplendent in jeweled gowns in pale silvery colors, their hair done up in artisanal styles that must have taken hours. They could greet the dignitaries and speak with them across a silver rope, but were off-limits for conversation to everyone else but *bhísroti*.

Aila tiptoed into the grand room, mesmerized by the people and costumes and décor, unsure what to do. "You're staying next to me, right?" she asked Masákh.

"My place is at the side with the security personnel."

"Aren't you supposed to translate for me? Aren't you supposed to test my drink?"

"I am unsure. I have never attended an event as high as this. I will ask Ráhnif about correct protocol. Remember you are *dáhneg*; I cannot act without your permission."

Aila bowed as her name was announced. The room seemed to hush, then break out into louder murmuring. People elbowed each other and pointed at her. Several gaudy females started toward her, giggling and shoving, daring each other to speak to her, like any Union women would if they spotted a celebrity. A man stepped in front of her, blocking their approach.

He was middle-aged and taller than Masákh, perhaps taller than Haghíde, and he gave off an aura of power that said he was used to being in control. Unlike the majority of the room, he wore a brown dress uniform, loaded with commendations. His chin hank was thick and dark, wrapped by a braiding of metallic threads. At each crossing of threads a small red rhinestone glittered. His ID and rank pins identified him as a Level-Five General.

Level Five?

Generals rarely made it past Three, and fought tooth and nail to make Four, which put them in the running for political appointments. General Tokh made Four only because Aila, under his care, had broken the ice between governments. And this guy was a Five? What the hell had he done, then?

Careful, Girly. Big careful.

He bent his head and smiled, polite and not overly ingratiating. He spoke to her – in flawless Standard.

"Welcome to Kerasím, Aila Perrin. I have long wanted to meet you. I am *fáhganid* General Five Trannor. It is an honor to meet the female who brought two hostile worlds together." He held out a hand the Union way – an ungloved hand.

Fáhganid, the one caste no one seemed to trust, all power and little accountability. Aila smiled in return, but curled her hand against her chest. "It would be unfitting for a *dáhneg* to touch a *fáhganid*."

He almost seemed put off, but lowered the hand with a tip of his head. "You are quite correct." His arm slithered around Aila's shoulders. *Dáhneg* could not touch *fáhganid*, but *fáhganid* could certainly touch *dáhneg*. Trannor glanced at Masákh. "I will introduce the Councillady to several people she should meet. Dismissed, Major."

Aila glanced at Masákh. He froze. A pained look crossed his face. He could not speak against a *fáhganid*, nor a General. "I will be at the side when needed."

"He remains with me as translator," she said quickly.

"I will translate if needed," Trannor said. His arm pulled her along. "Come."

He stopped at the first group of gathered men. Two wore uniforms, three were dressed outlandishly in bright brocades with metallic trims. The youngest might have been sixty. "This is General Four Ojahn, General Four Galdek, *Bhísroti* Vilom, the Minister of Education;

64

Bhísroti Rolapad, the Minister of Galactic Outreach; and *Bhísroti* Sarkulang, Minister of Employment. *Daran Aila Perrin, Union Council for Kerasi, vimnarhesu khomina Triskaris Tokh.*"

The cluster of men gave a simultaneous gasp of pleasure, and hands reached out to pat Aila on the shoulders and arms, while General Ojahn grasped her hand and swung it back and forth, trying to look like he knew what he was doing. Words came at her from five directions and she couldn't concentrate to follow any of them. The hands remained polite, but Aila felt as if she were being pecked apart by ducks. Was she even allowed to speak to *bhísroti*?

Trannor smiled again, still accommodating. "They are most pleased to meet you. They have heard many wonderful things about you, and it is an honor for them to say they have spoken to you, even touched you." Sure enough, personal comms came flying out of pockets, and they began to photograph each other standing next to her. Aila managed to lean in and smile each time.

"Isn't that a little backwards? I'm just an honorary *dáhneg*."

A hand grasped Aila's elbow and her head snapped around. Secretary Kel pulled at her. "Miss Perrin! You wandered off. You belong with the group. We are having audience with the Emperor's own wives, and you need to be there."

"By all means, Miss Perrin," General Trannor said with a bow. "They should be your first priority." Secretary Kel led her away.

"Thank you! Thank you, Secretary," Aila said with relief. "I wasn't sure what to do or how to get out of that. They seemed nice enough, but you can't trust a *fáhganid*. I've never met a *bhísroti* before."

"What did I tell you about wandering off alone?"

"It wasn't my doing," Aila insisted. "He spoke Standard, and he kind of just grabbed me at the door."

"Where's your guard? I thought that's why you brought him, to protect you?" Kel was stern, but more concerned than angry.

"He was outranked and ordered to the wall with the other guards. There was nothing he could do."

Kel's bright blue eyes bored into hers, parental and disapproving. "Do you see the problem now? He can translate, but he's not going to be able to help you with security. You just said yourself, you can't trust

65

anyone in the room. Now stay together. Blame me if you have to, but Don't. Wander. Off."

"I won't, Sir. Thank you again." He steered her forward toward the roped-off wives.

* * *

Masákh left the wall and moved to follow Aila, but a hand on his shoulder stopped him. He didn't give more than a slight glance. General Five Trannor held him in place. His voice was low and hard to hear over the noise of the room.

"You know General Tokh was banned from the city for security purposes, and communication is most restricted. He wishes you to know that if needed, the emergency frequency is blue. Please pass the word to Captain Haghíde. Stick to your orders, Major. Do not be intimidated by anyone below Thósikh, including me. Your orders come *tansohr Keralihn*. Remember that. I will support you."

Masákh continued to look ahead of him, smiling as if Trannor had told him something humorous. He'd never met the General, never heard of him, but Trannor seemed to be familiar with his private orders. "Thank you, Revered General. Your command be done."

* * *

Aila bowed and spoke to the Emperor's wives, though Kel made sure she didn't linger. She bowed to dozens of *dáhneg* and *fáhganid* who stopped to speak to her, their eyes saying more about their decision than their words, but Masákh had made sure she showed no extra skin, unlike the *bhísroti* women whose necklines often plunged to their waists. She fielded the same questions over and over, able to reply in fairly clear Emperor's Tongue.

What do you think of Kerasím? What do you think of our Emperor? Why does your husband allow you to travel alone? May I inquire if you have rooms for the night?

I am in love with your beautiful planet. Your Emperor is powerful indeed, and his hospitality awes us. I am unbonded and here under the approval of my father, a powerful Admiral in the Union fleet. I thank you for your offer, but I have lodgings this night.

66

Masákh had just returned to Aila's side after disposing of her empty *lunahl* glass when a man Aila hadn't noticed before slid in front of them, dressed in a rich black and silver outfit with a trailing cape falling from his shoulders. Two jumpy servants hovered behind him as if trying to anticipate his next thought. He was older and heavier than many of the others, his skin a deep bronze, his height and the width of his shoulders commanding on their own. A thin ringlet of metal sat atop his graying hair, and his chin hank was tied with a gold band from which hung a dozen tiny chains, each chain ending in a different small gemstone that sparkled when he moved. He was nothing less than high *bhísroti*, with an attitude that took up half the massive room. Masákh glanced up, then took to both knees as if he'd collapsed; Aila copied him without asking why. A moment later most of the room around them was bent on the floor in a rustle of expensive fabrics.

Who the hell is he?

"You are the female Aila Perrin, envoy trained by General Tokh dar-Giláhn?"

Aila didn't dare raise her head. *"Yes, your Reverence."*

"My father His Royal Majesty Emperor Nághtas requests a meeting with you, alone."

Aila studied the smooth blue and white stone inlay of the floor. *"I am most honored, but my aghát must assist me."*

"That is acceptable. You will come now." He turned and walked away.

Super Solar Shit! If his father was the Emperor, then that man was the heir to the throne of Kerasím! *Shit!* The Emperor – the freaking Emperor! Nághtas himself had requested to meet her personally! *Oh, where was Omi Kel now!?* Aila would have loved to see the look on his face, but she didn't have time to hunt the room for him.

Masákh helped Aila to rise and rushed them to follow. He whispered in her ear, "Nadigh, heir to the throne of Kerasím, and *thósikh* caste. It is most dangerous to separate from your group. I urge extreme caution. I do not know what Nághtas desires, but no one can refuse the Emperor a command, *no one*. It is quite possible you may be opposed to what he requests, and there is nothing I can do to stop him. *Nothing*! This is exceptionally risky."

"Protocol?"

"Extreme humility and caution."

Nadigh led them out a side door, through a corner of the massive throne room, into a ready room in the back.

The room was large, made larger by the two-story ceiling, every inch of the room, including the ceiling, decorated in gold leaf and murals of battles and lurid sexual exploits among the soldiers. Massive mirrors covered one wall, lest the Emperor not notice he'd forgotten a gemstone. To Aila's horror, a huge bed dominated the center of the room, easily twice the size of anything she'd ever seen. It, too, was coated in shimmering golds and reds. Furniture stood against the remaining walls: tables, chests, wide padded chairs, *lunahl* racks and glassware – anything an Emperor might desire at the last second before an appearance.

No one can refuse the demand of the Emperor.

You may be opposed to what he requests.

A chill of terror seized Aila, one she hadn't felt in a long, long time. *Could a Kerasi nearing eighty still do those things? Would Masákh and the son watch?*

A rear door opened. Nághtas, Emperor of All Kerasím appeared; Nághtas, on whose whim every person on the planet's fate hung; Nághtas the Mighty, grand enemy of the Union for fifty years, whose plans for societary reform had included kidnapping Union citizens. Two armed guards in gold attire preceded him, marching in perfect synchrony. Two more followed, with two servants after them. The Emperor wore an informal black shirt and pants with only a single large emblem on a chain around his neck, and a cape made of what looked like a silver metallic fur. He was grossly fat, to the point where walking seemed painful. His hair and chin hank were white and unadorned, bright against his skin, but his fingers were covered in large rings of precious metals and gems. A silver belt was strapped below his great stomach, keeping a sword at his ready. Nadigh dropped to a knee; Masákh fell to his, forehead to the ground. Aila did the same, watching from the corner of her eye.

"Rise." The command seemed annoyed. Perhaps it was frustrating staring down at the backs of heads all day.

A guard frisked the guests. Masákh's energy pistol and service knife were placed on a receiving table, in sight but too far away to be used. Nághtas dragged himself toward a stone-topped table, waited for his cape to be removed, and dropped onto a wide chair with a grunt. He raised a finger, and a servant scurried to prepare him a tray of refreshments.

"General Tokh's emissary, Aila Perrin, as requested, and her translator, *aghát* Major Masákh gha Lil, of General Tokh's command," Nadigh said.

Nághtas lifted his head, surveyed the room. "Nadigh, guests: stay. The rest of you, out." The finger waved again. His two servants and all four guards left the room, two in each direction, to stand outside.

"Now we have privacy. Come! Let me see you." Nághtas beckoned, and Aila took several steps forward, then bowed again. Fear crept up her spine but Nághtas made no attempt to touch her.

"Small, for such a powerful human." His face softened, the lines and wrinkles increasing as he gave a smile that, with the white hair and whiskers and the full curve of his rust-red lip, would have looked appropriate on a gnome. His voice was low and gravelly, and he didn't rush his words. "I have wanted to meet you for some time. I wanted to extend my gratitude for breaking open negotiations with the Union. It was a surprise and a delight that you were able to do that. That was our goal, our only goal, no matter what your Union wanted to believe. President Mijono is a difficult enemy, but he makes better use of his strength as our ally."

Aila kept her head bent. "It is my pleasure to serve your great cause, Excellency. You have done me highest honors by giving me *dáhneg* privilege. Perhaps the honor belongs more to my teachers, *Triskaris* Tokh and his *aghát*. Without their good teachings, I would never have understood the task."

Nághtas motioned to the table beside him. "Sit with me. Dine with me. You were treated well by Tokh?"

Nadigh brought a smaller chair and placed it beside the table. Aila bowed, thanked Nághtas, and sat. Masákh stood behind her. Nadigh retrieved the servant's tray of fruit and creams and small puffs of spiced pastry and put it on the table. He placed several on a golden plate for his father, several items on a smaller silver plate for Aila. She, Human Female, was being served by no one less than the Heir of Kerasím himself.

"I had some moments of distress, but yes, most times I was treated very well. Much better than Union propaganda led me to believe."

"What is the Union's stance on my proposed reforms?"

Politics. Aila didn't need Masákh's warning glance to tell her to tread carefully. "I hear both sides of the debate. Both sides make important points. There is worry that the laws and beliefs of our worlds are in too much conflict, and that allowing citizens free access will result in great misunderstandings and legal issues, creating further difficulties. Others feel that if openness is achieved in small increments, those fears will be irrelevant as we come to understand each other better."

"And you? What do you think of my reforms?"

Aila bit her lip. She wanted to be truthful, but she didn't dare insult the Emperor, either. "I think you are the bravest leader for wanting the best for your people, especially when it places you in a difficult position. It is not easy to implement changes that may be unpopular, even if it is in the best interest. If I understand your plan correctly, to open new paths for females, even to take the throne, then you have my full and unwavering support, and I pledge to fight for you within Union councils. If I can do more, please do not hesitate to ask."

Nághtas smiled once again, showing the points of his teeth, yellowed and worn with age. "I am most pleased with your support." He waved his finger; Nadigh opened a bottle of spirits and poured two glasses. He sipped from one, nodded, then handed it to his father. He placed another before Aila. Direct acceptance of objects by a female from a non-familial male was forbidden; fingers could touch, skin could contact, the giving could be misconstrued. Nadigh, heir, wore no gloves. Aila did not turn her head but lifted the glass and held it up to her shoulder. Masákh took it, drank from it, handed it back with his approval. She wiped the lip of the glass with a cloth from the table and swallowed enough to be gracious. Sweet, light, possibly *lunahl*, or at least something similar. She wasn't about to ask the Emperor if she could check the label.

Naghtas's face grew harsh and dark. "You imply my glass is foul?"

Aila tipped her head in deference as Masákh so often did, but kept her eyes toward the table. "You designated me *dáhneg*, your Excellency. My guard is only *whátaral*. While his task is to keep me safe and he has the heart of a *dáhneg*, it does not remove the caste difference between us."

His Excellency sat back and stared hard at her from under the bushy white brow ridge. Then he began to laugh just as hard. Nadigh joined in, slapping his father on the shoulder. Masákh smiled politely, and at last Aila smiled, though she didn't understand.

Nághtas patted her hand, skin to skin. Aila's insides crawled, unsure of the meaning. It might have been just the Emperor showing approval; for all she knew he might have just marked her as his territory. "I have never seen anyone understand us so well. You are within your rights. Does your guard bed you?"

Aila's heart missed a beat, but she held steady. Thank goodness she could still speak the truth without fear, even if they scanned her. She could feel the giant bed behind her breathing down her neck like an open invitation. "No, Your Excellency. He does not bed me. In the Union, it is an abuse of power for a teacher to bed a student, or any other leader to bed a person of lesser position merely for personal gain. It is often a punishable offense."

"That is a shame. Does he support me?"

"Your Excellency, I have heard him and his officers complain about many things in their lives, but let me be as clear as I can: in more than a year of captivity, in four years of working with them in an official capacity, I have never once heard them utter a word against you or your policies, even when they did not know I was listening, even when they had been drinking spirits. General Tokh and his *aghát* are among your most loyal supporters and never tolerated the least insult against you. Even when faced with great personal difficulty in Union prison, they treated your orders as law above all else and defended them even at risk of personal danger. Few in the Union are that dedicated to their leaders."

Nághtas bowed his head at her. "May your praise be truly deserved. Loyalty should be rewarded. *Aghát*, come here." He leaned to the side and tried to pull his sword from its sheath, but his fat got in the way. Nadigh helped him free it.

Masákh rushed around Aila to kneel at the Emperor's feet, head bent.

"Do you know him, Nadigh?"

"He is General Tokh's second *aghát*."

"And how does Tokh speak of him?"

"He spends much time behind Union lines, spreading peace. Tokh relies heavily on him, and speaks many praises."

"That is good enough for me." Nághtas gazed down at Masákh. "You are *whátaral*?"

Masákh's throat was dry as dust. "Yes, Your Excellency."

"You swear your allegiance to me above all else?"

"If it pleases his Majesty, I will give my head here and now."

Aila jumped from her seat, restraining herself at the last second from throwing herself between them. "Then I will require a new translator!"

Shit! Chalk up a major social blunder in front of an Emperor, you stupid female! At least no one from the Union witnessed it. She sat down in embarrassment.

Nadigh gave a hard snigger and looked away. Nághtas gave a wheezy chuckle, jiggling the mountain of fat in his lap. Three quick taps of the sword touched the back of Masákh's neck. "By my order, you are granted *nhásarwharl* privilege above your caste, extended to your wife and heirs now and for all time. Nadigh will see to the change. The female may keep her translator."

Masákh remained kneeling. His voice choked. "I thank you most graciously, Your Excellency. May I never disappoint you. Loyalty, Duty, Honor to the Emperor." He backed away, bowing with each step, until he stood behind Aila's chair once more. Nadigh helped replace the sword.

Nághtas went on to question Aila for at least a half hour on Union policies, which she explained with as much detail as she could. The Emperor seemed pleased.

"One more thing," Nághtas said.

Aila took a deep breath and held it. *Here it comes.* She could hear the rustle of bedcovers behind her.

He leaned forward over the table, almost knocking his plate to the floor. Nadigh grabbed it and moved it safely away. "*Khip Orahnj, Spayce Khadet.* It is a Union entertainment. Do you know it?"

Aila paused, not sure if she understood him right. Kip Orange was a B-grade videotainment loved best by pre-pubescent boys. It followed the story of bumbling Kip Orange, an accident-plagued man who happened to wander in and out of adventures without meaning to. It was inane, relied heavily on slapstick comedy and many gags about

72

bodily functions. They barely contained any dialog at all. She'd seen them with her brother Ramie. On the other hand, what better thing to transcend cultural barriers than physical comedy with few demands for language?

"*Sukh*, I know it. He is trapped on a ship by accident and is taken into space."

His Royal Majesty Nághtas, fearsome Emperor of all Kerasím, crowed with delight and shook his fists in victory.

Nadigh explained, "That is my father's favorite Union entertainment. He watches it almost every day. He wishes to know if there are more stories like that, that he may enjoy those as well."

What the... ? This was diplomacy? Aila took a deep breath. "*Sukh*. There are two others I know: *Kip Orange On Vacation*, and *Kip Orange Circles the World*. I can recommend several others that are similar, if it pleases your Excellency."

Nadigh bowed his head to her. "My father would be most grateful."

Nághtas ended the meeting with a wave of his hand. A finger signaled to his son. Nadigh went to a cabinet and brought out a small vial. Nághtas slid himself around the seat with difficulty, and with perhaps more difficulty Nadigh wrestled his hands under the heavy stomach and to Aila's horror unfastened his father's pants. Masákh's hand pressed down on her shoulder, keeping her in her seat.

Nadigh opened the vial and proceeded to dribble rusty-brown liquid on his father's underclothes. He stoppered the bottle and wrestled his father's pants closed again. "You are a female dignitary. My father is expected to bed you to maintain his dominance," he explained. "We are aware this is not the way of the Union and wish to abide by their laws in the name of diplomacy. However, that is not acceptable here. We ask in the name of friendship between our governments that you agree you were dominated."

"You're faking it," Aila realized. With Naghtas's age, his weight, his physical condition, Aila wondered if it was more like he just plain *couldn't,* and this disguised that fact more than anything. Either way, she was glad for it.

Except for her parents.

What would her parents think, when word got out? What would their friends think? How would her coworkers treat her? She'd be the laughing stock or the pity party of the entire Universe.

No.

"I cannot allow that. The Union will not take kindly to such action, whether real or implied. That would be a terrible setback to relations between our worlds. There will be great consequences."

Nadigh stepped toward her, fierce and terrible under his cape. Aila could not help cowering back against her seat. "One does not correct the Emperor. If you cannot abide by his request of agreement, then I will uphold our laws by completing the act."

Aila burned at the threat. She didn't doubt for a second he was up to the task. Masákh hadn't moved his hand; his thumb rubbed invisibly against her back. There was no choice. "I will join your secret, but only on Kerasím. I will inform my government it is a secret move by his Royal Highness, made from the goodness of his heart, knowing that more aggressive behavior would be frowned on by the Union, and reinforcing his desire to make peace. That is the best I can do. But while I am on Kerasím, it has been my greatest honor to be chosen for service to His Majesty the Emperor, and I thank him for the opportunity to bring him pleasure."

"Acceptable. I remain impressed by your training," Nághtas said. "Tokh has done exceptional work. You will have my personal protection whenever you set foot on Kerasím."

Aila slid to one knee. "Your kindness is exceptional, your Excellency. Thank you."

Nághtas needed three tries to stand from his chair, at last relying on a hand from Nadigh to steady himself. He led them from the room, Nadigh bringing up the rear. As they exited, the security guards fell into formation, one before and one behind. Nághtas entered the banquet.

"All bend before His Majesty, Emperor Nághtas, Emperor of All Kerasím!" barked the guard. The room fell to its knees, including the Union personnel. Every bare inch of floor seemed to be taken up by trailing capes or wide *bhísroti* skirts.

Nághtas grabbed Aila's hand and raised it high. With the other hand, he released his trousers and they fell to the floor, revealing the stain. "Relations with the Union have officially begun!" he announced with delight, and the Kerasi crowd let loose a loud roar.

Aila's eyes never left the floor. Her cheeks burned with fire. She barely felt Nághtas let go of her. Nadigh raised his pants for him. Nághtas signaled his wives and they followed him out of the room.

"Get me out of here," Aila whispered through clenched teeth.

Masákh rushed Aila around the edge of the room, out the main door and to the closest lift, shielding her from the crowd. As the doors closed, Aila released a strangled scream. Her arms flapped and flailed, and it took all her sensibility not to punch him. "Does it ever stop with you people? Can you ever interact with a female without humiliating her? I've got to call my mother. I have to let her know it's a sham before she hears it on official channels. What the hell's the matter with you?"

Masákh stood with his face in the corner of the lift. He sighed as if exhaling his entire life, as if he hadn't breathed at all during their meeting. The lift stopped at the guest wing and he pulled himself free. As the doors closed again, he leaned against the wall of the wide hallway. A sheen of sweat covered his face, and he was trembling. *Masákh* was trembling.

"What the hell's the matter?" she repeated. "Are you sick?" Was it something in the drink he tasted? Was it something catching?

Masákh seemed on the verge of a panic attack. His breath came in stentorous gasps, and he tried to slow it. "I cannot begin to explain. You are not Kerasi; you cannot understand. The Emperor is... almost a religious figure. He holds that much power. I, a *whátaral*, have just knelt before His Majesty in person, swore my loyalty before him with my own breath, offered him my life, and he gifted me *nhásarwharl* privilege without anyone's petition. I beg forgiveness for my lapse of professionalism, but I am overwhelmed by my emotions at this time."

Aila looked about the empty hall in disbelief. Her arms slapped against her sides. "Great. All my coworkers think I've been viciously raped by the Emperor of Kerasím, and you're doing backflips." She stormed off to her guest room.

In the room, she opened a direct message line to her mother. "Mom, Dad, you might hear something disturbing on the official channels about me and the Emperor. I want to tell you beforehand it is, under all circumstances, not true, and I have witnesses to swear to it. I am perfectly fine and unmolested, so please don't worry. I understand the reason it was said, I don't approve, but in the name of diplomacy I had to allow it. I'll explain in detail when I get back home. I've got stories you won't believe and theories I'm pretty sure are true, but meanwhile, please don't believe the rumors. I was actually very excited to meet with the Emperor, and overall I was rather impressed with him. And *bhísroti* are every bit as boring as I was told they are. What a bunch of spoiled twits. Love you both. I'll be in touch again soon."

She took off her shoes and jacket and was shaking her hair free when someone knocked on her bedroom door. Aila peered out.

Vanora Aikerman grabbed her wrist. "Aila, are you all right?"

"Fine!"

Aila opened the door. Wodu Mosi and Secretary Kel followed Vanora into the room.

Mosi put a concerned hand on her shoulder. "You're sure you're all right? What happened in there? What was he claiming?"

"I'm perfectly fine. It's a sham, meant to save face for him before his people. I didn't know what else to do, so I agreed to allow it. We sat and talked, drank their wine, ate their delicacies, he asked me about Union comedy videos he's enjoyed. He thanked me for my efforts at opening relations between us and asked many questions about my captivity. I told him what I thought of his policies. And then we parted. That's the God's honest truth, with Masákh and Nadigh the heir as witnesses. By Kerasi standards he must bed any female dignitary sent to him, in order to maintain his image among his people. All that's on him is dye. In all honesty, if you watch him up close, I don't think his health is strong enough to actually do anything. Nadigh claimed it was out of respect for the Union, but I'm not sure I believe that."

Aikerman looked horrified. "That's obscene! You never should have gone alone, Emperor or not. You should have insisted Omi go with you."

Kel's mouth pinched in anger. "Did I not tell you in no uncertain terms to stay with the group, not wander off? You don't know how lucky you are to be back here, let alone in one piece."

"I do know, and I also know that was the freaking Emperor himself, and not one of us would have declined his invitation. Masákh was there. It is an insult," Aila agreed, "but I didn't want to offend him or start a major scene, so I promised to promote the lie among his people but not ours. I just finished messaging my mother, so she heard it from me first."

Vanora gave her a brief hug. "That's very responsible of you, dear. I'm sure she'll appreciate every word."

"Where's your bodyguard?" Kel asked. He took several steps to peek into the empty bathroom.

"I sent him back to his room. The Emperor granted him some privilege or something and he practically had a religious experience over it. I don't think his feet are touching the ground."

"Bastards," Kel spat. "All the more reason we need to show restraint. Nághtas promises reforms from one side of his mouth but then pretends to have raped our youngest delegate so his people believe in him. He can't have it both ways. How can we trust him? We'll never know which side of his face we're talking to. If he asks you to meet with him again, you tell him I must be present or you cannot meet. Is that understood? I am the voice of the Planetary Union for this accord. I need to know what's done and said."

"I understand. I don't blame him," Aila said. "I honestly think he's doing the best he can. When you meet him you'll see for yourself. His ideas are worthy, but he's got a tough road to get them past all those air-headed *bhísroti*. I think he's playing a waiting game until after this conference is over. Once we're back off the planet, he can make stronger moves without having to worry about us."

Mosi shook her shoulder affectionately. "You're absolutely certain you're okay?"

"You know me, Wodu. I'd tell you if I wasn't," Aila insisted. "I'm better than fine, actually. I just met the Emperor of Kerasím – had drinks with him! I'm the first Human female in the history of the Universe to do that. I guess I'm a bit over the edge with that, too, when I think about it. Wow."

Ten

A promise to an Emperor could not, under any circumstances, be broken. Aila spent a full hour researching Kip Orange entertainments on her hand unit, and others of a similar vein. She packed all the programs onto a data chip and sent it via Masákh to Nadigh to give to his father, or Nadigh's servant to give to Nadigh to give to his father, or whatever crazy chain they followed. Aila suspected the difference in data systems wouldn't be an issue.

Comedy programs. She'd given the tyrannical Emperor of Kerasím a gift of moronic comedy programs. Aila couldn't stop shaking her head.

Morning came too fast, keeping up with the pace of the day. Today they would leave the palace for a two-day tour of the cities and countryside, an overview of Kerasi life, until they returned to the palace for the big ceremonies and peace accord. While the thought of seeing the people and society she had spent almost a quarter of her life studying was a dream come true – the number messed with Aila's head when she thought about it – the thought of the coming pomp and circumstance seemed far more interesting, and she hoped the days would speed by. One day, just one day, and already it was the trip of a lifetime.

True to Naghtas's word, the *aghát* Ráhnif knocked on her door before breakfast. He handed her a small ID card in Kerasi and a smaller box, then disappeared with a quick bow. Inside the box was a small pin, barely the width of her pinkie, two gold swords crossed over a circle of cobalt enamel. She messaged Masákh, who appeared within minutes.

"Who was it that gave this to you? You should never open anything until I examine it," he reminded her. "It is the Emperor's promise. By wearing the badge, you announce to all who see it that you have the direct protection of the Emperor. The card states it in writing.

If you are harmed, it will not be a random *dáhneg* or *fáhganid* who will deal with the accused, but the Emperor or his guards themselves. It is an insurance policy that cannot be bought, only gifted." Always alert to things Aila would never think of, he scanned the badge with his hand unit, and when he was satisfied it contained no listening technology, he pinned it onto her shirt next to her caste and bravery badges.

Masákh removed a small cloth from his pocket and polished the fingerprints from them. "For a non-Kerasi, you are gathering quite the assortment of commendations." His head twitched to the side as if he had a tic, not just once, but several times. He caught her eye, glared at her, and twitched it again.

Aila frowned. "What?"

Disappointment crushed his face. "Blind female! My *whátaral* badge! I received the documentation this morning. The silver disk behind it indicates privilege, the silver of *nhásarwharl* surrounding my brass *whátaral*."

Aila grinned from ear to ear. Her first instinct was to kiss him, but instead she bent forward and gave him a perfectly correct bow. "May I be the first to congratulate you, and the first to bow to you as a *nhásarwharl*. Did you show Haghíde yet? Will he be mad? The Emperor couldn't grant you the full caste?"

Masákh returned her bow. "It would be far more complicated and create many problems. Privilege is ninety percent of the caste and far easier to grant. I am certain Haghíde will have much to say about it. As *aghát*, we operate outside the bounds of caste, so it will change nothing between us."

"As long as you're happy with it. But you still can't touch me," she said with a saucy wink, and closed up her travel bag for the next part of the trip.

Day one was every bit as exhausting as promised, filled with so many sights Aila would never remember all the details even looking at her photos. The wake-up call for the second day seemed to come just minutes after she fell asleep.

The longer breaks for transport on the second day allowed for napping, and the slower pace of countryside made the day seem more relaxing. Aila had been to zoos, but even back in school she could not remember ever having visited a working farm. *Bagresh* were adorable little animals the size of tiny goats, friendly and large-eyed and bouncing everywhere like hyperactive puppies on springs. The short-haired varieties were used for meat and dairy purposes and the long-haired varieties for textiles, but thousands upon thousands of them in the same place gave off an unbearable stench that rolled across the open meadows and corrals with every slight breeze. At times Aila found it hard to keep a smile when she was choking for air, but she was glad she wasn't one of the two or three representatives who wound up vomiting, made worse when they were offered samples of various dishes made with *bagresh* meat.

The second stop of the day, a two-hour flight away, was a *trobe*-fruit orchard. *Trobe* was the main fruit used in the manufacture of *lunahl*. To Aila's great relief, the orchard didn't use *bagresh* fertilizer and the air smelled fruit-sweet, with the ground giving off a sun-drenched faintly toasted smell. Rabihrkal *Lunahlery* was one of the most respected distilleries on Kerasím, makers of various types of *lunahl* for several hundred years. Aila didn't understand the whole fermentation process, but the white berry fruit looked very pretty hanging down from the purple-black leaves of the *trobe* vines, row after row after row, as far as the eye could see. The vines were trained to grow in great horizontal wheels, leaves up, berries down, making them easy to harvest. After the tour of the vineyards and fermentation rooms and bottling, they were treated to a great display of local delicacies and the chance to taste twenty different types of *lunahl* made on the premises, from light sparkling clear to dark amber in color.

"Remember, the word is taste," Masákh warned her. "Do not take more than that. I am not responsible for the others; I have no desire to be wiping your vomit from the aircraft."

"I'll be careful," Aila insisted. A bowing worker offered her a small glass from a tray, and a card in Kerasi that explained the type. Aila accepted it and returned the bow.

Masákh yanked the glass from her hand, pulled his probe from one of his million hidden pockets, and stuck it in the liquid. The light on top stayed white. He handed the glass back.

Aila gave him a sarcastic eye. "You really think they're going to poison us here, with their reputation at stake?"

Masákh wouldn't be shaken. "And would you suspect them if you became violently ill tomorrow? I was hired to keep you safe; I will continue to do so, whether you approve or not."

Aila shrugged. "Whatever makes you happy." She took a small sip of the approved *lunahl*, a sparkling white. It was sweet, but had a sharp aftertaste that dried her throat and made her want to drink something to make the feeling go away. Maybe that was the point, but she didn't care for it. She reached for a candy sample in the shape of a *trobe* berry instead. It wasn't chocolate, wasn't the same color, but the consistency and sweetness were similar, and she liked it better than that particular *lunahl*.

The delegation had broken into four groups, one around each of the other *aghát*, who explained the type and content of each glass, and why it was significant. Aila was on her third clean taste when murmuring broke out among Haghíde's group.

Vanora Aikerman turned around to Aila. "My dear, have you tried this one? This is delightful, best one yet. I may have to bring some back with me." She held out her glass, filled with a ginger-colored liquid.

Aila paused, embarrassed by the inevitable grab. Masákh took it, but fumbled the probe and it rubbed against the outside of the glass.

The light on top turned orange.

Masákh stared at the light, not quite believing it. He wiped off the probe, reset it, and dipped it in the liquid. The light stayed white. He wiped it again, this time touching it to the side of the glass. The light turned orange. He examined the readout, face absolutely neutral but Aila could see his eyes were already thinking three steps ahead.

He placed the glass down. "Councilwoman Aikerman, may I see your hands, please?"

Aikerman turned a shoulder to him. "My what?"

"Your glass has raised a concern. I would merely like to test your hand to see if you have come into contact with a chemical."

Aikerman grew alarmed. "What kind of chemical?" Those around her now turned to watch. Haghíde's head came up sharply, eyes intent on the probe. Vanora put her palm out.

Masákh touched the probe to her palm, then her fingers. The orange light continued to glow.

"What is it? What does it mean?" Vanora demanded.

"Can you test me?" Reqi Posht asked, and held out a hand. Several others made the same demand. "Why isn't anyone else testing this stuff?"

Masákh gave a small bow and a crafted smile that Aila had long ago learned meant pure bullshit. "It means none of us washed our hands between touring the vines and sampling the product. You came in contact with the dust of a fungicide during the tour. If you would care to wash your hands, nothing further needs to be done."

Haghíde's group disappeared in a rush to the nearest lavatory, making the other groups take note. Several other council members followed them. Masákh tried to wave Aila to go with them, but she hung back.

Masákh flashed the readout discreetly to Haghíde.

"That is not a Kerasi compound." Haghíde said just above a whisper.

Masákh shook his head just enough to be seen.

Eleven

The guard opened the door to the Emperor's quarters. Nághtas lounged in his private sitting room, his youngest wife at his side, a pretty waif-like thirty year old with a very pregnant belly. A Union comedy played on the wallscreen. Nadigh strode in, followed by his daughter Rimas. Both took to a knee.

Nághtas wrestled himself up to a sitting position. He ordered his wife to shut off the video and leave with a tap and a wave of his finger. She kissed his neck and obeyed. He waved the guard out next.

"Come, come," he said to Nadigh. "Sit with me. Do I not receive affection from the daughter of my heir?"

"Of course, Wisefather Emperor," Rimas said. She bent before him and pressed her lips to his hairline, then bent further so he could kiss her on her throat. "Thank you for receiving me, Wisefather." Rimas gave off the same aura of power, the same sense of intensity her father carried. Her dark brown hair swirled loose around her shoulders, accented with several bright pink stripes near her face. She didn't care for the crazy fashions of the other *bhísroti* women but wore black silk bloomers and a silver blouse that wrapped around her figure. She moved about with a comfort that defied the *bhísroti* air of privilege that garnered so much resentment from the other castes.

"Sit, my special one. You have made your mark on the Council, that is for certain. A strong start. They will not underestimate you again, but there is much you will need to know if our plan continues to flourish. Report, Nadigh. How are the delegates fairing on their tour?"

Nadigh bowed his head. Even as Royal Heir, he still had to adhere to most protocol. There was always the possibility he could lose favor, be executed, and his brother Moragh would take his place. Highly unlikely, but a legal possibility nonetheless. "All eight *aghát* report favorably, your Excellency. No unscheduled events took place during the tours. One almost took place, but the guards dealt with it most swiftly."

Nághtas glared. "What type of incident?"

"A *nhásarwharl* demanded favors from an escorted but unmarried *rhibáni* in the marketplace. The female's father pleaded otherwise."

"And the result?"

"The *nhásarwharl* was castrated by the authorities."

"Were the delegates aware?"

"No, your Excellency. It is not believed so. They were led from the area at the first sounds of trouble."

Nághtas breathed a sigh of relief. "Good. And our star dignitary? What did she have to say about what she saw?"

"She was with Dihr's group today. He said she was most impressed by the new school for females, and applauded your efforts. She bought numerous gifts at the markets, asked questions about the local governmental structure from Governor Plengh, and took many photographs of the Governor's gardens which she then sent back to Union space with great approval."

"When they return, I want you to meet her, Rimas," Nághtas said. "She is an amazing little creature. Sometimes a mistake can be the best fortune. We had no idea their female young were so intelligent. She is barely past childhood and already adept at the play of diplomacy."

Rimas laughed. She flipped her hair back and crossed her legs, quite at ease. "You would not have given me the same credit, Wisefather, if Father hadn't insisted. I would still be planning parties and nursing infants."

The Emperor swatted her words from the air. "Yes, yes, but you were a process over time. We did not set out to make you a commander of men from the start. That was your father's idea. Had your brothers lived past infancy, none of this would ever have come to pass. The Perrin child was an error on our part, but a very good one. The Fates delivered her to us for a reason. She is like you, Rimas, quick of mind and strong of will. She has been an unfailing advocate for us, even when we made mistakes. You must get to know her, friend her."

"I saw her at the reception. She is barely older than my son Targha."

"Age is irrelevant. I have two wives younger than you; we still find things to talk about. Together you will learn much about the other. She remains our greatest link to success. Her and that other one. Mohsih."

"Wodu Mosi," Nadigh filled in. "The councilman for adding new worlds. I spoke with him on the first night. He is already aware of Kerasi etiquette, and attempts to speak our language. That is a most favorable sign. He asked important questions and gave favorable replies to ours. He is someone we will be able to work with. The *aghát* have dealt with him often and find him to be fair."

Nághtas sipped at his glass of *flehdan*. It made his feet swell and his heart race, but it was night, his physician wasn't here, and he was the Emperor of All Kerasím, by the stars. "By word of the *aghát*, he has supported the Perrin girl from the start. He will be a worthy ally. Rimas, what should our next move be?"

Rimas looked up with a start, unprepared for the question. "Your Excellency?"

Nághtas belched. He scratched the skin behind his chin hank. "If you plan to rule, you must always think like a ruler. If I put you in charge tonight, what would you do to ensure this accord goes in our favor?"

Rimas looked panic-stricken. She searched the corners of her mind. "I would say we must be perfect. Show them exactly how they wish us to be, that we are more similar to them than they realize. If we show them our best, show them how we are trying to achieve their goals, they will see we are true to our words. We are honorable, and deserve a chance."

Nághtas frowned, the sagging bronze cheeks drooping to cover the corners of his mouth like stage curtains. "A goal, yes, but our weakest one. We could show them a videogram that plays like a holiday advertisement but it does not mean they will believe it. Good will does not forge bonds by itself. Nadigh?"

Nadigh had been trained to rule since birth; he not only anticipated the question but was two years down the road on planning. "We need something big. Something to catch the eye of the galaxy. You should sign something major into law during the accord. After they give their speeches, we make a grand gesture that they cannot ignore. The question is, what. Too much and there will be a backlash while they are

85

present. Too little and it will not have the impact we need. What are their greatest arguing points?"

"Assault on females. Capital punishment without due process. The position of the *ghinadín*. What they term a 'slavery' issue with *ghinadín* and consorts. The list is annoyingly long." Nághtas sipped at his *flehdan*.

"I would vote for improving the rights of consorts," Rimas said, "but too large a change would create an unworkable counterattack. A single law will do nothing to stop the random assault of females; it would have to be enforced, and that is too easy to sidestep."

"Without doubt. That is something that must be tackled slowly."

"The easiest to fix is that of capital punishment," Nadigh said. "Make it illegal for any citizen below *bhísroti* to take the life of another without an order from a court, or forfeit their own life. It may clog our courts for a while until we expand laws and courts to handle the cases, but it will show that we are willing to give due process and are not executing citizens randomly for petty offenses of which they may not be guilty. Should a mere insult be worth a life, even a *soláhrin* life? That is a major step that should please them. It will cause grumbling, but not uprising."

"The *fáhganids* will scream like a female on her wedding night. What about the military?"

"Exempt," Nadigh said. "Strictly a civilian law. Although it should include reckless military executions of civilians."

"I like that," Nághtas said, fingering his *flehdan* glass. "It is bold, but will not create undue stress on the structure. We have another day until they return. We will sit with my lawmaker and write it up tomorrow, and announce it the night of the accord."

He leaned forward with a grunt and reached out to chuck Rimas under the chin as if she were nine instead of thirty years past it. "Patience, Rimas. I will make this a world for you to rule yet. Your father and I will pave the path, one way or another."

Rimas smiled back at him, the favored small-child of the Emperor's forty-five small-children. "I know you will, Wisefather. I will make you proud."

Twelve

Secretary Kel was right. Diplomatic tours were an exhausting pain in the ass. There was nothing glamorous or impressive about being dragged at high speed around a planet, face cramping from a perpetual polite smile, stomach churning from so many funny smells and foods, and always the fear you'd do or say something wrong and insult the host, defeating the whole purpose of being there. And that was not counting the fact the palace was six hours ahead of ship's time, giving everyone a rotten case of flight lag. Tonight would be the main palace event, council with the government of Kerasím, dinner with Emperor Nághtas, and spectacular festivities that were being touted as firsts for Kerasím. All Aila wanted was half a day to catch her breath, lie on the bed in her grand guest suite and rest up, but no one would have that chance.

Masákh caught her lying down and clapped his hands sharply. "Up! You leave for a museum tour in thirty of your minutes. You will disturb the condition of your clothing lying down."

Aila pulled herself up and endured his tugging and smoothing until she was once more presentable by *aghát* standards.

"There. I will see you when you return, and I expect you to remain presentable."

Aila snapped her head around. "What do you mean, when I return? You aren't going? You have to go!" She circled around him, her hands, her face, her whole body involved in the begging. "You're my translator! You're my bodyguard! I need you next to me. What if I have questions? What if something goes wrong? What if I need you?"

Masákh rubbed her cheek with the back of his gloved finger. His eyes met hers, holding the gaze so long he seemed to caress her with it. The finger left her cheek, traced her lip back and forth as if deciding whether it needed kissing, then slid down and gave her a chuck under her chin. He broke the gaze and flashed a faint smile. "It is a simple museum, in perhaps the safest city on the planet. The Emperor's *aghát* will be there, as well as Haghíde, and you know Haghíde can handle anything I can. Ráhnif has my full trust, should you need help. I have errands to make while you are out."

"They're not political, are they? Nothing where you could get hurt?"

"You are concerned about me here, on my own world? Is it care about me, or concern over losing a bodyguard? Haghíde will gladly take my place."

His words hit a chord. *Damn him!* She was trying so hard to stay focused. Aila turned away to hide her face. "Haghíde is a dear friend and I always trust him, but it's not his name I whisper in the middle of the night."

They were alone in the room, unseen. Masákh wrapped his arms around her from behind, allowing himself to hold her, just hold her, his cheek against hers. Aila leaned back against him and a little thrill shot up her spine at the contact. "I know your words. Do not worry about my duties. One of them is to find you something proper to wear tonight. There is nothing among your clothing that is adequate by Kerasi standards. The meeting will be televised live all over Kerasím, even into the *ghinadín* cities via mobile community viewscreens. There should be one Union delegate who the people can believe in, who understands our people, supports their customs and businesses and appreciates their culture. Sometimes a visual speaks louder than words."

She leaned her head back to look at him. "You're not going to dress me like a *bhísroti*, with my neckline to my waist, are you?"

He released her from his arms. "Not when you are a lowly *dáhneg*. Your mother would demand my head. And Haghíde would lose his mind."

"Mm. Could you do me a favor? Grab something small for Mrs. Aikerman – a pin, a scarf, a hairnet – I don't care. Anything Kerasi that could go in her favor, too."

"As you wish."

* * *

Aila had not been gone half an hour when Masákh was escorted into the small discussion room, his weapons having been removed in the hall. He had no idea what to expect or why he had been summoned, or even by who. He did not question the Emperor's guard who whispered, "Major, your presence is requested on the third floor." *Whátaral* allowed inside palace walls did not question.

His heart sank as he entered the room. *Was this fortune or foul?* Heir apparent Nadigh sat in a casual chair, raised several inches above the floor. A small folding chair stood opposite. Behind Nadigh stood two guards in gold, fully armed with swords and painful control sticks in their hands, ready for action at the slightest provocation. Off to the side sat Nadigh's daughter Rimas, silent but shrewdly attentive. Masákh dropped to his knees and bent forward, head to the floor.

"Rise. You are Masákh gha Lil of General Tokh's *aghát*, publicly hired as escort for the Union emissary Aila Perrin and privately assigned by my father as her personal guard. We met in my father's presence three days ago."

"Yes, your Majesty."

"You may sit."

"You are most gracious, your Excellency." Masákh rose and took the small chair. It was hard and uncomfortable beneath him. This was not regulation. Nadigh was *thósikh*, controlling every citizen on Kerasím except his father. Masákh could not refuse him. He had no idea what he would do if Nadigh demanded he act against the Emperor. To disobey Nadigh would be a death sentence; to break his oath to the Emperor would be a death sentence. He did not like either choice.

"You have sworn your loyalty to the Emperor."

"Yes, your Majesty."

"What is your opinion of the Human emissary?"

Masákh sat back but kept himself no less at attention. What was Nadigh after? What did he wish to hear? Masákh could not lie to a *thósikh*, but he was not willing to sacrifice Aila, either. "She is young, but gaining experience rapidly. She has internalized the Emperor's plans for change and feels it to be her personal duty to help Kerasi females find their voice in their world, as her females once did. Within the Union there are no limits placed on females, of any kind."

Nadigh nodded slowly. "Do you bed her?"

"No, your Majesty. That is a scannable truth."

89

"Have you bedded Human females before? Do you wish to bed her?"

Again Masákh tread with care, unsure where the conversation was headed. The wrong order could place him in a very difficult situation. "I have, your Majesty, when I was sequestered in Earth's past. Humans have mating rituals which are not easily decoded and mistakes can cause legal difficulties, but as on Kerasím, there are those whose favors can be bought. Should the correct opportunity present itself and she agree, I would not be opposed to bedding the emissary."

Nadigh gave a contemplative hum. His body language was relaxed, indicating friendly conversation, but his face gave away nothing more. His chin hank was bound in gold cording wrapped in shining blue threads, and his fingers twisted absently at the tuft of hair at the end. "I forgot Tokh and his unit were involved in time experiments. But you have restraint. You work with females within the Union. Do you find it difficult to work with them? Distracting? How are they able to work without caste order?"

"Most of them do not have the same behaviors when working as when they are not. They are focused on their tasks, which allows one to focus on his. One accepts as law that they cannot be touched, and it prevents misinterpretation of signals. As for caste, it is often replaced by a gradient of positions, such as in military ranking. One may speak or act one way to coworkers of the same level, but must show restraint and respect when interacting with those of higher position. The greatest difference is mobility: anyone may be born on the level of a *ghinadín* and with education and opportunity rise to the level of *bhísroti*, male or female."

"And you have no difficulty with this? You have taken orders from females?"

"Yes, your Majesty. I have accepted orders from higher-ranked Union females in my duties. *Aghát* can be from *whátaral*, *nhásarwharl*, or *díhnarwharl* status; by directive we work together as *aghát* free of caste interference. That has helped smooth the transition."

"You've commanded those of higher caste, without difficulty?"

"As an *aghát*, yes."

"Fascinating." Nadigh's interest seemed genuine, as if he hadn't expected such answers. "Then you would have no difficulty accepting a female as Emperor, with rule over males?"

Akh! So that was where this was leading. But why? "Your Majesty, I was among the first group chosen for the *aghát* program, before the age of ten. My entire life since has been with the goal of assisting the Emperor with the proposed plan to disable the caste system and place a female in power. That has been my life's objective; I cannot believe in any other vision."

"And you would submit to mind scan over the same information you have just given me?"

"Without fear, your Majesty. My answers will not change."

Nadigh sat forward as if he'd stumbled onto a winning prize. "Excellent. One more question: if you were required to trust another with your life, who would you choose?"

"I have trusted my life to General Tokh and all of his *aghát*. He has picked a most excellent unit of men. If I had to rely on one, I would chose the *aghát* Haghíde. I know his competency, and our philosophies are closely aligned."

"Haghíde..."

"*Aghát* Captain Haghíde Kitáhl, of General Tokh's unit."

Nadigh gave a satisfied sigh and sat back in his chair. "I was among those who chose General Tokh to head his program unit. He has proved himself exceptional for many years; it is no surprise he chose exceptional men for his team." His eye lifted toward Rimas; Rimas gave a slow blink without changing her expression at all.

"Let me explain," Nadigh said. "I trust you understand the information is not to leave this room."

"By my honor, your Majesty. Your word is law."

"By my father's current plan, if all goes well at the accord, he will step down on his 80th birthday, turning active rule over to me. I will have perhaps twenty years to finish carrying out his plans to increase the participation of females in society and decrease the stranglehold our bloated caste system has on the people. When I am of similar age, if nothing dreadful has befallen me, I will then step down and turn rule over to my daughter Rimas. Rimas will be the first female Emperor of Kerasím. There will be great backlash and unrest, an outcry for my brothers or her son to take the throne; it will be a most difficult position to maintain and she will require advisors and protectors she can trust implicitly. I am already in the process of screening potential candidates for positions starting after I am Emperor. You have passed my first assessment. Does the candidacy appeal to you?"

Masákh's heart had stopped beating two sentences before. He fought hard just to make his lungs inflate. Such a position was beyond prestige, but also a double-edged sword. Should he fail the Empress, she would have his head. Those who envied his position would also be hard after his head. But the honor, just to be interviewed! Far beyond anything he could ever have imagined. Not here. Not on Kerasím. Not for a *whátaral*. This was fantasy at its strangest. His words struggled to find air. "I am most humbled by your gracious offer, your Majesty. I exist to serve you. I would be honored by any position his Majesty feels appropriate for me."

Nadigh broke eye contact as if his business was now concluded, but after a pause he spoke again. "You are trusted by the Union delegates. I will set you a test: My father's plan was to show them how civilized we are. I want them to see our worst. Show the delegates what we fight against, what they must help us change. Fire up the egos of the males who think they can change us. Make the females weep in empathy. Pull them tighter into our cause. Can you do that?"

"Of course, your Majesty." Masákh answered before he had even the faintest plan in his head. "I will need access to an official vehicle, and a driver familiar with the city. When may I begin?"

Nadigh's eyebrow crawled upward at the speed of his response. From the corner of his eye, Masákh could see Rimas staring at her father with the same expression.

Nadigh granted permission with a wave of his hands. "I will authorize a vehicle in your name immediately."

* * *

The museum proved tolerable; the exhibits interesting, the artwork sublime, Dihr and Ulan's explanations and guidance *aghát*-perfect, and Haghíde's chatty curiosity kept her mind off other matters, but Aila was relieved when it was over. She returned to find numerous boxes and plastic-wrapped packages waiting on her bed.

From a square box she removed an exquisite pair of shoes, black velvet with glittering gold swirls and a boxy heel. Aila tore off her Union shoes and tried them on; not only did they fit, they were comfortable as hell. She ran to the wall mirror and twirled around. They were dressy, but looked just as wonderful with her brown pants and rose-colored tunic. A slim package revealed a long veil of black and gold lace. Aila had wrapped it around herself like a ribbon and was prancing in the mirror when Masákh knocked and entered.

"Is everything to your liking?"

"I haven't unwrapped it all, but these shoes are to die for." She wiggled her hips under the ribbon of veil. "If I were a more naughty type, I would wear this and nothing more."

Masákh raised an eyebrow. "I would be most interested to observe that, but it would be deemed disrespectful for public greeting of the Emperor, and you would be turned away."

She dropped the veil and danced over to him. "What does my dress look like, then? What color is it? Black or gold like the shoes and veil? Is it gold? It's gold, isn't it!"

"All-gold formal attire is reserved for *thósikh* only." He took his knife from his belt and slit the wrappings on the final box. "Go to the mirror. Close your eyes."

Aila ran to it, too eager. His hands pulled at her tunic.

She pulled it back. "Hey!"

"*Shu, shu!* Do you trust me or not? Keep your eyes closed." He removed her shirt but restrained himself from looking at her pink undergarment or its lacy little straps, or the way one strap slipped off her shoulder and folded itself so delicately on her arm, or the direction of the soft fuzzy little hairs on the sweetly curved back of her neck, nothing but business. Masákh slid the dress over her head, cool and silky as a sheet of rain. When her arms were in and he'd fluffed it into place, he said "Eyes front."

"Ohhhhhh!"

The mirror took her breath away. The dress was pure overkill Kerasi glory. The monstrous skirt fell to the floor in four ruffled tiers in a kaleidoscope of forest, wine, and gold swirls. The bodice clung to every curve, armpits to hips. The neckline, edged in shining gold appliqué, left her upper chest bare but her breasts fully covered. The sleeves began off her shoulders and ended just past her elbows. Masákh curved the train off to the side so she could see it, six ridiculous feet of it. He folded it up and fastened it to straps at the waist, resulting in a cascade of puffs and ruffles down the back. With sparkling clips, he gathered and folded and fastened the veil so it hung from the back of her head down to the puffs.

Aila stared, speechless. "I can't imagine... It fits perfect! How did you know?"

He pulled out his pocket interface and aimed it at her until it beeped. "I scanned your measurements. Now you are fit to walk among the *dáhneg*. Almost." He went back to the bed and opened the smallest box. "The clothing was bought on state *dakra*. This is a gift from me."

He fastened a piece of jewelry around her neck. When his hands came away, a choker of sparkling burgundy stones encircled her throat, while a sunburst of clear rays fanned out across her chest. The rainbows of refraction as she turned said there was no way in a supernova the stones were anything but actual gems. She spun to face him.

"I'm not even going to ask. It's far too much! *Soyavoh! Soyavoh!* Oh Masákh! It's lovely! *Oh!*" Etiquette be damned! She threw her arms around his neck and gave him a fast squeeze before stepping back.

He didn't return the embrace, but bowed with a smile, still proper. The dark eyes glowed with a tenderness she'd never seen, hugging her without touching. Aila felt her heart shiver and her blood rush to her cheeks.

"You are more worthy than almost anyone who will be at the display tonight. Now you will look the part."

"You'll do my hair to match, won't you?"

He bowed again. "Of course. Now, I have other work to attend to. I suggest you change back to your street clothes and rest yourself. Tonight will be long."

Aila was fetching herself a bottled fruit drink from the apartment's kitchenette when her interface gave a soft tremble against her leg. She pulled it from her pocket and read Masákh's silent message.

Do you have four or five associates who share your viewpoint that you can trust? If you can get away without alerting the entire party, meet me on the first floor by the lifts in ten minutes. There are things you should see that are not on the itinerary.

I'll be there, she messaged back.

Aila ran through the list of envoys in her head. Who did she trust? Who wouldn't be missed for a little while? What the hell was Masákh up to? What had he stumbled upon? What would happen if they got caught? Would she be jeopardizing everyone's job? Kel couldn't destroy her if she was with others. If it wasn't on the itinerary, what would happen to Masákh if the Emperor found out?

"Vanora, do you trust me?" she said softly.

Mrs. Aikerman had been gazing out a tall window, studying the acres of back gardens and the people in them. She turned her head. "Yes, I suppose so."

"Can you think of two or three other people you can trust among the delegates, people who share an allied viewpoint? They're more likely to listen to you than to me."

"Perhaps. Wodu is strongly in favor of open relations. Perhaps Marisi Belenn. He's usually adventurous, or Hawet Quin. She's a good sort. What's up?"

Aila checked her small carry bag. She made sure she had her ID, water-treatment tablets, and enzyme tablets in case she had to eat anything non-official. She knew from experience not all Kerasi food digested well in Humans. "Message them. If you want to see something important that's not on the official tour, meet me by the lifts on the first floor in ten minutes. Keep it secret, and don't be late."

Aikerman frowned at her. "Where are you going? We have a formal event in just three hours. You can't leave without an escort."

The apartment *aghát* wasn't in sight. "I know," Aila said, and slipped out the door alone.

Thirteen

Four of the delegates appeared out of the lift several minutes after she arrived. Aila hadn't expected more than one or maybe two to show. Masákh and Ráhnif waited with her. Side by side they looked like cousins, Ráhnif being shorter, his bleached skin a shade or two more tan, and his black hair wavy to the point of curls. His goatee was trimmed quite short, perhaps to keep it from curling. Aila could still spot some of the fading scars from his facial surgery; he wasn't made *aghát* more than a few years ago. That would put him in his early twenties.

"Follow me. Stay close, stay quiet," Masákh instructed.

Wodu Mosi was perhaps the second most senior representative of their delegation, Commissioner for Non-Union Worlds, responsible for investigating and representing any world doing business with or applying for membership in the Union. Tall, dark of skin and almost hairless, he was easy to spot in any crowd, given to wearing loose robes in the brightest mix of colors and patterns. Aila had known him for at least four years, and considered him a friend. She should have known Wodu would jump at the chance to see something unofficial.

Mosi held up a hand. "Wait. I would like to know what I'm getting into so close before this evening's events."

Masákh tipped his head. "I apologize for the timing. This is nothing but a street tour. You will not even leave the vehicle. It will take perhaps an hour at most."

"I don't like this," Hawet Quin said. "Why so secret? We aren't supposed to leave the safety of our group, let alone the building."

"I am charged by the Emperor to ensure your safety," Ráhnif said. "I will be accompanying you. There will be no danger. That is truth."

"This is entirely voluntary," Masákh said. "No one is required to attend, no one will face consequences for not attending. It is for your own information only."

"I'm staking my life on this," Aila said. "I wouldn't be doing that if I didn't think it was safe."

"If Wodu thinks it's okay, I'm in," Marisi Belenn said.

"Let's not be silly. I won't let her go alone and I'll never talk her out of it, so I guess I'm going," Vanora Aikerman said.

Mosi gave a nod. "Okay."

Quin raised her hands. "I'm in, then."

Masákh gave a nod to Ráhnif, who bowed his head in reply. They walked down the long corridor, around a corner, and entered another lift that took them down to a service level, where they climbed into an official-looking silver hovercraft, the windows mirrored to protect the riders.

"May we know what we are about to see?" Mosi asked as the vehicle left the underground parking area and emerged on a side route out of the palace grounds.

"You have toured the best Kerasím has to offer," Masákh said. He stood backwards in the vehicle, leaning against the control panel in a slight crouch. The vehicle was a long luxury transport, seating up to fifteen people in a great horseshoe of gold-trimmed ivory *muuht* leather instead of rows. "You marveled at our factories, schools, and our medical facilities. You have been blinded by the palace, seen the glory of the cities, the depth of our artistic endeavors, the wondrous might of our military and the variety and pleasures of our food and drink. These are things we take pride in, and you should be properly impressed. What you have not seen is anything below *nhásarwharl* in caste, the top of the middle castes. This is a tour of the places you are not supposed to see. Since this is not an official tour, please be discreet and do not discuss it with others until you are back in Union territory."

Mosi nodded. "May we ask questions during the tour?"

"Of course. The vehicle is clean."

Mosi paused, then nodded. No spybugs.

They cruised several miles to the outskirts of the city on smooth, paved roads busy but not jammed with traffic. The walled villas gave way to housing rows and clusters of high-rise apartment complexes. Garden plots, park-like areas with trees and simple fountains, playgrounds, and private markets manned by men and women lent a livelihood to the area. The higher floors bore balconies, and many buildings were painted in bold, bright colors. On cross streets, businesses were crowded together. Aila could read the signs, but most bore pictures so illiterate women could find them: clothiers, bakers, bankers, video screens, shoes. Long transit trains made of several linked cars, known locally as Public Eels, snaked their way through the streets, carrying large volumes of passengers. There was still an abundance of private vehicles, but most were small and similar in design, and all had tires, no hovercraft. Everything was bright and orderly, not much different than a dozen cities Aila knew.

"This is the middle-caste section of the city," Masákh said. "*Rhibáni* will occupy the lower floors, *whátaral* the middle, *nhásarwharl* the top. Single dwellings may house low *díhnarwharl*, sometimes the top floor of the housing units. Occasionally a *nhásarwharl* with special assigned duty may also have a small private residence."

"It's nice enough," Aikerman said. "It's clean. Prosperous. Similar to any number of worlds."

Masákh agreed. "Most middle-caste cities do well. There is low unemployment, adequate services, public utilities. There is low judicial presence – what you would term a police force. The people do not wish to call attention of the *dáhneg* and *fáhganid*, so most crime is small and dealt with on a local level, or by private negotiator. There isn't the grandeur of the upper castes, but for the average Kerasi, it can be a very pleasant life."

Ráhnif continued straight on the same roadway, until a bridge crossed a river. An invisible curtain seemed to span the river, for on the other side of the bridge, a different world appeared. Private vehicles became fewer, and the vehicles were old, in poor repair, and often doubled as transport trucks, with bundles of items tied to the roofs. Shops with bars on their windows lined the bottom of four-story buildings, with walk-up dwellings above. Short trees with thin, droopy branches and airy, tumbleweed-like scrub grew thick in abandoned areas, and young children played among the rubble of a demolished building. They stopped and stared at the hovercraft going by; some tried running after it, while a woman called to them.

"*Tápatihn?*" Aila said.

"And *Soláhrin*. Some of the less-wealthy *tághinet*."

"The lower classes," Belenn said. He had his pocket com out, recording video through the windows, as were most of the delegates.

98

Aila kicked herself, and took hers out as well. "And there's no upward mobility at all?"

"There are better neighborhoods than this, and other cities both better and worse," Masákh said, "but the person would still be limited to a *tápatihn* or *soláhrin* neighborhood."

"So they can improve their property, but not change to a higher neighborhood."

"Correct. Many times the insides of apartments are more impressive than the outsides. The lower castes are fiercely jealous and will destroy the property of anyone they feel is living above their caste. Improvements are kept private."

Ráhnif didn't stop, but continued farther. He turned left and followed the river. After a short buffer zone of emptiness the ramshackle buildings became an outright slum glued together by mountains of garbage, and the road became a treacherous dirt alley between the rows of shelters, so narrow it didn't seem as if their craft would make it through. Construction blocks, plastic sheeting, boards, broken airwings and rowboats made up the walls of dwellings like a castaway's camp. People were everywhere; women wrapped in colorful montages of fabric, men wearing only pants, children both half-naked and naked ran between the multitude of small fires women were cooking over. Every adult bore a scar or symbolic tattoo on their face. Before one dwelling a man was beating a skinny child with a stick. Further down, an argument between two women turned to screeching blows until the vehicle approached and they ran. By the corner of a side alley, a man was having sex with a screaming woman atop a pile of garbage while two other men watched. As the vehicle eased down the narrow street, most of the people scattered like beetles into hiding.

"This is a *ghinadín* village," Masákh explained. He kept his voice factual, neither glorifying the misery around them nor apologizing for it. "Reliable wages are difficult to find. Most survive by picking through the refuse from the upper cities and selling items back for recycling. There are few amenities here. Some of the better off have solar converters and thus rudimentary electronics. There is little private sanitation. Facilities are built for them, but they are quickly destroyed and the fixtures sold for profit. Law enforcement does not venture down here unless a major crime has been reported, or a riot or fire has broken out. That is why they hide when they see us; they think we are officials looking to round them up for labor. Occasionally officials will sweep through and look for the healthier children to take away to be trained as workers. Sometimes there is a call out for the military or to fill jobs in industrial fields that no *soláhrin* or *tápatihn* will work, such as mining or sewers."

"This is disgusting," Marisi Belenn muttered as they passed a much more affluent building with a half-dozen women before it. Three bared their breasts and shook them; a fourth bent over and wiggled a bare backside at the vehicle. "And you allow this squalor?"

"These are the people who would be helped most by the Emperor's plan to disband the caste system," Masákh said evenly. "They will not improve overnight, but those with ambition will move up quickly to *soláhrin* or even *tápatihn* levels. With education and nutrition, their offspring could move higher. After a generation or two, most of the *ghinadín* should be assimilated."

Ráhnif continued through the gully of filth for a while before taking another turn, closer to the river. Here, under a smaller bridge, huddled an open-air camp. A few tarps could be seen, but the main shelter seemed to be the bridge itself. A dozen or so people of both sexes lay on the ground or sat on larger stones or overturned buckets. Most didn't move at the approach of a vehicle, didn't move much at all. The men's hair was as long as the women's, and their chin hanks so overgrown they looked like ragged beards. A wizened old man was the only one who seemed to take notice of the vehicle.

"These are the *thanak tohr*, the southern people. They are not mentioned even in Kerasi society. Many began as *ghinadín*, but even the *ghinadín* will not touch them. Some are criminals, some are physically incapacitated or elderly with no offspring, many have minds that are no longer coherent. Prisons do not want them, and they are of no use as laborers. They form their own societies and look out for each other. They cause no harm, but are the only ones *ghinadín* may release frustrations on, so many perish from young *ghinadín* looking for entertainment."

Aila'd never imagined such deplorable suffering, didn't have the words to convey it. A word came to her head, but not a human word. "*Trixahg?*"

Masákh nodded. "Yes. If a female is labeled *trixahg*, this is where she would end up."

"And that means…?" Mosi asked.

"A woman so disgustingly filthy and disease-ridden that even the *ghinadín* will not assault her," Aila said. "If she does not run away, they will beat her to death. Not for a crime, but simply because she lives."

There were several sighs around the vehicle. Ráhnif opened his window, took a package from the seat next to him, and tossed it on the ground. He closed the window and pulled the vehicle away, navigating it over the bridge and back into sensible *tápatihn* territory.

"A charity package, from a *díhnarwharl* welfare society. It will contain small coins, unspoiled bread or fruit, measures of grain, perhaps common medications they cannot otherwise acquire. Occasionally it may contain clothing. Nothing can be of too high a quality, or a *ghinadín* will come and take it from them, with or without violence," Masákh said.

They rode back in silence, save for one last pause within the limits of the upper-caste confines. A beautiful building stood on a corner, pink and white and brown-flecked stone surrounded by columns covered in carved vines and animals. A huge sign sat atop it covered in flashing lights, tacky and out of place with the grandeur of the area.

Aila squinted, lips moving as she sounded out the symbols. "Does that say what I think it does?"

In the front, Ráhnif nodded. Masákh did as well. "It is an auction house for consorts. Those with enough status may come here and purchase a female as their private consort. A consort is property; a wife has legal rights."

"Slavery," Marisi Belenn acknowledged.

"Yes, but the only work they do is on their backs, with no say in the matter," Aila mumbled. She remembered only too well the plight of General Tokh's consort Mímihn, a beautiful young blind girl, so lonely in her isolated world, and how becoming a consort had been one of the greatest fears of Aila's captivity. She switched to Kerasi to avoid embarrassment with her coworkers. "*Masákh, remove us before I cry.*"

They were back at the palace within minutes. Wodu Mosi stopped Masákh before they entered the lift. "Thank you for the tour. But why show that to people who already support your cause? Why not show it to those who are undecided, or don't see the point?"

"Your eyes are open now," Masákh said. "Those who are undecided would be ashamed of what they saw, and ignore it. Those opposed would say it is too big a problem and cannot be fixed, so there is no need. You already believe you can make a difference; now you know the situations that will benefit most from your actions."

"Why? You're from a privileged position. What's your stake in this? What do you get from the dissolution of the castes? Money? Power? A better house?"

"I have little to gain from the destruction of the caste system. I am middle of middle. I might gain some, but not greatly. My reasons are patriotic and personal. That is my scannable truth."

The words caught Mosi's ear. Nothing was more infamous, more feared, than the Kerasi mind scanner. "Can you get us a demonstration of your notorious mindreader machines?"

"I regret, no. They are few in number and are considered highest security. I do not have necessary clearance, nor do I know the locations of such machinery."

Mosi bowed from the waist. "Forgive me, it's my duty to ask."

Masákh bowed in reply. "Quite understood."

Aila made it back to their apartment before the tears broke loose. All the times the *aghát* had drilled the misery of the *ghinadín* into her, how they practically spit the word in disgust, told her over and over that as a foreign female even *ghinadín* held power over her, so she'd better behave. She'd run into *ghinadín* during her captivity, mousy little man/boys stunted from a childhood of malnutrition, terrified of not performing a duty correctly, the scars on their face ensuring no one ever mistook them for anything but the lowest of the low, their eyes never leaving the floor lest they offend. They were the punching bags of the entire planet, and they lived like rats in a trash can, for no reason of their own.

Mrs. Aikerman put an arm around her. "What's the matter, child?"

"Those people! Living off garbage – With no shelter – I can't – I heard about it, but now I've seen it with my own eyes, and it's real, and I still can't imagine. How? How do they let people live like that?"

Vanora pulled her into a grandmotherly hug. "Don't let their poverty get to you, child. I've seen it before on a half-dozen other worlds. There's still a few isolated pockets like that on Earth, if you dig hard enough to find them. It just looks a little different, less permanent. It was good of your friend to show it to us, so we can show the rest of the galaxy. I hope he doesn't catch trouble for it."

"He wouldn't have done it if it wasn't safe. You just – you don't know. You never spoke with some of those women. You never lay awake nights worried you could become one with one word from a captor," Aila cried. "Everything they ever frightened me with – I just saw it, and it wasn't just a made-up threat, it was real. The vote has to go through. They can't keep those people living in those conditions. They can't!"

Mrs. Aikerman rocked her side to side. "Yes, I have talked with women like those in my years. We call them by many names. The difference is we made it illegal in the Union, and when we find it going on, we have the right to rescue the women immediately and lock up the dealers. It's just public here, that's all. You're young, child. I'm seventy-four years into this life; I've seen the evils in the world. A diplomat's work is never done. You can't save the entire universe, but every person you do save is a victory. And I agree. I took enough video during the tour; you can be sure I'll be giving a lecture on it during the flight home. Shush, now. Go wash your face. We have a banquet to attend, and you can't be looking like you've just come from a funeral."

Aila wiped her eyes and gave a wan smile. "Thank you." She felt bad for misjudging Mrs. Aikerman. She was old, she was a nosy busybody who thought she knew everything, Aila would stake big money she was reporting to her mother at least twice daily, but all in all, she was all right.

Fourteen

Aila stood in the hallway with the other delegates, waiting for the last few stragglers. She had to admit, she had never looked more stunning in her life. Masákh had rolled her hair up from the sides and pinned it until it hugged her head in smooth waves, leaving a single curl to dangle on each side, very Kerasi. The shimmering black and gold veil stood up from the back of her head on sparkling veil-pins and hung down her back like a waterfall. She'd gone lighter than Kerasi-standard on her make-up, just enough to give her face a soft bronze sheen and some color, and her green eyeliner not only matched her dress but made her eyes stand out. The fabulous dress made her slender waist seem slimmer and her small breasts rounder, and the glittery necklace lit up her chest. *Hell in a supernova!* She was prettier than all the one-eyebrowed nobles in all the paintings lining the walls. Several of the hall guards saluted her, and everyone, right down to the Emperor's *aghát*, paid her unrehearsed compliments. She sent a dozen photos of herself to her parents, not one of them with Masákh.

Those she kept to herself, outside of one she sent to Thayer without any explanation. That was about as sordid a detail as she had at the moment.

Masákh and Haghíde stood apart with the Emperor's *aghát,* all of them in their dress uniforms, right down to their gloves and swords and shining boots. From what Aila could overhear, they were discussing which Kerasi dignitaries and which Union ones were most likely to make fools of themselves at the dinner, and how awful it was to be on duty when surrounded by so much free Pepper Rum. Once everyone left the guest floor duty would prevail, and they would not have time to speak to each other the rest of the night. Aila stood with Vanora, who was delighted with Aila's gift of a silver net dotted with blue beads that she wore over her short hair, complementing her navy and silver pantsuit. Vee M'para and Chedna Kerek appeared at last, Vee with shoes still in hand, and they boarded the lift down to the main floor.

Secretary of State Kel's hand shot out, blocking Aila's path. "Miss Perrin, may I speak with you privately?"

"Of course." She gave a nod to Vanora to continue without her.

Masákh stopped dead before the doors. Haghíde was at the end of the line; he gestured for Masákh to go ahead; he would cover. Masákh joined the party in the lift.

"I asked to speak to Miss Perrin *alone*," Kel emphasized.

"I will move aside if you desire more private conversation," Haghíde said, "but the task of bodyguard requires Miss Perrin to remain in my reach at all times."

"You aren't her bodyguard. Masákh gha Lil is."

"He is on a break before we begin and I am relieving him."

Kel put his arm around Aila's shoulder and pulled her farther down the hall. *"What the hell are you doing?"*

His tone caught her off guard. It was cold, angry, accusatory, and it frightened her. She'd never considered anger when he asked to speak to her. Not from anyone in the Union. Her interface was in a small wine-colored silk bag looped around her wrist. She clutched it tight with both hands until she could feel the outline of the interface. One press to activate it, one press at the top where Masákh's link should be. She held the bag to her chest, link open, the better to capture every word. "What do you mean?"

"This!" Kel grabbed a handful of ruffle and shook it. "Whose idea was this? That damned Kerasi whispering in your ear? This was not approved by the State Department. A veil, a necklace, even a handbag, fine, but all out like this in imperial colors? Are you trying to tip the scales? Why don't you fill in a third eyebrow, take it all the way? Is there some secret agenda you're playing, or did the Emperor ask you to do it the other night while you were screwing him?"

Aila didn't give a damn what kind of incident she started, what she got charged with, or if they fired her from the council. They couldn't arrest her until she got back on the Union ship. The little pin on the shoulder of her dress said the Emperor promised to protect her. Dad would understand. Hell, he'd even approve this one. She slapped Kel's face as hard as she could with the hand that wasn't clenching the bag.

"How dare you!" she hissed. "How dare you! Excuse me for showing support for my hosts, like a good ambassador should! Excuse me for trying to be a role model for the billions of Kerasi women who so desperately need one, with or without Union intervention. Excuse me for being a good guest and dropping a little money into their economy. I will not even discuss the other comment."

She turned to leave, but he grabbed her arm and spun her back. Haghíde was at her side in an instant, his hand resting on top of Kel's. "Sir, you will release your hand," he ordered, as cold and intimidating as Masákh. They clung to each other, stalemated.

"Did you ever think of the other side of that coin, Little Girl? What signal you're sending to the Union? That we're sucking up to the Kerasi, that things may already have been decided and we're not being truthful to our own people? That you're ashamed to dress like your own people, show off the work and designs of your own economy and artists, win the women over with our society? That with all the televised coverage, companies wouldn't have paid a fortune for you to endorse their formalwear? You never should have come. I told them you were too young, too messed in the head, too much of a liability thinking you know everything. Every time I look away, you sneak off. I'd send you to the ship right now on charges of insubordination, but the cameras will notice your absence. You will be back on that ship one hour after tonight's festivities end if I have to escort you there myself. Keep the accessories, but I want you out of that dress before you go down there."

Aila looked him dead in the eye. "I'm not wearing high-fashion Union clothing because the two designers I spoke to at home didn't think we'd make it back alive, and didn't want their names linked to corpses. And you'd be the last person on the planet to see me without this dress on, even before I file harassment and misconduct charges. And if you touch me again in such a manner, my bodyguard will break every bone in your arm. Don't say you weren't warned. Cover me, Haghíde." She yanked her arm back and stalked to the lift, the huge skirt antagonizing Kel with every flounce.

"You are not fine," Haghíde said in the lift.

"No." Aila gave a sniff, trying to hold herself together. She grabbed her interface, hit privacy with a shaking finger, and held it to her ear. "Did you get all that? Did you do that to me on purpose? Was this dress a set-up?"

"I heard it." Masákh's voice said. "Is he with you now?"

"No, just Haghíde. What the hell did I do wrong?"

The doors opened on the crowded floor. Masákh was waiting by them.

"Did you do that to me on purpose?" Aila repeated.

"No," he swore. "You said you liked the color green. I thought the colors went well with your hair. I almost chose a tricolor blue, but blue is more of an unofficial *bhísroti* color, and *fáhganid* are often seen in red, so I chose the dress more fitting to a *dáhneg*. I did not consider any other consequences. I take full responsibility. I apologize for the distress it has brought you. I will keep a closer eye on the Secretary."

Mrs. Aikerman appeared from the crowd and took her hand. "Are you okay, dear? You look upset. No one that ravishing should look upset."

"I am so beyond upset, I can't speak," Aila said. She ran her hands over her face with care so as not to disrupt her hair or cosmetics. "I don't have time to begin to explain it right now, but I will tell you every word later. Short form: if you see Secretary Kel within ten feet of me tonight, you better step between us, because there will be bloodshed. I don't even know where to start. How does one file assault charges against a Galactic Secretary of State?"

"Oh my. What stupid thing did he do now? Maybe you better not wait too long to tell me," Mrs. Aikerman said. "Stay close, then; I'll protect you. He wouldn't dare pull anything on me." The Union news team approached, camera lights blinding them.

"Can you tell us your name and who you represent?"

Aila leaned toward the outstretched microphone. "Aila Perrin, Union Council on Kerasi Affairs."

"Can you tell us what you're wearing?" said a female voice behind the light. "Is that Kerasi?"

Aila brightened up. "Oh yes! I have no idea of the name of the designer, but I fell in love with it and I had to have it! I'm hoping it's not too fluffy for tonight's festivities. Isn't it gorgeous?" She gave a twirl for the camera. "And you know what's even better than the dress?" She picked up the front of the skirt. "These shoes! Are these not the greatest shoes? I think they're the most comfortable thing I've ever worn. If we have shoes like this at home, I want to know who makes them, because I'm buying a dozen of them when I get back. Is it really bad if I do something tacky? Can I say hi to my mom?"

"Go right ahead!"

Aila smiled and waved to the camera, the perfect picture of youth excited to be included in government. "Hi Mom! Hi Dad! Thayer, can you totally believe this dress! We've got about ten minutes and then we go in to conference with the Emperor himself! Unreal!"

Fifteen seconds of fame up, the camera moved on. Aila breathed a sigh of relief. She'd managed to work in a plug for Union shoe designers, so Kel could eat shit right now.

A Kerasi newsman beckoned her. "Yu-nyon feemayl! Yu-nyon feemayl!" He motioned her out onto the front steps of the palace, where a news crew and cameras waited. Aila gave a wink at Vanora and headed toward them.

"Aila! I urge extreme caution," Masákh whispered. "Crowds are not safe. You will be a target to anyone in range."

"I'm only on the steps." Aila stopped short with a gasp as she looked out from the doors. Tens of thousands of citizens lined the main thoroughfare from the palace gates to the steps. They pressed against barriers, waving and shouting, as guards walked laps slapping them back. Dividers broke up the spectators by caste; the higher the caste, the closer to the palace they could stand, hoping to catch a glimpse of *fáhganid* red or a *bhísroti* in a feathered headpiece arriving at the doors.

Never had she imagined this kind of spectacle.

"Why do you wear Kerasi dress?" the newsman asked. His questions were simple, she could understand them, but the noise of the crowd kept distracting her, and Masákh had to fill in some words for her.

"In the Union, females wear what they like. This dress is the most beautiful I have seen, so I wanted to wear it to honor your Emperor."

"What do you think of Kerasím?"

"I am awed by the beauty of your cities and country. I love to eat *m'vat*. I like it very much. And *lunahl*," she giggled. "I am very fond of your *lunahl*."

The newsman laughed. He wore a ridiculous-looking purple satin striped shirt, and his chin hank was braided with gold cords, split and waxed and curled until the end looked like two big fishhooks. "You are much like Kerasi females. Are Kerasi males desirable to Union females?"

Aila smiled, but she couldn't stop the blush. *Look anywhere, anywhere, just not at Masákh. Don't look at him.* She gazed down the alley of people to the giant statue of the Emperor, as if she were thinking.

"Yes, many of your men are pleasing. I'm sure there are many Union women who would like to meet them."

"Have you bedded a Kerasi yet?"

Aila laughed nervously. Her answer would be broadcast live across the Union and Kerasím. "I have been invited by the Emperor himself, but I must wait my turn. He has many dignitaries. He is a very busy man."

The interviewer gave a braying howl of laughter and chucked her under her chin with his knuckle. "You are pleasing for a Union female. When the Emperor is finished with you, may I take you as my consort?"

Aila laughed again, but with a touch of hysteria. She shot Masákh a polite but frantic glance. "In the Union, females choose whom they wish to be consort for. At the moment, I belong to the Union government, and you would have to petition them for permission."

The newsmen on the step laughed. The women by the steps screamed and waved to her.

"May I greet your females?" she asked. If nothing else, it ended the interview before it got worse.

"Please do."

Aila thanked him and bounded down the steps

"Aila, no!" Masákh ran after her. "They will tear you apart for a scrap of your dress."

"Someone must give them hope." She reached for the outstretched hands, but Masákh slapped her back. He pulled green gloves from her bag and slid them over her hands.

"You are dáhneg!" He bent and straightened her train, feeding the image of royalty for the cameras. Aila reached and stretched and grasped hand after hand of women desperate for two seconds of recognition from an upper caste, from a foreign dignitary, from a *female* foreign dignitary, from a *Union* dignitary. All were polite; not

one even pulled at her gloves. Those not reaching for her took photos with their hand coms.

It wasn't right, though. She was pressing hands with *dáhneg* and *díhnarwharl*, who already had many privileges. She should be among the lower classes.

Good luck. She gazed down the endless mob; if there were *soláhrin* and *ghinadín* here, they were a quarter mile off by the gates. She didn't have that kind of time.

"*Morae! Morae! Morae!*"

Hello!

She rushed down the line, Masákh cursing behind her, until she made it to a few *whátaral* hands, then crossed to the other side and worked her way back, well aware of the news cameras following her.

Screw you, Kel. These are the people that need us. He should have been out there, too.

When she reached the steps again, she stopped and turned to wave one last time before entering the palace, and the crowd screamed.

Wow. So that's what it's like to be President.

Fifteen

Inside the front entry hall, Masákh snarled in her face. He snatched the gloves from her hands and stuffed them into her bag. "That was extremely foolish! That is not done on Kerasím. A dignitary does not risk their life for something so worthless." He reset the train short and fluffed the puffs into place.

"You're wrong on that," Aila said. "We already risked our lives just coming here. That was an insurance policy from the people. It's all very real to them now. They've been touched by the outer world, an outer world that's dressed just like them. They will never forget it."

A bell sounded, a prelude to an orchestra playing The Emperor's March, the official anthem of Kerasím, commanding and dignified. Masákh tapped her arm and she followed. They found a spot in the monstrous front hall, bowing as the *bhísroti* paraded by into the council room, many in bright blue robes or blue capes, noses in the air, as if they'd had to walk through a cloud of flies. Next came *fáhganid*, often in red. Many were in military uniforms, elite of the elite and supremely dangerous, some of them no more than walking executioners. Their eyes shifted side to side, waiting for just one poor soul to break protocol so they could punish them. *Dáhnegs* filed last. If Aila had been Kerasi and male, she would have walked with them.

The imperial senate stopped at *dáhneg*. Chosen *díhnarwharl* might be in the public balcony, but the rest would watch the televised proceedings on monitors in the public rooms. Nághtas did not walk among the common folk; he had begun the assembly by entering the room from the back, shouting a call to meet, banging a jeweled staff on the floor to command it, and taking his throne.

Masákh pulled Aila into line with Vanora and gave her a nod. He would be standing against the wall behind her, with the other *aghát* and security officers. A whisper wire wrapped the back of his neck and sat

111

against his cheek to feed into an earbug she wore, so he could answer questions without having to be next to her.

One by one the Union delegates were announced, along with their positions. They walked the length of the council room, bowed before Nághtas seated on his throne, and walked to their seats. Council boxes were taken with Kerasi; the delegates had comfortable but lesser chairs arranged off to the side at the front. A two-story flag hung from one wall, while buntings of imperial red and gold draped the balconies like a holiday display. Nághtas seemed well-rested, or had taken something to ease his pains, for he stood and sat without help. He looked the very part of Emperor, dressed in gold cloth with white trim and his silver fur cape. A simple ancient ceremonial band nestled on his white hair, the front bearing the Emperor's Crest, a large orange stone set in the center with a small white stone off-center at the top, mirroring their suns.

To the Emperor's right sat his personal council. Nadigh, heir to the throne of all Kerasím, the only other *thósikh* male, no less commanding than the previous encounter; *bhísroti* Moragh, Naghtas's middle son, and Turwheg, his youngest, and four of his most trusted advisors, two of them Naghtas's own brothers. To his left sat the Union members who were giving speeches: Secretary of State Kel, Wodu Mosi, Hawet Quin, and Vee M'para. The main balcony ran around the sides and back of the room, filled with various high-caste officials who weren't part of the council, while the small upper balcony, high in the back, was filled with the wives and consorts of the officials present, another first for Kerasím. Naghtas's twelve wives sat in a corner to the side of the main floor, along with his granddaughter, Rimas.

Nághtas opened the floor, which meant everyone had to remain standing. One did not sit if the Emperor stood, and even if he sat, no one could sit unless he gave permission. Only Nadigh was exempt, sitting while his father spoke.

Aila was impressed. Naghtas's words were clear, thoughtful, and strongly spoken. Perhaps he was simply tired the other night, after a day of walking the miles of halls his palace had. Perhaps he'd been drinking too much. The speech was being translated to Union text as he spoke and fed to a giant screen on the wall behind His Majesty. Aila caught about half his words without translation. A quick check with Masákh proved that the translation was indeed accurate. Nághtas spoke of progress, of the next stage of Kerasi development, of a need to join with the rest of the galaxy if progress was to continue. He spoke of doubling the strength of their economy by allowing the other half of their citizens – females – to have enough education to assist with businesses, perhaps even be in charge of their own trade for the housecrafts they made. It was a tiny step – so tiny – but for Kerasím, it was a giant leap. He continued onward into a speech about peace among the people, and Aila's attention wandered from the screen to watch the reactions of the men in the audience.

Masákh's voice rang in her ear, startling her. "Are you paying attention? This is revolutionary. He has just erased a significant portion of *fáhganid* powers." He translated Naghtas's words for her, not waiting for the scroll on the wallscreen.

"… There is no greater peace than citizens living without fear of death. A system of lower courts will be provided for addressing complaints. A higher court will be instituted to deal with potential capital offenses, made up of three persons of similar caste to the defendant and a *bhísroti* judge capable of carrying out sentence. This ban on random execution extends also to the military; military officers wishing to address crimes by non-military citizens must go through tribunal first. Military crimes within the military ranks will remain the issue of the appropriate commanders. This ban on executions begins today. Complaints for redress may be filed immediately, but courts will not begin for two weeks. Thus is my word as Emperor of Kerasím, infallible and immutable; follow my law."

"Holy Star Systems!" Aila whispered back. "He just wiped out our complaint of death squads. Now we just have to see if he keeps his word. He's really pushing this reform thing, isn't he?"

Nághtas sat to an equal amount of polite knee slapping and rumbling whispers as the information sank in. Nadigh stood next and spoke briefly, lending support to his father's proposals. As the father of only daughters, he knew there was nothing they weren't capable of. Secretary of State Kel stood up, and the room heaved a noisy sigh as Nághtas gave permission to sit. The translation captions switched to Kerasi. Kel spoke about the long road the Kerasi had before them. He praised the Emperor for his foresight, and for the measures he had already begun to take. Much of the speech was taken up with neutral backpatting and diplomatic gibberish. He had to ad-lib comments to the ban on capricious executions; it must have killed him inside to acknowledge their effort, and he stuttered through his praise. Aila spent the last five minutes watching the Kerasi symbols on the viewer so she wouldn't make faces at him. After three robotic claps, she leaned over to Vanora.

Her hand blocked her mouth from camera view. "Nod and smile," she whispered. "Just to warn you, I slapped that bastard upstairs, after he accused me of dressing like this because the Emperor told me to while I was having sex with him. Among other things."

Vanora faked a laugh and nodded. "Oh, that overreactive bastard. I would have beaten him with the heel of my shoe, left a good mark he'd have to explain," she whispered back.

"That might not have been wise." Masákh's voice rang in Aila's ear, having picked up the exchange on the spybug. Aila pretended to scratch the back of her hair while giving him an obscene finger gesture.

"I mean, seriously – Do you see a problem with my dress?" Aila asked. "Look around at the other women – this is really pretty tame. Okay, the skirt is fluffier than I'd choose, but it's not that different than what you'd see at any state dinner, really. Is it? I don't see where I'm out of line at all here."

"No, no." Vanora patted her hand. "I think you look lovely, Child. Are you outshining the rest of us? Are you more attired to your age and less to the dignity of the event? Perhaps from our point of view, but you look ravishing. And if that brings some attention to us, perhaps it's not a bad thing. I told you, Omi's just nervous about making everything come across right. You suddenly changing your outfit just upset him, that's all. Don't take it personally. If he bothers you again, call me over and I'll put him in his place. That's the beauty of being retired; they can't fire me."

Aila smiled and squeezed the hand back. "Thanks, Vanora. I appreciate it."

Hawet Quin stood up next, Ambassador at Large for the Union. Kerasím was on treaty and truce, Ross Halian was chipping at the ice, but there were no formal diplomatic arrangements. Quin liked challenges, and was quick to accept the nomination for Ambassador. If they wanted to open up relations, they'd have to deal with women in power, and Quin had decided she was stubborn enough to be the one. Of Noorish origin, she was short, squat, and just as gray of face as she was of hair. Her black pantsuit took away some of the squat but gave her skin a bluish cast. She was a nice lady, well-respected, very people-oriented and outgoing, someone who truly enjoyed learning about other cultures and seeing what she might be able to do to help them. Aila knew her position on Kerasím was quite favorable, but she wanted to know how Quin planned on phrasing it, and tried to pay attention.

After several minutes, Vanora leaned over. "Do you hear that? That high-pitched whistling? Or am I imagining it? Is it feedback from your earbug, or their sound system?"

Aila paused, listening. "Yes, I do hear it. Just barely. Masákh, do you hear that?"

There was a pause. "Yes. I'm not sure what it is. It could be the air system. It sounds almost like a ..."

A flash of yellow-green light pulsed across the room. Nághtas gave a loud grunt, as if he'd been punched in the stomach. He slammed backward on his throne so hard he nearly stood up, then slumped downward, a huge burn mark in the center of his shining gold shirt. His ceremonial headpiece rolled to the floor. Brownish-red blood oozed up from deep within, not cauterized by the blast.

The room silenced in a single breath, a thousand people staring at the same impossible sight, until one of Nághtas's wives stood up and screamed. Women screamed from the upper balcony, men shouted, and a stampede began toward the main doors at the rear. A crush of people formed; the doors opened inward, against the flow, and no one could move. Nadigh dove for the floor, disappearing under an escape hatch on the podium. Moragh ducked low, slithered over and pulled his father to the floor. A second bolt flashed, and Hawet Quin jumped and dropped in mid-run. As the stampede worsened, a tremendous blast shook the room from outside the closed doors, rumbling through the polished flooring and making the chandeliers rock and dance high overhead. A smell of explosives and thick dust drifted across the room. The stampede stopped, tried to reverse direction, but the rear was still surging forward, crushing those caught in the middle. People jumped or fell from the balcony, smashing down onto the crowd below.

Vanora crouched on the floor, inching toward the front, but Aila sat, frozen, staring at the back of Naghtas's throne stained with blood. Her finger pulled the bug from her ear, and she started to stand. Powerful hands reached under her arms and pulled her up and over the back of her seat until her feet touched floor, the giant skirt slithering after. A third flash sizzled through the row where she had been sitting and lit the back wall; another wave of screams followed, but Aila didn't see where it hit. Dignitaries in their finery crawled on the floor, hiding between the rows of chairs. Security officers wrestled open the side doors to the adjoining meeting room and tried to herd people through.

Masákh's arm propelled her forward as he hurled chairs out of the way. He shoved her through the door to Naghtas's ready room and went to slam it shut, only to find Haghíde behind him, weapon drawn, covering his back. Masákh shut the door after Haghíde. "Run!" was all he could say. Aila grabbed up her skirt and ran for her life across the long room. A servant entered, carrying a tray for after the speeches. Masákh seized him around the neck and shoved his own weapon against the servant's head, even though the man was certain to be of higher caste. The tray and glassware smashed onto the floor.

"The Emperor's emergency door! Which is it? *Which is it!*"

"There! There!" The servant pointed, and Masákh allowed him to press the hidden panels that opened a secret door in the wall.

Masákh released him. "If you or anyone in the building wants to live, I suggest you run now. Hiding might not be enough." The man nodded and ran back toward the kitchens.

"What about – We can't just leave them!" Aila pointed breathlessly at the council room. "We've got to help them! Vanora – I didn't see her – We have to – ! You're security, Haghíde! You've got to help them out!"

"She was seeing to the woman Hawet," Haghíde said. "The Emperor's guard will see to her. My Union orders were just overridden. Go!"

Masákh slipped through the narrow door; Haghíde pushed Aila through and followed, shutting the reinforced panel behind them. Sounds of a crowd leaked through the wall door; others were escaping. Haghíde pushed her forward. Motion lights flickered on ahead of them.

A claustrophobic corridor barely wide enough for Haghíde's shoulders led to a steep staircase, just as narrow. *How the hell could the Emperor's stomach fit?* Masákh headed downward.

"Is he dead? Why? Why would they do that? What the hell happened?"

"I don't know, but I don't wish to join him. Move!"

Masákh rushed, but Aila gave a screech and grabbed the walls, to the sound of tearing fabric.

"I'm sorry," Haghíde said. "The dress is trailing on the stairs. I cannot avoid it."

Masákh growled and ran back up to them. He pulled out his knife, a wicked-looking military issue, stabbed the gorgeous skirt between the second and third ruffle, and hacked at the voluminous fabric. Haghíde did the same on the other side. There was barely enough room on the stairs for them to move their arms.

"Watch my legs! Don't cut my legs!"

"Trixhor pan khar," Haghíde swore after a minute. He beat at the massive underskirt as if it were attacking him. "How much dress is there?"

Aila shrieked. "Haghíde! How dare you use that phrase! That's inexcusable!"

Haghíde stopped cutting. "How dare you know that phrase!"

"That's no excuse for such vulgarity!"

"This isn't standard operating procedure!" he snapped. "I apologize, this is my first assassination! Then it is bullshit! Bullshit, bullshit, bullshit! I know you say that one yourself."

"Shu!" Masákh hissed. "You do not know what is beyond the walls!"

Haghíde dropped his knife and tore at the fabric with his hands; it ripped in a perfect line. Masákh did the same, and in seconds they'd torn the lovely skirt off at her knees. Aila abandoned the long wide underskirt on the stairs, the shed skin of something pale and monstrous.

"Now go!"

The stairs switched back two more times before stopping. Masákh went first, weapon ready, Haghíde prepared to fire over Aila's shoulder.

A door exited them into a security holding area, but it was empty. All personnel were dealing with the nightmare above. Masákh opened a door on the opposite side of the room; a vehicle stood waiting, as nondescript as any upper-caste transport. He motioned them in.

The start stick was in place, ready for a sudden need. Masákh activated it and they emerged from a tunnel on the far side of the rear gardens.

"We will be spotted," Haghíde said, watching every direction. "You are stealing a *bhísroti* vehicle. That's death on a good day. They will assume we are guilty of the assassination as well."

"They will think another *bhísroti* took it, and I will claim military need. There are greater worries at the moment than misplaced vehicles. Once we get to the city proper, we'll leave it."

Aila watched out the rear window. Aircraft were flying thick toward the palace, ground vehicles streaming up the main drive and out across the lawns. Thousands of people fled across the gardens and grass like waves on a shore, *tághinet* musicians and their instruments running alongside *bhísroti* and neither one of them caring a whit less. Private craft fought to retrieve their *fáhganid* or *bhísroti* owners; some didn't care what they flattened in the process, be it landscaping or people. A line of smoke rose above the palace.

"What do we do?" she said helplessly. "What will happen to everyone?"

"Hide. Survive. Regroup when it's safe," Masákh said. "Whoever was firing wasn't doing it on a whim, and they weren't stopping with the Emperor. The addition of the explosion means this was not a simple attack by an angry citizen but a planned operation by someone who knew what they were doing. If they're targeting Union personnel, then you are in great danger. You hired me as a bodyguard; I am keeping you safe. The Emperor's staff will see to the others. They are sworn to protect just as loyally."

Aila glanced behind with distress. "Maybe, but Kel's going to fire me when he finds out I'm gone again."

Masákh abandoned the vehicle in the downtown proper where it would be easy to locate. The assassination had been broadcast live to every household; the city was chaos with panicked servants running for supplies and ground vehicles gridlocking as people tried to flee.

Citizens spotted the *aghats'* uniforms and clamored around them. *"Please help me get to safety! What direction should we flee? Were you at the palace? Is the Emperor all right? The broadcast cut out before we could tell. Escort me to the flight fields!"* A *dáhneg* stuffed a fistful of cash in Haghíde's face.

Masákh brushed each one aside with authority. "Return to your homes and wait for the all-clear announcement," he ordered. "Clear the

118

streets so emergency vehicles may get to the palace. The difficulty is confined to the palace. You will be safe in your homes. We have our duties, let us pass or else!"

"What if they recognize her from the broadcasts?" Haghíde said.

Masákh glanced at Aila for no more than a second. The lacy gold and black veil still hung from her fancy hair like a mantilla. He flipped the fold over Aila's face, covering her to her shoulders. "Now you are no more than another fleeing *dáhneg*. Perhaps no one will recognize a shorter dress."

"I can't see that far."

"All you must do is follow, and not speak."

He led them through a shining office building, its security officer fled from his post, out a courtyard on the other side, across that, and several blocks outward, away from the worst of the crush. They came to a long factory of fire-red glazed brick and shining brass doors. It was dark and empty, all workers sent home early to watch the accord. The main entry was set back in a welcoming alcove, with potted plants, benches, and mosaic tiles on the step, part of the Emperor's initiative to keep his city beautiful.

"Chch!" Haghíde motioned with his head toward the alcove. Masákh steered Aila to a bench behind a tall potted fern, and she flipped the veil out of her face. Haghíde tapped at his pocket interface as if punishing it.

Aila's little red handbag was still wrapped around her wrist. She slipped it off and pulled out her own interface.

"What are you doing?" Masákh seized it from her.

Aila made a grab for it. "Sending my mom a message. She'll be totally freaking out. I have to let her know I'm alive."

Masákh flipped the device over, looked for the seams, opened the back, and removed the operating chip. "Absolutely forbidden. It must remain disabled. If it's live, you are traceable."

"I'm traceable anyway. You think we weren't tagged before coming on this mission?"

"Where?" He pulled out his interface, tapped to the proper instrumentation, and began to scan her.

"Back of my left shoulder."

119

His screen blinked, analyzing. Masákh made an unhappy face. He tapped the screen again and saved the data. "It must come out, but I cannot do it here."

"Moving now. Three minutes," Haghíde said.

Aila put her defunct interface back in the bag and prepared to walk, but a vehicle glided down the street at a crawl, the windows as black as the paint. All three of them pulled back into the shadows until Haghíde's interface gave a yellow flash. He burst out to the stopped vehicle and slid in the back. Masákh rushed Aila ahead of him and climbed in after. Masákh slammed the door and sat back with a sigh of relief.

"Injuries?" said the driver in Union standard.

"By the Grace of the Emperor, none," Haghíde said.

The driver glanced back. "Hello, Aila. It's nice to see you again. I saw your interview on the broadcast. You were quite charming. Your speech is much improved."

Aila stared. She knew only a handful of Kerasi by name. "Ghírandar? Goodness! What's it been, three years? How are you here?" Ghírandar, no more than a raw rookie straight out of training when she was captured, and here he was running covert stuff with no one over his shoulder. He was dressed as if he'd come from the palace, too.

"Anyone of any ability is in the city this week. We were chosen as a unit by General Tokh; our duties may be different now, but we are no less a team. Masákh covered you, Haghíde covered him, we covered Haghíde. And that was our side. I know there were Union plants watching your back as well, but I don't know their names."

"I'll bet anything Secretary Kel wasn't one of them. Probably Davion Foote; I guarantee he knows my father, and I'd guess Vanora, too. She's defense council like my dad and she's female. They probably pulled her out of retirement just so she could room with me."

"Word?" Masákh said.

"Nadigh lives," Ghírandar said. "He's calling all moves from a safe location. There are no counts yet; they are still clearing the council room. The main hall was severely damaged in the blast; they have to wind their way through the side and rear doors. Sources say there are at least six Union dead, many more Kerasi. I do not have names yet. Most were trampled to death trying to escape. It was planned to create a maximum amount of panic and disorder."

"Six of us? That's a quarter! Why? Why would they do that?" Aila cried. "But I liked him! I sat and spoke with the Emperor, drank with him, and he was most pleasant. Why would they kill him?"

"Power does not come without many enemies," Masákh said. "You met him for one hour and he liked what you said. There were many with much to lose from his reforms, and they also had great power."

"Did you know? Did you know they were going to kill him in there?"

"No," Ghírandar said. "If there was a hint, we would have prevented it. Do not assume we are not as grieved as you. We are Kerasi, we are born to this. Nághtas has been Emperor for fifty-one years; most have never known another. He was our existence, our very culture; you cannot understand the depth of our grief."

Aila bowed her head in shame. "On behalf of the Planetary Union, I extend my sympathies to you and the Kerasi people. Know that there are many in the Union who grieve with you."

"We thank you for your grief. Any time there is a large public event, the Emperor is at risk. Inviting Union persons increased that risk by drawing out dissidents. We prepare on the chance, but it has been three hundred years since the last assassination. Until we know who is responsible, know what the Union plans to do, we will bring you somewhere safe."

"Get me off the planet. I need to get back to the Union ships. That's where I'll be safest."

Haghíde gave a snort. "How? Where are your escorts? Where is your Union party? Who will give you clearance to leave, and how will you make it out of our space in one piece? Our Emperor is dead, our government in crisis. All spaceflight was grounded when your ships entered orbit. Air traffic will now be grounded as well. All military will be on full alert. All military ships will be brought to orbit, prepared for invasion fleets. The Emperor wished to reform Kerasi society, but he has brought upheaval upon us. Do not expect communication with the Union for at least a day or more. Until we know what is happening, your safety is our priority. We must find a secure location."

Aila knew her mind had been tampered with at the end of her captivity, memories of locations erased, but she remembered her wire cage, two stories underground, with blinding clarity. "Oh no! I'm not doing that shit again! You are not locking me underground ever again. I'll take my chances on the streets! Is that was this is all about? Recapturing me?" She threw herself over Masákh, reaching for the door. He flung her back with annoyance.

"Do not flatter yourself," Ghírandar said. "You're not that important."

Aila flashed angry. "What do you mean, I'm …"

Masákh silenced her. "Enough. There will be no prisons unless we are in it together. Of that I am certain."

Sixteen

They skimmed through a high-caste suburban neighborhood, the vehicle disguised by location. The farther they went, the more exclusive the neighborhoods, until high walls and shrubbery hid private homes from view. After an hour the landscape shifted; the stunty Kerasi trees became sparser until glimpses of water were seen. Soon Ghírandar was paralleling a waterfront marina; vehicles like theirs were parked helter-skelter as servants scurried to load up watercraft with valuables, their desperate owners shouting abuse from the decks. Craft were leaving in fleets for open water, safer away from land. Ghírandar stopped at the far end, by a sign reading *Palinet Marina Air Landing. Caution.* A folded-wing craft sat on it, dark blue with military insignia, including the marks of a level-four General. The wings were locked upright in the air, waiting.

"Smooth travel," Ghírandar wished them as they climbed out. "I hope I can see you again." Aila thanked him, and Masákh led the way to the aircraft.

He spoke to the pilot, a captain in brown, as Haghíde helped her with the flight restraints. Masákh sealed the hatch, the wings came down in a hydraulic squeal, the engines whined with increasing fervor, and they lifted off immediately.

Masákh waited until they were safely in flight, then reached into a bin on the side of the craft and passed out containers of water and several sealed bars.

"I know it will disappoint you, but we are not headed to a prison, just a safehouse," he said.

Aila sipped at the water, but tried to wave away the food. "I can't eat right now. I'm too upset. I'll be sick."

"Eat," Masákh urged. "First rule of military: if there's food, eat it, because you don't know when you might eat again and you will need your strength. It contains protein and carbohydrates. I believe the banquet is no longer an option for our dinner."

The banquet. Here she sat in the remnants of her fantasy dress, still in the beautiful shoes, the wonderful shining necklace, and a million pounds of crushed hopes and dreams caught like dust in the veil around her shoulders. The longer the day went on, the more the events sank in, the heavier her heart felt. Aila unwrapped the bar and picked at it. It was soft and sticky, full of a fruit puree with a protein paste she didn't want to think about. Not great, but she'd tasted worse on Kerasím.

She tried to hug Masákh, desperate for comfort, but he pushed her off with a quiet retort. He did allow her to cling to his arm, and she didn't let go for quite a while despite Haghíde's scathing glance.

Eventually the scenery caught her eye. They were flying low and fast, following the seacoast. Up here, Kerasím was as beautiful as ever. Boats were thick on the sparkling green water, heading for safer harbors, but the white beaches themselves were empty. Villages went by, their colorful roofs bright against the sandy ground. Anyone outside who saw the aircraft ran for cover, not knowing what it would do. To their right rose rocky hills, the white cliffs dense with homes in an unending variety of brilliant colors; to the left lay the far shore of the inlet. Halfway up one of the crowded hills overlooking the water stood a huge estate of white and gray stone, offset by a red-tiled roof. Formal gardens and patios terraced to the side, following the mountain, with a small swimming pool in the center. Aila sat up when their craft made a swooping turn and headed straight for it.

They hovered a moment over a landing pad not far from the building, then touched down. People ran out toward the pad, including what looked like children.

The Kerasi that met them wore black tactical clothing. His face was frightening and familiar, the military cut of the dark chin hank showing the first signs of graying. He wore a *díhnarwharl* general's rank, and a deadly sword strapped to his side. While Aila never doubted his strength or agility, his stomach still hung out over his belt far more than regulations allowed. Every hair on the back of Aila's neck stood up.

No. Not again.

He clapped Masákh on the shoulder with a wide grin. "Masákh! You made it out safely! We worried, until Ghírandar informed us.

Congratulations on your honor! *Nhásarwharl* by privilege. Nothing less than you deserve. Haghíde!" He clapped Haghíde's shoulder with just as much enthusiasm. "Excellent job."

"Thank you, General," Haghíde bowed.

The General ran his eyes over Aila, watching for a recognition, a reaction. Four years could not change history. They hadn't parted on the best of terms, considering at the time she couldn't even curse him without causing herself pain, and here she was dressed up like Kerasi royalty, apparently at his current fortress, begging for shelter on his doorstep. Masákh might be that desperate, but she wasn't. Aila stared back, harsh and distrustful, surprised at how raw and fresh some wounds still were.

He bowed low before her. "Our experiment gone right. Welcome to my home, Aila Perrin. You do me and my household great honor. As my guest, whatever is mine is now yours. May you rest well here."

Tokh, who cut off heads as a form of discipline. Tokh, who ordered her tortured for trying to escape his prison. Tokh, who kept her caged for more than fourteen months of her life and gave the orders that stole her speech for three of them. Tokh, who risked his life standing up to nosy *fáhganid* to keep her safe, who executed at least five of his own men just for thinking of harming her; Tokh, who despite her fears and those few separate incidents, really did treat her decently. This was the last thing she needed to deal with on this day. The crushing confusion returned, hard.

"Tokh dar-Giláhn," she sneered, and wouldn't do more than tip her head. Speaking his whole name wasn't a mistake this time but a deliberate stab to let him know she wouldn't be played with. She held power over him, and she wasn't afraid to use it. "Please tell me Kassán is not living in your basement, or I will jump from your cliff."

Tokh paused to think her words through, then threw back his head, his laughter echoing off the building. "No, no. But I know where he is. He is on loan to the Emperor, and I'm sure he will be extremely busy very soon. Do you remember my wife, Mímihn? She will look after you while you are here. She remembers you with great liking." Mímihn peered around from behind Tokh at the mention of her name, her long black hair down and loose around her shoulders, as young and beautiful as ever.

"Consort," Aila said with a frown. "She's your consort."

"My second wife Umara died of a medical issue. I made Mímihn my full wife the following year. She is now mother to Umara's children, Joralan and Kesseh."

"That was very kind of you."

Mímihn walked straight to Aila and greeted her with a warm embrace. "Ah-lo, Ai-lah! Hahppy see!" she said in halting Standard.

Aila replied in Kerasi. "I am honored to meet you again, Mímihn."

She stared up at Aila, squinting, and broke out in a huge grin, showing small, even, pointed teeth. Her fingers poked and prodded Aila's cheek and fancy hair, fingered the necklace, touched the fabric of her dress, squinted closer at it, ran her hands over the remaining ruffles, and sighed with longing. "You are more beautiful than I imagined! Like a *bhísroti*!"

"You can see?!" Mímihn had been totally blind when Aila had met her, the fate of far too many consorts.

Tokh explained. "A year ago I kept my promise to restore Mímihn's sight. After three surgeries, she has fifty percent vision in her left eye and fifteen percent in her right. They will try to gain more in a few months. Or when they can," he said with a sigh. "No one knows what will happen now. But come, friends. You've been in a most tragic battle. Eat, rest, then we will attend to business. You will be safe here. I am under the Emperor's protection and have already submitted my oath of loyalty to Emperor Nadigh."

How a man of any race could be so brutal yet loving and compassionate only added to Aila's confusion. "You are most honorable, Lord Tokh."

Tokh brayed with laughter again. "The *dáhneg* is calling me Lord!"

Mímihn seized her hand and dragged her toward the house. "Khome! Khome!"

Tokh's home was decorated in a style that fit a Kerasi General, as far as Aila could ever have imagined, a rustic lodge of masculine stone and beam, right down to a massive stuffed *dhastal* head hanging over the main door. More people waited inside the great hall.

Tokh gave a nod to the crowd. "May I present Aila Perrin, Union Council on Kerasi Affairs, an associate of mine from my greatest mission."

Aila snorted. "Associate. Like it was voluntary. On my world, we call it prisoner. I will not be your prisoner again."

If Tokh was annoyed, he didn't show it. "Refusing my honor is your choice."

He pointed to a tall, thin, sharp-faced woman in her fifties. She was pretty enough for her age, her hair and cosmetics well-done, but her narrow hawkish nose added to the image that said she would be vicious if provoked. "My first-wife, Zheníhda. Her sons are grown, off in the military." Zheníhda bowed but said nothing, her face never softening at all.

He pointed to a pretty, younger woman still in her twenties, with short purple hair, white eyeliner, and a toddler on her hip. While Zheníhda dressed conservative-spinster, this woman wore a stretchy shirt and loose pants that came half-way to her knees, ready to take on anything from a hike in the park to dinner and dancing. Her feet were bare, her ankles and toes covered in rings and fine chain anklets. She bowed to Aila, keeping the baby upright.

Tokh sighed as if embarrassed. "This is my son Kitras's wife, Dalo, mother of his children here. He has been on a difficult assignment for several months, so we brought her here. Zenak and his wife are stationed at Nar Rhede; we don't see them often. These here are my children with Umara. There were no classes today for the conference; I'm not sure now when they will resume. Go! You've seen the Human; now let us speak." He waved everyone away, but not before the two little girls in the cluster bowed, bursting with excitement.

"Ah-lo, Yu-nyon Laydy! Ah-lo, Laydy!"

Aila bowed with a smile. "Hello to you." The girls squealed and grabbed each other's hand.

"Khome! Khome!" Mímihn pulled on her arm.

Aila looked to Masákh, but he sent her off with a nod. She followed Mímihn to the upper floor.

"You may stay in this room," Mímihn said in Kerasi. "It is restful. This is my side of the house. The *hyrak* lives on the other side."

The room was far more feminine than Aila expected, filled with soft colors, swooping draperies, and a bed loaded with pillows and silky linens; Mímihn's sanctuary, not Tokh's. She took her shoes off and unclipped the veil from her hair. "*Hyrak*? Isn't that a bird?"

Mímihn's sweet young face folded into a foul glare. Her skin was lighter than Zheníhda's, a lovely golden oak accented with just enough makeup, and like Dalo she kept her eyebrow thin and fashionably styled. "That is what I call Zheníhda. She hates me. She is like a *hyrak*, peck-peck-pecking me all the time. When Umara died, Zheníhda would then inherit all of Tokh's property if he died. Even at her age, she would attract a new husband who would want her property. I was consort; I was part of that property. She walked around like a *bhísroti* and spit on me, thinking she was wealthy. Now that I am his wife, too, she will only get half of the property and she cannot sell me for money. She is furious at Tokh, and hates me very much. Tokh does not talk about it, but that is how Umara died: Zheníhda pecked her until her heart broke."

"Well, I like you, Mímihn."

Mímihn brightened again. "Yes. Now you speak enough Kerasi, we can truly be friends. We will fight the *hyrak* together. Go! Wash! I will find you something easier to wear."

Aila rinsed her face in the attached washroom, fighting back the hard rush of tears that wanted very much to surface. The day was killing her, from the elation of the conference to the horror of the assassination, the deaths of her coworkers, to finding out her cold-blooded Kerasi captor from before had a home, a family, even grandchildren hanging about him, twisting her mind in so many directions she might as well have been floating alone in space. How did one figure out the world again when your worst sworn enemies turned out to be the best friends covering your back all along? She'd always felt a sort of kindred spirit in Mímihn, both prisoners at the whim of their captors, but right now all she really wanted to do was sit in a corner and cry her stress out, preferably on Masákh's shoulder. She was never quite sure if he was lying to her or not, but even a good lie from him right now would be a comfort.

Mímihn swirled into the room, a manageable skirt and blouse in hand. "Here. These should fit." She helped Aila out of the remainders of her dress and into the every-day clothes. The blouse was loose, but the skirt fit well. Mímihn's feet were tiny, so Aila left her beautiful fancy shoes on. The necklace didn't match; Aila fingered it, but decided not to remove it. Masákh said he'd paid for it himself. Better to keep it close.

Mímihn smiled, noticing. "That is beautiful. Did he buy you that? Is he kind in bed?"

"What?!" Aila's hand flew from her neck.

"Masákh. I can see now. He watches you move, and your heart flies through the air to him. He is very magnificent in uniform like that."

"I do not bed him!"

It was Mímihn's turn to look confused. She sat on the silky bedcover. "Why not? A male does not gift a female with a necklace like that unless he loves her very much. It marks her as betrothed and off limits to others. Or do you bed the other one?"

"Haghíde? NO!" Aila shouted. "I bed none of them! In the Union, females do not bed males unless there is heart behind it."

"You do not want to bed him?"

Aila sat next to her. She wasn't sure what she should say, how the words might be carried to the wrong ears, but Mímihn felt like an old friend and sex was a public topic on Kerasím. "It is not that simple. Almost. I almost did. We were this close," she placed her palms together, "but we both know duty must come first. So we did not."

"That is bad," Mímihn decided. "You must go to him tonight. He had much stress today; he will welcome your comfort."

"No. Even if I did, he would turn me away. We agreed, it should not be until after our duties are finished. But now I do not know when that might be. But do not say a word! No one must know! I do not wish it to be a mark against his duty."

"I understand. It is very hard, when your heart is attached. I never loved anyone until I met Tokh. He is my life-breath. I fear today's trouble will pull him away on a new mission and I will cry every day I am alone."

"Never?" Aila said. "You never had love before? How many years have you?"

"Gah!" Mímihn snorted. Her little slippered foot stomped the carpet, and she clenched her jaw angrily. "I am now twenty-three. I have my fourteenth nameday, dreaming of a young and handsome cadet, someone who will tell me sweet words and give me little gifts, like the boy who worked at the marketplace, and the next day, I am married to an old *nhásarwharl* colonel, sixty-eight years old."

"Sixty-eight!? After one *day*?"

"All gray and fat and nothing but business. He lost three sons to battles, so he wanted a new young wife for a new son. I did not want to marry him, but my family gave me to him. I did not want him to touch me, but he held me down. He was very bad at it. He was too old." Mímihn held up a finger and let it wilt downward with a giggle.

"He tried for a year to give me a child. Then he beat me because I did not have one. He shared me with his friends, and still I did not have a child. When I became seventeen he could divorce me, so he sold me as a consort. I was bought by the son of a *dáhneg*, with wives and children already. He shared me like a bottle of *muhr*. One day he accused me of liking his friends too much, so he took me to a place where they put me to sleep. When I woke up, I could not see. I screamed and cried, but it could not be fixed. One day he had men in; one of them was a friend of his father. The friend was Tokh. He saw my owner beat me because he lost a game, and it made him mad. When the betting was very high, Tokh bet against ownership of the consort. Tokh won. I was very scared – I did not know who he was, where I was going, what he would do to me. He did bed me that night, but he was very kind about it. He had sweet words for me, the first male who ever did. He has always been very kind to me, and I love him very much."

The day had numbed Aila too much to respond. Five years. Mímihn was just five years older than she was, and she'd been through so much, it made Aila's kidnapping look like a school trip to a park. "I cannot believe that the General I know, who cuts off heads and hurts young females, could be so kind."

Mímihn grabbed her hand and squeezed it. "You must never confuse the duty with the man. I know what he does as General. The man Tokh hates it. When he was a student, he was forced by a superior to kill another student. He says that every time he must carry out an execution, he sees only the student's face. Out there he is a General of the Military. Here at home, he is only the man Tokh. Here, he can be himself."

"I'm glad you know only his kindness," Aila said. A girl ran into the room, Mímihn's stepdaughter Kesseh, followed by Dalo's daughter Faelihn, Kesseh's niece. Both were around seven. Kesseh was a smidgen shorter, her hair brown against Faelihn's black, and done up in two knots, Mímihn's specialty. Kesseh's jaw and eyes looked exactly as her father's, while Faelihn looked more like her mother. They stared at the guest and bowed with great seriousness.

"Father says the Great Lady must come down right now."

"We will come," Mímihn said. She pulled Aila up. "And try not to make faces at the *hyrak*."

Tokh sat at the dining table in the great room, his belt knife and a variety of small items laid out next to him. "You will sit. Masákh says you have a tracking tag. It must be removed."

Aila'd forgotten about it, but Masákh never forgot anything. Her heart skipped a beat, but one did not show fear to Kerasi. Not if you wanted to be taken seriously. She sat on the chair before Tokh and pulled her arm from the blouse. "Left shoulder."

Mímihn began to fret. "I'm so sorry, Aila! Hold my hand. You can squeeze it when you yell. Tokh is very good. He will be very fast."

"Do not get blood on my floor, Tokh," Zheníhda sniffed. "All they need to find is a trace."

"Quiet, female! Do not tell me my business." Tokh scanned Aila's shoulder with an instrument and located the spot with his finger. "Just below the skin. Simple. I have a cream to ease the pain, but I do not know how deep it will go. Masákh and Haghíde will hold you."

If she wanted to make a good impression, now was the time. When on Kerasím and named *dáhneg*, one had better act it. She just hoped she could pull it off. Aila turned to glare at him. "I am Union! No one holds us down. Remove it, and do not waste your useless creams."

Tokh bowed his head to her. "As you wish." His glance at Masákh said, *Stand ready*.

Aila put her elbows on the table, folded a hand over her fist, and rested her face on her hands, the better to hide any tears. Tokh found the spot with his finger and made a small nick with his knife. Aila tensed up but didn't so much as grunt. The wound stung, but his knife was so sharp he needed just one pass. A push with his finger, a tug with the tip of the knife, and the tiny microchip sat on the table before her, in less than twenty seconds. Yes, it hurt, but she could think of a dozen things that hurt worse – most of them also inflicted by Tokh.

131

Tokh blotted the wound, painted it with sealant and kept the tension with a tiny adhesive strip. Aila put her arm back in her sleeve. "The next time my mother insists on a tracker, I'm going to make sure it's put into her instead."

"Impressive," Tokh said with admiration. "You have the bones of a Kerasi. Mimi, get her a glass of *durwah*."

"Ka!" Aila called after her. "Not unless you are testing me. *Flehdan* is good."

Tokh bowed his head. *"Flehdan,* then. You did not move. Kerasi women are not that strong."

Mímihn placed a small glass of *flehdan* before her. Aila studied it, prayed it wouldn't knock her on her ass, and pushed her luck. She tossed her head back and downed the glass all at once. The bite of the liquor hurt worse than the kitchen-table surgery. She could feel Masákh's disapproval burning into her back.

Oh well.

The glass clicked on the table as Aila put it down, loud against the surprised hush of the room. "One learns to be strong under your command."

Tokh's frown suggested he'd been insulted. "Explain."

Aila didn't smile back. Some things hadn't been forgiven. Her voice bit back like the liquor. "Spending a year with you on Kye was no party. I learned then how to be strong. You underestimate the strength of women, especially Kerasi women."

Aila turned in the chair and felt the room spin with the rush of alcohol. *Whoops.* She switched to Kerasi for the women's benefit. "You think I am strong because I do not scream when you cut me? You do not know Kerasi females. Look at your wife." Aila pointed a finger back at Zheníhda. "She brings your sons. She must stay behind when you are away. She must be as strong as you to fill your place. Mímihn – she lived years of terrible pain and still she gets up, filled with happiness. If your females cry, it is because they must be strong for too long, but you choose to look away."

"I thank you for such a quick surgery, and the *flehdan*," she said to Tokh, and returned upstairs.

Seventeen

Dinner was superb for Kerasi fare, but Aila ate only enough to be polite. She drank far more of the *lunahl* Mímihn poured for her than she intended, sitting by Masákh and listening to the men's conversation far more than the women's as they sat around drinking *lunahl* and *muhr* and picking at the bright red nut-cake Zheníhda had made. On the back wall a news program played on a viewscreen, sound minimized and captions on, replaying the catastrophe over and over. Aila tried hard to keep her eyes from it. She couldn't read Kerasi fast enough to follow most of the flashing captions anyway.

"Moragh is safe," Tokh insisted. "He has six sons; all are in hiding. He turned himself in immediately, demanded to be scanned for truth, which he passed. Moragh did not have a hand in it. Turwheg, however, is still among the missing."

"It does not seem logical that Turwheg would be involved," Haghíde said. He and Masákh had shed their dress jackets and looked oddly informal, if not still almost identical, in their liner shirts. "If he was after the throne, he would have to murder not only Nághtas, but Nadigh, Moragh, and all of Moragh's offspring. It would be unreasonably difficult to do so and not be caught."

"Where there's power, there's money, and where there's money, there is always a willing hand," Masákh replied. "I do not suspect Nadigh. All of this maneuvering was to put his daughter in the line of succession for the throne of Kerasím; why would he undermine it? I spoke with him this very morning; his words did not hint at gaining power for several years."

"That's a worthy question," Tokh said. "Turwheg has always been a bit of a renegade. He knows he will never inherit the throne, but he has almost unlimited wealth and privilege, and being *bhísroti*, the only person who can discipline him is the Emperor. He has never had limits to anything. He was even failed from the military – Nághtas claimed he

133

pulled him out because he was needed elsewhere, but the truth was that he was incompetent in any position."

"He could have funded the activity," Masákh said. "Remove everyone at once through misfortune, and he will step up with great grief to honor his father. He will have the sympathy of the world and no one will think twice." Everyone agreed.

Tokh played with his *lunahl* glass. "What disturbs me more is the coverage of the incident. There are no fewer than eight cameras covering every angle of the room. The shooter is in the top balcony, with the females. He is veiled, so you cannot see the face, but the hands and measurements are too large for a female, and there are flashes of green uniform behind the rail. The compartment that hid the weapon was found. Only someone able to bypass a weapon scan, or whose access to the room was unquestioned, could have placed the rifle in the balcony. But watch." He called up footage from the house computer onto the room's viewscreen with a hand control and replayed the assassination. He pointed up at the screen and ran the footage at half-speed.

"This was the live feed. Watch the council members in the background. The female ambassador is speaking. Nadigh looks bored, looks at his hands; Nághtas leans over to speak with him. Moragh crosses his arms, tries to look interested. Turwheg bends down out of frame to fix his shoe. On the Union side, the male Wodu is listening to the speech; his eyes are focused downward, intent on the words. But watch the Union Secretary. He is watching the balcony. He moves his head – a Union signal for yes, for approval – and as Nághtas straightens up, the shooter begins to fire. Coincidence?"

Haghíde sat back, understanding the implications. "A Union plot? Or the work of both sides in cooperation?"

Tokh raised his hands. "Unknown at this time. But the Secretary Kel is the only surviving member of the Union delegation sitting in the honor seats."

"Why?" Aila demanded. "Why would he sacrifice his own people? I don't believe a word of it. Wodu Mosi is dead? He was such a supporter of the project! He was one of the people who was instrumental in getting the discussions off the ground, getting the *aghát* released from detention! He backed me up from the start. He was still backing me and Masákh up just earlier this afternoon...."

"And the Secretary's stance on opening relations?" Tokh asked.

Aila's head bent. "Unfavorable. I fought with him more than once, the last time to blows."

Tokh smiled at the news. "So you are difficult for everyone, not just me. Your fire never ceases to impress." He changed the screen back to the news program.

Aila frowned. "Hey! That's my face up there. Why?"

All heads turned to the screen. Tokh blasted the volume to life. Masákh translated it for her as the newsman spoke. Footage from her hand-shaking escapade rolled across the screen.

"The question of the moment is 'Where is Aila Perrin?' The Member of the Union Council for Kerasi Affairs is not among the dead and has not been located among the living, nor has her Kerasi bodyguard. Is she wandering injured? Is she kidnapped? Was she part of the plot to destroy the land of Nághtas and made a getaway with her fellow plotters? Or has she defected from the Union, seeking amnesty among the chaos? The question is who will find her first – those that want to save her, or those that want her to pay?"

"I'm a sitting duck," Aila mumbled. The room stared at her, oblivious to the reference. "A sleeping *hyrak*. Something that is easy to kill because it does not know it is in danger. They will trace Masákh to you, and assume I am with him."

"You are safe for the time being," Tokh insisted. "Have no fear."

The urge to cry came on strong again, fueled by too much *lunahl*. Aila pushed her hands over her face, scraping away any evidence. Assassination and its aftermath was never considered during the planning of the delegation. "General, may I beg a request?"

"My house is yours."

"May I please send a message to my mother, let her know I am still alive and uninjured. That might stall a Union invasion fleet for a little bit longer."

Tokh sat back with a sigh. He made several indecisive faces. "We are ordered to keep to official communication only, but I will make the exception. Thirty seconds, no more. A tight beam, scrambled, with multiple relays and echo should be sufficient. Follow me."

Mom? Dad? No time, but I want you to know I'm
alive, unhurt, and in a very safe location with known

135

friends. Trying to figure out if it's safe to go back, but all flight is blocked. What the hell happened? Love you both.

Aila sent the message, thanked Tokh, and went upstairs instead of rejoining the group. The tears would wait no longer. She threw herself on the bed and let them come, crying until she gasped for air. The images would not leave her head: Nághtas addressing the crowd so nobly vs. Nághtas splayed backward in his throne, face shocked, chest smoking and bleeding. The screams. The stink of ozone from the weapon fire. Hawet hitting the floor not ten feet from her, not a nice neat drop with eyes closed like a video program, but her head bouncing on the floor, mouth open, spit flying, eyes staring into nothing as her grayish face darkened, smoke rising off her clothing. Masákh stayed controlled but she could hear the panic in his voice, and then to wind up at Tokh's estate, Tokh the Slayer at home with his family. And to find out she was on the Kerasi Most Wanted list.

Mom was right.

Too much!

A brief knock tapped her door before it opened. Masákh stood in the doorway.

"You did not return. I came to check. You are upset."

The last thing Aila felt like was listening again about Kerasi cultural taboos about crying. She choked out, "No, I didn't. I'm human, and I'm crying, and I don't care, so if you have a problem with that, get lost!"

Masákh entered and shut the door. He stood by, watching. He wasn't wearing his gloves, but after several minutes gave her back the faintest of pats, as if afraid to touch her. Aila sprang to her knees and grabbed him in a fierce hug, crying on his shoulder.

"How?" she sobbed. "How do you do this? How do you not let it affect you? That was your Emperor, all your world in one person. How do you walk around without crashing?"

Masákh stood stiffly, hand patting her as if it controlled itself. "*Shu.* I do not know. Many years of training. Do not think about what you see. Focus on duty. Do not worry about that which you cannot change. If something has already happened, you cannot change it, move on. We are trained first as soldiers, only then as *aghát*. I can

136

commiserate with Haghíde and the General, but we each know that mourning does not bring back the dead. We have an Emperor, but his name is now Nadigh, and Nághtas will join his parade of ancestors. In time that was to be expected. Our loyalty is to the Emperor; we now serve Nadigh, and await his order. We will work hard to find who is behind this and see he is brought to great justice, whether Union or Kerasi. Though I now suspect it will be both."

Aila's tears eased a bit. "It doesn't bother you, the loss of life? Everything we worked for, gone in an instant."

"You have worked hard for four years, but I have worked twenty-five years for this day, only to see everything disappear in a flash of light. My life's work: support the Emperor, prepare, prepare, prepare for the day you will be called on to make his ideas happen. Work hard, Masákh. You are smart, work hard! You must be in the top of your cadet class to move on to diplomat school! You must be top of your diplomat class to be chosen for *aghát* training! You must be top of the *aghát* if you want favor with a good commander! Masákh, the responsibility for the project is now yours! The Emperor is counting on you!"

He stopped patting and squeezed her, as if by pressing her against him he could force his emotions into place. "I am as upset as you. I have been denied the common pleasures of life for twenty five years for just one goal: to generate a peace deal with the Union. Today was to be that historic day, and our well-earned victory was stolen. I am angry. Much more angry than sad. And I wish to be there when justice is served. Everything is now about following the trail backward."

Aila sniffed. "Is there a trail?"

"Most assuredly. You should sleep. You will have better spirits in the morning."

"Sleep? I'll never sleep here. This is Tokh's house, and I have not forgotten a thing of what he does. I don't trust him farther than I can spit. Please don't leave me! I know nothing bad will happen when you're with me, especially when Tokh is in command. Just – hold me. Tell me what you know. Tell me I'm going to make it out of here alive."

"*Shu, shu.* Tokh will not harm you. He …"

The door tapped again and Mímihn poked her head in. "Oh! Forgiveness!"

137

Masákh released Aila so fast he seemed to throw her away from him. "No! Come! She is upset by the day. I'm sure she would appreciate your company far more than mine. I will have a cup of *gohr* sent up to help her sleep."

"Of course I will talk," Mímihn said. "Make it two."

As soon as Masákh left, she glared at Aila sitting cross-legged on the bed. "Foolish female! That was your chance!"

Mímihn spoke with Aila late into the night. They couldn't always find the words they needed, but more than enough to work their way to understanding. Several times Aila referenced her comm unit to look up the proper word, cursing Masákh for disabling any function that called for connections to be made to an outside server.

Aila shook her head. "I cannot sleep. I will know what we are doing in the morning, and then maybe I'll sleep."

Mímihn rubbed her arm. "Sleep is the best thing after a stressful day. The bed is most comfortable. Tell me what I can do to make it better."

"Get me back to the Union ship. I will not be held prisoner again."

Mímihn frowned. "You are not a prisoner. Tokh brought you here as his guest."

Aila laughed without humor. "That's what he told me last time, 'You are a guest of the Kerasi Coalition.' Then he held me in a cage, tortured me, and did something so I could not speak. That is not what you do to guests. I cannot walk out of your house and return to my ship. That makes me a prisoner."

Mímihn tried to speak a half-dozen times, but each time stopped short as words failed her. "I'm sorry, Ai-la. I don't know everything Tokh did then. I was trapped in my rooms, too. I am very sorry if he hurt you, but I tell you truth now, he is beyond the stars to see you again, and he speaks of you only with pride. He is most honored to be able to help you at this time. I told you, do not equate the soldier at home with the soldier following orders. He made the order to bring you here, to remove you from the danger of Keranihn. Please believe me, you are very, very safe here."

Aila took a large swallow of her drink and made an awful face. Her hand covered her mouth, forcing the liquid down. "I can't trust him. I can't. I'm afraid I will wake up in a cage in your basement. I'm afraid of the bad dreams."

Mímihn wrapped her arms around Aila and squeezed tight. "*Shu! Shu shu shu shu!* I understand, Ai-la! I do understand. That happens to everyone who has been through something bad. I still have bad dreams about my before-times, but in my dreams, the pain and screams come out of the darkness, and when I open my eyes it is dark in the room, so I do not know if I am dreaming or if it is real or if I am safe. Only if I feel Tokh next to me do I know I am truly safe. *Shu.* I will stay with you tonight and hold your hand. I promise on my sight, nothing bad will happen to you here. The house is built onto the cliff; there is no basement."

She released Aila and leaned around to see her face. "Now, if you'd listened to me and stayed with that nice-looking *aghát* officer, you would truly be safe from everything."

Aila broke into a smile at last.

Eighteen

The *gohr* did its work. Aila slept a sweaty, dreamless sleep, Mímihn curled next to her for comfort, and as a result she awoke late. Mímihn had left her clean clothing and a simple breakfast of thin bread, fruit, and sweet-nut butter. Kerasi bathtubs were teacup shaped, with a shelf across one side for sitting on; the one in her washroom was large enough for three people. Aila washed, dressed, and slipped down the stairs.

As she entered the kitchen, Zheníhda stared at her with disapproval. "They are outside. Be aware, I will allow no other consorts kept here."

Aila took a moment to grasp her meaning. She walked up under Zheníhda's thin nose. "You are speaking to a *dáhneg, díhnarwharl*. Show respect! Do not call me consort. I am consort to no male, least of all a graying *díhnarwharl* general." Aila was in no mood for pissing games. She stalked toward the door. The insult to Tokh was unwarranted, but she wanted Zheníhda to know her place. If Zheníhda was jealous of younger females, the insult would be a nice twisty knife in the wound.

The beauty of the day belied the upset of the people living it. Warm orange sun and clear green skies, the water and surf rolling far below, the cliffside views, an ocean breeze – truly, the most idyllic place Aila had ever been prisoner. Across the gardens and pool, by the far edge of the property, the men were holding shooting practice with an electronic target. The new Emperor Nadigh was still in hiding but starting to give orders. All states were currently under martial rule until Nadigh emerged, and in the crisis all commissioned officers were considered to be on active duty. Weapon practice was common sense.

Mímihn sat off to the side while Tokh's ten-year old son Joralan practiced shooting a handweapon, coming remarkably close to the highlighted points. Tokh watched with approval, his smallson Lanag, a year younger than Uncle Joralan, watching safely next to him.

"I don't know whether to be frightened by a child with a pistol, or happy to know even a Kerasi child can cover my back," Aila said.

Mímihn laughed, even though she didn't understand a word. "Bright day, Ai-la! You slept very well for all your worry. Sit! Sit with me. This is fun." She patted the cement ledge next to her.

"I scored thirty," Lanag told Aila. "My *bo* is a sharpshooter. He taught me how to shoot when I was six. I'm better than Joralan, but he's better with swords."

Aila shook her head. "You scare me." She walked up to Masákh. "Your uprising killed my friends. Teach me to kill in return."

Tokh laughed. "A female does not have the spine to kill."

"We do in the Union. Get between a mother and child and she will kill you without second thought."

"I have met your mother. She can kill by tongue alone," Haghíde said, and took a fast shot at the target. It hit dead center, just below the eyes.

Tokh waved a hand. "She is my guest. Let her play."

Aila raised a sardonic eyebrow. "You wouldn't let me anywhere near weapons last time, even when my life was in danger."

"I did not trust you then. I will trust you now. It is bad fortune to kill one's host."

Masákh bowed and handed her his weapon. A consummate marksman, citations for excellence made a full row on his uniform. He explained the parts, showed her how to sight it, how to get the best accuracy. He stood behind her, his arm under hers supporting the aim, pressed together cheek to cheek, far too familiar for any type of polite instruction. Aila focused on her task with cold determination. The target was some forty feet away, a full-sized outline of a male. Her first shot, steadied by Masákh, hit the edge of the outline, but did hit it.

Masákh straightened up. "A minor wounding. He would shoot you in return and you would die."

Aila raised the weapon and fired a half dozen rapid shots in the direction of the target. Two made it. "There! I chased him back to cover. Do it again."

Masákh bent over her once more. "Your leg out here with mine. There. Find your center of balance. Elbow tight." His chest pressed against her back, his groin against her hips as she leaned back against him. His voice was low in her ear, giving directives.

"Fire."

Aila raised her hands in victory as the shot hit the target's neck. Not the chest she was aiming for, but a lethal hit just the same.

"Maintain position! You opened yourself to return volley. Now you are dead. Do not celebrate until you are told the threat is clear." He leaned in again, counted off, but her hand twitched at the last second. Instead of the belly, she took out the target's groin.

Joralan and Lanag burst out laughing. "Gah! She blew off his *hihvat!*"

Mímihn laughed wildly, a high-pitched noise like a bird shrieking. "There will be no celebration after that shot! Stay far away from Tokh if you must shoot."

Haghíde's mouth pressed tight, as if he were holding a bitter tablet on his tongue. Not a trace of humor tainted his words. "Perhaps if she wasn't supporting your weight, she might be able to move her arms properly."

Masákh gestured Haghíde to take his place. Haghíde stood next to Aila, never touching.

"You will never hit a target if you are locked up. A good shot is a natural move." He twisted about, loosening up. He turned his back to the target, focused his mind, then spun around, bent his knees, supported his wrist on his other arm and fired the weapon, all in one smooth motion. He just missed the heart, but the resulting wound would also have been instantly fatal. "See it in your mind, then do it."

Aila took a deep breath, placed her feet, bent her knees, tucked her bottom, rested her shooting wrist on her other forearm, sighted, and pushed the trigger. The shot went dead through the target's solar plexus. This time, instead of jumping in victory, she squinted and fired off three more shots without breaking position. Two hit the target, both deadly.

Haghíde bowed his head. "Much better. Do three more sets, with a focus on consistency."

"Can I try to beat her?" Joralan asked, and Tokh consented. His shots were not better, but no worse than Aila's.

"Good, for a first time," Tokh said to the *aghát*, "but a target is not a battle. Shooting a computer image is a game. Put her in battle with men running toward her and firing their own weapons, people around her screaming as they die, let her see the life fade from someone's eyes and she will fail. You should not fill her with false success. Like a cadet in war, it will be her death."

The target sounded a bell; three lethal hits in a row. Aila twirled around and shook her backside in a victory dance. Mímihn laughed and clapped for her.

Tokh sighed. "She would get an entire squadron killed." He shouted over to Aila, "Yes, but you'll never swing a sword without severing your own foot."

"I will if you teach me." She returned the pistol to Masákh.

Tokh hesitated. His sword was his life, more familiar to him than a spoon. "Mimi, go inside and bring me some fruit – nothing smaller than a *basaringa.*" She returned minutes later with several large vegetables and fruit in a tote.

Aila was practicing her first lesson – holding up the sword. It was far heavier than she'd expected, or she was far weaker than she'd ever believed. She couldn't hold it steady with her arm outstretched for even a full minute.

"Can I go first?" Joralan asked. "I want to show her how good I am."

Tokh gave a nod. "One swing, and you will move back with Mími."

Joralan's own sword was short, no longer than Aila's forearm, but far sharper than a child should have had. Tokh set a tall gourd on a decorative pillar of the low wall overlooking the cliff. Joralan bowed to his father, drew his sword, took a well-practiced stance, swung a graceful arc from his wrist and shoulder, and sliced the vegetable in two. The top fell on the ground, but the bottom merely rocked and sat still again. He bowed to claim his victory.

"Excellent." Tokh clapped his son on his back as he sheathed the sword.

"Will you show them your trick, *Dihnarbo*?" Lanag said. "Show them your trick! I want to see your trick."

"Please, *Bo*?" Joralan added.

Tokh gave Joralan a playful swat to his rump. "Go ask your new mother for her hair ribbon."

Joralan ran back with her neck scarf. Tokh waved him away and Mímihn pulled him back with Lanag, well out of range of any blade. Tokh set up another gourd, studied it, faced the opposite direction, and tied Mímihn's scarf over his eyes. He pulled his sword, waved it about to warm up his arm, then concentrated. When ready, he pivoted on one foot and swung, sword in perfect control. The vegetable still stood. He pulled the blindfold from his face, observed his work, then bowed to his audience.

The onlookers cheered, except Aila.

"You missed!" she laughed.

"Did I? Bring it here."

Aila grasped the vegetable by the top and lifted it. The top half jerked up. He'd sliced it so cleanly the halves never knew they'd been separated. Aila stared at him, open-jawed. She bowed to him. "My apologies for doubting you."

"You still have not learned. Replace it. See if you can knock it down, at least."

Aila's bravado fled in the face of such a display. Tokh was a master and she was a fool. He handed her his precious sword, the grand separator of heads, and talked her through positioning. The vegetable was already cut. All she had to do was hit it. She needed two hands for even that much control, but managed to knock the top free without hitting the pillar.

Masákh clapped his leg. "And you did not cause yourself to bleed. That is a great trick indeed. I dare not practice with you."

The words hurt, but she was too proud to ask for Joralan's blade. She whirled on Tokh. "Something harder now."

Tokh removed the gourd and replaced it with a dark purple fruit, a soft thing the size of a child's head. "Weight on the forward foot, swing from the shoulder, not the elbow. The sword is an extension of your arm, just another length of it. Slice as if drawing a line across; do not hack as if cutting wood. Aim for the center."

Aila eyed the round purple ball.

It's you or me, fruit. I'm done being laughed at. You're an evil fruit. You killed Wodu Mosi and now I will kill you. This is my sword, Separator, and I will have your head.

Part of my arm. Smooth and straight and controlled. Follow through until clear. Come on, Sword. It's head-shaped. You know what to do with heads. Just do it.

Two hands on the hilt, Aila swung outward from her shoulder in a gorgeous smooth arc. The tip hit high on the fruit, scalping the top two inches down. Red-pink fruit juice splattered back at her as the piece went flying. The rest of the round fruit rocked, tipped, and rolled off the pillar. It smashed on the tan paving stones, exploding chunks of red puree over Aila's legs like so much brain matter. Dark red juice bled outward in a stain.

Aila flashed back to the one beheading she'd witnessed during her captivity, and for a split second the melon became that head, the fruit juice an obscene amount of blood. The patio began to spin. She dropped the sword with a clatter and ran to the wall over the cliff, where she promptly lost her breakfast.

Over a damned piece of fruit.

Aila could hear the men laughing and slapping each other as she fled back to the house.

She locked the bedroom door and would not come out, not to Masákh's request, Haghíde's inquiries, or Mímihn's gentle pleadings. Aila refused to join the house for lunch, a terribly rude thing for a guest. In mid-afternoon the lock disengaged and the door opened. Tokh stood in the doorway, stern and cold.

"You will accompany me, or I will lead you by your hair."

Aila rose from the bed, silent but compliant. No one else could be heard in the large house; she was alone with her Prison Guard. Pleasant host or not, Tokh's authority still scared the wits out of her. Where the hell was Masákh?

He led her outside, wandering the walkways between the sections of lawn and gardens surrounding the small swimming pool, as private as they could get.

"Strong females are a novelty to us. We are not used to their attempts at male activities. For a first attempt, your aim with a pistol was admirable. I would suggest practicing as much as you can until you are proficient. However, sword work requires years of practice and skill. Masákh is not wrong to suggest you will draw your own blood. It is strange, your fearlessness. I cannot imagine Zhenihda shooting a pistol, even with her life in danger."

"I can see that," Aila said. "Many women in our history never did more than raise children and make homes. Others began that way, but when their husbands fell in battle, they took their man's place, either at weapon or at running their business. Others never wanted to be tied to home and learned to fly or fight or play sport every bit as well as a male."

Tokh paused. "How? How are females educated? Are there special academies, or are they taught at home? When do they start, when do they stop? What programs are they taught? Are there special female teachers? And how are they taught?"

Aila laughed to herself. "You still don't get it. Union females are taught in the same classrooms as male children, all together. The teachers are male or female; it doesn't matter. They learn the exact same subjects, whether it's math or music or rocket science or army combat. Yes, we have female generals. They all start by four or five and they must continue until seventeen or eighteen, but most study at least four to six years more. Doctors and surgeons and specialists, maybe ten years more. Whatever the boys do, the girls do too."

Tokh frowned. "That is not possible on Kerasím."

"Of course it is. You just have to do it. You did it to me; why are Kerasi females any different? Are you telling me your own daughter is not as smart as me? Someone somewhere knew I could learn, and they told you to teach me. I never wanted to become a diplomat; I filled the position you created me for. I never expected to need to learn to fire a weapon, but now your people want my head. I must learn to defend myself or I will die. I refuse to die on Kerasím, therefore I must fight. It is very simple, really. May I ask, how many heads have you taken with that sword?"

"This? This was a gift from a general whose favor I won." He paused to think, then resumed walking. "In forty years? Perhaps thirty? I have not kept count. I performed my first execution at seventeen, not by choice, a regret that has never faded. You accuse me of great acts of brutality, but I find the task most distasteful, unless in self-defense. But that is what the duty of a Kerasi General requires. I do no more than I must. You are not Kerasi; you are not military. I do not expect you to understand."

"I am trying. And I am military. My father is an Admiral."

"I did forget that."

Tokh's head turned from her, eyes watching the clear sky, the cliffside, the boats moving through the inlet far below. "Nadigh is sorting out his forces. He has my pledge of loyalty. The *aghát* and my officers made theirs this morning. Once he has amassed enough troops he trusts, Nadigh will take control and all will be settled."

"I want to do the same. I met him when I met the Emperor. I want to make a statement to him, that I recognize him to be the one true leader of Kerasím and pledge my loyalty to him and no other pretenders. I hate not having contact with the other members of my group. I would represent us to him."

"No. Do not be seen on camera, anywhere. I will relay your message to him myself."

"But…"

Tokh stopped walking. They were by the wall at the far end of the property, overlooking the hillside where the land tumbled down into the sea, a jut of ridge that blocked the view of the next property beyond it. A breeze blew upward, shook the twisted red-leafed trees clinging to the hillside and whipped at their hair, fluttering Tokh's unclipped chin hank.

"I forbid it. I did not want to distress you with too much information. One hundred sixty five people died yesterday in the attack at Derahl Nohr, between weapon fire and panic; more than fifteen percent of the attendees. Nineteen Union officials survived the attack, and four of their security guards. Three died later of injuries, leaving sixteen officials. You are the only one unaccounted for, and that has created speculation and multiple bounties, men looking for favor from the new Emperor by returning his missing dignitary. The problems begin in that someone may wish you dead as well, and they will hunt you down in name for the bounty, but in truth to dispose of you. The Emperor knows you are here but will not tell your people until he feels it is safe. Several of his top aides also disappeared in the confusion, at least one of them at the end of a weapon. There are several rumors circulating, but few facts. The Emperor wishes you to remain away from the palace until things are in control. You are at extreme risk, and you must maintain absolute secrecy."

Aila realized a bigger horror. "If they are hunting for me, every second I'm here I put your home and children at risk. I cannot allow you to do that. I have to leave. I have to go back."

"I am working on that," Tokh said. "A plan should be in place by morning. Most likely I will send you out to Yomebor, where one of my sons will meet you and keep you secure. It is a risky distance, but you should be safer."

"Masákh will accompany me?"

"And Haghíde, at minimum. Two guards means one is always alert while the other rests."

Aila bowed her head. "I thank you most deeply."

Nineteen

Aila was quiet the rest of the evening. The adults sat in the great room after the children were all upstairs, drinking *lunahl* and watching Nadigh's first world address on the large viewscreen. Everything seemed so strange and so very familiar at the same time. Aila tried to pull back, to observe the scene as an outsider, as a diplomat, and it hurt to see that Kerasi home life, at least here, was as normal as anywhere in the Union. Aila wanted to record it, to blast it into every Union home, *these people are just like you, if you give them a chance.* Monogamy wasn't a requirement in the Union; some Union cultures had group marriages, so the fact there were two wives wasn't a big deal. A caring husband, a blended remarriage, multiple generations under one roof, happy children running about – and there were people in the Union that wanted to destroy that for no reason but some unfounded prejudice. Friends and family sitting together, watching an address from their leader, sipping wine and eating pastries, watching newscasts during a worrisome world crisis – it was so blasted normal Aila wanted to cry.

And there was a price on her head for wanting to share this scene with her people.

It was General Tokh's personal home, Tokh the Slayer, Tokh the Torturer, Tokh the Imprisoner, and she didn't want to leave.

* * *

The mood in the dignitaries' apartment was somber at best. Everyone had been moved into a single communal apartment for security. The belongings of the deceased were packed up and readied for removal back to the ship. So many of them had been murdered in a matter of minutes, along with countless Kerasi. Omi Kel paced the apartment in a fury, while the remainder of their party sat quietly on the sofas or watched out the windows, too shocked to do much else.

He got up in Rahnif's face, nose to nose, cheeks dusky with anger. "You have no right to hold us like this! If you do not release us, my government will consider this an act of hostility. Do you understand that term, act of hostility?"

Ráhnif bowed in apology. "I do understand the term, Secretary Kel. It is beyond my power to change the situation. All airflight has been grounded until the situation stabilizes."

"Why did you send Ross Halian back to the Union Embassy? Why couldn't he stay here with us, explain things to us, someone we could trust? Why couldn't we be sent to the Embassy with him, house ourselves with our own people?"

"Captain Ross felt he could be of more use at the Embassy. He is in contact with both us and your ships. I assure you, you will be released without harm at the first opportunity. It is not our intent to detain you for anything other than your safety. If we had bad intent, we would not be allowing you full contact with your ships, or escorted movement anywhere on palace grounds."

Kel accepted the information with a grunt of disgust. "Yeah. Then tell me where Councilmember Perrin is. Why isn't she with us? Where are you holding her? She's not at our embassy."

"I apologize, but I do not have those answers. You have the Emperor's word, her location is of prime importance to our investigators, and we are working very hard to find her."

"Fuck your Emperor!" Kel snarled. "You think we're that stupid? We spoke with our ship. We know she was flown two or three hundred miles south of here. We know that for a fact, even if you yourself weren't told that, which means your word of all airflight being grounded is a lie. If we know where she went from up in orbit, then your not knowing is also a lie. Then she disappeared off our screens. If she was dead, we'd still know where she was, but she's alive and in hiding by her own message home, even if we can't trace the signal. That means you're holding her for some other purpose. I want her returned to us immediately, and alive. At the very least I demand to speak with her on camera, tell us herself that she is unharmed."

Rahnif's face didn't change, but his pupils widened. He bowed again. "My apologies, Secretary, if I have been misinformed. I will request an update and notify you immediately."

"You do that. And don't bring me any lies this time, either."

Ulan was on duty when their dinner meal was brought to them. The apartment kitchen was stocked with small items, but three formal meals fit for dignitaries were brought to them from the Emperor's kitchens on tall rolling carts, the table set, and the meal presented by their *aghát* and two kitchen staff. Mealtime conversation was light and sparse; only one thing was on the dignitaries' minds, and none of them wanted to talk about it. Not in front of *aghát*.

Kuana Raveset, Councilor at Large from Vega, spoke with Halden Kane, the councilor from Centauri. "Now, you said your granddaughter was out by Neptune. She's doing research?"

"Yes. She's aboard the Johann Galle Research Station, studying particle theory. Been there two years now. She's got a year or so left. She's thrilled to be out there."

"She doesn't mind the lack of sunlight?"

"They have a floor of gardens with artificial sunlight timed to the Earth calendar, so no one's natural cycle gets too disturbed by perpetual darkness."

"That's wonderful," Raveset said. "What kinds of things do they grow? Flowers and such, or food they can eat?"

"A little bit of – Ow!" Kane leaned sideways and looked under the table. He pulled his leg back and rubbed his ankle. Kel was sitting to his left; he looked under the table as well, curious.

"Sorry, it felt like something bit me. Must have been something sharp on the chair when I moved my leg." He brushed at the chair leg, hoping to find it. "Must have fallen down."

"It's not a flea or bedbug or something?" Kel said. "Does anyone have any idea what kind of insects they have here? Where the hell is Perrin when we need her? She probably knows the whole catalog."

"Oh God! I hope they don't have spiders," said Vanora. She sliced off a thin section from the roast *hyrak* squab on her plate and dipped it in a dish of sweet vinegar heavy with *dann* and *sunelli* spices, rather tasty on the *hyrak*. "I can tolerate anything but spiders. Had a big black and yellow thing crawl up my pantleg one time; hated them ever since. Ugh!" She gave a hard shiver.

Kel signaled to Ulan. "You! Mr. *Aghát* there. Do you have any insects in the palace? Mr. Kane thinks one may have bit him."

Ulan stepped to the end of the table. "Were you able to see it? Insects are an affront to the Emperor. We do not tolerate them inside the palace. If you see it, I will dispose of it immediately."

Halden Kane waved him off, shaking his head. He was one of the older delegates, heavy-set, with an impressively large white walrus mustache, something that seemed to fascinate Kerasi men, for whom mustaches were considered primitive and uncivilized. "Don't bother yourself. I just clipped it against the chairleg. Seriously, I haven't seen an insect here yet."

"Just the same, I will be checking my clothing most thoroughly," Aikerman said. "You can't be too careful."

Yoma Calti of Fornax put her fork down and rested her head on her good fist. She'd sprained a wrist in the stampede and wore a new brace to support it, forcing her to have someone else cut her meat. "I don't want to think about insects. I don't think I can take any other stress right now. I want to go back to the ship where I don't have to worry about them."

Kane started to chuckle. He sipped from his cup, a half-empty glass of *muhr* he'd been drinking throughout the meal. He'd taken quite a liking to it in the last twelve hours. "Did you ever hear the joke about the man who went to the doc because he had a pain in his..." Kane's chuckle turned to coughing. His face darkened, first dusty blue, then a deep periwinkle. His breath roared in wheezing gasps.

"Halden?! Are you all right?" Kuana said with concern.

"You swallow wrong?" Kel said. "Put your arms up, stretch it all out."

Kane grasped his chest, gave a horrible rattly wheeze, and keeled over onto Kuana Raveset, upsetting her plate and spilling her glass across the table. Raveset jumped up with a scream.

"Get a doctor!"

The table took to its feet. Kel lowered him to the floor, but Kane's ivory face was already purple, the bluish Centauri mottling nearly black. His eyes stared upward at the ceiling without blinking. "Kane! Can you hear me?" Kel began pressing hard on Kane's chest.

"Don't just stand there like a landed fish!" Aikerman snapped at Ulan. "Get a doctor up here! He's dying!"

Ulan bowed rapidly three times and pulled his interface from a pocket. "Immediately, Lady Aikerman."

Twenty

Tokh had kept a night watch, just in case, allowing both *aghát* to rest. He roused the household before sun-up.

Mímihn bumped into everything in a nervous frenzy. She shoved a tote bag at Aila with several changes of clothes. Then she shoved fruit into it. Ten minutes later she wrapped half a cheese and added it to the bag. Then it was a tiny bottle of *flehdan* spirits and a box of herbed wafers. Halfway through breakfast she ran up the stairs and returned with a bottle of perfume and tucked it into a corner of the bag.

"Useless female!" Tokh snapped. "What in the Emperor's name does she need perfume for? She is going into hiding, not to consort training!"

Mímihn was near tears. "In case she needs it!"

Zheníhda smirked over her breakfast. "Not everyone beds their way up the castes, *trixihn.*"

Mímihn's cheeks turned a deep shade of bronze. She flapped her arms and made screechy percolating sounds like a *hyrak.*

Zheníhda flew from her chair, but a loud crack stopped everyone cold. The flat of Tokh's sword had slapped the table.

"The next sound will receive the next blow," he said, cold and powerful as the General Aila feared. Zheníhda returned to her seat. Aila put her arms around Mímihn, who began to weep.

Tokh added several small tools to the bulging tote bag.

"It's time," he said.

The sky was starting to glow. Mímihn had trouble seeing in dim light, and kept a hand on Aila as they left the house. To confuse their trail, the travelers would meet a fishing boat that would take them to their transport, three villages up the coast. A paved road led partway down the cliff, to stairs that went to the beach. Masákh would go ahead alone, watching the road. Haghíde, and Aila hidden under a veil, would

154

follow, looking as any other couple walking to the water. Aila had left her precious necklace in Mímihn's hands; either she or Masákh could return to claim it later, but it would stay safe.

Aila said goodbye to the children, thanked Zheníhda for her hospitality, and was crushed by a hug from Mímihn.

"You are my only friend!" she wept into Aila's ear. "Now I am left with the *hyrak*, who pecks at how I raise Tokh's children. I wish you could stay!"

Aila hugged her back. "I will keep contact, send you pretty things from my home when I get back. I am happy that you are living so well now. You are my greatest friend on Kerasím. *Soyavoh.*"

Aila stood before Tokh. One did not hug a General, no matter how grateful one was to them. Aila bowed instead. "You confuse me, General Tokh. The last time I saw you, you reveled in my pain. Now, you show me every hospitality of an old friend. I am most grateful, but I fear I will never understand Kerasi."

Tokh clapped his hand on her shoulder as if she were a comrade. "You must learn to separate Kerasi duty from Kerasi the person. What I did was not against you, the person. I acted as the situation needed. You broke orders, I enforced them. There was no malice intended. Not much, at least. You inspired us with your abilities then and continue to inspire us today. You would be a brave warrior even if you weren't female. My house is always open to you."

Aila bowed again. "I thank you most graciously, Lord. You are a most honorable host."

Tokh's head tipped, listening. His eyes scanned the brightening sky behind her. Up and down the hillside, lights were starting to glow as the servants began their day. The air was chill and damp with the fading night, and the waves could be heard rolling far below. Nothing could have been more peaceful.

He pushed her to the side. The *aghát* studied the sky as well. A faint buzzing drifted on the air.

"What?" Mímihn pleaded. "What is it? I cannot see that far."

Inside the house, an alarm began to whoop.

Dark dots appeared against the pale mint sky. Tokh pointed. *"There!* Inside! Everyone inside!"

No one moved, watching. Three dots were growing rapidly larger, bearing straight at them.

"Vorex-class Daggers!" Tokh shouted. He shoved Aila toward the house. *"Get under cover!"* The women scattered.

Aila pulled Mímihn. Masákh and Haghíde ran up behind and pushed them faster.

The first shots hit the far edge of the property before she touched the house. Aila stopped to watch under the shelter of the balcony over her head. Plasma strafes pounded the grounds, blasting holes in the shadowy gardens, the paved walks and patios, the pergola drenched in the red-flowered *whenir* vines. Shots landed in the pool, vaporizing clouds of water that hung foggy and gray in the thin light. They raked across the courtyard where everyone had been standing just moments before. As the craft flew off, one last blast struck directly on Tokh's landing pad. His aircraft exploded in a fireball. Aila shoved Mímihn in the door, while the *aghát* hit dirt. A wave of searing heat poured over them, but the 'pad was a safe distance from the house for exactly such a reason. Mímihn shrieked and danced in place, arms protecting her head. Zheníhda didn't yell but shielded Kesseh, cowering near the cooking unit in the kitchen. Dalo screamed and dragged her children under the dining table, huddled in terror.

Only Tokh seem unperturbed, standing like a statue in the destruction of his front yard as chunks of ash and aircraft rained down around him, daring to be made a target. "No markings at all, and no deviation from course. Those were not imperial craft. It's a warning, meant to frighten me. They don't know who is here. They are probably targeting everyone with high rank." He raised his sword to the sky and bellowed, "I declared my loyalty! Long live Emperor Nadigh!"

He turned to the travelers by the house, coughing on the cloud of smoke from the burning 'craft. "The neighbors will be here any second! Don't waste a distraction! Go!"

Aila watched the smoke dissipate from the water's edge as a fire team arrived to put out the burning aircraft high above. The boat they boarded was a small working fishing vessel, wet, slippery, and stinking of *dinkorhat* and *marmu*. The dwarf dot of white sun rose first, soon blotted out by its larger twin in a beautiful orange ball reflecting off the water. The sea breeze was salty and fresh, whipping her veil back from her face, but Aila clung to the rail on the seaward side as the jade water slid by.

Haghíde leaned on the rail next to her. Even in a seabreeze, *aghát* hair didn't ruffle much. "Does the boat make you ill?"

Aila turned to look at him. He and Masákh left their uniforms at Tokh's in favor of Kerasi street clothes, and the sight of Haghíde in a mustard-gold shirt and brown trousers was driving her crazy. She couldn't take them seriously without their uniforms. It was wrong.

"No. My heart is very sad and I don't feel like speaking. I'm upset about Tokh's beautiful home. I hope I did not put his family in danger."

"I think Tokh was right. It was only a warning, or they would have targeted the house direct. They damaged his property but did not hurt him. That is important."

"It's a wonderful home."

"Did you know it was a gift from the Emperor?" Haghíde said. "Not even a *díhnarwharl* general can afford such an estate. It once belonged to a *fáhganid* who owed too many taxes on it. Tokh was the only general to complete the emissary project successfully, so Nághtas gave it to him as a reward. That could be another reason it was targeted. To seize the property of a *fáhganid* and give it to a *díhnarwharl* would make many enemies. They used the situation to retaliate. There is much of that happening at the moment."

Aila nodded in agreement. "Haghíde, you would tell a friend the truth, wouldn't you? How safe are we going to be in… Yomebor? Who is it we're running from? How do we know who to avoid?"

Haghíde thought a moment. "We should be removed from the worst threats. No one should expect to find us in Yomebor. There are too many spices in the mixture right now to be certain who is at fault. A group calling themselves The Birthright has claimed responsibility, but they are too small and disorganized to infiltrate the palace. In the last hundred years there have been several major unrests in the region of Kanok Sohr demanding independence from Empiric rule, but the dissidents are denying involvement, nor have our contacts heard of secret claims. There are always middle-caste agitators, but none of them has the power or finances to do anything this involved. That was not a regular weapon but a military assault arm meant for use in war; I rank Captain Two, and I would not have access to such a weapon. It has to have come from very high. Nadigh has frozen all banks and lenders, threatening them with death if they do not obey, until he has analyzed the accounts of every *bhísroti*, looking for traitors. His offspring understand, but there are others who are quite angry. He has locked down the palace and is clearing his staff one by one, putting them through the mind scanner to prove their innocence. Unfortunately, Nadigh's memory expert was kidnapped during the assassination, so it is taking far longer than it should."

"Hmph." Aila had no love for the Kerasi ability to mind-sift. Through drugs, hypnotism, and the finest computerized neurography, the Kerasi possessed the ability to sort through memories – even image them if done right, separating actual memory engrams from verbal truths, weeding out liars and fakers. On low power with a cooperative subject, the procedure was brief, painless, and safe. On a resistant or uncooperative subject, the power could be ramped up, but the procedure became painful and dangerous as individual nerves stressed, overloaded, and died. The subject's mind could be irreparably damaged, rendering them mentally and physically inert. Despite a tendency for insubordination and a sadistic streak that troubled even the General, Tokh believed Kassán kai-Imahr to be the finest neuroinvestigator on Kerasím, and chose him for his personal team. It was Kassán who had manipulated Aila's brain and tortured her on command. Aila had survived at least three scans that she could sort of remember, too scared to give even the slightest resistance. The last was used to cross-wire her own nervous system to induce seizures when she spoke. Even though Union medicine was able to restore her speech, she still hadn't forgiven Tokh for that.

Her sarcasm was palpable. "Perhaps they should bring in Kassán. I'm sure he could speed everyone through."

Haghíde looked off into the water, as if he didn't want to be seen saying the words. "Kassán was assigned to the Emperor. It is he who is now in enemy hands."

* * *

Nadigh's personal servant, a *dáhneg* by birth, entered the Emperor's chamber, one of very few people allowed in at the moment. Nadigh sat, jaw resting on his fist, his elbow on the arm of his blue chair. He stared off into space, possibly thinking, possibly just in mourning. "Your Majesty? I bring you news."

"I hope it is good."

"Lassehne, youngest of your father's widows, has given early birth due to the upset of your father's death. She has birthed a son, your Majesty, a new brother for you. He is healthy and well. The physician understands you have much to occupy you, but has asked if you would please visit her as soon as possible."

Nadigh raised his eyes with contempt. "Why would I need to visit a newly-birthed widow?"

"The physician pleads for Her Lady's health. She cannot stop crying from grief, and she fears that because the child is male, you will kill it as a rival. She begs to be allowed to name it Nághtas, after his father. The physician feels a kind word from you may ease her grief. Such grief in a mother is bad for the child's health. He is the son of your late father, your Majesty, the same as you."

Nadigh sighed emptily. "I will try to make time later tonight. In the meantime, you may tell her I give my word she may keep the child, but he will never be allowed claim to the throne. I will write that in the book of laws as well, so all may know it. Nághtas, son of Nághtas and Lassehne, is of royal lineage but due to the postumousness of his birth and the inability of his father to acknowledge him, he has no claim whatsoever to the throne of Kerasím, and any attempt to seize it in his name is to result in his death."

"I will inform the physician at once, your Majesty. Also, *Aghát* Captain Ulan waits to speak with you, your Excellency."

Nadigh's eyes and one finger directed the approval.

Ulan approached with caution, kneeling before the Emperor with deep reverence. Nadigh's very brief reign had resulted in the executions of almost thirty people so far, people Nadigh considered to be conspirators and enemies of the state. He had arrested his own brother after a manhunt, ordered him to be worked on by a mind investigator. This was not the time to make mistakes of any kind.

"Your most gracious Majesty, I bring you information you will not like hearing, and request your instruction on how you would like it handled."

The hand lowered and Nadigh sat up. "Stand. Speak."

Ulan stood but kept his head bent. "The death report on the Centauri dignitary came back from the investigator. The dignitary Halden did die from a stopped heart, however, no vessels were blocked to account for it. A fast-acting cardio-toxin was present in his blood in great enough quantity to stop the heart. The toxin could not have been ingested; it could only have been injected."

Nadigh's eyes went wide under his heavy brow. He skipped a breath. "That cannot be."

"The investigator was very clear on that, your Excellency. Heating it in food, or the acids in *muhr* or the stomach would destroy it."

"How? You said yourself you were present in the room, and no one approached him. Who sat near him? How would he not know someone injected him?"

"He sat between the Secretary Kel and a female dignitary from the star system Vega, what we call Onigar. Your Majesty, I do not wish to speculate on the incident, but there was a minor event not long before the man Halden stopped breathing."

"Speak."

Ulan bowed again and continued. "The man claimed to have felt as if an insect had bitten him. It became an amusement among the dignitaries and was ignored."

"Did you mention that to the death investigator?"

"Yes, Your Excellency. He found a small puncture wound just above the left ankle. The concentration of toxin was strongest at that location. He did not feel it was caused by an insect, as no insects carry that toxin."

Nadigh sighed and rested his forehead on his fist, eyes downward. Speaking seemed to take more energy than he had. "And who sat to his left?"

"The Secretary of State Omi Kel, your Majesty."

Nadigh's face squeezed tight in pain. "Was he an old man?"

"Yes, Your Majesty. Seventy years."

"Then my official word is that he died of heart failure of age, brought on by the stress of the current situation. Mention nothing else to the Union. This is impossibly delicate. I cannot accuse a high Union official of killing one of their own inside my palace without irrefutable proof. I would send them back immediately, but now I have vital questions and must find answers first. Give them my sincerest condolences, and tell them it will not be much longer. Make whatever concessions you can for them, but keep the male Omi Kel under close supervision."

Ulan bowed low. "It will be done."

Twenty-one

Leaving the fishing boat was more treacherous than boarding it; *dáhneg* did not board fishing boats unless to inspect one they owned, and even then the inspector would not be female. They walked the docks and up to the streets until they found a vehicle for hire, Aila hiding from the public under her shimmering black and gold veil.

"To the nearest flight hangar," Masákh ordered. "The Great Lady's boat began to founder, and we were rescued by a stinking fish trawler. She must get home as fast as possible. My Great Lord has managed to reserve seats on a military flight for us."

The driver of a public vehicle would not caste higher than *rhibáni*, most likely only *tápatihn*; neither should have looked directly at a *whátaral*, let alone a *dáhneg*, yet the driver stared so long he seemed to be reading Masákh's lips. He studied Aila as if he could see through her veil.

"I can do that," he said at last. "Get in. Your Lord must have a lot of pull, with all flight grounded. Where are you headed to?" he asked after they were seated and the vehicle began to move.

"Down to Lodahm. My Great Lord has a home there. With all the unrest, he's afraid of looting and wants his Lady in residence to monitor it," Masákh explained.

"That makes good sense," the driver said. "I wouldn't want to be anywhere near the Emperor's city right now. Too many people dying. Much safer to stay out of the way, no?"

Aila could feel Masákh growing restless from the small talk. Masákh was not one to squirm. On her other side, Haghíde watched out the side glass, ignoring the chatter and gazing at the clouds.

The vehicle passed through a variety of neat and pretty neighborhoods, the narrow roads empty of traffic as people remained safe in their homes. It wasn't until a vegetable farm went by that

Masákh said something. "Isn't the flight hanger off the main artery? Shouldn't we have come to it by now?"

"Yes," the driver said, "but you are not familiar to this area. With all the panic, there was an accident and the traffic is backed up. A good driver knows all the back routes. This is a lovely road, much nicer than the *soláhrin* slums by the artery. The Great Lady does not need to be offended by them."

Haghíde lunged forward, grabbed the driver by the shoulder over the seat and held his plasma pistol to the back of the man's skull. "I have watched the air traffic overhead. We are not headed toward the flight hangar. You will get us to the hangar in fifteen *fasim* or your brain will cover the controls and I will take us there myself."

"Yes! Yes! I know a faster route to the artery! I can do that! I will do it! There is no need for impatience! *Tápatihn* are here to serve! You may put the weapon down!"

Haghíde released him, but maintained his weapon. The vehicle changed course immediately and doubled its speed.

Aila sprang sideways onto Masákh when Haghíde lunged. She knew, she knew for fact that all *aghát* were trained by the military, that they were Kerasi first and foremost, that corporal punishment and raping and killing were deeply entrenched in their society and not one of them was innocent, but seeing Haghíde become aggressive and threaten someone burst his bubble of virtue. Haghíde, the least violent Kerasi she'd ever met. Haghíde was someone you trusted to run a child care center. Cold, hard, and killing had never applied. Masákh said nothing, didn't give her the least reassurance. Obviously he knew Haghíde far better than she did.

They slid onto the flowing artery in no time, and exited onto the lead road for the hangar not long after. "See! See! I told you my way would save time!" the driver said, grinning as if he'd planned it all along. He sped them along the lane that led to the field for private aircraft, searching for the proper pad number.

"Here. Stop here," Masákh ordered. The driver pulled over to an empty pad and they got out.

"I am sorry for the misunderstanding," the driver said. "This ride is on me; no charge for the Great Lady in a hurry."

"White craft, two pads down," Masákh whispered to Aila. "Hurry, but don't run."

"No, this one's on me," Haghíde said, and blasted the driver just once in the chest. "Liar."

Aila shrieked, staring. Masákh grabbed her elbow and pulled her forward. "Why! Why did he just shoot that man? He was only earning a living!"

"*Shu!* He recognized us," Masákh hissed through clenched teeth. "*Aghát* do not look like normal Kerasi. Our faces are wanted as much as yours. Two missing *aghát* accompanied by a veiled female – he was bringing us elsewhere to claim a bounty." The craft door opened as they approached; he hoisted her up the steps and shoved her in. "If you want to live, you leave no loose ends."

"Loose ends!" Aila exclaimed. She clawed the veil from her face and flipped it down her back. "You just murdered someone in cold blood!"

Haghíde entered and slammed the door behind them. "Go!" he said to the pilot.

Masákh took a seat in the plush passenger area of the luxury craft. "He did what was necessary. If he did not, I would have."

The pilot sat sideways in his seat, as he had since they'd entered. "And greetings to you, too, old friends," he said with a touch of hurt.

Aila looked up, only to recognize the pilot. The shortest of Tokh's *aghát*, stockier in the chest and shoulders, with rounder cheeks and waves to his black hair. Tótoghar, fourth of her captors. He'd left his Union assignment two years previous.

"Hello, Tótoghar," she said. "It's nice to see a familiar face. Is this coincidence, or are you all following me?"

"I go where I'm sent."

"When you are being hunted, you need people you trust," Masákh said. Tótoghar flipped controls; the craft gave a loud whoosh of engines and lifted upward.

"That's quite true," Aila snapped. "How nice to trust you won't be shot. Have you killed anyone today?" she asked Tótoghar.

"No, but the day is not finished. Is there someone you wish dead?"

"Possibly, later. May I sit copilot next to you, then?" she said bravely. "I don't want to sit back there."

Tótoghar motioned to the empty seat. "Yes, but do not touch anything."

Tótoghar flew steady, not too fast, not too high, as insignificant as possible. They dined on thick sandwiches with spicy sauce that he had loaded in the small galley, then Masákh and Haghíde napped while they could. Aila felt safer awake.

"I thought none of you could pilot?" Aila asked. "Masákh can't."

"That was realized to be an oversight," Tótoghar said. "I've spent the last two years in intensive training for everything sub-orbital. Because so few *aghát* are licensed, it keeps me in high demand. Since I am one of Tokh's men, every time I'm requisitioned by someone else, Tokh gets a fee and I get a bonus. It's a profitable arrangement. Of course, now every General thinks they should have a diplomatic pilot, so my bonus days are numbered."

"Have you been to Yomebor? What's it like there?"

"Just once. A long ocean coast on the east, a high mountain range to the south. Warm and humid. Many trees. The capitol is Bihndorahl, Birel in the local dialect. It is a small city, just half a million people, very – I know you have a word for it. Excitable?"

"Joyful? Lively?"

"Yes. Full of life. It is not as orderly as Keranihn. You will be entertained by it."

"It sounds very exciting." Aila kept an eye on the sparse airtraffic. Haghíde, murder aside, had been able to tell so much just from watching the patterns of aircraft. What could she learn? What could she figure out? She felt stupider than a drained power cell. In two hours, she'd seen just two or three flights in the distance. No help.

"What will we do there? Where are we staying?"

Tótoghar smiled. It was a friendly smile, but Aila knew better. "Your contact will have that information. I retrieve and deliver. Sometimes I am involved in discussions, sometimes I am not. But I guarantee it will be a safe place."

"Hmph. I'm tired of hearing about safe places. Fornax was supposed to be safe. Kye was supposed to be safe. The Emperor's Palace was supposed to be safe. Tokh's home was supposed to be safe. There are no safe places, Tótoghar. There are only friendly and hostile ones."

Tótoghar nodded. "I believe you have discovered truth. But I am delivering you to trusted friends. It is only three days since the assassination. I would expect the Emperor to have everything under

164

control within two more. Then he will lift restrictions, you may return to your people at the palace, and return to your ship."

"Is anyone from the delegation still alive?" Aila said without hope.

"Of course. They are not happy and are making many demands to leave, but this morning there were at least a dozen in protected holding. I do not know the names. I do not mean they are in holding cells," he corrected himself. "They share an apartment in the palace. It makes security easier."

"That makes sense." A finger tapped Aila's shoulder. Haghíde motioned her out of the front seat.

"Please exchange seats."

Aila glared at him. "Are you going to shoot me if I don't?"

Haghíde glared back. "You are not fair. Perhaps you prefer to be taken prisoner again, by persons who have already assassinated an Emperor and whose behavior cannot be assumed to be less violent than mine. You continue to criticize me for saving your life as well as mine and Masákh's. Masákh, too, has killed to keep you from harm. Do you criticize him, or do you forget because he is warm above you?"

Masákh stood up in the passenger area. His voice was sharp, a command from someone used to giving commands. "Haghíde, you go too far!"

Aila rose from her seat while Tótoghar pretended to focus on his instruments. Haghíde was taller than Masákh, a full six feet or a smidgen more, with a chest and shoulders well-sculpted from weightlifting. Haghíde didn't need a weapon; no doubt he could kill her with his bare hands if he was ordered to. She stood right under his nose, cold and steely. "Are you accusing me of misconduct?"

He backed down. "No. I question your behaviors, but not to the point of misconduct. If I overstepped my privilege, I apologize, but I will not be reprimanded by a foreign civilian for performing my correct duty."

Aila backed down as well. "I'm sorry, but the sudden and seeming randomness of your action has disturbed me greatly. I thank you for your unfailing attention to your duty. I just wish you'd warned me first."

"Understandable."

She gave Haghíde her seat and moved to the back, as far from Masákh as she could. She threw him an angry glance, but there was nothing he could do.

Aila watched the planet slip by beneath her, a colorful array of cities, forests, lakes, and orderly suburbs linked by modern-looking roadways, many thick with ground-traffic. From high up, it wasn't hard to pick out the upper-caste private retreats from the sometimes smoldering refuse-dump camps of *ghinadín* slums. Clouds passed by the craft, casting shadows on the landscape below. It could have been Fornax. It could have been Centauri. It could have been Earth so far below. Yes, there were cultural divides, and some of them were very wide, but at the heart of it, the people were all the same, wanting nothing more than a decent living, good health, and loved ones who cared about them. It was crazy, all this hatred and killing because of profound ignorance. Aila thought of Wodu Mosi, probably the person she most trusted in the delegation, and her heart grew heavy.

The men had slipped into conversation in Kerasi. Aila stopped paying attention unless her ear caught an easy phrase. The discussion consisted of everything ordinary – people they knew, General Tokh, the rank of sports teams, whether the new Emperor would favor the old Emperor's team or a new one, what the new date of the Emperor's Birthday holiday would be. Nothing about the situation. Nothing about where they were going. Nothing to make her feel better.

The craft's console gave a beep, and a blue light flashed. A Kerasi voice spewed out of a speaker.

"*Aaka!*" Tótoghar growled. He touched several controls. "We've caught attention."

Masákh held onto the back of the pilot's seat, searching the control board for information he couldn't decipher. "Where are we?"

"Two hours short, outside of Bhon. I must answer. *Flight Asabar 6195, responding*," Tótoghar said into the com.

"*Airflight is currently restricted, Asabar 6195. All flights are subject to confirmation. Please state destination, origin, and authorization.*"

Masákh hurried back to the passenger area. Another aircraft appeared off starboard, a one-manned Spearhead. It was small, silver, shaped like a needle for ultra-fast flight. Aila gasped, pressed back in her seat, and pulled her veil over her face. The windows weren't tinted; if she could see out, no doubt the other craft could see in.

Not a tremor sounded in Tótoghar's voice. The years had done him well; he was as calm and nerveless as any of Tokh's senior *aghát*. *"Received, Bhon flight control. Authorization U-R-M-5-6-0-0-1, Prihnsoohr to Bihndorahl. Pilot, two technicians, wife of one technician, carrying emergency repair parts for a public water facility."*

"Confirmed, Asabar 6195. Please maintain current trajectory and speed for scanning."

"Received, holding for scan."

A beam of red light passed over their craft, starting at the front and passing to the back. Aila turned away, even though she knew it wouldn't help. "I'm a giveaway," she whispered. "I'm not Kerasi. They'll pick me out of the scan."

"Trixohran!" Masákh swore under his breath.

"Don't panic yet," Tótoghar said away from his voice pickup.

"Asabar 6195, we're getting a false reading on personnel. Please land at Bhon flight hangar for visual inspection."

"Received, Bhon flight control. On approach, Bhon flight hangar. Changing trajectory now. Landing ETA seven fasim."

"Is this just harassment? Are they looking for payoff?" Haghíde said.

Masákh tapped his pocket interface. "Emergency signal sent. If we go quietly, say nothing, it is possible that imperial troops will intervene before long. Aila does have imperial protection. That may save her."

"If they honor it," Haghíde said.

"We're not going quietly," Tótoghar said. "My orders come from higher up than a flight hangar, and they do not include side stops in Bhon. Strap down. Evasive maneuvers in thirty seconds." He began adjusting controls to build power.

Aila's heart squeezed tight. "Look at the shape of that thing! We can't outrun them! We're just a personal luxury transport. They'll shoot us down! I'm not Kerasi! They lift my veil, I'm done!"

"We are still in flight." Masákh noticed Mímihn's tote bag on the floor by Aila's feet. He grabbed it, crammed food and water containers into it, and forced it to close. He unfastened Aila's restraints, looped the handles of the bag through the restraint straps, and clicked it tight again. "Don't lose it." He belted himself down in the seat next to her.

Tótoghar changed course as if circling to approach the hangar. The escort beside him also began to bank and descend. When he felt the escort was far enough in the lead, he flipped to emergency speed and shot downward. Aila screamed as the nosedive sent them into freefall for an agonizing twenty seconds. The totebag floated upward in front of her, tethered by its handle. Masákh's hand closed over hers where she gripped the seat, squeezing it until she clung to his instead. He didn't even reprimand her for shrieking like a female.

They leveled out, flying at maximum speed and dangerously low, just clearing the tops of the taller buildings. Aila pulled the veil back from her face. One look out the glass, one look at the closeness to the ground, and she knew they would all die. She scrunched her eyes shut, bent her head and shrank small in the seat, waiting for the explosion when they ran into a building, or maybe a signal tower.

The speaker on the control board shouted orders, then threats. The silver Spearhead returned, speeding alongside them, visually directing them to land. Tótoghar dipped lower still, riding the canyons created by apartment developments. The escort was forced to retreat behind them. Tótoghar flung the ship in a tight left, then a tight right, shaking the tail. When he rose above the buildings again, two additional Spearheads now escorted them.

"Gah! Not good, men. We've got two *fasim* at most," Tótoghar said. "I might lose one, but not three. Plan?"

"We must land," Haghíde said. "They will blow us from the sky."

"Take our chances," Masákh agreed. "Maybe we have bought a little time for imperial intervention. Perhaps they will signal air control to let us go."

"I will find a place to set down," Tótoghar said. "We land and we sit tight. We are a ship under imperial protection, and we will not move until we speak to imperial troops."

"Good," Haghíde agreed.

"Do it," Masákh said. "Relay it now. Maybe they will ease up."

A warning shot pinged off the rear flank of the ship, rocking it. Tótoghar fought to maintain control. Aila put her head in her lap and pressed the hem of her veil over her eyes. *I will not be captured. I will not be captured. Not again.*

"This is Asabar 6195. We are under imperial protection. We will land only on imperial command. Please confirm imperial directive."

A second shot missed, blasting a nearby building. Chunks of concrete fell into the street below. A third shot hit directly into an engine, rolling the craft until Tótoghar stabilized it. Smoke poured from the side in a thick trail.

"Asabar 6195, you are ordered to land immediately or be shot from the sky."

"Sorry, men. She's going down on her own. I've got less than ten percent engine function and forty percent navigation. Hold tight, I don't know how well she'll land. I'm going to aim for that patch of forest up there after that building. Maybe it will buy us time."

"Bhon flight base, controls are dead, engine failing. Coming down. We are under imperial protection. I repeat, imperial protection."

"Brace for impact." Tótoghar cut speed to momentum and brought the craft down until they skimmed the tops of the trees, branches clawing the belly like so many desperate fingernails to slow the craft. Sensors screeched, lights on the display board flashed manically, *collision imminent.* Using the remaining thruster power, he braked hard and brought her down into the trees. The body of the craft wrenched back and forth as tree fought metal, shearing the stabilizers and wings from the fuselage and buffeting the passengers. Tótoghar managed to keep it pointed in a straight line, gouging a furrow between the trunks, and they came to a stop listing only thirty degrees to port. A strange silence blanketed them, interspersed with odd ticks and pings from the overworked metal.

"Injuries?" Masákh said. One by one they shook their heads. The men unstrapped and checked to make sure their weapons were still with them.

"Excellent flying," Haghíde said to Tótoghar, and clapped him on the shoulder.

Masákh removed Aila's restraints and claimed the totebag. He pulled her from the seat by her hand and kept her from sliding downward against the angle of the fuselage. "Our cover won't last. You two circle north. We will head directly into the city, find refuge until we receive new orders. Tap every two hours; we will meet there if possible. Go!"

Aila's head still spun from the crash. Her limbs felt weak and shaky and her stomach never wanted to eat again. Tótoghar and Haghíde helped her out through the gaping hole where the wing used to be. "But Tótoghar said to sit tight when we land – wait for confirmation."

"They ignored our claim of imperial protection, information they would have had access to. It is not safe. A distress signal has been sent." Masákh and Haghíde clapped shoulders as they passed.

Masákh took Aila by the hand. "Go!"

Twenty-two

Mímihn served Tokh his lunch at the table. At the other end, Zheníhda was coaxing food into their one-year old smallson, Niboh. From back in the office came a chiming beep.

Tokh lifted his head and looked at the time. "Too early. They have not arrived yet."

Mímihn rubbed his shoulders. "Then ignore it. You can take a break from your war games long enough to take some food. A General is mortal, too, you know."

Zheníhda rolled her eyes toward them. "Not if you listen to him."

The chime repeated, a higher, insistent pitch painful to the ear. Tokh pushed away from the table. "I must take it." Mímihn gave an annoyed sigh and sat by his plate to wait for his return. His voice carried loud from the other room, and she rose to stand by his doorway instead.

"What do you mean, went down?" he barked.

"Asabar 6195 was shot down over Bhon," Kitras said on the screen. "We heard the whole thing over wavecapture. Scan picked up a human on board. They followed every procedure to the letter, identified themselves several times as being under Imperial protection, their flightplans and numbers were perfectly legit. Someone had to give an order for that kind of harassment. Someone had to know. Tracking showed the craft stationary on the ground for several minutes before it was blown up."

Tokh's copper face paled to a sickly mustard. "What! Survivors?"

"At least two," Kitras confirmed. "Someone hit the emergency beacon after the crash, and we've picked up locator pings from Masákh and Tótoghar, moving in different directions."

"He wouldn't have left her," Tokh said. "Heading?"

"One toward Bhon, one circling northward."

171

Tokh split his screen, opened up a map of the area, pulled it in tighter. "A decoy. Are you still in Bihndorahl?"

"Yes."

"Where is General's One?"

"With General Rhigandir at the moment."

"I will speak with Rhigandir. Get to Bhon immediately, find out what's going on. Infiltrate anything suspicious. Have General's One set up there; scan all levels, leave nothing unmonitored. At most they have six hours of daylight left. Get them off the street at all costs. I want every locator mark sent to me immediately. Make Masákh the priority. Don't fly directly into Bhon, consider them hostile for now. There's a military hangar twenty minutes north; land there. I will arrange transport from there."

Kitras gave a sharp nod. "It will be done, General. With flight, we should be there in two hours."

"Like a rocket, Kitras. The Emperor wants her alive."

"Yes, Lord General."

Tokh cut the call and paged General Rhigandir. "Rhigandir! What's going on? Why are my men being shot from the skies on your watch? This is not a good time to be making enemies."

Rhigandir was a good ten years older than Tokh, and every day of it showed. He bowed his head and raised his hands in supplication. "Forgive me, Tokh. We don't know why. It was not my men, that I assure you, by my word. The order came down from a *fáhganid*, that's all we know. No one will dispute a *fáhganid*, not even you or me."

"Bihndorahl is Perdilon Vor's territory. He doesn't care what goes through his air, as long as his supply of *dhurwah* isn't interrupted."

"Perdilon's trapped at Derahl Nohr, with the other *fáhganid*," Rhigandir said. "That's the problem; all the governors and magistrates went to the palace for the celebration. Some made it out, but the rest are being held awaiting interrogation by the Emperor. There is a complete void of power out in the regions. No one has realized it, or there would be riots starting. Perdilon will pass interrogation; he knows nothing and his loyalty is to his liquor. I do not see any such order coming from him."

Ideas began to swirl through Tokh's head. "Where there is weakness, there is opportunity. I'm sure with the right amount of *dhurwah* he will be happy to tell someone what he knows. Is there a

172

master list of who went to the palace? Who has returned? Anyone still there we have connection to? Perhaps they will exchange information for a speedy release."

"I will work on it," Rhigandir swore. "Anyone who has returned is sitting silent, pretending they aren't home. I know at least five *fáhganid* were executed. Some are screaming at the *bhísroti* to do something, others are shaking in their robes and dumping files and bank accounts to make themselves clean. The *bhísroti* aren't about to help them; they're in the same escape pod. They're all trying to distance themselves from each other, in case they ever raised a glass with someone who's drawn Nadigh's ire."

Tokh nodded, thoughts already running a day ahead. He had access to the databases listing all *fáhganid*; that was a privilege of a general of the army. *Fáhganid* were the distant heads of the military, sitting back with clean hands and never involved in fighting – he himself reported to one, but they were the top brass and Generals were expected to be able to work with them. The list of those executed would be available on news waves. He would put out his feelers and see who had escaped the immediate purges. He could find out who downed his craft, but it had to be fast. It would be a sleepless night.

"Get my men to Bhon as fast as physically possible," Tokh told Rhigandir, "and I will share my information with you before midnight. Tokh out."

Mímihn hung on the doorframe, fighting to keep her tears in her eyes. There was a little-girl tremor in her voice. Even her black curls seemed to wilt. "My beloved General, what did he mean, shot down?"

Tokh growled lightly at the disturbance, until he glanced at her troubled face. He paused long enough to press her hand to his lips. "They crashed near Bhon, but they walked away. Masákh is with her. I am twelve hundred *nalis* away; if you want me to rescue them, you will not interrupt me again."

"Yes, my Lord."

173

Twenty-three

The Spearheads circled low, watching the downed craft, scanning and searching the area for survivors, the engines of three planes deafening at low altitude. The building Tótoghar had missed hitting was a school; Masákh and Aila made it as far as the vehicle park before one of the Spearheads spit fire and Tótoghar's aircraft exploded, buried in the trees. A fireball rolled upwards, thick with smoke, while the Spearheads passed back and forth, looking for runners. Windows in the school flew open and heads fought for a better view. Boys outside at exercise stopped and pointed amid shouts of awe. Learning stopped for the day, no matter how the schoolmasters threatened or beat.

Masákh halted at the building and turned around to watch, allowing Aila to catch her breath.

"Shouldn't we be running while they're distracted?" she panted.

"If you are working and there's a sudden explosion outside, what do you do?"

"Run and see what made the noise," Aila realized.

"Correct. To be the only person running away from an explosion is suspicious. Wait, watch, then do what the crowds do." People poured out of the building, surrounding and insulating them without question, just another pair of spectators.

Sirens sounded in the distance as ground response vehicles headed for the fire, and they used the distraction to leave and walk farther into the city. Aila pulled her veil down far enough to shield her eyes. "What now?" she asked. "What do we do? Take a public train to Bhindorahl? Shouldn't we be sending a signal or something?"

"It is obvious someone doesn't want us in Bhindorahl. Haghíde will send notification as soon as he's far enough away, draw eyes away from us. We need to find a safe place and stay put until we receive orders. I am not familiar with this region; I don't know the generals, *aghats*, or safehouses." Masákh tried to make his stride match hers,

174

unable to push her to move faster; a difficult task as she spoke over her shoulder.

"You'd trust a random *aghát*? What if their orders were to take you out?"

"I would have to know their General first. Only then."

"Why are you walking behind me?" Aila persisted. "I can't talk to you back there."

"You are a *dáhneg* woman on the street. I am your *whátaral* servant. *Nhásarwharl* servant," he corrected. He paused, face registering awe as the idea settled in. "That is the first time I have said that. It is most strange. I have not had time to adjust my thoughts. Either way, I walk behind you. Look around you. Do you see any other *dáhneg* females holding hands with their servants?"

On the busy sidewalks, men in finery knocked people over without regard as they walked. Others were low-caste servants, even *ghinadín*, scurrying as fast as possible with their hands full of packages. Some were women, never less than three to a pack, chaperoned by an older male. Some seemed to be couples, a man and a woman, some with children trailing. About one in ten might qualify as a female with servant, and almost all had their faces uncovered. Scariest were the street corners where local military officers in green, weapons displayed, kept peace during the crisis. Masákh bent his head each time they passed one, hiding his face with feigned respect.

"I don't know. I can't pick out anyone but *ghinadín*. Everyone looks alike to me. Can't you walk in front of me, then, clear the way, things like that?"

"Yes, that I can do," he said, and took the lead. Overhead, a Spearhead passed a block away, loud and low. They were not the only ones to gaze up at it, but Aila was sure it didn't give anyone else the fear it gave her.

"So what do we do? Where do we go?"

Masákh turned to look at her. "You are a *dáhneg* female. The first thing we must do is get you different clothes. If they are looking for a *dáhneg*, they will not pay attention to a *nhásarwharl*."

"But I got them from a *díhnarwharl*. What about you?"

"It is not my clothing that will give me away." His hand hid his chin as he spoke, a chin trimmed into a tight goatee with no manly Kerasi goat-hank of chin hair. He might have been able to pass with just his brow ridge reduced, but the bleached skin and flat teeth were a flashing sign that there was something funny about him.

"What about your black glasses?" Aila suggested. "You always had them back on Kye."

Masákh shook his head. "This was supposed to be a quick private flight. They are with my uniform, at Tokh's."

Aila entered the public lavatory dressed as a *dáhneg* carrying a shopping bag and a tote bag, and left it dressed as a *nhásarwharl* with just a tote bag. From a Union viewpoint, she didn't see much difference. The fabrics weren't as satiny, the colors as bright, but the styles weren't that far off. The purple veil was just as sheer as the black and gold, like gazing through a window curtain. The shoes, however, were nowhere near as nice as her *dáhneg* ones. Mímihn's clothes were stashed in the tote bag. Masákh wore a new pair of sunglasses; some disguise was better than none.

They walked, side by side this time, as a *nhásarwharl* couple could. Street markets, window shopping, almost an hour spent torturing a *tághinet* street musician, tossing him *harím* coins every time he stopped playing just to see how long he could go on. They perused an electronics store, watching the planetary news channel on the display screens for information on the crash or on the missing dignitary, but the news was silent. Masákh browsed the personal interface displays.

"Wander to the next row and make a small distraction," he said under his breath.

"What?"

"Wander to the next row and make a small distraction. Do it now. You are an ignorant *nhásarwharl* female. Gather attention."

Aila walked as if she were bored, poking displays, fingering packages, pointing to letters on signs and sounding them out. On the next row stood a variety of printers. She found one with the operation panel glowing and touched as many controls as she could. The printer began making noises, flashing, spitting out printouts of an advertisement, and finally began beeping.

"*Ka! Ka! Shu! Hoxt! Ka!*" she told it, banging at it until the catch tray fell to the floor with a clatter. Aila gave a little shriek and tried to put it back together. The shop clerk hurried over. He slapped at her, cursing her out while he replaced the tray.

Masákh rushed around the corner. He shook her by her shoulder. *"Stupid female! I told you not to touch! Apologies! Apologies! I will take her out immediately. My apologies."*

On the street again, Aila raised her veil to glare at him. "Can you tell me what that was about? I don't appreciate being hit by a storekeeper."

Masákh took her arm and walked. "It is called teamwork. My father owns a similar shop. I am familiar with the items sold. I took the operating chip from a display that has the same one my interface requires. No one will be tracing the identification number. I use mine sparingly for checking on official business, and switch out for accessing the planetary network for any information we need, no worries involved. When we find somewhere to sit, I will find us a place for the night."

Aila smiled under the sheer cloth. "You. Are a genius."

Genius until the sun fell. There was still no word from Haghíde as to orders, no lead on where to find safety. If there was a worse place to spend the night, Aila wasn't sure she could think of one. She hung back, refusing to go farther, the precious totebag slung over a shoulder. The only reason she had reached the streetcorner was knowing that Masákh carried a weapon on him. The building was modern enough, brown concrete and glass sandwiched between two similar-looking buildings, three blocks and a dark alley from the main thoroughfares. No personal vehicles navigated the road, and it was far too narrow for public transportation. Noise and light spilled out from a bar across the street. Couples hung on each other as they climbed the steps, groping each other in public. Some of the women wore veils, some of them didn't. Half of them looked and sounded drunk.

"Isn't there an abandoned building we could break into?" she pleaded. "A storage shed? What about under a bridge?"

"It is my understanding females prefer lavatory facilities. It is merely a Discretion House. It is the safest place for us in the city. Come. You must trust me, and do as I say." He held her hand, coaxing her forward. As she came close, he put his arm around her shoulders.

177

"You have two choices. Be familiar with me, or fight me as if you are intoxicated. I would suggest the former."

"Don't you let go of me for a minute! I'm serious, Masákh! I'm getting freaky. They're speaking funny; I can't make out what they're saying."

"It is the local dialect of the Yomebor region, not Emperor's Tongue." As they neared the steps, he turned to her. "Jump."

"What?"

"Jump." She gave a hop, and he lifted her up and hung her over his shoulder, holding her knees, and entered the building. Men and women were gathered in the lobby, a lobby with very low lighting, and everyone seemed to have a very deep interest in each other.

Masákh bowed his head to the hotel clerk while Aila kicked her feet. "I would like a room for the night." The clerk responded with a bow, checked the inventory, and readied a key.

"Faster!" Aila said in Emperor's Tongue, and slapped him on his backside. She meant it, too. The lobby folk were scaring her, too numerous to fight off if they decided to attack. She lifted her veil and draped the other half over Masákh's head, hiding his face as well, laughing as if she'd done something funny. "I see you now!"

He placed currency on the counter, then leaned in to the clerk as best he could while covered by the sheer veil. "Forgive me, I told her *nhásarwharl* but she thinks I am *díhnarwharl*. Is it possible to give me a *díhnarwharl* room?" He pushed two more bills across the counter. The clerk shrugged, handed him a different key, and pocketed the cash. Masákh signed in.

He put her down in the lift, sliding out from under the veil. Neither of them spoke until they reached their room on the eighth floor. Voices and laughter could be heard through some of the doors. Masákh locked their door immediately upon entering. Aila tore the tiresome veil from her hair. Her eyes darted around the small room. If this was *díhnarwharl*, what the hell did the others look like? Tawdry, garish, worn, with a stain on the bedcover, stains on the chair, and a faint stain on the carpet that looked like it had been blood.

"That was excellent thinking, using the veil," he said. "It protected both of us."

Aila backed into the corner by the door and stayed there, hugging herself. A braying burst of laughter leaked in from the hallway. "I can't believe you brought me to a whore house!"

Masákh unloaded his pockets onto a small table. There were no drawers for clothing, no computer desk or even a coat rack. People didn't stay long enough to care. "No. Not in the Union sense of the word. It is a Discretion House, common to every major city. Yes, some of the lobby females may be for purchase, but most of the patrons are made up of couples who do not wish to be seen together. It may be a *dáhneg* female pairing with a *whátaral*, a male bedding his brother's wife while he is away, two young people who do not want their parents to know, two males who wish silence. They come here. No one asks questions. No one checks ID. If you look at the registry, there will be at least fifty people with the name of *Tansohr Kheralin,* By Order of the Emperor. No one questions the order of the Emperor. That is exactly as I signed in. We are invisible." He swapped operating chips in the interface, powered up, glanced at the screens, and shut it back off.

"Everything still good with Haghíde?"

He paused a fraction of a second too long. "Yes. I was hoping the directive had come in, but nothing yet. I will keep checking." He peeled the window curtain back the width of his eye and peered out into the city. Eight floors up, *díhnarwharl* level, meant no one could enter through the windows. Below, the lights of the bar across the street flashed their colors with regularity. No one stood unattended on the street or by the doors. No vehicles crept where they didn't belong. No uniforms were visible. Blocks away, the lights of the city made a pretty tourist photo against the black of the night. Farther in the distance, the ground-traffic arteries showed a steady flow of blue vehicle lights. "We are safe for the night. I suggest you sleep."

"Uh-uh. I'll never sleep," Aila swore. "We're going to catch some hideous disease here. We were better off with my under-a-bridge idea." She pressed her hands over her face, pushing tears back. "Ohhh goodness! If my mother knew where you brought me, my dad would kill you, and I'm not sure I'd stop him."

Masákh touched her arm. Touching her in the line of duty was one thing; touching her intentionally was another. When she didn't object, he put his hands on her shoulders. She fell against him and held on. There was no one to witness him; he dared return the gesture. He bent

179

his head and kissed her on her temple. "*Shu, falahndi*. It is only until daybreak. We will leave at first light, before the others. I swear it."

Aila held him tight. "Right now, I just want to go home. I'm done. Take me back to the palace and I will face the Emperor myself."

He tipped her face to him, traced her lips with a finger, then dared himself to touch them with his own. She returned it just as lightly, and he repeated it with too much intent.

Aila flinched hard and pushed him away. She cringed back against the wall. "What are you doing? Is that why you brought me here? You think you can force yourself on me, be the Kerasi the Union thinks you are, instead of the one I thought you were?"

His face went blank, except for the flashing anger in his eyes. They bored into hers, snake eyes black and unblinking. "If I meant to force you, you could not stop me, here or anywhere else. I meant to offer comfort and distraction. Unless you wish to force caste. As *dáhneg*, you may order me to perform acts for you, and I cannot refuse."

Aila drew a shaky breath and tipped her head back until she pulled herself together. For whatever reason the ceiling, at least, was free of stains. "No. That won't be necessary. I'm sorry, Masákh. I'm just really, really freaking out right now. It's been one hell of a day, you know? We started out the day dodging aircraft fire, murdered a man doing his job, survived an air wreck after being shot at, and now I'm hiding from an unknown assassin in a whorehouse, hoping to be rescued by someone who hasn't been in contact yet. I can't take any more!"

Masákh never broke his deadpan expression. "Welcome to the Kerasi military."

His humor worked. Aila broke into laughter. "Sometimes I really love you."

"Come." He took the tote from the floor, drawing out the treats Mímihn had packed. "I will force you to eat, with or without your permission. We will celebrate being alive and hidden."

Twenty-four

Masákh dozed on the bed, but Aila refused. The metal frame, with two spindles bent forward as if the occupant had been tied there and tried to escape, made her nauseated, compounded by slapping and crying noises in the next room. She stayed curled in the corner of the floor, her veil as a blanket and one of Mímihn's skirts rolled as a pillow, and managed a few hours' sleep. As he promised, Masákh roused her at first light, and they slipped out unnoticed by anyone but the night clerk.

"Don't you ever, ever, bring me to such a place again." Aila's words were so cold they fell to the sidewalk instead of rising with her breath. "I'll take my chances sleeping in a doorway."

He led her through the alleys toward the center of the city. The streets were deserted in the pale light of the coming dawn, save a *ghinadín* picking through a trash bin behind a clothing store, and the occasional pre-dawn walker of *ghoosh*, a common small pet with the tail of a raccoon, the cry of a lonely cat, and the face of a bug-eyed loris. After two or three blocks, Aila realized Masákh kept turning his head to the side every time they passed a signpost, or a large display window, or the occasional delivery truck out for an early run.

"What's wrong?"

"Press against me," he said under his breath.

"What?"

"Press your side against me. Leave no seam between us." Aila shook her head, but she moved in until they bumped with every step.

He reached inside his shirt and removed his weapon from its holster, lowered his arm, and grasped her hand, transferring it. "Keep looking straight ahead. Do not look back. Understood? We are being followed. Watch the reflections in the windows and you will see."

Aila watched carefully at the next intersection. Half a block behind them a figure moved. Her breath caught as she realized, "That's a greenshirt! What do we do?"

"You are going to take my weapon. We are going to circle around to the next alley. When we come to a commercial refuse container, you will walk behind it and hide yourself. I will confront him."

Aila's heart raced. "What if something happens to you? What will I do? How will I ever get back?"

Masákh gave an irritated sigh. He took out his interface, pretended to answer it, then handed it to Aila. "Pretend to have a conversation while I speak. *Ab Kherisi*, foolish female! When done, put it in the tote bag. If for some reason a problem occurs, you may use the interface to call Tokh direct and ask for help. Once you do, anyone who intercepted the signal will know where you are. It will then be a race to see who locates you first, but you will have a chance."

They rounded a corner down the back side of a row of buildings. When they came upon an industrial-sized trash collection bin, Masákh let go of her hand. "Go. Hide yourself and do not come out until I tell you."

"But!"

"Shu!" he hissed, and she burst forward and ran behind the bin as he spun and ran the opposite direction to confront their follower.

Aila was torn, wanting to see what was happening and not daring to move. She waited behind the big black bin, pressed against the wall of the building, weapon in hand, watching her unprotected side for any sign of intruders, her heart pounding until she feared it would overload and stop altogether. She knew Masákh had caught their tail by the voices rising and falling, Masákh's much louder and angrier, but she couldn't make out the words. After several minutes she could hear a struggle, then a softer noise, someone choking, or perhaps vomiting. She scrunched her eyes shut, hoping to Earth the noises weren't coming from Masákh, but she was too scared to keep them closed more than a few seconds. Footsteps approached; she readied the weapon before her with shaking hands.

Someone tapped the side of the bin. "It is Masákh. All is safe. I am coming around to you now." He appeared, hands out, black gloves on. Aila breathed a sigh of relief and lowered the weapon. He reached into the trash bin, found a piece of discarded wrapping plastic, and wiped his gloves off. They left brown streaks on the plastic. He removed the gloves, folded them, and put them into a pocket in his trousers.

Aila held on to the weapon. "Masákh, what did you do?"

"My duty, both as Major and as your guard. I will take the weapon now."

"You killed him?" Aila stepped around him to gaze down the alley. The greenshirt was slumped against the building, the front of his shirt soaked with rusty-brown blood. "You said confront, not butcher!"

Masákh's hand closed over hers. "I will take the weapon now." The words were low and calm, but an order not to be disobeyed.

Aila released it, searching his face for answers. She fought a growing urge to run, but there was no point; he would catch her before she got ten feet away. "Why? What could he possibly have done to deserve that? Sometimes you scare the life out of me, Masákh. I'm not always sure I want to know you, and right now is one of those times. Will you at least give me warning before I piss you off so bad you kill me?"

Masákh's nostrils flared, his mouth pinched tight, his eyes piercing her with that icy black glare. "Why do you always assume I am randomly killing people for enjoyment? Do you ever consider what my emotion might be on the subject? Do you ever consider I am weighing one life against yours? I am trained as a diplomat, not an executioner." He pulled a strange interface from his pocket and flicked it on, holding up the screen to show her several photographs of the two of them emerging from the discretion house. Aila's veil wasn't down; their faces were clearly visible in two of the photos.

"This is what cost him his life. The pictures have been downloaded to a server. He claims to have been acting on the orders of a captain who reports to a *fáhganid*, who is offering large bounty on our location and capture. I can trace the assignment of a Captain Dorbatal, find where the threat lies, but he did not know the name of the *fáhganid* beyond the term 'The Red Man.' There are ten million *fáhganid* across the planet, four million of them male; the term is all but useless."

Aila hung her head. Why did he always have to have solid justification to back him up? Or was it all a smooth lie, to keep her in line? Even four years ago she was never sure, but the photos were pretty damning. "So what now? They'll know we're here."

Masákh tore open the officer's interface, removed the power supply and the operating chip. He shattered the screen against the corner of the trash bin so hard it bent the case and obliterated the circuitry. The chip, with all its treasonous information, he dropped inside his right boot for later decrypting.

"If the local military had orders to find us, they would have surrounded the city and left no building unsearched. Tokh has thus not notified them, which means he has suspicions and is using only trusted networks. The fact we walked around the city yesterday, passing officers that paid us no attention means they have not been put on alert from any other source, either. Therefore this is something covert, without open military order. Since we cannot distinguish normal officers on patrol from those on secret missions, all military officers must be considered suspect. We cannot leave the city; any help Haghíde sends will be looking for us here as well. We need the commercial sections for population to blend into. We will put several blocks behind us; if they are searching here and we are elsewhere in the city, it should buy us some time. I expect Haghíde's answer to come through any moment now that the sun is up."

He took the tote bag from her and held out his murdering hand, spatters of blood on his cuff and the skin beneath.

For the first time Aila's spirits began to flag, and the day began to feel like an ongoing nightmare she had no escape from. She understood his reasoning, but couldn't help feeling bad for the dead officer lying on the pavement. Was he promised gain? Was he just following his orders? He hadn't meant her personal harm; she knew that in her heart. He probably had no idea who she was, and Masákh had knifed the life out of him. Masákh's hand was waiting; the pause was becoming lengthy, but she didn't want to touch him at the moment. Would he get angry if she refused?

Aila turned her face from him and began to walk.

They zigzagged through the city, grabbing a small breakfast on the way. Aila had nothing to say to him, and they walked the distance in silence. Masákh continued to check his interface with obsessive regularity, the intervals growing shorter as his patience decreased.

"What do we do if no directive comes?" Aila said at last.

Masákh gave a heavy sigh. He was unfailingly punctual; there was no reason a transmission shouldn't be, especially from a fellow punctualist. "If I do not have a directive by noon, I will use the secondary chip and place a message directly to Tokh. Once I make contact the new chip will be useless and we will lose our access to world programming, but we will have our answers."

Hour by hour the city came alive again and they blended into the crowds, just a *nhásarwharl* couple sitting in the fresh air of a little parklet, enjoying the morning. The sun was warm on Aila's back, the absence of conversation dull, the drone of traffic noises steady and soothing, and the lack of sleep caught up with her. While Masákh obsessed on his interface, Aila dozed under the cover of the veil.

"Have you noticed something odd?" Masákh said quietly.

Aila's eyes flew open and she scanned the little public garden where they sat in front of an office building. A *díhnarwharl* sat reading something on an interface and frowning. Three women sat at a table, drinking cups of *raffin* and laughing, someone's grown son waiting impatiently as escort. A *dáhneg* toddler climbed on and off a bench while he and his nanny shared a dish of *m'vat*. Nothing caught her eye through the slight blur of the veil. No one was looking at them. "Like what?"

"Where is security? *Don't turn!* Use your eyes, not your head."

Aila tried very hard not to be obvious. She looked up at Masákh from under the veil. *"Time?"* she said in Kerasi. He showed her the clock on his interface, holding it at such an angle she could focus innocently in the proper direction. A green uniform had moved into a corner of the sitting garden, standing sentry at the rear exit. He pretended to watch beyond the garden, but every now and then his eyes would fix on them. And only them.

"We should get going," she said aloud, and stood up. Another guard stood against a building across the street. Not watching them, not threatening, not at all unusual for a large city whose government was on high alert, but Aila took it personally just the same.

Masákh took the lead for several blocks, then held a door for her at a sweet shop. Aila took her time, pointing to more than half the inventory and questioning the staff on the flavors before choosing just two items. When they exited the shop, the same two green *bhántanok* officers were waiting, one at the next corner, the other still innocuous across the street. Anxiety gripped Aila's chest. If the guards cornered them, it was unlikely they could be reasoned with, and Masákh didn't have enough *dakra* on him to pull together a bribe that would be enticing for two. Unless he was fast beyond belief, he wouldn't be able to shoot more than one before the other shot him and then shot her.

"What do we do?" she whispered. "Sit tight, hide, or confront them?"

"If they were going to arrest us, they would have. They're just tailing. Ignore them." But he reached into his pocket and sent a locational ping, off-schedule.

They strolled aimlessly, window shopping. Every time they stopped, the greens were the same distance away, never closer, never farther, remaining inconsequential.

"Do not look at them," Masákh whispered. "Do not engage. Let them think we don't know."

At a corner shop, Masákh lingered inside, then led Aila out a back exit to a less-congested street, down an alley and out to the next main street. He crossed again, herded her another block, and turned right.

"We have to get off the streets. Find the nearest Eel stop. Even if we ride in a circle around the city, we're not as visible." Aila nodded. The nearest was a block back the way they came. As they reached the busy stop, a *bhántanok* officer strolled by.

Obviously Masákh felt none of the panic Aila did under her veil, didn't feel tears of fear and frustration trying to surface from under three hours' sleep. His stride was confident and even, not wobbly-kneed and dizzy like hers. He tipped his head to the Greenshirt as they strolled past. "Bright day, officer," he said.

"Bright day, Major," the officer replied, even though Masákh wore dark shades, was not in uniform, and displayed no rank at all.

Masákh turned at the next intersection, down a street of back doors and loading docks, a parking area for street vehicles, and a recessed door to an industrial building with a crude sign plastered to it reading *"Use entrance on Gulwahr Street."* He yanked Aila up the two steps into the recessed doorway, cramming her into the corner. She pulled the veil back to see better.

Aila's voice shook. "They're going to follow us forever. Masákh, you're going to have to shoot them."

He pocketed the sun shades and gave her a cold eye. "The one who accuses others of unnecessary force is suggesting unprovoked murder of two military officers, on a city street with witnesses everywhere? Do you think their commander will accept the reason of 'they frightened my client' as a worthy excuse?"

Aila looked down at the ground. "I'm sorry. At the moment I feel my life is very much in danger, and the force is justified."

"I do not disagree." His hand slipped inside his shirt and removed his weapon, removed the safety, and hid it in his hand. "Stay back. I will have only one chance to get both."

Aila pressed backward against the door, trying both to be shielded and peer around him at the same time, listening for the sound of boots on the pavement. Focused forward, she never heard a thing until the door gave way behind her, taking her off balance. The first hand clamped over her mouth and the second slipped around her waist and lifted her off her feet, pulling her inside the building.

Twenty-five

Nadigh stood over the table in his planning room, Rimas, Moragh, and two of his trusted uncles with him. The table top was a computer screen in itself, with the option of 3-D visuals or flipping the entire display over to a wallscreen. Nadigh knew he was trying to accomplish too much in too short a time: cleaning house, restructuring, passing laws, investigating his father's death, and so much more. He'd slept a total of six hours in the past forty-eight. He would try to catch two more soon, before he collapsed. And there was still a state funeral to plan.

Moragh's interface chimed. He was currently intercepting and handling all communications, one less thing Nadigh had to attend to.

Moragh glanced at the text on his screen. His finger jammed the privacy switch and he held it to his ear. He stepped away from the table, but the urgency in his voice removed all conversation in the room. "Where? When? Who was with them? Have you viewed the surveillance? Get someone on it immediately. I will inform the Emperor. Moragh, end."

Nadigh turned his head. "It wouldn't be good news, would it?"

Moragh bowed several times. "I'm sorry, my brother. There is another major incident among the delegates, one that may require direct intervention. Dihr brought the four females to the roof for exercise. While there, the Prime Minister of Koos jumped to her death."

Nadigh tipped his head back and clenched his pointed teeth in a fearsome grimace. "Witnesses? Was the Secretary Kel near her?"

"No, Excellency. He was not on the roof. Another female tried to grab her, but was unable to stop her fall. It is worse than that. The females messaged the males; they ran upstairs to the roof. The last one in line was the Naborine councilor, Vis Na Wa Din. He was stabbed from behind on the sixth-floor stairwell. He was dead by the time everyone returned inside. It was felt the Prime Minister's fall was a suicide, until the discovery of the councilman. Now it is uncertain."

Nadigh gave a scream of rage and slammed his fists on the table screen hard enough to shatter it in two places. Rimas took a step back.

"Breath," Uncle Durghid, Supreme Head of the Empiric Senate, told him.

Nadigh leaned over the table, hands gripping the edge hard enough to flip it over if he chose. "This is not Turwheg's doing! This is not my doing! Why are they killing their own? I will know who and why! One of them is involved in my father's death and I will prove it or they will not leave. I have been sympathetic and accommodating to this point. No more! I will not be made a fool of by a petty dignitary in my first week as Emperor. Rimas! You will see to the remaining females. Interrogate them separately. I want to know what happened to the female jumper. When you are done, interrogate the men. I want cameras every six paces any place they go, or they are not allowed to go there. You will put cameras everywhere but the private lavatories. Guards will be posted within the apartments at all times, no matter what the objections. There will be one empty seat between them at meals; all food will be served by my guards. No one is to touch another's dish. The *aghát* will adjust their schedule accordingly. I want all persons and their items searched and inventoried. Rimas and her sisters will see to the females so there are no objections.

"Moragh, ready my broadcast room immediately. I will speak with the Union President Mijono before I approach the delegates. I will be open and honest about the treachery, and my reasons why I will not release his people. He will either support me in my quest to learn the truth, or I will charge them with the death of my father and send them to my scanner to find out. They stole my royal technician during the assassination; I cannot guarantee the condition of anyone following the procedure. In fact – tell them that. Tell the delegates I will no longer play their games. If the person responsible for the deaths of their own does not step forward in the next twelve hours, I will have them strapped down one by one and the information extracted by memory scan, beginning with Secretary Kel."

"And this missing delegate Perrin they keep asking for?" Rimas said. "Is she alive, and if so where? What should I tell the delegates? They are persistent."

189

Nadigh still leaned on the table, jaw clenched, face a sanguine brown, exhausted eyes locked on a crack across the broken tablescreen. "I know precisely where she is. She is in the care of one of my trusted Generals, safer at the moment than any other delegate in my care. That is all you need to know, and you can thus honestly tell them everything you know. The people adored her energy and fearlessness, and the fact she could speak directly to them. They need her right now as a symbol of what we can achieve. I will not bring her back here to be murdered by her own people, and I will tell Mijono as much. Everyone, to task."

Twenty-six

Aila screamed and tore at the hand on her mouth. She kicked Masákh before being pulled inside. Never had she seen such a look on his face, a murderous rage as he spun around and saw what was happening, a desperation that defied all reason. He dove after her, never losing contact. The door shut behind him, the sudden darkness blinding them for several seconds. His hand seized upon the arm that held her as he jammed his weapon against the holder's head.

"Let her go or die!" he ordered so harshly he choked on the words. He began to count, *"Veh! Moh!"*

"Put the toy down, Masákh." Arrogance and disdain dripped from every word. "If you cared to look, you'd see I've already released her. If you want to live, you'll get in here and follow me."

Masákh breathed hard, waiting for the adrenaline to fade. His eyes adjusted to the shadows, and his hand lowered. Two other men, one in green and one in brown, stood behind him. Anger flared up so hard spit flew on his words. *"Trixhor pan khar,* Mátokhan! I was one second from killing you! Announce yourself!"

The door to the street opened and both stalking greenshirts tried to enter. Masákh spun, weapon out, while Aila launched herself at the door with a shriek, crushing the leader.

Mátokhan grabbed Masákh's arm. *"Ka!* They are mine. They were sent to steer you here. We aren't trusting communications. Come."

Masákh couldn't move yet. "Communications?! I was about to kill them! You could not have had one of them slip me a paper, 'Here, citizen, you dropped this?', or better yet, 'General's One is having a special on safehouses, would you care for the address?'?"

General's One referred to Mátokhan's position. He was Tokh's Number One *aghát,* older than Masákh – General's Two – by at least ten years, higher in rank, higher in caste, and his duties had always been well beyond what Masákh did. While Masákh was tutoring imprisoned little Union girls on how to act like proper Kerasi ones, Mátokhan worked alone, without direct supervision, and had the Emperor's permission to bargain with Union representatives in his name. When negotiations finally began and Aila had Union permission to barter a preliminary deal, she had sat down with Mátokhan to broker the first steps because at the time she was the only one who knew how. Aila was not fond of him; his arrogance and superiority went well beyond any Kerasi she had ever met below *fáhganid* caste. She'd learned to deal with him by being as strong and icy and unyielding as she could, never entered into his baiting games or allowed his arrogance to get the best of her – skills she stole from Masákh himself. Although he had never threatened her, Aila didn't trust him farther than the next molecule. But he was here, and he was Tokh's man every bit as much as Masákh was, and she was very relieved to see him.

Mátokhan used a thumbprint to open an inner door and motioned them through it. "You didn't give us a chance. Do you have any idea how hard it is to tail an *aghát* who knows he's being followed? It was all they could do to keep you in sight. We covered the area with code markers for you to come in; you never responded."

Masákh frowned. "I saw them. Without other communication, I feared they were a trap."

They entered a grimy yellow corridor and climbed a wide flight of stairs at the end.

Aila broke her silence at last. "I thought you were preaching the Emperor's cause on Mensara?"

Mátokhan eyed her with the same amusement one gave a barking puppy following at heel. "The Emperor is no fool. Was no fool," he corrected himself. "All diplomats, troops, and probably most of the spies within the Union were recalled for the Accord. Nághtas wanted every person fluent in Union Standard, every person with diplomatic abilities who understood Union custom on hand if needed, to the point of assigning someone for every dignitary. You, I see, were quick to pick old favorites."

Aila gave him a greasy, sarcastic smile. "I didn't see you in the audience. I suppose, after all your years of begging to get people to listen to the Emperor and reporting back to him, being in his presence must have lost some of its glory."

Mátokhan whirled around, finger outstretched so far that Masákh flung his arm out, blocking Aila. "DON'T speak to me about Nághtas! I was allowed within his presence many times, receiving my orders directly from him so there would be no misunderstanding. I was one of very, very few people he trusted to speak for him, even if only on a limited subject. That is a privilege not even Tokh had. And I was in the balcony at the far left side, sitting above Naghtas's wives. I had full view of the assassination, and no way to protect my Emperor. Because of the crush at the exits, I wound up lowering myself over the side of the balcony and assisting his wives and smalldaughter to safety while you all ran and saved yourselves. You may have the stronger hand playing Union games, but you are here on my world and I will not tolerate a Union female criticizing me."

Aila shrank back against Masákh. She bowed her head and mumbled, "Apologies."

Masákh's arm still blocked her like an iron gate, pushing her behind him, shielding her. His words were cold and threatening, as much as his face. "Stand down! We are all equally wounded, and you would do well to remember that."

Mátokhan shut his mouth and tipped his head in acknowledgment. In the upstairs corridor, he again opened a door with a thumbprint scan. Inside was a small reception area, empty of everything but a few padded benches. He opened a final door and they emerged into a long conference room. Milky-white glass set high in one wall let in a diffuse light. A table stretched the length of the room; ten Kerasi officers sat five to a side, some in green uniforms, some in brown. All wore earbugs, intent on the computer screens before them.

"This our mobile field office," Mátokhan explained. "General Rhigandir's safehouse. I have two shifts of ten men. We can set up or collapse operations in fifteen minutes. We've been here half a day. Now that you are brought in, I'm sure we'll be moving out again soon."

"Any word on Tótoghar and Haghíde?" Masákh asked. "We were moving in opposite directions, but their signal is ten hours overdue."

"What?!" Aila said. Damn Kerasi evasiveness!

"Picked up eight hours ago by our men. They requested food and sleep; both should be back on assignment in the next few hours."

"Why did they not signal they were safe?" Masákh demanded. "That is protocol. I depended on that signal for my next move."

"It was felt you would stay on the surface if you thought they were trying to find you. If you went underground, you'd be harder to find."

Masákh accepted that truth.

"Go through that door," Mátokhan ordered Aila, pointing to the end of the room. "It is my office, so to speak. You may rest while we discuss the situation." He eyed Masákh with disdain. Masákh had not shaved or bathed in a day and a half; he was dishonorably unkempt, the goatee nowhere near regulation. "Perhaps you would first care to borrow my kit and clean yourself before someone puts you on report. There are no facilities beyond the sinks in the lavatories and the temperature of the water is not guaranteed; do your best."

"I would welcome the courtesy, Brother *Aghát*, but after a briefing. We have been too long in the dark."

Aila slipped partially behind Masákh again. "I am a Union representative. My people are dead as well, others trapped here. I will know what is happening, so I may relay the information to my government when I am able."

Mátokhan gave her a long, blank-faced, fish-eyed stare. "I have worked with many dignitaries and authorities in the last several years, but you are the only one I cannot get to follow my directives. I do not have time to waste. Come."

Out of the work room and across the hall was a small room that held nothing but a table and a scattering of worn chairs. Mátokhan called back into the workroom, and a moment later a greenshirt brought them cups of hot *raffin* and some type of fruit-laden cakelets.

"Bring me up to date on the last day," Masákh said between bites of cakelet. "We have had little access to airwaves."

"It's not pretty," Mátokhan said. "Nadigh is furious. He emptied the palace of everyone but his family and Naghtas's wives and young children, and a few guards and servants he trusted. Moragh was scanned and he passed; he and his family are also sequestered in the building. Every other person was escorted out by the imperial guard. Anyone who wishes to gain his approval must pass a scan. As Naghtas's technician was kidnapped in the coup, it took time to get a qualified specialist to the palace. They are managing to clear up to ten people a day under Moragh's supervision. Nadigh is gaining ground. He has declared the *bhísroti* dead and disbanded, as well as the *fáhganid*, which I do not need to tell you has upset many. *Dáhneg* is now the top caste below *thósikh*, and if things do not settle Nadigh has threatened to demote them all to *nhásarwharl*, because they are not noble enough to be called *díhnarwharl*. He wishes to build a democratic cabinet to oversee what used to be caste duties, but he hasn't had enough time yet. There is talk of retaliation, but the military swears allegiance to the Emperor, not the *fáhganid*. He has promised the military will still receive their pay on time, no delays, so he still has their full support. Well, below *fáhganid* level. At least one hundred have lost their heads in his purge."

"And the shooter? Did they capture the assassin?"

Mátokhan gave a slow bow of his head. "With full confession, of course." His eyes rolled toward Aila, then back down. "I do not think we need to discuss the details of his fate before a galactic audience. We may know he is dead, and that is enough. His wife and children were dealt with more civilly. He was a simple *rhibáni*, paid one million *dakra* up front. He was too smart to put it all into a bank at once, so most of it was seized from his home. He never saw a person, just a voice on his interface, and the voice referenced a Citizen Red who was the voice's superior. Weapon and payment were made through a public package delivery, no questions asked."

Masákh sat back. "I disposed of a tail who mentioned reporting to 'The Red Man.' I believed it to mean a *fáhganid*."

"There are many things that seem to point that way, but it could also be a decoy. It could be someone whose name is actually Red."

"What about the remaining Union delegates?" Aila asked. "Where are they? Who is still alive? Are they being returned to the ships? Are the ships still in orbit?"

Mátokhan pulled out his interface. He tapped through several menus, then handed it to her. "I trust Masákh has taught you to read Kerasi."

It was a list of the Union deceased. Aila sounded out the translated names whose phonetics were not always close to the Union equivalent.

"Hawet Quin. Wodu Mosi. N'ua. Chedna Kerek. Oh no! Vee M'para. She was so sweet. Melli Vergara? Kuu Taam. Oh thank goodness, Masákh! I don't see Vanora's name anywhere here. She must have made it. Wait – Prime Minister Moann? She wasn't on the list I saw at General Tokh's. Was she among the injured? That's not going to go over well on Koos." She handed back the interface.

Mátokhan gave her that cold greasy smile, attempting to mimic Union mannerisms and never quite understanding why it didn't work. "Nine dignitaries and four guards died as a result of the shooter or subsequent injuries. Three more have died in the last three days in what are assumed to be further assassinations, meant to shed suspicion and distrust onto the Emperor. One was poisoned, one stabbed, one thrown from a roof. None were by Kerasi hands."

"What?!" Aila stared, stupefied. It didn't make sense. No one in the delegation would murder another delegate. No one. It had to be a disgruntled Kerasi guard, someone else the Emperor had trusted. Poor Vanora, caught up in the middle of all of that, wondering if she might be next in the crosshairs. How could anyone sleep even an hour in such a situation? Even Masákh sat back, silent. "I don't believe it! There has to be someone else involved. That's more than half of us! What the hell is happening?"

Mátokhan raised an eyebrow at her. "Do you not know your delegates?"

"What do you mean?"

He handed back the interface. "You are nothing more than a cadet on your first mission; your eyes are blinded by glory and you never *question* anything. How many of your group were for diplomacy and how many against?"

"In talks onboard ship, there were ten of us who were staunchly pro-diplomacy, and about seven who were opposed. The rest were undecided until they could observe things for themselves."

"And after?"

Aila counted back down the list and tried to remember everyone's positions. "Ten of the deceased are pro- or neutral. Only two are from the against list."

"And you don't think that's strange?"

"Possibly, but it doesn't have to mean anything. It's just bad luck."

"Tokh questioned the Secretary Kel," Masákh said. "Aila herself had difficulties with him. I heard some of his more aggressive comments, and they were not favorable to Kerasím."

"That doesn't mean he would murder his own people," Aila argued. "In the Union we have the right to disagree, even with authority figures, without fearing retaliation. That's part of living in freedom."

Mátokhan sat back with a sigh. "You sit in meetings and play games of Let's All Be Friends, travel to places and tell others how they should live, like a flock of new young wives. When you learn to suspect everyone, especially those with authority, only then will you truly be a diplomat. This Kel – the leader of your group – was kidnapped from the palace last night while you were playing tourist."

"What? How? Who would take him? Why?" Aila's voice held sympathy. Just when you thought you were safe, they came to grab you in the middle of the night when you were too confused to think straight. She knew that feeling all too well.

Masákh's eyes narrowed. "How can that happen? They were under imperial guard. No one noticed? There was no surveillance?"

"That's the question now, isn't it," Mátokhan said. The crumbs from his cakelet played against his *aghát* sensibilities and his finger rounded them up into a very precise pile on his plate; chaos contained. "Nadigh is outraged over the last two deaths, and threatens to put the dignitaries through a scanner if no one confesses. Soon after, two *fáhganid* guards – certainly not out of place at the palace – show up at the door, say that Nadigh wishes to speak with the secretary in charge. No one questions an order from Nadigh. He walks out the door escorted by two guards, and no one thinks of it until someone in the Union asks when he might be returning, many hours later. No weapons, no bloodshed, no objections, just *pah*! Into another dimension. What would you think? Nadigh neither requested nor spoke to him."

"That would depend on if he's alive or dead. If dead, it could be anyone from the Emperor downward. Alive? My guess is that he made a deal for his life and left his cabinet to suffer what fate awaits," Masákh said.

Mátokhan turned to Aila. "And you? He is your superior. What do you believe?"

Aila glared back. She didn't know what to think. Omi Kel had been Secretary of State for the Planetary Union for six years. For at least ten before that he'd been on various councils, before that a player in Centauri politics. No one could question his loyalty to President Mijono or the Union, including Aila. His personality grated on her, but that wasn't a crime. She didn't share his viewpoint on this matter, but she had no doubt he believed he was acting in the best interest of the

Union. He was no coward; a coward would never have come to Kerasím in the first place. He would not leave his people to die.

"If I were to guess anything," she said, "I would guess he cut a deal; he had all the high-security knowledge: take him, learn what they wanted, but in exchange guarantee his people are returned unharmed. That would be the Union thing to do."

Mátokhan's expression said he hadn't considered an unselfish rationale. "That is also a possibility. The question then is, to whom did he make the bargain?"

The comment went unanswered, and the conversation paused.

"So what now?" Aila said. "Do I wait here in this office until I can leave? Obviously it's too dangerous to head deeper into Yomebor."

Mátokhan shook his head. "You are safe for the moment, but I am sending you back to Tokh. He feels it is now too risky to place you anywhere else. You should be closer to the palace, either to be sheltered with your people there or taken back to your ship. We will finalize plans tonight."

"Unless this is settled and I am heading straight to the ship, I won't go to the palace," Aila decided. "I won't be the final victim."

Aila dined with Masákh and Mátokhan on the same simple rations the crew ate. She didn't ask what it consisted of, and Masákh didn't explain. It kept the hunger away.

"You may take my office for the night," Mátokhan said, showing her the little room off the work room. It had a field cot, and a washroom so tiny that closing the door took some shuffling. "Masákh and I will bunk with the crew."

Aila pulled Masákh into the room. "I can't do that!" she whispered. "I can't sleep alone with ten Kerasi officers on the other side of a door. That's suicide. You have to stay with me."

"I cannot. It would be most suspicious." His hands rested on her shoulders, fingered the fabric of her shirt. She leaned against him; he buried his face in the top of her head. "You must trust Mátokhan, and trust his men."

"That won't happen. Give me your weapon, then. Come on! Give me it! I need some way to defend myself. You can have it back in the morning. I suggest if you choose to check on me during the night, you knock first and announce yourself."

Indecision weighed on his face. To be weaponless was to be powerless, but he reached inside his shirt and handed it to her. "You remember how to remove the safety, and how to steady your aim?"

"I do. 'Don't hesitate; if you aim, fire first, do not be the one fired at.' I remember."

He bid her goodnight and shut the door.

Mátokhan caught him exiting the room. His smirk said he approved. "A quick dalliance before being separated for the night? You're a lucky man. What's she like?"

Masákh's pause gave away too much. "I am hired to guard her, not bed her. I made sure she was secure for the night."

"Truly, Brother *Aghát*? You take no liberties at all?"

"She is Union. You know their rules. Females must first grant consent or there are severe penalties."

"Hmph. If you won't, do you mind if I do?"

Masákh spread his hands and tipped his head, the sliminess of his smile saying he already knew the answer. "You have dealt with her before. You know the strength of her mindset, but you may ask." He knocked on the office door. "Aila, it is Masákh. I am with Mátokhan."

The door opened just enough for her to peer out.

"As commander of the facility, Mátokhan offers to stay and protect you, if he may bed you once during the night."

Aila's face twisted in horror. "*What!?* Absolutely not!" She raised the weapon and pointed it at him through the gap. Her thumb remembered the safety switch. "How dare you! One hand on this door and I will shoot whoever comes through it, sight unseen. Tokh himself taught me to shoot, so be assured I will not miss." She slammed the door and locked it. A loud scraping noise sounded before a thud hit the door.

"That would be the desk," Masákh surmised. "I have seen her target practice. If you value your *khatas*, I would not recommend offending her."

Mátokhan shrugged a shoulder. "*Gah.* She will not sleep tonight, thinking of me."

Exhausted as she was, Aila didn't sleep much, every light on and her ear picking up every voice and sound in the main room, one hand resting on the weapon. She waited for Masákh to give her an all-clear in the morning. The weapon was returned, as promised.

They killed time in the workroom, listening to the short bursts of coded information coming through the underground channels. Nadigh was still cleaning house, reassigning former *bhísroti* to different positions, assigning his uncles as directors of cabinets, changing out regional presidents, heads of security, making new loyalists and new enemies. Anyone he felt couldn't be trusted, anyone who failed a memory scan, was executed. It was far too early to tell if his measures were warranted or if he would be a tyrant of an emperor, but in a day, with the stroke of a pen, he'd given females three new huge rights: the right to refuse a marriage, the right to divorce a husband providing they remarried within a week, and the right to hold public office with the permission of her husband, paving the way for his daughter Rimas to gain the throne. Outside poured a steady rain, so even a walk one block to get something better to eat was not a pleasant idea.

"Mátokhan, you're sending all kinds of encrypted stuff," Aila said when she thought about it. "Can you get a message to one of the ships in orbit?"

"Impossible. I might send to a relay, but I would not attempt direct contact without permission of superiors. Everything is monitored."

"Can you send one all the way to Earth?"

"Earth is too far for this equipment. It would take more than a year."

"Can you relay to Tokh to relay to a ship?" she persisted. "I want my parents to know I'm still okay. Masákh disabled my interface."

Mátokhan gave a nod. "That I can do. Twenty seconds, no more, and it will not be private, so do not give information."

"I know the drill," she assured him.

A dark rainy night made it harder to track anyone. Mátokhan's arrangements had them leaving after dinner and running a ground vehicle straight through until the next night, when they would arrive at Tokh's estate on the cliffs of Imahlva. Masákh and the driver, a *nhásarwharl* Captain named Gurih, would take turns navigating and sleeping.

"They'll tail us," Aila insisted. "Faster is better. As much as I don't want to set foot on a plane right now, we should be flying."

"No," Mátokhan said. "You will leave in a vehicle from a storage lot two streets over, half an hour after our decoy. Our decoy will also have three passengers; it will go directly to the air hangar, where personnel will be exchanged. We have not been here long enough to attract attention. Airflight is still restricted and public transportation not secure. A personal vehicle is the safest journey."

Aila sighed, out of options. "I don't like that at all."

For the first hour or two Aila watched out every darkened window like a camera, wary of any passing vehicle, checking to make sure someone from the other direction didn't spin around and follow them, but nothing seemed strange at all. The dark, the rain, the steady hum of the vehicle, the hour creeping toward midnight after two nights of little sleep, the relief of having Masákh so close even if he resisted all efforts to touch him, made her drowsy. It didn't help that the local airwaves Gurih located played nothing but slow, somber music to honor the late Emperor Nághtas. She lay flat on the rear seat, her head jammed against Masákh's leg but not on it, her hand tucked invisibly under his knee, his hand petting her hair in the dark of the back seat, and she slept several hours.

They stopped, stretched, ate, and switched drivers twice before suns-up. Gurih sat front passenger when Masákh piloted, allowing Aila the entire seat to spread out on. Cities went by, countryside, hills and valleys and their alternating vistas, the short red and purple-leafed trees so common to Kerasím and its functional orange sun. No wonder the Kerasi had blended so seamlessly into Kye's society when they'd infiltrated the Union. The rain and clouds lifted mid-day, leaving an inviting brightness Aila wasn't allowed to witness except through the dark tinted glass of the windows.

The sun crept downward and set behind them as they moved northeast hour after hour, and the windows blacked out once more. They stopped to switch drivers, and Masákh came into the back to sit with her. His hand slipped down in the darkness and squeezed hers; she held onto it and didn't let go. "Very close now. Perhaps one more hour," he told her. "We've made excellent time. We may already be close enough to appear on the General's sensors."

"Good. I'm so tired of sitting. I'm going to run laps in his yard for half an hour."

Masákh snorted and freed his hand. "That is not fair to Lady Mímihn. She cannot see to run after you in the dark. You will need to rescue her from the pool."

Aila laughed. "I can just see her doing that, too."

"Trixohr!" Gurih exclaimed. He jammed hard at the braking control and tried to spin the vehicle sideways to avoid the large transport truck blocking the road, its warning lights flashing, the driver waving frantically. Aila and Masákh slammed forward against the seat, then slid back when they came to a stop.

Masákh grabbed her by her shoulders. "Are you injured?"

Aila shook her head. "No, I'm good."

Gurih put the vehicle in reverse, but something slammed the side with a staticky buzz. They stopped moving and the console lights went out, plunging the vehicle into darkness, save the odd blue lights flashing in front of them.

"We've shorted out," Gurih said. His confusion lasted only a second. *"Trap!"*

"Down!" Masákh ordered, and shoved Aila flat on the seat. He reached for his weapon, but the shorted-out doors were yanked open.

Before Masákh could pull his hand free, he was hit with a stun stick. He arched backwards, then collapsed on Aila. Gurih got off a single shot before he, too, was stunned.

Aila was seized from behind by at least four hands. She couldn't make anyone out; hands seemed to be everywhere. She grabbed for Masákh but was yanked belly-down half-out of the vehicle, her hands wrenched behind her and bound while she screamed and twisted and kicked. The invisible hands hefted her under her arms and dragged her away.

Masákh managed to fling an uncoordinated arm in her direction. "Aila!"

Twenty-seven

Aila breathed deep, trying her hardest to stave off panic. Her hands were locked in heavy metal loops, an adhesive strip covered her mouth, a cloth was bound over her eyes so tight she saw stars. The bench in the back of the delivery truck was hard and slippery, and she fought to maintain her seat over every bump and jiggle. No one spoke, but she could hear men breathing around her.

Keep your head, Girl. Don't panic. Don't panic. You've been captured before, and this time you know how it works. They want you alive or you'd be dead right now. They want you in one piece, or they'd be all over you. Think! Don't be a whiny whimpering female, think like Masákh. You're an Admiral's daughter. What information would you be able to tell a commanding officer?

Aila pushed her fear down as far as she could – it wasn't far, but it was enough. A male was on either side of her, sitting but not touching. She could smell they were male; most Kerasi just smelled – well, not Human, but sweaty males were the worst, especially if they hadn't washed in a while. They must have been low-level officers; *aghát* didn't smell that bad. The transport was loud and rattly, but by the sound of breathing and shuffling boots, she guessed there were at least six of them. No light came in around the edges of her blindfold, therefore the back of the truck was probably dark. She filled her mouth with spit, then worked her wet tongue at the edges of the adhesive over her lips until she had a corner free. If they decided to seal her nose as well, she wanted a ready means of getting air.

Kerasi women do not call attention to themselves if they want to live, Masákh had drilled into her, so Aila played the dutiful prisoner and pretended to be part of the wall, counting off potential minutes in her head. Time equaled approximate distance. She was only an hour or so from Tokh's; she wanted to remain in that area.

By her estimate, twenty minutes had elapsed when Aila felt the transport leave the main roadway. The turns were sharp and the road too bumpy to be anything but dirt; the wallowing of the transport sent those on the benches into a ballet of counterbalancing to keep their seats. They came to a stop inside a building somewhere; all traffic noise had stopped; voices took over. The rear door opened; light filled the edges of her blindfold. Hands pulled her to stand, lowered her from the transport, guided her to walk. By the sharpness of the curved nails, they wore no gloves.

"Take her to the office level; they've got a room up there."

Eighteen steps across a floor, up two flights of sixteen stairs, a door, a left, eight steps forward, a right, a long corridor with many voices and a wall to her left. The acoustics were poor; it was an open area.

Come on! Come on! You could have walked the Kye embassy blindfolded, you knew it that well. Concentrate!

A short flight up, a right, thirty-five steps, and a door on her left was opened. She was directed in six steps, the adhesive was pulled from her mouth in a fast painful yank, and she was pushed downward until she sat on the floor. The boots retreated; the door shut and clicked. She could hear the sounds of the open area outside, and foot traffic past the door. Boots shuffled back and forth; at least one guard was posted outside the door. Not a breath could be heard from inside the room; she was alone.

Good work, Girl. You're doing fine. You're helping yourself get out of here. Masákh won't let you be here long. Losing you violates his promise of protection, and I wouldn't want to be in the way when he gets hold of the person that did it. If he notifies Mátokhan, he'll be out for blood as well; I have imperial protection, and I guarantee he'd swallow his own teeth before he disappoints the Emperor.

As time dragged, Aila ran out of things to console herself with. She tried to rub the blindfold off against her knee, but it was tied well. The metal hand locks chafed her wrists; her shoulders and elbows began to ache, but there was no pulling free. She rolled to her knees, then up to her feet. Leaning against the wall, she backed up six paces and found the door. Ten paces across the room to the far wall, twelve paces down the length, ten across the opposite wall, ten to the door, two for the door, and six back to where she started, and she sat back down. Not once did her shoulder bump a window or another door, or a single piece of furniture; escape was not likely. A dim glow came in around the blindfold, so they'd left a light on for her. After a while the floor grew hard against her butt-bones, and she slid over to lay on her side.

She must have dozed off, for she woke to a heavy boot tapping her backside. Aila rolled to sit up, but hands pulled her to her feet. They picked at the knot in the blindfold, removing it. Aila blinked her eyes at a dim empty room with no windows and a bare light beaming down from a corner of the ceiling. The dirty walls were the gray-green color of an overboiled eggyolk, an order for repainting at least thirty years overdue. A single guard in brown stood before her, lieutenant by insignia, a blaster rifle slung down his back by its strap. Someone wasn't playing games. He motioned her forward with his head, kept a heavy gloved hand on her shoulder to steer her. Out the door and around a corner to her left. The building looked industrial, perhaps some sort of abandoned factory, with an open warehouse floor and a balcony walkway with offices. On her fast glance, Aila saw at least a dozen people, greens and browns. Down the side corridor they stopped at a door. Her guard unlocked her hands; Aila's shoulders were ever thankful, and she rubbed her wrists to remove the red marks.

He opened the door before her and held up a hand with all fingers spread. *"Tavi fasim."*

Aila entered possibly the filthiest lavatory she'd ever seen. The dirt on the walls could have been used for archeology practice. Each step of her shoes needed a small tug to unstick them from the floor. And that didn't take into account the stench. Seven ancient pipe toilets festered in a row, not even a curtain separating them.

She'd been granted five minutes to pee before the guard would haul her out. She managed it in one and a half, and spent the remainder of the time searching the room. The small windows were high up, and when she climbed up to the sill, she looked straight down a three-story drop to pavement. No good. There was nothing to be had in the room to make a weapon, not even a mirror to shatter, unless she could figure out how to disassemble plumbing with her fingers. Maybe she'd try it next trip. Someone was bound to drop something at some point.

Aila tapped at the door. The guard opened it immediately. He bound her arms in front of her this time, and marched her back to the room. The door was shut and locked again.

A plate of food waited. *If this doesn't bring back memories.* Except it should have been Masákh escorting her through the halls, and even then she wasn't tied like a farm animal. Her stomach growled at the tantalizing smell. It was presented in a civilized manner, too classy for the common troops. A vegetable salad, an herbed bread round, a mound of seasoned grains with bits of fruit and several slices of spiced meat; nothing like the slops the crew probably ate. Aila stared at the plate until long after the food had grown cold, at last deciding if they were going to poison her, they wouldn't have wasted time preparing the food so well. It was Kerasi, but High Kerasi, fit for a *dáhneg*, and she wound up eating the entire thing.

She knew morning had arrived when the door unlocked and she was ordered to stand. The lavatory ritual repeated itself. This time, instead of having her hands locked again and being directed back to her room, she was led farther down the hall to what appeared to be a cafeteria. Windows lined the outside wall, making the room painfully bright. Guards were stationed at each corner of the room. The table in the center was set for two, and sitting opposite to the door was a familiar face, white Centauri hair sticking up as if he were surprised at her presence.

He gestured in apology toward the empty place setting. "Join me for breakfast?"

Aila stared. She slid into the seat across from him. "Secretary Kel. How long have you been here? Is everyone else here as well?"

He picked at his breakfast. "I was taken from the palace two days ago. Be careful what you say and do; there's one of those high-up fellows with the red robes you need to be careful of. He's got a rather difficult temper."

"Red usually means *fáhganid*," Aila said. "They're the enforcers. They buffer issues before they get to the *bhísroti*. They're used to having their orders followed."

"How long have you been here? They haven't hurt you, have they?"

"I'm guessing maybe twelve hours. So far I'm okay."

Kel pushed a serving dish toward her. "You're more used to Kerasi kidnappings than I am. You have an advantage over me. We were rather frantic when you were unaccounted for after the massacre.

Where have you been? What happened to your guard? Were you kidnapped from the palace, too?"

Beware The Man, Girly! Don't you trust him! He'll turn on you the minute he gets what he wants. Aila could hear Thayer's derisive voice warning her. Aila had managed to survive her trials by trust; Thayer had been knocked around so much she didn't trust anyone, which was probably why she never kept a boyfriend that long. While Aila was thrilled to see someone she knew, someone from her world, someone with the authority to make real decisions and get things done, it seemed odd that he would show up here. On the other hand, he was not only the head of the delegation, but a top government official. If you were going to take a hostage, he was probably the one to take. But his comment about kidnappings had made her mad.

Last time he spoke to you he accused you of misconduct. It doesn't matter who he is: don't be stupid. Play it like an aghát.

She took a disk of bread from a plate and smeared it with sweet-nut butter and a sprinkling of sautéed fruit, took a bite, and chewed it for a while. "I hired a bodyguard for a reason. I was taken to a place of safety."

"Obviously not too safe, or you wouldn't be here. What happened? Did he turn on you?"

"We left it too soon. So what do they want? Why are we here? Are they kidnapping the rest of us, too? What have you found out?"

Kel maintained his friendly air, as he did when they were in council sessions. It couldn't have been the change of fashion; Aila still wore Kerasi clothing, a red blouse and loose bronze bloomers of Mímihn's. Maybe he just really hated that party dress.

He shrugged his shoulders. "I know very little. I don't have your advantage of speaking their language. I understand why they'd take me; that's a risk of being Secretary of State. But you're just as important."

Aila almost choked on the bread. Her whole face screwed up in a frown. "Me? Why would I be important? I'm a lowly little junior council member. I have no power at all. Even if they mind-scanned me, I know nothing."

Kel held up a finger. "Ah! That's where you're wrong. I warned you about how you were dressed, but you preferred to listen to the whispers of those *aghát*, without ever thinking why. That's the error of inexperience, and you made a big one. Your little handshaking stunt was seen not only across the galaxy, but across Kerasím. All those ignorant women saw an Earth woman dressed like their royalty, coming out and making contact with the peasants. You're now their idol. You filled their heads with ideas. They want to be like you. They want their royalty to be like you, and that pompous fool Nadigh is making it happen. The Union saw you out among the Kerasi riff raff, dressed like a damned queen. You showed them live that Kerasi women are just like them, fashion-conscious and celebrity-crazy and eager to accept Union folk. Your camera stunt tipped the balance of power. Your trick has destabilized an entire planet, caused the deaths of hundreds, and Divinity only knows what will happen now. And don't say such things aloud; I've been warned they have a scanner operator here. If we want to keep our wits, we've got to play their games. Do exactly what they say, and we'll get out of this in one piece."

Aila gave a snort. Kel had just managed to lose any sympathy she might have felt for him. He couldn't step away from pointing the finger at anyone but himself, oblivious to the real danger he was in, especially if there was a *fáhganid* lurking about. That explained the fancy dinner last night.

"I've been scanned before. I have nothing to hide. I greeted the women because I felt sorry for them, banned from attending the festivities simply because they were women and below *dáhneg* caste. That was my only rationale. And that act had nothing to do with the assassination of Nághtas. That assassination was planned out long before I set foot on Kerasím. I would think, as Secretary of State for the Planetary Union, your office would be working to help the Emperor find the parties responsible, get us the hell out of here."

Kel paused to chew a bite of his breakfast, bits of fried animal fat mixed with a porridge and fried into cakes. He waved his fork at her for emphasis. "Oh, I offered! I offered! Nadigh is understandably upset, but he's taking it out on his own people, trashing his government, making radical changes that may prove quite dangerous to the Union."

Aila shook her head. "I don't see how allowing Kerasi women to divorce abusive husbands is a threat to the Union. They've been given a few basic universal rights; they don't even have a right to vote. Most of them can't read, so it's not likely they're writing manifestos to overthrow the Emperor who gave them the rights."

Kel's voice took on a more irritated tone. "This. This is where your inexperience will cut your own throat. Stop looking at just your special interest. Look at the whole picture, Aila. *It's not about the women.* It's the fact Nadigh has just cut the power of the upper classes. Imagine if the Union did away with business ownership, government, and military control, overnight. Your own father would be out of a job, his position negated, hoping somehow someone will make a job for him. Our civilization would dissolve. Just as theirs will. If the military starts siding with the upper castes, Nadigh is as good as dead, and his Empire with him. Imagine all that weaponry in the hands of rebels with no unifying government; anarchy on the ground, all his underlings vying for power, enemy ships gone rogue, *time itself* at stake if they break the moratorium."

One could only tap a broken circuit for so long. Nadigh wasn't going anywhere. And even if he did, there was a chain of power that would take over. Their government had been stable as carbon ten times longer than the Union had been around. Aila changed tactics. "So what do they want with us?"

Kel shrugged, the sad defeated move of someone who had tried and failed. "They haven't told me a thing. I assume they're going to try to ransom us."

"You've been here two or three days, and you don't know why? What's the point of ransom? Money to fund a cause? If they had enough money to buy an assassination, it's unlikely they'd waste time demanding money from the Union. What are they after? Weapons? Ships? You have to know something, Secretary, even if you don't want to share it with me. And since it's my life on the line here, too, I consider that rather rude."

Kel wasn't that stupid. Aila finished her breakfast, downed a glass of pale green *harfa* juice, and stood up. She held her wrists out to the guard at the door to be bound again. She was done.

"If you happen to see the *fáhganid*," she said over her shoulder, "tell him I am insulted. If he wants my cooperation, he'll get a detail in there to clean that lavatory. See you at dinner."

Aila stewed in her dank little room. Something wasn't adding up. *The enemy of my friend is my enemy also.* Who held a really bad grudge against Nághtas? What did Ross Halian know? Was he negotiating with

Nadigh? Or had he been seized as well? She understood why she might be taken. A pawn against the Emperor. A bargaining chip. A tidy ransom if not from the Union, then from her father, which would be a very Kerasi thing to do. But so was direct execution. Much less messy than hostages.

Why why why.

They didn't kill Masákh. They stunned him.

Why? Why leave him uninjured? Did they mean to shame him? Was it too big a risk of hitting her? Was he taken to a different location? Or just a different transport? It gave her hope for rescue, but the Kerasi way was just to kill something. Was it because *aghát* were sworn to the Emperor, and to kill an Emperor's officer was to anger the Emperor?

What am I missing?

Masákh would see it.

Not speaking to her, not telling her what was going on, keeping her in a dark little room – that was typically Kerasi. After her first imprisonment, it didn't worry her nearly as much as it should have. She needed to buy time. That she was sure of. To buy time, she'd have to keep time. She crawled around on the floor, sweeping her bound hands ahead of her, until she found a piece of gravel that might have fallen from a boot tread. Pinching it in her fingers, she scratched her name and the date she thought it was, and two little lines on the dingy wall; two meals.

Think. How would the aghát work this?

Trick me into giving information, and give back nothing.

But the Kerasi hadn't asked her a thing. That too, was suspicious.

Aila formulated a plan. She would give Kel one last chance to tell her what was going on – if they let them speak again, and then she was going straight to the *fáhganid.* If Kel couldn't negotiate with his captors, she sure as hell would negotiate with hers, and Kel wasn't going to be part of her bargain.

A midday lavatory trip broke up Aila's day; the lavatory looked no different, so either Kel hadn't seen the *fáhganid,* or the *fáhganid* didn't care. No loss. Diseases could be cured later. Dinner was on schedule; two meals a day, which meant she'd start trying to save some of her meal or take extra back with her, if they'd allow it. She was led once more down the hall to the cafeteria; and sure enough, Kel was already there. Nothing she'd eaten yet had caused her to question the food, but the fact this was the second time they'd eaten together, and the second time he'd gotten food before her, made her skittish about its purity.

Kel smiled and waved a hand at the chair across from him. "I'm glad to see you, Aila. I asked if they'd let you eat with me again, but I wasn't sure they'd allow it."

Aila didn't grab for the food right away. "Really? They have a translator? What's his name? Is he *aghát*? I'd like to request to speak to him."

"You already speak their language. You aren't talking to your guard? Pester them. Eventually they'll answer just to make you shut up."

Aila smiled, the same little nonchalant smirk Masákh would give her, saying, *Your foolishness amuses me.* Regular grunts didn't speak a word of Union Standard; only special elite did. Masákh had told her that the first time he met her. "I haven't spoken to anyone but you. And my Emperor's Tongue isn't as good as you seem to think. That's why I had a translator for a bodyguard. A guard generally knows nothing except his direct orders and what time he gets off duty. Those are not points for deep conversation." She spooned food onto her plate and began to eat.

Aila waved at one of the guards and motioned to the food. *"Ka lunahl?"* The guards relaxed, shifting feet and chuckling.

One broke his silence and mumbled, *"Dehn yar."*

We wish.

Aila bowed her head in sympathy.

"What did you say?" Kel demanded.

"Come on, Secretary. Even you should be able to say, 'What, no wine?'"

"Aila, don't get friendly with them. They can't be trusted. You know they can't. Start chatting with them and they're going to think you're open to other activities you might not like. These are men that rape women – rape men! – in broad daylight on city streets, and no one stops them. You don't want to draw attention to yourself, like you did at the palace."

"Is that why the big silence around me? I figured it was because I might be able to overhear something. There's something you don't understand about Kerasi, Secretary," Aila said with seriousness. "Almost all information is on a need-to-know basis, and if you disobey orders you face punishment, which can be anything from a public beating to torture or beheading. Therefore, most orders are followed pretty well. Don't misquote me, I don't trust them, not in the least, but if assault was the first thing on their minds they would have done it when I was tied up and blindfolded in the back of a transport with at least six stinking men. There's another purpose here; I just don't know it yet."

Kel reached across the table and grabbed her hand, caring and friendly. He held it tight between his, pleading with her. "Aila, I mean it! I'm worried for you. I'm still the leader of our group. I'm still responsible for you. I have to answer to your parents, to the President. The last thing I want to have to tell …"

And like a bolt of plasma fire, it hit her. Aila stared down at his hand holding hers, and she knew exactly what was going on.

His wrist was smooth.

Aila's wrists had been bound behind her for the better part of a day; the unnatural position, the lying down, the off-balance standing up, the being lifted, all pulled at the bones and skin until her wrists were raw and bruising. For the last twelve hours or so they'd been bound in front of her, better, but hard metal still rubbed her skin with every movement. The only time they were off were lavatory breaks or her meals with Kel. Even now, without the binders on, her wrists were red and chafed between the light bruises.

Kel's were unmarked.

He'd been here longer than she had and he was unmarked, which meant he wasn't being restrained at all. Males were a threat on Kerasím, but never females.

Kel was toying with her.

She'd been annoyed with her capture, far too indifferent based on her previous captivity. Now she was frightened, and it wasn't because of the Kerasi.

She took a deep breath and gave him a polite smile. "I thank you for your concern. Be assured, I am being as cautious as I can. I'd just like to know what I have to do to negotiate my release. Who's in charge here? What are their demands? Surely, you must know that much. They'll try to negotiate with a powerful male like you long before

212

they'll ever say a word to me. You're the one that has to get us free. Do your job, Mr. Secretary. Do it soon, because I don't want to be in the crossfire when the Emperor's troops come to get me." She took two pieces of fruit from a bowl on the table and went to the guard at the door to be bound.

He let her keep the fruit.

Twenty-eight

Aila's night was long and restless. The noise outside died out, save the pacing of her guard's boots, but her mind wouldn't quiet. Tokh had suspected Kel. Masákh questioned his involvement. Mátokhan tried to make her see. Aila's heart still didn't want to believe, but those wrists.... Every time her binders rubbed her skin, she thought of Kel's wrists without a single scrape on them. She was locked in a windowless room; the least he could be doing was pleading for them to unbind her.

Deep breath, Girl. One full day had passed, and she was no worse for wear. Was Masákh on her trail? Was he making progress? Tokh seemed to have contacts everywhere; Masákh would have notified him, and Tokh would have started a hundred trails to find her. His men tracked her down within hours of escaping his compound back on Kye; this was his homeworld. There was no way in hell he would fail the Emperor. Time, time, time. There was no way she was going to get a message to him. Not with Kel as her only contact. For over an hour she debated whether or not to have breakfast with him or ask the guard if food could be brought to her instead. What would he do then? Seek her out, or throw a tantrum in private? In the end she went not just to get relief from her binders and the boxed-in feeling of her room, but to prove to Kel she didn't suspect anything. If he was her only contact, then she needed every bit of information she could get.

"I'm glad to see you looking well," he said with a smile. "You had a good night?"

"Where's your cell?" she pried. "Do you have a window, or bedding, or at least anything to read?"

Kel glanced at the guards. Was he judging if they spoke Standard, and would know what he said? Was he going to give her information, or was he lying through his teeth? "I'm a floor up. I have a window, but it's useless for escape. Too high."

"Have they made demands of you yet? What information do they want?"

He hemmed and hawed. "I'm not sure, but it's political in nature. Who's in charge of what, who reports to who. That kind of thing."

"That's public knowledge available on any infolink. They already know that. I want information," she said. "I want names. Someone is in charge here. Find out who. You're awfully content to just sit here, Mr. Secretary. You're a lot more aggressive in chambers."

The barb went under his skin, and his cheeks and forehead flushed a pale blue. "Forgive me, it's my first kidnapping and I don't know what to do. You want the truth? You want to hear me say it? I'm afraid of them. Yes, I am the Secretary of State for the entire Planetary Union and I am afraid. Don't anger them, Aila. If we want to live, we must stay model prisoners and get on their good sides. Tell them what they want to hear, do exactly what they ask you to do, and maybe we'll come out of this alive with our minds intact."

Aila glared in reply. "You keep trying to instill fear in me, but you can't give me solid reasons as to why. If you can't give me real information, then I can't believe you."

She returned to her cell room angry and annoyed. The fear hit when she hunted for the piece of gravel to scratch off another meal. Her hair stood up, her spine crinkled, and her breath stopped for too long. Just above her tally, someone had scratched crude Union letters in the grime.

SIGNAL SENT

Twenty-nine

Son of a bitch.

Aila glanced back at the closed door, heart racing. There were no windows or peepholes; she couldn't see out, they couldn't see in. The gap at the bottom was minimal. She'd hunted the room well and hadn't found a single hidden camera. Somewhere, someone knew her, knew she was there, and knew who to call. Someone risked their life to leave her a message.

There was no way in hell it was Kel.

Who? Where? Signal to whom? What kind of signal? When would they get here? What would happen?

Her life was in someone's hands; she hoped she didn't wind up trusting the wrong person.

It was too early for the mid-afternoon lavatory break when she heard the door unlock. The guard motioned to her. *"Come."*

This time she made sure to look at the ID patch on his shirt. *Sidehn,* said the symbols. "Where are we going?" she asked, but received no answer. "Do you know I have *dáhneg* privilege, and I have the Emperor's protection?"

They didn't turn left, but went straight and then right around the balcony of rooms above the open main floor. Sidehn knocked, then opened the door at a room with a curtained interior window overlooking the work floor. Aila paused to offer her wrists to be unbound, but he merely thrust her into the room and shut the door.

At a conference table sat Secretary Kel looking subdued and still not bound, and at the end of the table, his chair taller than all others in the room, two red-suited guards behind him, sat an aging *fáhganid* in a red shirt and a wide red cape, the shoulders trimmed in feathers. The pinched curve of his nose matched the curve of his brow ridge and brown shadows invaded the hollows of his copper cheeks and brow, giving him the appearance of an old dried mummy. His eyes didn't even turn toward her as she entered, staring like an owl at the wall. Foreign females weren't worth his time.

Aila approached him half-way and knelt, keeping her eyes downward. She waited. *Fáhganid* were exceptionally dangerous because only *bhísroti* could give them orders, and a *fáhganid* whose powers had just been stripped by the government was likely to be very irritable indeed.

"Sit," Kel said. "Our friend Mr. Red here has made some demands, and you need to go over them. Once they're complete, they promise we'll be able to leave. Sit, so we can discuss this."

Aila bowed her head and spoke in Kerasi. *"One does not sit in the presence of a superior unless told to."*

The hawk-like nose lifted as if he'd smelled something wonderful. *"Ahhh,"* he sighed. *"The female knows proper respect. She has my permission to sit."*

Aila bowed again. *"Thank you, your Reverence."* She slipped onto one of the cruddy metal chairs at the table.

As Kel spoke, he paused now and then for the *fáhganid*'s translator, the guard on his left. The translator was slow and stumbling, checking the database on his interface for words he didn't know.

Kel pushed a paper forward. "I told you it was going to come to this, but you wouldn't take my warning. His Excellency here has agreed to let you go if you do two things. One is sign this document. The other is reading it before a camera for televising. Then you will be released in a safe location."

Information. Information is the key to both sides of a door. Aila didn't touch the paper. "And what about your conditions? What gets you released? Why release just one of us?"

Kel smiled nervously. He looked down at his hands, his fingers twisting around each other like a box of worms trying to find the way out. "They brought me here to strong-arm you. It's Kerasi logic; you should be familiar enough with it. I am your supervisor, therefore I control you. Don't get flustered, I know that's not how it works in reality, but that's their way. You do this, we both walk out of here alive. You mess up, they'll take it out on me."

217

Gender aside, the fact she was still in restraints and he wasn't still didn't sit right. She was seen as a threat, but he wasn't? There was a thread of truth to the logic, but it was too complicated. No *fáhganid* was going to risk losing his head for the kidnapping of a foreign official when all he had to do was beat the female into submission. Yes, on the outside Kel was right, but that wasn't the way it worked in the Kerasi mind. Not from a *fáhganid*. Aila pulled the paper forward and read it.

It was a two-page declaration stating that she, Aila Perrin, Member of the Union Council for Kerasi Affairs, due to the unfortunate circumstances she had survived, was adding her voice to the fact that the situation on Kerasím was too volatile, too dangerous, and for the sake of both cultures, it would be in everyone's best interest to cease further development of relations at this time, blah blah blah.

The wording of the document was far too smooth and eloquent for the level of translation the *fáhganid*'s guard was working at.

Aila stole a sideways glance at the *fáhganid*. *"Your Reverence, how may I address you as to rank and name?"*

The dark eyes looked down over the hooked nose with as much warmth as if he'd been addressed by a pile of dung. *"I am a Grand General of the Army of Kerasím."* He didn't say the words so much as decree them. *"Your Secretary calls me Mister Red."*

"Revered Grand General, are these words from your honored mouth, or did the Secretary write them?"

Mr. Red turned his head to look at her, the middle of his thick gray eyebrow arching upward. He seemed to understand exactly what she was asking, and why in his language. "Meestahr Frehnd. *I approved.*"

"Thank you, Gracious Revered."

Kel tapped the table with a finger, drawing her attention back to him. "He's got translators for a reason. I was conversing with you, not him. That was quite rude. One more reason you shouldn't have been on this mission. Your attention to protocol is abysmal."

"I'm sorry. I think it's ruder to have to filter everything through a translator when I can ask directly how he likes to be addressed."

He pushed an ink stick across the table. "Please sign this, and we'll be back to the palace by nightfall."

Aila picked up the writing stick. Kel hadn't volunteered a single bit of information yet, but was it from skill or a true lack of knowledge?

She tried to play him like she used to play Haghíde, distract and conquer. "How are we getting back?"

"I'm sure they'll pack us in a transport and drop us somewhere."

"We're around three hundred miles from the palace. Wouldn't it be easier to fly us out? Or will they just drop us at the nearest city?"

"I have no idea."

"How long after I sign will I be released?"

Kel twitched with irritation, his shoulders shrugging, face grimacing, hands waving, like a child about to tantrum. "I don't know! That's not my decision."

"Can I call someone to meet me somewhere? Should I ask Mr. Red? Is it okay if I ask him directly? I'd like to know."

Kel slammed a finger on the paper with a raised voice. "Sign the document!"

"I'd like to know the details of my release before I sign it!" Aila shouted back.

"Sign the document!" Mr. Red ordered.

No good. *Well, screw you then, Kel. I'm not playing.* Aila placed the writing stick on the table and bent her head. "My apologies, Revered Grand General. I cannot sign it. I disagree with every word in it." She waited for the translator to finish speaking. He did pretty well with simple words, but it would be a whole hell of a lot easier if she could just speak directly. She braced for impact; Aila fully expected the *fáhganid* or one of his guards to reach out and whack her, if not with his hand then with the painful "incentive" rod they always carried.

Mr. Red stared at Secretary Kel with such anger that his eyes seemed ready to pop out from under the shaggy brow. He growled another decree.

"You will make her sign," said the translator.

"Aila, don't be a fool. You don't want him angry at you," Kel warned. "They don't play nice. I shouldn't have to tell you that."

"Angry at me, or angry at you?" she dared at last. "I'm not the fool. I sign that, I'm dead. You get my last words on record saying they're too dangerous and then they get to kill me, to underscore the point. You get released, you both get your ways, and no one is left to know just what a traitor you are. No."

"Traitor! You're calling *me* a traitor?! The girl who kisses up to the Emperor himself?"

She turned to Mr. Red. *"Ka. Kho dag an fi."* *I am sorry.* Aila tore the page in half, stood up, and opened the door. The guard outside spun around and stood at attention, startled. She motioned with her head and walked back to her room on her own before him, the *fáhganid's* raging voice following her all the way down the corridor.

* * *

Aila curled up in a corner of her cell room, weeping just a little. Everyone had been right all along. Kel was blunt and sometimes crass with the way he treated his many underlings, but never, ever would she have suspected him of being an outright traitor to the Union. Was she really that young and naïve, or was he really that evil? He had to be in on everything from the beginning. As Tokh pointed out, he was the only survivor of the whole row of Union personnel. If you're going through the trouble of assassinating top officials, why not shoot the leader, unless he made arrangements? He was here, in league with a *fáhganid* who wouldn't give a name, and he wasn't tied up. He probably helped assassinate a foreign leader, and she was too raw and new at this game to see any of it coming.

So where does that leave me? Aila desperately wanted to tell that to Nadigh, to help him get justice for his father, but if she ratted out the Union Secretary of State to a foreign power, did that make her a traitor to the Union, too?

Mom, if ever I needed your lawyer skills, it's now. Any hope she had went wriggling out under the door.

No, not true. She still had the secret message-writer, unless that was done by Kel to throw her off track.

Four years ago, escaping from Kerasi hands the first time, she'd been terrified of being located by Masákh. Now she couldn't think of a way to make him find her fast enough.

The door opening stopped a third hour of stomach-churning. The guard led her to her lavatory break, but this time didn't return her to her cell room. Men had gathered in the open area below the balcony, perhaps a hundred. Most were green uniforms, a handful of browns, some in black tacticals or gray service uniforms. A few browns stood on the balcony not far from her room. Mr. Red left his conference room and paraded out, his long cape flowing behind him, followed by Kel and his two guards. The gathered men fell to one knee at his presence; Aila followed suit, making Kel the boor once again.

Mr. Red ordered them to stand with a flick of his wrist.

Kel approached her, penitent and pleading. "Aila, you have no idea how angry you made him. I warned you, they aren't going to play games. What he plans to do – It's despicable beyond reason. I don't want to see you hurt. I mean that. Sign the paper. You don't want to have to go through this, and I certainly don't want to see it happen."

Fear ran cold up Aila's spine. The chance he was bluffing was only fifty-fifty. The *fáhganid* was most likely going to beat her for disobedience and that was going to hurt like hell, probably leave welts or bruises, grace forbid break a bone. She hoped that was all. "You certainly seemed to have the stomach to watch a beloved Emperor be assassinated. Why should this bother you? Because I'm human, not Kerasi? Are you really that bigoted, Mr. Secretary?"

Kel's nostril's flared. He leaned into her face and waved a finger at her nose. "Damn you, Aila! I tried. I tried to save you, and that's what I'm going to say to your parents. Don't say I didn't try. Whatever happens to you from here on is your own damned fault, thinking you know everything. Who knows? You like Kerasi so damned much, maybe you'll enjoy this, too." He stepped back and gave Mr. Red the stage.

Mr. Red raised a hand, and the floor went quiet.

"I have before me a Union female, unattached. She is young, unmarked, and undisciplined. I will hold a lottery for her. In one hour, I will draw ten names. Of those ten names, I will hold a contest. Five hand-to-hand combats. The five winners will be allowed to have her for one hour."

Aila's heart stopped. *Oh no.*

A deafening wave of shouts echoed in the cavernous room. Men climbed on the work tables for a better view, grabbing their genitals and cheering. Obscene requests were shouted up from the floor.

Mr. Red pointed a finger at Aila. She thrashed and kicked with everything she had, bit someone in the arm, but two guards pinned her while one of Red's guards unfastened her blouse. Mímihn's dainty undergarment was held together by a single clip; in less than a second it, too, was gone. The guard wrapped his fingers in her hair and rammed her up against the railing of the balcony, pushing her forward, bare breasts pointed at the horde below. Aila took a deep breath and imagined skewering Kel through his empty chest with Tokh's sword, and this time she wouldn't throw up. She pulled her arms in to cover herself; the guard yanked them over her head by her binders, exposing her chest.

"Does this please you?" It didn't seem possible that the shouts could grow louder. The bolder ones tried jumping up to touch her. The crowd ran a serious risk of losing control.

"Those who are not under disciplinary action may file their name with the shift manager."

The floor cleared in a stampede of boots. Red turned and headed back for his conference room, guards and Kel in tow. He waved a finger at Aila's guard. The brown shirt dragged her backwards to the wall of the balcony. Large industrial pipes ran up the wall; sewage, water, fuel, gas, Aila had no idea what they did or where they went. Her guard unlocked her binders, held her arms and locked them behind her, bound to a pipe. She was to remain on display, humiliated before a squadron of lower-caste Kerasi who hung out on the floor below, punching and daring each other to get closer.

Aila turned to her guard. "If you had honor, you would close my shirt."

He eyed her breasts with appreciation but didn't break his stance. *"Ka."*

"I am under protection of the Emperor. There will be great reward if you get me out of here; I can guarantee that. I have benefactors here, and my father is a great Admiral in the Union fleet. I can gain audience with the Emperor himself if needed."

The guard smiled. He kept his face forward. "You talk sweet, but I like my head."

"I will get you a commendation from a General. He will protect your head."

He took a step away and raised his hand in threat. "Silence!"

Several times admirers walking the balconade stopped too long or came too close; Aila's guard pulled his weapon into place and urged them on. He may not have been able to be bought, but he did follow orders well. Aila grew tired of standing still, but any shifting caused the tight binders to pull on her wrists, throbbing and raw after fighting. Pulling and tugging at the pipe to test its strength only made it worse. She had to settle for alternating between aching legs and screaming wrists.

Damn you, Kel! You knew! You knew he'd do this all along, and you allowed it. Wait. Just you wait until I tell Nadigh.

After an hour, Red made another appearance. He held his hands out to Aila, withered old mummy hands, presenting her like a sideshow attraction to the roar of the crowd. He flexed them, breathed deep, tipped his head back in divine inspiration, and wrapped the leathery digits over her breasts, squeezing them with overblown pleasure as the crowd exploded in shouting.

Aila stared straight ahead. Her heart pounded so hard with nerves she swore it was making her vision jump with each beat. His fingers were cold and bony, his nails too long, and his pinches hurt. *Don't make a show. It's only boobs. Be glad you're wearing pants, not a skirt. He's doing this to humiliate you. They want you to react. Don't blink. Be glad they're not as big as Thayer's. You still have time. You still have time. Think about that signal. Maybe it was a locator ping, like Masákh used. Maybe it was a whole SOS. Hurry, Signalperson!*

Please hurry!

Red turned to the crowd with a sweep of his cape. *"I will begin."* He drew two names from a container to a mass of cheering. Men cleared the tables off the main floor to make an arena, while the first combatants readied to fight.

"There's still time, Aila," Kel whispered to her. His eyes started out on her face but kept drifting downward to her chest before he pulled them up again. "You can stop this now. Just sign the papers. You don't have to believe them, you just have to follow orders. They're going to throw you into a room with five of these animals and record the whole thing. Only you can stop them."

Aila fought the urge to vomit. The men punching each other below had arms like small trees. All the self-defense classes in the world wouldn't help her. "You would do that to my parents? Show everyone how I was assaulted and killed, while you did nothing? You're sicker than I thought, Omi. You pushed too hard. You blew your chance. You know those men aren't going to take the word no at this point, no matter how many pages I sign. I'm dead. And you can't get anything from a dead man."

The combat was fierce; two trained Kerasi soldiers, bare-handed, could take and give each other quite a beating, and it was a good half-hour or more before a winner was declared. Mr. Red decided to have one combat per hour, enough time to clean the floor and keep the men in a frenzy. Aila's guard was changed on the hour as well, so no one could be too tempted standing next to her. The second guard wouldn't even acknowledge her attempts at bribery. He slid her blouse backward until it hung from her elbows, and every so often he'd poke her in the side to watch her chest jiggle.

By the third hour, Aila was light-headed from lack of circulation. Pain radiated up her legs in long sharp daggers from standing in the same position so long, until she gave in and sank to her knees. She pulled and twisted at the binders, anything she could to loosen them just a little, but the pain was too much. Her new guard didn't say a word as she sank, watching the fight before him.

When all the backs were to them and all eyes were on the combat, he knelt down beside her. He held a piece of something before her mouth. *"A sweet, for energy."*

Aila stared at him. He was perhaps thirty and wore a brown uniform. There was something vaguely familiar about his face, but Aila was certain she'd never met him before. She knew only two, maybe three brownshirts by name, and none was that young. What difference would poisoned food make now? Everyone was entitled to a last meal. She accepted the bite. It was sweet and chewy, like honey and dried fruit.

He pulled a container from his pocket and offered her water. Aila didn't hesitate this time. "My name is Kitras," he whispered in Union Standard.

Aila shook her head. The name meant nothing. He held up another sweet for her, and she wolfed it down.

"Kitras," he repeated. "Kitras dar-Giláhn, son of Tokh. My father says you are strong. You must be strong little more. We are soon ready."

"*You* sent the signal?"

"Yes." He held the container once more so she could drink.

224

"I'd kiss you if I could. Thank you. Thank him." She struggled back to her feet, wincing at the pull on her wrists. Kitras helped her up. He pulled her blouse back over her shoulders, took the loose ends and tied them together, pulling it closed enough to cover her. He slipped her a third sweet.

Kitras's shift as her guard lasted only an hour, but for that hour Aila was braver than brave, knowing a dar-Giláhn was covering her back. Too soon he was rotated out by a leering little *tápatihn* not much taller than Aila, who smelled as bad as the lavatory.

"This isn't going to get us anywhere," Kel said to Mr. Red as he announced the next combat. "A dead man can't sign a confession. You have one of those memory-pullers here; can't he convince her to sign?"

The guard translated as fast as he could. Mr. Red stopped to think, his mind focusing inward until it looked as if he were staring at the hook of his nose. "Mmm. He has been more difficult than she has, but I will send word for him to prepare."

Thirty

Two new guards approached her pipe. One kept a weapon at the ready while the other released her, then bound her arms in front of her. Aila could have cried from the relief of a new position. Her shoulders were stiff, her hands swollen, her legs barely able to walk from lack of circulation.

Where to? They hadn't begun the last combat yet. Was Kel giving her one last chance?

"Lavatory?" she asked, and one of the guards graciously granted her three minutes while they waited. They circled her in a new direction, down a flight of stairs beyond the cafeteria, Aila stumbling several times on legs too painful to bear her weight. Guards were posted outside of a doorway at the end of a dark corridor. Was this where Kel would beat her for not cooperating, or were they moving her to the room she'd soon share with five over-eager Kerasi males who would probably kill each other to get to her first?

That's an idea. One or two of them dead is that many less I have to deal with.

There was yelling in the room ahead of them. Two voices, male, arguing. The walls, the speed at which the words came, the distortion of the volume, meant Aila could make out little. She knew *dihnarwharl*, and Colonel, and prisoner; not one of the words made her feel better. Despite her efforts to drag her feet and wriggle away, one of her escorts opened the door and the other threw her into the room.

Aila stumbled and caught herself. It was a plain room, hastily furnished with a large dining table, a bright floor lamp with adjustable boom, and laid out on a countertop by a dirty industrial sink, several large metal chests, their open drawers displaying a frightening arrangement of pointy medical tools and vials of unknown substances. Aila glanced at the arguers and the horror of all her nightmares took over, a terror so encompassing she stopped breathing, her vision blacked out, and she fell backward onto the wall until she could see.

Kassán.

Kassán the sadist.
Kassán the torturer.
Kassán, shredder of minds and stealer of voices.
Kassán the insane.

Kassán, the finest neuroanatomist Tokh had ever seen, the only one whose emissary had survived intact, the only technician good enough that the Emperor requested him for himself.

Kassán, who still made Aila wake up screaming at night, four years and countless hours of therapy later.

His lab clothing was gone, replaced by a rumpled brown uniform. A hand's length of citations and medals paved the side of his shirt along with a Colonel's rank, which meant he was no lower than *nhásarwharl* in caste. Aila'd only seen him out of his filthy lab gear once and that was a dress uniform; this brown looked out of place, as if he'd been kidnapped from his bed and had to borrow the clothes. The wisps of hair still clinging to his balding head were as white as his chin hank, in bad need of a combing, though his bushy eyebrow was still gray. Scars covered his scalp, his face, his hands, battle wounds from patients or victims or his own botched experiments. His shoulders were bent from decades of hunching over tables pulling pain and confessions from the guilty and the innocent, his squinty eyes straining to find the exact entry point, the exact vein, the exact nerve to take advantage of. His temper was short and fierce, but it was the coldness of his laughter, his elation at the fright he created, that brought the worst terror. Nothing silenced a room faster than someone mentioning Kassán and amusement in the same sentence.

And he was here.

No.

No.

No one was taking her speech this time, if she had to kill every Kerasi from here to the exit. Let the blood drip from her hands, let it paint the floors, let her go down in history as one of the bloodiest murderers on twelve planets, but she would not be tortured again.

The young brown officer arguing with him shoved Kassán so hard he fell against the chests. Kassán grabbed a scalpel from an open drawer and pointed it forward. "I'll slice you so thin your own mother will eat you for dinner and not think twice," he spat. "I will slice you from the bottom up and feed you the slices myself."

Aila didn't doubt the threat for a second.

"You've been given your duty, Old Man. Do not make me get the *fáhganid.*" The officer turned and stepped toward the door.

Kassán threw the scalpel; it sliced so close to the officer several hairs were caught in it when it drove into the wall behind him.

The officer eyed the scalpel and drew his weapon. "Do not make me punish you."

"You don't know how." Kassán gave up the argument. He mumbled to himself, hands gesticulating through the air, a string of curses so foul Aila didn't understand most of them. "Get him up here."

Aila screamed as the guards moved in to grab her. She dropped to the floor, kicking and twisting and clawing as hard as she could. Four years of self-defense training were paying off. One of the guards raised a hand and began to slap her.

The pitch of the screaming caught Kassán's attention. His head snapped up and he came around the table. "A female? You never mentioned a female! Stop!"

"It does not matter. The task is the same. Banukh requests cooperation."

"I ordered you to stop!" Kassán barked. The guard put his hand down. Kassán spoke in Union Standard. "You! I know you. You are Tokh's experiment. I have worked you before."

"Worked me!" Aila screeched back. "Torturer! Voice-stealer! Pain maker! Fuck you! Fuck you back to the hell you came from!"

Kassán motioned for her to be brought to the table. Anger controlled Aila's fear for the moment. As they dropped her onto the table, her bound hands shot out and tried to grab his throat. The guards pinned her down.

"I'll kill you! I'll bite your fucking throat out! No more! You're not touching me again!"

228

"Hold her still," he said to the guards. One grabbed her by the jaw and pulled back, immobilizing her head while two held her legs.

Kassán bent down to tap her neck for her carotid. "Play my game and you will not be harmed," he whispered lightly in her ear. There was no gloating, no condescension, no maniacal laughing, no psycho sniffing or licking, just rapid little words in thickly accented Standard meant only for her. "Be still. In the name of Tokh, you have my word."

Aila panted from stress and struggle. "I know you were taken against your will from the palace. I can help you. I can get word to the General where you are. He'll get word to the Emperor. I am under protection of the Emperor. You don't want to do this."

Kassán was filling a syringe. "Tell me more."

"No! Don't touch me! Don't you hurt me! I won't say a thing if you touch me!"

"Ab Kherisi!" growled the lead guard. "I need to know what she's saying!"

Kassán stopped to glare. "She does not speak Kherisi well. Do you want the information or not? If she will squeal without force, don't you think I should let her speak? Or do you want to answer for an overdose?" The guard shut up.

Kassán plunged the needle into her arm. "This is a half-dose of tranquilizer. It should not affect you much, but you may pretend it does. Understand?"

Aila felt a tingle take over. Her heart slowed its frantic race, but her head remained clear. He wasn't kidding. He was as angry over captivity as she was, and he wasn't cooperating, either. What was that saying about politics and strange bedfellows? Never in a hundred years would she have thought she would make a bargain with Kassán. She stiffened up, gave a small cry, then relaxed herself with theatric flair, rolling her head in protest.

"Better, no?" He waved the guards back. Aila moaned on the table.

He made a show of taking a baseline pulse. "You are damaging her!" he barked, pointing to her wrists. "I will not be blamed for that. They are too tight. You want me to work, you will remove them. I need access to the wrists and veins and they cannot be constricted. If you fear a female that much, you are a shame to Kerasím." One of the guards removed her binders. Aila let her arms fall to the table with a heavy thunk, too grateful.

Kassán attached monitors to points on her chest, ankle, neck, her tortured wrists. "Tell me more," he purred. "How do you get information out?"

The tremors in her voice were no act. "Then what? You erase my mind and leave me here? One trust at a time."

He checked the damaged skin on her face where she'd been slapped, pretended to check her eyes, leaning close. Aila could not help a nervous cry. "Fool! Do you see my equipment anywhere near? They give me a box of potions and expect me to make the dead dance. I get better results with clamps and flame. I'll give them nothing. *Speak.*"

Aila gave a grand twitch. The monitors picked up the motion and flashed something incomprehensible. She breathed twice as fast; different monitors bounced around. A twitch of her leg set a yellow light flashing. She was in control of Kassán's show. She whispered, "There is one in the building who is not who he seems. He is a direct line to the one you swore an oath on. Please! I'll play any game, just buy me time. I need you to buy me time. You must keep me down here. I promise, I will get you out of here when they come for me."

Kassán laid out tools at his ready: needles, clamps, retractors, tubes, and several vials of medications. He filled another syringe.

"You are playing well, but you must play harder. If they suspect, it is your head before mine. This is sterilized water. Fight, but give answers to satisfy them, or I will have to assist. Understood? You do not want me to assist your answers. *Ab Kherisi*, if possible." He stabbed her with the syringe, tapping it sideways until she cried out from the sting.

"*Sukh!*"

He nodded to the guards. *"You may question now."*

Thirty-one

How much longer, Kitras? Aila wondered as she was dragged back up the stairs. Lying flat on the table, filled with relaxants, had eased much of the pain in her legs. She'd managed to waste at least an hour with Kassán, maybe more, yelling, rolling, pleading, shrieking; without ever being in harsh pain or giving important information. Kassán could fake it as hard as he gave it. He coated her wrists in a slippery salve and made sure they replaced the binders far looser than they'd been; with a little effort, she just might be able to pull her hands through the restraints. Either way, it helped ease the rubbing. Masákh had warned her long ago that Kassán was not always a team player, his loyalty lying where it best suited his needs, which at the time had been with Tokh. Thank goodness he remained a man of the Emperor, with a great respect for Tokh. She didn't trust him – wouldn't trust him even if he were the one tied to pipes and being eaten alive by rats – but she was deeply thankful they shared a common enemy.

Back to her pipe. Someone realized her shirt was still tied shut and pulled it loose to expose her again. Mr. Red left his dinner to announce the final contest. The four previous winners were getting restless, ready for their prize, hanging from the balcony railing and calling obscenities to her, asking her to choose which one she'd like first.

Hurry, Kitras! I'm out of time.

Kel gave it one more effort. "I can still stop this, Aila. I can get you out of here. It's all up to you." He didn't have the balls to touch her bared breasts but traced little circles on her stomach instead, while his eyes did things his hands didn't. "I'm sorry about this. I really am. You have no idea how much I'm dreading it. Please, Aila. Principles are just words; they're not worth someone's life. Signing the papers isn't enough; just read the statement before a camera and I will make sure he lets you go. I don't want to see what's left when they get through with you."

Pound for pound, Aila had more respect for Kassán at the moment than Omi Kel. She spat in his face. "Is that before or after you get off watching on the monitor?"

Kel's ivory face darkened to pale blue and his mouth drew up in a tight line. His hand hauled back and slapped her face, hard. Aila's head slammed to the side, her vision turned to sparkles, and the binders tore viciously at her wrists as she twisted. Blood oozed onto her tongue where her teeth had cut into her cheek.

Ow. She straightened up. "I guessed that right, didn't I."

Before he could hit her a second time, a tremendous explosion shook the building from inside the vehicle bay, large enough to shift the air pressure in the huge room and release a cascade of dust from the ceiling high overhead. The entry door blew open from the force; smoke poured onto the floor in a roiling ball. All activity ceased as everyone stared. From the floor above came the sound of pounding boots. Glass exploded inward from a window high overhead. A canister hit the floor and began pouring a vile yellow smoke, followed by a second, then a third. Muffled shouts sounded through the entry door.

"Arms! All hands to posts!" shouted the *fáhganid*. "Bring her with me!"

Her guard fumbled in his hastiness to unhook her. Caustic smoke drifted up from the main floor, making him cough. Aila took her one chance. The second her hand was released, she beat him with the loose end of the binders, clocking him in the side of the head as he coughed. Aila tried to run toward the smoke, but he grabbed her on the second step.

Aila gripped the balcony railing, coughing. "Help me!" she screamed into the smoke. "Upstairs! On the balcony! Help me!"

The guard fought her to let go. Aila clung to the railing until he grabbed her around the middle and yanked her free. She flailed, she arched her back, kicked her feet, grabbed for the railing again while screaming, until he lost patience and yanked her by the binders still dangling from one wrist. Aila gave a cry of pain and followed him to the office at the corner. She was sealed into the room with Mr. Red, Kel, and the two guards. The Kerasi were armed; Kel hadn't been trusted with weapons.

Sucker.

Aila dragged herself into a back corner of the room, panting hard. She tied her shirt closed again, dabbed at her bleeding wrist with the hem. "I told you I was under imperial protection. You've pissed my friends off. I should make them lock you in a room with five pissed-off Kerasi males and watch your own humiliation," she told Kel with a bloodthirsty glare.

The *fáhganid* was peering from behind the curtain over the interior window. The smoke made it impossible to see anything beyond the balcony railing. He turned and looked down his nose at her. *"If you speak, I will remove your tongue."*

Weapon fire sounded in the hallway, the zapping sizzle of plasma as it hit, the screams of anyone touched by it. The *fáhganid* guard opened the door a crack. He picked off anyone he saw, not caring which side he was killing.

"Aila!" came a shout in the smoky fog. "Aila!"

Aila knew that voice. It had yelled at her plenty, consoled her some, droned on about subjects she never wanted to learn about in the first place. A voice she wanted to hear more than any other in the universe.

She rushed to the doorway and ducked under the red guard's arm. "Masákh! Here! There are four of them!" An elbow crashed down on her skull, sending her to the floor. She crawled back to her corner. A second later, the glass on the window blew inward with a direct hit. Some of the curtain shredded but it made the glass fall downward instead of showering over them. Kel and one of the guards flipped the heavy conference table over, making a defense to hide behind. The guard locked the door. They ripped down the shreds of curtain and fired out the open hole to the hallway. Smoke drifted inward but it was dissipating, more of a chemical smell than an obstruction.

"Give up the female and you may go free," said Masákh's voice. "Your men are dead or seized. You have no escape. Send the female out."

"She's not the only hostage!" Kel yelled from behind the table. "Omi Kel, Secretary of State for the Planetary Union. I was taken from the Emperor's palace four days ago. Get me out of here and I guarantee you will be rewarded well beyond your means."

Aila glanced around for anything to use as a weapon. Chairs, the table, a regular little industrial office. She inched forward, only to hear the rattle of the binder still locked on one wrist.

The binder.

Aila rubbed the remainders of Kassán's salve over her hand, squeezed the bones as close as possible, gritted her teeth and shoved the binder as hard as she could down over her hand. She twisted and pushed on the wounds, trying hard not to scream at the pain, and slowly, slowly, her hand came through the hole. She was free.

Aila stood up. Weapon fire pinged high onto the wall, putting the suffering paint out of its misery in a firework of sparks. The guards returned it, shot for shot. Kel crouched behind the table, while Mr. Red stayed out of range tucked in the inside corner, safe from weapon fire.

Three shots pinged off the back wall in rapid succession; more than one person was shooting. The guards strafed the balcony side to side. Someone outside shrieked. Aila pounced. She looped the binders over the near-guard's head and pulled the ends tight around his neck with all her strength. The guard backstepped, twisted, and bent, sending her over his shoulder and onto the floor. The second guard took a single step to help him and took a direct hit. He flew backwards and landed draped over the edge of the table, the charred remainder of his face staring directly at Secretary Kel. Kel ran to the side of the room with a yell.

"THREE!" Aila yelled from the floor. She rolled to her feet, brushing off broken glass.

A double-shot caught the remaining guard in the shoulder. He dropped his weapon and clutched his arm. As he bent to retrieve the weapon, he caught another shot high in his chest.

"TWO!" Aila shouted.

With the guards dead, Mr. Red had no translator. He shouted at Kel in rapid Kerasi, motioning to the fallen weapon and pointing to the window.

"You're the Grand General!" Kel shouted back. "You take over! I don't know a damned thing about weapons!"

Several shots fired into the room, making everyone duck low. Kel reached out and snatched the weapon of the downed guard, then leaped and seized Aila by the hair, hauling her to her feet. He shoved the weapon against her head, shaking her. Mr. Red waited in his safe corner for the action to stop.

"Listen out there!" Kel shouted. "You want the girl? I've got her right here, with a weapon to her head. You want her alive? You will let me walk out of here unharmed!"

And from the haze in the hallway, Masákh emerged. He wore black clothing under body armor. His meticulous hair was rumpled every which way. A raw burn from a near-hit showed brown and shiny through a hole in the arm of his shirt, and soot marked his yellow-tan face. Never had Aila seen him look so blastedly gorgeous and heroic. Behind him appeared Haghíde dressed the same way, a scanning interface over one eye. Kitras and at least a half-dozen other officers in battle gear stood behind them.

Masákh raised his hands. "Let her go and you will both leave here alive. That is my truth."

"You think I'm going to believe you? I walk down this hall, you shoot me in the back. I am the Secretary of State for the Planetary Union. You want me alive."

Masákh took another step forward. "At the moment, there are no threats against you. You are a missing dignitary and we are prepared to return you to your group. Any legal action will be handled by your government."

"He plotted to kill Nághtas!" Aila said, struggling. "Don't believe him!"

"I'm guilty of nothing but protecting myself and the worlds I swore to defend!" Kel snarled. "All I provided was funding and a list of personnel. You want guilty? There's the untrustworthy bastard that sold out his own people! There's the one you should be after!" He pointed his weapon hand at Mr. Red. "A hundred million interstellar credits. That's what he was paid. Half from someone inside his own government. He's the one who coordinated everything."

Mr. Red stepped out from the corner. He inflated himself to full pompousness. "Do not think of raising a weapon to a *fáhganid*. I want a safe escort to my aircraft on the roof, and safe flight from the area. What you do with that one is up to you. He has no respect for his own people, let alone Kerasím. He changes loyalty faster than a clock changes time. He is not worth the shit of a *trixahg*."

Aila began to laugh, a laugh of deep relief tinged with a hint of hysteria. "Hah! He just sold you out. He just bargained his way out of here and left you to die. He's *fáhganid*; no matter what his crimes, only a *fáhganid* or *bhísroti* can stop him and they know it. He's free as a bird."

"Yeah?" Kel whipped his arm out and fired directly at Mr. Red, not ten feet away. The shot hit the *fáhganid* square in the chest, sent him flying back against the wall, arms jerking as the nerves overloaded before he slumped to the ground, his clothes and flesh smoking. Aila screamed.

The room exploded. Masákh's warning shot went so close to the side of Kel's head even Aila felt the heat. Kel flinched sideways. Aila swung a fist down and backward, hitting him in the groin, and he let go of her. She ran for the back of the room, crouching with her hands over her head. A blast hit the door, destroying the lock and handle. Someone kicked the door open.

"Aila! Now!" Haghíde called, but Aila didn't dare. With three bodies, six chairs and a table sprawled on the glass-littered floor, getting to the door was a hazard in itself. She wasn't about to be hit by a random shot.

Masákh didn't wait but vaulted over the window frame to grab Kel by the arm, bending his wrist backward. Kel got off one shot that hit the ceiling before he dropped the weapon. He grabbed Masákh by the hair and pulled him off balance, smashing his head on the edge of the overturned table twice before Masákh twisted out from the grip. Kel grabbed one of the metal chairs and swung it. Masákh backpedaled out of the way, but as he raised his weapon he tripped on the body of the guard bent over the table. He lost his balance and flipped backward over the table just as Kel brought down the chair. There was an audible crack as it smashed against his leg, and Masákh gave a hideous yelp. His weapon skidded across the floor as he landed.

Masákh slid backward toward the wall. His breath came in heaving waves as he fought to stand on one leg. Kel came at him once more with the chair.

"*Masákh! Move!*" Haghíde's weapon was trained and ready. "I can't get a clear shot!"

"Kel! NO!" Aila shrieked.

Masákh raised his arms and tried to hop backwards, but the chair caught him in the side of the head, and he dropped.

Aila dove for his weapon. In one smooth move she snatched it up, rolled, swung her arm and fired, nailing Omi Kel between his breastbone and his shoulder.

His face took on a most astonished look and he jerked backwards, hitting the ground with the sound of a bag of wet sand.

Aila dropped the weapon. She stared at Kel splayed on the floor, his clothing smoking, and she began to shake.

"Excellent shot," Haghíde said. "I could not have done better." He raised his interface and holstered his weapon before picking his way into the room. Kitras entered behind him and rushed to Masákh.

Aila gave a shriek and launched herself over Masákh. "Don't touch him! Don't touch him!"

Haghíde knelt beside her, dared to put a hand on her back. "He is hurt. We must get him to help."

She clung tighter as tears began. "No! You'll hurt him worse! Wake up, Masákh! You found me! Wake up!" She caressed his cheek, tried to touch his head but her hand came away bloody. "Make him wake up!"

"He's alive, just injured," Kitras said. He pulled the cape from the *fáhganid*, cut a strip free with his knife, and pressed it against Masákh's head wound. "I've sent for a medic. You must move back."

"Kassán! Kassán's in the basement!" Aila gasped between sobs. "He's got medications down there! He's got equipment." Haghíde sent an officer running.

"Masákh! Masákh!"

Haghíde tried to move her again, but Aila elbowed him in the face. She lay her head on Masákh's chest, feeling it rise and fall, listening to his heartbeat.

Haghíde left her alone until the medics arrived, just before Kassán. "I must insist you allow them to work." With much coercing, he got her to sit up. In the melee her blouse had come untied and now hung loose, exposing far too much. "Fix your clothing," he whispered urgently. "There are many eyes in the room." Aila didn't respond, sobbing so hard she couldn't breathe. "If you will forgive my touch," he said with embarrassment, and proceeded to fasten her blouse. Aila's eyes never left Masákh.

Kassán surveyed the medics' equipment, shot Masákh with something to stabilize him and something for pain. "Get him out fast. Get that leg splinted, or he'll never run with it again."

To Aila he said, "You spoke truth. You have honor, for a female. I will commend you to Tokh and to his Majesty."

Aila didn't respond, didn't reprimand him for not saying thank you, didn't even notice him, Kassán the Nightmare. She sat quietly, holding the limp hand, kissing it, until the medics attempted to move Masákh to a stretcher and she threw herself at him once more.

"No! No!"

Haghíde could no longer play games. "Aila!" he commanded, seizing her in a bear hug and moving her away. Her eyes focused on his face. "You may accompany him for transport, but you must walk by yourself. You must stop this behavior! It is undignified. I know he would reprimand you most harshly."

Aila managed a deep breath, and the sobbing slowed. She followed the stretcher to the helicraft on the roof, never saying a word. She didn't fight while Kassán and the medics continued to work, and Haghíde reported in to Tokh. Landing reinstated her panic. Haghíde tightened his grip as Masákh was carried out into the hospital and Aila was not. Aila screamed and fought, but the craft lifted up again.

"Aila! You must stop!" Haghíde grabbed her face. "You would not be allowed in; it is a hospital for males only. Kitras is with him; Kitras will make sure he gets good treatment. You are injured as well. We are heading to a hospital for females so you may get treatment."

"No!" was all she managed to sob.

Aila's treatment was short. The doctors had never seen a human before, had no access to data on medications or dosages or even what normal was for them – information held only by the military. They washed and tended her wrists, the cuts and bruises on her face, and the dozens of little cuts from the broken glass. Haghíde stood by and translated, but the word *medical scanner* sent Aila into full-blown panic, and Haghíde would not allow it. On Haghíde's order, two brown-uniformed soldiers stood at attention outside her room, combat arms at ready, checking the identification of anyone entering. It was nearing midnight before a General strode down the hall in full uniform, several officers at his heels. He barked reports from the bowing doctors before entering the room.

Tokh stopped short. Haghíde sat next to Aila, his arms around her to keep her still, a forbidden touch. Any attempt to let go sent her into a frenzy of clawing at him until he held her once more. Her sobs had grown faint and infrequent, but she shuddered and twitched without end, staring ahead without seeing anything. Haghíde shook his head at Tokh.

Tokh clapped his gloved hand on her shoulder. "You are the bravest of brave, my female warrior. I have been told your aim is to be feared. I came to bring you to safety. Mimi is most excited for your return. My craft is waiting."

The twitching and shaking wouldn't stop. Aila reached forward and put her arms around his middle. Tokh stiffened at the improper contact but she didn't let go, didn't make a sound. He snorted with embarrassment, tried to push her away, but when she didn't let go, he bowed his head at her, lifted her in his arms, and carried her from the building without a word.

Thirty-two

Aila had little memory of the next three days. She was in a bright, quiet place, the voices she heard were familiar even if she couldn't understand the words. The gentlest hands touched her face, her hands, her back, and held her so tightly when the nightmares hit. Aila couldn't even call them nightmares; a nightmare had form and substance and surrealistic reasoning. This was sheer black emptiness, a bottomless void of overwhelming terror that threatened to drown her as she fell downward into it, screaming so hard her throat bled.

She woke one morning in an extravagant bed, on satiny sheets of silver-pink, surrounded by a cloud of pillows, wearing a sleeveless blue lounging dress silky against her skin. The furniture was ornate, a whitewashed wood painted with idyllic scenes of courtly life, the scrolled trim painted in shades of gold with black detailing. Plush lounging sofas of *fáhganid* red stood off to the side near a sizable wallscreen. Sunlight poured in from glass doors to the balcony over the kitchen courtyard.

Aila sat up, only to have Mímihn pop up out of the pillows next to her.

"Bright morning, Ai-lah. Are you with the living today?"

Aila took a deep breath and nodded. Yes. Her head had come back from the brink. She would live.

"This is your room?" she managed to say.

"Of course. I will send for some food and tell Tokh. He will want to know." Mímihn messaged the kitchen, then Tokh. Minutes later he appeared at the door, Haghíde behind him.

Aila sat on the foot of a lounge, but didn't stand when he entered. She'd stopped shaking, but showed no emotion at all.

Tokh sat on the opposite lounge. "You are up from bed. That is a good sign."

"Thank you," Aila said in a flat voice. "Thank you for rescuing me."

"You remember. That is excellent. I did not provide much more than logistics. Haghíde brought you out."

"*Soyavoh*. Thank you."

"I would not have left you," Haghíde swore. He hovered near as if he wished to do something important, but didn't know what.

The conversation paused. Aila could not compose a single thought to speak. A sob came out of nowhere and caught her throat, and she gave a hard shudder.

"You have combat sickness," Tokh told her. "You are strong, but even the strongest can suffer it when the battle is too intense. You have been receiving medication for it. Do you wish another tablet?"

"What kind? I have enough trouble with your food. How do you know it's safe for me?"

Tokh gave a small smile. "I spoke to an expert neuroanatomist who has dosed humans before. They are simple sedatives to ease your trauma."

"Kassán," she realized.

"Knowledge can be used to heal as well as harm."

"Yes. I think I would like one." Mímihn jumped to bring Aila the jar.

"In ten years I have never heard a word of praise cross Kassán's teeth, yet he had choice words to say about you. That is most impressive." Tokh's face was unreadable, but the dark eyes measured her. She sat on his lounge chair, a huddled empty mass of female human frailty, but he acknowledged no weakness.

Aila forced herself to mumble, "All I did was plead for my life."

"The remaining Union delegates have been released and returned to your ships in orbit. I sent word to the current officials in charge to inform your parents you are safe and recovering. They would like to send people here to speak with you, check on your condition. Do you wish to speak with them?"

Parents. Aila was not ready to deal with their hysteria yet. Not yet. *Sorry Mom.* "For a short time. Tomorrow, though. Not today."

"Understandable." He stood up. "I will leave you in Mimi's care."

"Thank you."

Haghíde bowed before her. "Pleasant rest. I will be on guard if you wish me."

She reached up and squeezed his hand, making the contact personal. "Thank you, Haghíde."

Kassán's tranquilizers were stronger than Aila expected. She slept hard, until Mímihn roused her for a brief attempt at dinner, then slept again through the night. She awoke the next morning to find Haghíde sitting on one of the lounge chairs, his interface in his hand, the wallscreen on silent with captions running underneath.

"Bright morning," he said. "I hope you do not mind I am in the room instead of standing outside it. Since you were sleeping, I used the time for duties. On my honor, I took no liberties while you slept."

"I believe you."

"You are improved?"

Aila nodded. "Yes, I do feel better."

"Lady Mímihn will be pleased. She is caring for her children at the moment. She will return shortly."

The question ate at Aila the day before, but she never found the strength to ask it. It was easier to take the tablet and forget. It seemed wrong to ask it of Haghíde, a tease, but today she needed to know. "Where is he, Haghíde? Did he die?"

"Masákh? You do not remember? He is recovering in a hospital. He has a head wound, several burns, and a broken leg. You are not wife or consort, or mother or sister, therefore you cannot visit."

"Understandable." The word made it out before her heart imploded like a black hole, so hard and so fast a whimper escaped her. "Out, Haghíde. Let me dress, and I will try to come downstairs."

Aila made it down to breakfast, but lost her energy halfway through. She collapsed on one of the grand sofas in Tokh's great room, too drained to climb the stairs.

Haghíde came and sat next to her. He said nothing at first, staring at her with an odd little grin until Aila began to get creeped out.

"You are truly a warrior in your spine," he said at last. "We seized the surveillance video from the building where you were held. You were most brave in a very dangerous situation. I most liked when you

242

hit the guard with the restraints. That was foolish and intelligent at the same time."

Aila couldn't summon the energy to glare at him. "Did you enjoy staring at my chest as well? I wish you'd thrown me a weapon when you first arrived; I would have shot every one of those bastards right between the eyes, and I wouldn't have missed."

"No, I did not enjoy that. There is no pleasure in the humiliation of friends, even female ones. Do not feel shamed. You won the respect of many high-level officers and officials."

The shakes returned, and Aila felt her eyes fill with tears. "I can't stop thinking about... If Kitras hadn't infiltrated them, if he hadn't let you know where I was... If Kassán hadn't bought me time... If your team had been just ten minutes later... I..." The tears won. She fell over with her face on Haghíde's leg, crying until she choked.

Haghíde looked about in desperation, but none of the house females was in sight. He patted her hair as if it would burn him. "Is this contact too personal? I apologize, it is my oversight my gloves are upstairs." Aila shook her head.

Tokh entered the room and eyed them strangely. Haghíde nudged her until she sat up and wiped her face on her hands. Haghíde stood up, but Aila couldn't even try.

"I apologize for my weakness," she managed.

Tokh sat before her, motioned Haghíde to sit. He didn't look pleased; if possible, he looked sad. "Apology is not needed. You have not had adequate time for recovery and you are still very much ill, but I'm afraid your day has become most difficult. I have had several unpleasant calls this morning. You are scheduled to meet with your Union representatives this afternoon. However, the government of Kerasím wishes to meet with you before then, to take your statement as to what happened and question you as necessary. I have informed them your health is most delicate. They insist they will speak with you first or the Union must wait until they do. I will do whatever I can to support you, but I cannot refuse them. Truth: I do not like this; Ghírandar cannot be here in time to give you legal counsel, and I do not know what they want. I suspect it is straight information. They have a visual record of your mistreatment, but not of conversations that occurred. However, there is a faint but real chance that because you are not a Kerasi citizen, you could be charged with treason. You were in the presence of one believed to be implicated in the death of the Emperor, and the murder of a *fáhganid*. I believe I can block that; I am waiting for guidance. I believe it will not be an issue. They will be here within the hour."

Aila drew a trembling breath. Mom couldn't help her here; maybe Kerasi law was something Mom should take up, help ease her fears. If Ghírandar could study Union law, then Mom sure as hell could learn Kerasi. "That's only fair, I guess. It's your planet, your issue. I will do my best."

Tokh studied her, a shivering mess of tears and sobs. His face was unreadable, neither disgusted by her shortcoming nor sympathetic to it. "You need a glass of *rhimahdia*." It came out like a command, but the voice was tinged with understanding. He rose and returned with a tiny glass of Kerasi pepper rum sized for a light-weight human female, the sides already turning pink.

"Drink – slowly. It will steady your nerves."

Aila didn't try to refuse. It took her a dozen painful swallows for what amounted to three spoonfuls. By the time she finished her mouth and head were numb but she'd stopped shaking. Tokh was right. She *did* need that. "I'm ready."

Unmarked aircraft circled overhead. One touched down on the empty landing pad. One landed in the front courtyard. Another landed on the side grassway, crushing a border of yellow and purple flowers to avoid the pool. Brown guards came running up from the side yard, formed a perimeter and stood at attention. From the landing pad, officers in gold uniforms marched forward, identical in the cut of their chin hanks, the angle of their belts, the shine of their boots stepping together so precisely it was hard to tell where one left off and the other started. They stopped at the third craft and waited at attention.

This was not a normal investigation crew.

The door to the final craft lowered. Two imperial *fáhganid* servants marched forward, officially demoted but still wearing flowing red robes, one to each side of the door. Aila assumed they were the officials sent to take her statement, but no.

"All kneel before her Royal Excellency, Rimas, daughter of Emperor Nadigh, Heir to the throne of Kerasím," shouted one of the former *fáhganid*.

Holy supernovas! All around her, people dropped like flies. Aila had never seen Tokh bow to anyone beyond a single *fáhganid*; usually everyone was bowing to him. Mímihn gave a squeak and threw herself flat on the ground; Zheníhda lowered herself with as much dignity as possible. Aila dropped to her knees behind Tokh, head bent but naughty eyes rolling forward to watch the daughter who had brought a planet to its knees.

"All rise," came the command in a calm but definitely female voice.

Haghíde helped Aila to her feet. Rimas bore a strong resemblance to her father, tall and broad in shoulder, and the same power emanated from her as she walked. She wore smooth black pants – not the baggy ones Kerasi women wore, but ones that showed the wearer had thighs and knees under them, and a bright blue shirt that left no doubt she was female, a woman with ample curves to her chest and hips, having birthed three children more than a dozen years ago. Tall black boots covered her legs to her knees, heels clicking against the stones. She wore no veil, not even a ceremonial remnant. The front of her long brown hair was braided back from her face in a half-dozen small braids that had been dyed a bright pink, while the rest ran long and wild over her shoulders. Her dark eyes held a sparkle of wonderment that said this was all new to her and she was still trying to feel it out. A blue belt circled her waist, and sure enough, a sword hung from one side of it and an energy weapon on the other. A blue cape draped over everything. Never had Kerasi men bent knee to a female. No wonder the *bhísroti* didn't want her near the throne.

She strode forward with confidence, not leaving a spare second to doubt her authority. "General, show me where we will meet."

The dining table in the great room had been cleared and polished to a gleaming luster. "With your permission, my wife Zheníhda will attend table," Tokh said. He froze in a deep bow, eyes to the floor. Zheníhda's face looked ten seconds from panic at the responsibility of serving a noble.

"As long as she does not speak. This is a private interview," Rimas said. She took the center seat on one side; her officers filled in on either side of her, while guards stood both inside and outside the front door, allowing no passage in any direction. A camera was set on the table before her Highness to record the interviewed, another at the end to get a wide view.

"The interviewed may sit. Her counsel and translator may sit with her."

Aila bowed and took the seat across from the camera. Tokh sat next to her.

"You wish to speak for the interviewed, Lord Tokh? Does the subject have ties to you?"

Tokh seemed as if he were trying to make up his mind. He took a deep breath and lifted his head. "Your Majesty, I was given care and supervision of the subject since she was of the age of thirteen, a task I took most seriously. She is as a daughter to me. She was given protection by the great Nághtas; I would grant her also the recognition of the line of dar-Gilåhn."

Rimas sat back. Her face didn't change, but it was obvious she hadn't expected that. "You are prepared to accept responsibility for her actions on Kerasím, good or bad, to discipline her as required, to care and shelter her as long as she remains unmarried, as it reflects upon you, even though she is a Human?"

"I am."

"You vouch for her loyalty to the Emperor of Kerasím above all others?"

"Not above all but equal to, as the facts of the previous weeks will show."

Aila stared at Tokh, unsure what the protocol was, unsure whether she was allowed to speak or not. It sounded as if he'd just adopted her. Did that mean she was trapped here? That he would exert pressure on her? That he thought he could control her, or keep her from the Union? Or was this the legal move he'd promised to use to protect her? If she opened her mouth, would it reflect badly on him before superiors – and Heir Apparent was almost as superior as one could get. Rimas was like no other Kerasi woman. She was educated far beyond any Kerasi female, beyond many of the men. She oozed upper-caste arrogance and power. Aila had no doubt Rimas was quite handy with that sword and would not hesitate to prove her command. Rimas was exactly what Kerasím needed to wake them up and see women as capable.

Rimas rapped her knuckles on the table, twice. "Let it be known from now forward Union representative Aila Perrin is acknowledged by

General Four Tokh dar-Giláhn, is covered by the protection of his name and is as one with his line and all property therein. She may use the name Aila Perrin daras-Giláhn for all purposes Kerasi and more."

Aila could just imagine the furor going through Zheníhda's mind right now. She bent her head. "Thank you, Lord Tokh," she made sure to reply in Union Standard. "I hope."

"Now," Rimas said. "You left the palace after the assassination. Please explain what happened after that, in every detail possible, so we will know what you know without needing harsher methods."

Rimas's interrogation lasted three interminable hours, prying details out of Aila she didn't want to remember. Aila spent at least an hour in tears, trying her best to form words in any language. Zheníhda brought her cold drinks, Tokh put his hand on her shoulder to strengthen her, but by far the turning point was Rimas leaning across the table – Rimas, Heir to the Throne of Kerasím, the very first *thósikh*-caste woman who was not the wife of an Emperor, grasping Aila's hand in her own, albeit with a glove on.

Her voice was caring, a mother's comfort to a despairing child. "Take your time. As my own family has discovered, betrayal is most difficult to understand, and leaves only pain and anger to swirl behind."

Aila knelt when Rimas left, but couldn't rise. Haghíde carried her to her room, Mímihn tried to feed her a bite or two of food, but Aila fell into a deep sleep. Tokh poked her awake with the collapsed thickness of his incentive stick two hours later, unwilling to touch a sleeping Union female, even one he'd laid claim to.

"I know you require rest, but the Union delegation will be arriving soon."

Aila nodded. She sat up, still weary. "What did you mean before, what you told Rimas? I am one with your line? What is that? I didn't want to question you in front of Rimas."

"That was the correct action." He clasped the incentive stick behind his back and paced the room. "As a foreign female, you have no legal rights on Kerasím. I did not believe Nadigh would use you to some end, but I do not know the will of the Emperor. I used a maneuver that would grant you legal protection, should such an incident occur."

"You adopted me?" Tokh stopped pacing and tilted his head, questioning the phrase. "You claimed me as one of your own offspring."

Tokh resumed pacing, from the balcony doors to the lounges and back. "If a female claims her child is mine and I deny it, she has the right to demand genetic testing. If she claims a child is mine and I do not deny it, truth or not the issue ends; there is no claim to prove. Although it is impossible for you to be my offspring, by acknowledging you as mine, there is no law that says I must prove it. Rimas could not deny me."

"You used a hole in the law that never existed before."

Tokh pointed his incentive stick at her. "Yes! I claimed you as my own offspring, accepting responsibility for all your actions and granting you full protection of my lineage. Should anyone call you traitor to Kerasím, they would also call me a traitor, and that would be most difficult to prove. Kerasi law does not extend into Union space, but while you are on Kerasím, your actions and behavior are now tied to me. Do not abuse my name and reputation; I warn you, I will treat you no differently than my true offspring. Bring dishonor to my house and you will not like the punishment."

Aila had no doubt of that; Tokh's past punishments had not been forgotten. His was a temper she truly feared. She slid off the bed to kneel before him, her forehead all the way to the floor. "You give me too much honor, General. I am beyond grateful for everything you have done for me. May I never disappoint you, and may my actions serve to glorify your honor."

Tokh stopped before her. He gazed down at the back of her head, and a thoughtful smile broke out. "They always have."

Thirty-three

The morning had spent most of Aila's reserves. She sat on a cushioned chair at an ironwork and stone table in the shade of Tokh's side patio overlooking the partially repaired gardens, staring off to where the water met the sky, unable to gather an ounce of energy. She saw the aircraft fly up the coast from the palace, heard it land on the other side of the property, but let Tokh take care of the greetings. She didn't pull herself from the chair until she saw who had been sent: Undersecretary Bindai Hhani, now acting Secretary of State; a doctor, Ellia Baisch; Vanora Aikerman; and Ross Halian.

Aila rose to greet him with a hug and a kiss to his cheek. "I'm so glad to see you, Mr. Halian! I was afraid you might have been among the wounded."

"I was far enough from the crush, against the wall," he said, returning her hug. "I'm happier to see you in one piece. You're a damned hard person to keep track of."

"Sorry about that, but I didn't actually have a scratch until a few days ago." She hugged Secretary Hhani, whom she also knew fairly well, but saved the biggest hug for Aikerman.

"I'm so, so happy to see you, Vanora! I had no idea what happened to you. I didn't see your name on any of the casualty lists, but I worried anyway." Aila sank back onto her chair. "I can't imagine what you went through."

Aikerman tossed the thought away as she sat. "Bah! I'm a tough old bird. If anything, I let you down, my dear. I'm retired intelligence, Child. It was my job to know where you were at all times, and your protectors slipped you from my grasp the split-second I stopped to see to poor Hawet. They know their stuff, I'll give them that."

"I suspected something like that. I know my parents."

Tokh sat to Aila's right. Zheníhda scurried in and out, bringing refreshments from the kitchen and disappearing just as quickly. The conversation dwindled to an uncomfortable silence.

Tokh picked up the cue. "Do you wish to speak with your people in private? I will return to the house until you call."

"Ka," Aila said, so quick and sharp it was more of a command. She grabbed his arm, holding him to the chair. "There is nothing I would say to them I would not have you hear. I have gone over my ordeal in every detail with your government; there is nothing I can add to that. You named me daras-Giláhn. You have every right to be here."

"Are you sure about that, my dear?" Aikerman asked. "We don't want to take up too much of the General's time. He's been so generous already." There was a leading edge to her voice that said *wrong answer.*

Emotion tried again to overwhelm Aila. She lifted her face to the green-blue sky, gazed at the stunted little trees on the hillside, Tokh's mangled gardens spread out before them and his little *ghinadín* servant Thrit working on repairs at the far end. The orange sun was hot on the patio, but cool air flowed up from the water far below, balancing it.

"I have seen so much beauty in the last two weeks, beauty of the land, of the country, of the people of Kerasím. I have touched the hands of the masses and those of the royalty. I have seen the greatest kindnesses from ordinary people. Yes, for two days I was caught up in a very dire situation, but even then I witnessed common decency, even among people whom I considered to be the purest form of evil. I would love to go over with you what I have learned and recorded, Mr. Hhani, and Mr. Halian, too, but it will have to wait a week or so until I've recovered a bit more. Everything else is public record. The General stays."

She stared without blinking into Ross Halian's eyes when she said "recorded;" he gave an understanding nod in reply.

"I'll mark you down first thing, a week from today," he promised.

They spoke for more than an hour, Aila officially recounting as much of her ordeal as she cared, and asking a number of questions of Halian and Hhani. She passed Baisch's simple physical exam.

"You look worse off than you are," Baisch said, and Aila knew it was true. She had fading bruises on her face, the multitude of small cuts had almost healed, and the gruesome-looking bruises and cuts were healing on her wrists.

Aila rubbed her wrists as if consoling them. "I'm afraid most of this was my doing. I couldn't stop trying to slide out of the binders. With a little help from Kassán, I finally did."

Baisch patted her arm. "You're a lucky lady. Outside of some stress and exhaustion, you're really in pretty good shape. A week or two of rest and you'll be on the lecture circuit in no time. The tranquilizers you're taking aren't my first choice, but they're not harmful at that dose."

"I haven't taken any today," Aila insisted. "I'm trying to get my feet back."

"If you're able to travel, we're ready to take you out of here," Halian said. "Your parents are in orbit on board the *Edge of Eternity*. They're very anxious to get you back up there."

Aila fell silent. *Home.* Mom. Dad. Thayer. Ramie. The safety of her own room.

A room for one.

No, she wasn't ready to leave. She arrived as two, she would only leave as two.

Aila shook her head. "No. I know my parents will try to create a diplomatic incident out of it, but I need to rest before I can deal with all that. I'm not up to travel. I can barely walk back to my bed. I would love to speak to them via comwaves if I may, twice a day if it helps. I feel very safe here, and I'm among good friends. I would like to wait a few days, maybe even a week, get some energy back, if I may."

"We're still working closely with the Emperor on this, so we're not leaving orbit too soon." Hhani said, "Nadigh's angry enough with his own people, but he's a bit shy of us right now, and I can't blame him. Doctor?"

"As long as she's not under any undue influence, I'm okay with that," Baisch said. "Halian's down here in the city; perhaps he can check in on her. Is that all right with her host?"

Aila knew the answer, but she asked it for the record. "General, you've been a tremendous host. Would I be asking too much to rest here a little longer? I do not wish to overstay my welcome."

Tokh looked as if he might have been insulted, but took it as a matter of protocol. He addressed the table. "I offer her my home as I would my own offspring. She may stay until she wishes to leave, with full protection of my unit; that is my word. Forgive me; I have never met another Human female. I may ask a question?"

Tokh seemed so serious. For a minute Aila worried he was going to do something rash, start an argument, make a bid to keep her indefinitely. She knew too well the power and command he could project. He must have been formidable indeed in military councils.

Hhani gave a bow of his head, the safest of all gestures on Kerasím. "By all means, General. Anything."

"Are all Earth females as strong as this one? Do they think tactically by nature? They are all able to speak other languages? Do you choose certain ones to train in military style, or is that part of all education? We understand you feel your females are equal at tasks to your males, but never did we imagine this could be so true."

The Union team looked around the table and gave a collective nod.

"Aila's certainly something special," Ross Halian said with a grin. "I'm sure you've realized by now she doesn't like to sit back and let others do all the work."

"We study whatever we desire," Baisch said. "There are basic requirements, but we choose our own specialties."

"Oh, I'd say at least half of us are go-getters like that," Vanora said. "I spent twenty years working in the space fleet, then went on to surveillance and covert assignments. In my younger days, I would have given you a good run for your money."

Tokh didn't understand the phrase, and questioned Aila.

"She would have caused you great trouble as an opponent," Aila explained.

"Which is why it makes me sad to have to do this," Vanora said. She stood up and took a step back from the table. She reached inside the back of her waistband and withdrew a hand weapon, trained on Aila and Tokh. Baisch gasped and ducked to the side. Hhani shoved his chair back with his feet.

"Vanora, what the hell are you doing? Are you crazy!" Halian said. He stood up, but Hhani sat between them; he couldn't grab her. Tokh's hand slid downward to his hip.

"Don't move, General! Keep your hands where I can see them. Ross – don't try it. I've got twice the experience you have, whether you want to admit it or not. You see, Aila, you weren't supposed to survive that hopeful little conference the Emperor had planned. I was there to make sure of that, but your paranoid Kerasi friend was too speedy for me. It's been a hard haul trying to stay even one step behind them, let alone ahead of them. Our intelligence isn't quite as good as theirs, and it was rather difficult to send info under the Emperor's nose. It was bad enough having to take De'a out myself, with the Emperor trying so hard to keep us nice and safe. If Kel wasn't such a spineless prick he would have just taken you out like he did Kane and the Naborine, but he wanted Banukh to make you a martyr, and even then he couldn't find it in himself to break you into retracting your support. I'm sorry to waste so much talent. You've been so nice to her, General, it's a shame to make you take the blame for the massacre of four Union officials here on your property, but then, you're still wanted for crimes inside Union space, so it's not a surprise at all. Oh, don't look so shocked. I know exactly who you are and what you've done. Once again, with my background to support me, I will be the only one who escapes to tell how it happened. I'm sorry, but there's now ample evidence the Kerasi are just too barbaric and violent a people to have open ties with."

Nothing was making sense. Aila watched Vanora speak as if in a bad dream. She'd *roomed* with her, for Space's sake! She'd trusted her, forgiven her for being old and most likely a snitch. How could Vanora kill De'a for no reason? How could she have that much hate? Was that what Defense Council did to people?

Aila turned toward the General in bewilderment, but Tokh hadn't flinched. He looked as calm and collected as if he were watching a theater production. "You will not leave my property alive."

Aikerman smiled. "You have no idea what I can do." She raised the weapon.

A shadow crossed the table, and something exploded. Bits of shrapnel hit Aila, followed by a wave of liquid and a blinding flash of weapon fire. Aila gasped and tensed up, knowing she'd been hit and the liquid was her own blood. She lifted her head in a panic, hands clutching her chest in what was likely her last breath, and was doubly confused to see Aikerman flat on the stones of the patio, a perfect gory shot deep into her chest, while Aila felt no pain. Tokh was on his feet, holstering his weapon.

Tokh bowed to Secretary Hhani, cringing in his seat with his hands up to protect himself. "My deepest apologies for the death of your delegate, but no one threatens me or my guests."

Hhani eased back into his chair. His head kept turning between the General and Aikerman's body. "My apologies, sir, for a danger I had no idea existed. You have my sincerest thanks, and those of everyone at this table."

"That's the fastest draw I think I've ever seen," Halian said with admiration.

Baisch dashed over to Aikerman, but it was obvious that if she wasn't already dead, she would be in another second. "What the hell happened? What exploded?" She dabbed at her shirt.

"I don't know," Tokh said. He poked at shards of glass on the table and came away with a larger piece that had the remnants of a gold *lunahl* label clinging to it. He glanced at the empty sky overhead, but there was nothing to explain the bottle. He glanced behind him, but the kitchen doors were closed and no one in the house could possibly have flung a bottle at that angle and made it land like that.

The doors burst open and Mímihn flew out onto the patio in a frenzy. She ran up to Tokh, speaking far too fast to be understood. She knelt and bowed like a flower in a breeze, pleading.

"Stand up, female!" Tokh barked. "Speak! I do not have time for nonsense!"

"Forgiveness, my great husband! I beg forgiveness! Please do not be too harsh! I hid on my balcony, listening to conversations when I should not. I wanted to watch the Union ladies. I did not know what they said, but when the older lady holds a weapon to my Tokh, to my dear friend Aila, I must do something. I close my bad eye and try to hit her with a bottle of *lunahl*. I missed and hit the table instead. I am most sorry for not minding my own business. Please, my dear husband, do not be harsh with me!"

The words sank in. Tokh's head tipped back and he let loose a braying laugh. He lifted Mímihn off the ground and kissed her throat. "My life saved by a half-blind wife!"

Aila began to shake again and laughed off her panic as she put together the sequence of events; Ross Halian explained it to the doctor and Mr. Hhani. Aila's shirt was damp with *lunahl*, but she was unharmed. She rose and gave Secretary Hhani a hard hug. "Please explain to my mother why I will be recovering here instead of with her. These people have my back at every turn. I feel far safer here than with my own people at the moment."

"At the moment, I do too," Doctor Baisch agreed.

Thirty-four

Chaos rocked Tokh's estate yet again. Hhani had to inform the Union of what had transpired; Tokh had to inform the Emperor. Officials from both sides flew in to examine the scene, interview everyone in the house, examine the body. Nadigh did not send Rimas but his brother Moragh instead, someone more experienced and far more ruthless in investigating issues that could affect the throne. Neighbors poured out of the surrounding houses, gathering at Justice Wahtegahn's house just above Tokh's, peering down over the walls and trying to guess what had happened this time, until hours later when the officials left and they could swarm Tokh proper. Tokh banished Dalo and the children to the upper floor, and his wives to the downstairs bedroom where he could keep an eye on them. It took numerous translators and much convincing from both Secretary Hhani and Captain Halian that no charges were being filed against General Tokh, that the Union was most grateful to him, and he deserved to be rewarded.

Aila slipped Ross Halian the chip from her interface, complete with the recording of her argument with Kel before the assassination and recordings of the conditions of the lower-caste cities. Halian would watch them, and direct them to the right people. Then she snuck off and took one of Kassán's pills and blotted out the rest of the day and night, so groggy and dazed she had trouble answering questions.

Oh Vanora! How I trusted you! How I believed you! I fell for every bit of false friendship you showed me, even when you warned me we were all expendable. Vanora, you hurt me through the heart.

"When you learn to suspect everyone, only then will you truly be a diplomat." Mátokhan had tried to warn her. How right he was.

How could she go home when the Union seemed to want her dead more than the Kerasi?

Aila waited until morning to speak to her mother on a direct line to the ship.

Leila Perrin's face was sharp and no-nonsense, leaning into the camera as if she could pull her daughter through the screen. "Aila, what is the problem? Why aren't you up here already? Everyone else is back aboard. You're free to leave, aren't you? You were supposed to leave with Bindai." Leila's worry came through loud and clear.

Aila sighed, a motion that seemed to melt her further into her chair, bonded and immovable. "After what just happened? I'm more scared to be trapped on that ship with no escape than to stay exactly where I am. You might not believe it, but I've got more people watching my back here, people I trust, than you have on that entire ship. I can't leave yet. Not until I calm down. It's a long way home, and I don't want to die on board."

"You're being overly dramatic again. How could you stay there after what they just did to you?"

"My friends didn't do that, Mom. The Emperor didn't do that. That was the enemies of the Emperor, including our own Secretary of State, and a former Union council member. Don't. Just don't. I need a few more days to build up my nerve. If you want to come here and visit me, hold me, even stay here with me, you and Daddy are more than welcome. I could really use a hug right now."

Leila gave a nervous laugh. "I'm trying to get you out of danger, not put all of us into it. You need to be up here."

Aila looked away from the screen for a lengthy pause. Her voice was sad but not accusatory. Home seemed so very far away right now, another life, another person, a piece of history growing fainter by the hour. At the same time, she felt perfectly at home right where she sat. Maybe that's what growing up was, a new home, a new family, a new life. "I knew you wouldn't do it, Mom. That's the difference between us, I guess. If it were you down here, I'd be with you."

Haghíde was more upset than she was, begging Aila's forgiveness every hour. "I failed in my duty as your interim bodyguard," he fretted. "I should have searched everyone arriving. I was falsely reassured by the fact I was familiar with three of the dignitaries. It was Tokh's home and I was unsure if I should be searching guests without his request. I will not be caught that way again. Please forgive my error."

Aila squeezed his hand. She hated seeing him upset with himself, especially without reason. "Haghíde, Masákh was well aware of my friendship with Aikerman. I truly suspected nothing. I slept in the same room with her, ate with her, sought her opinions, and I had no clue. She didn't raise any alarms with Masákh, so he would not have thought to frisk her, either. I cannot forgive what I don't blame."

Two days without anyone trying to shoot her gave Aila the rest she needed. She walked about the grounds with Mímihn or Tokh, helped Dalo with her baby, and played modified games of *rahl*-ball with Haghíde, Joralan, Kesseh, Dalo, and Dalo's older children Lanag and Faelihn. Haghíde never let her out of his sight, back straight, at attention, watching every direction outside lest he miss a danger somewhere, even when she walked about with Tokh.

On the second day, Nadigh gave his first public execution. Joralan was ordered to take all the children outside while the adults watched the event with the rest of the planet on a live-feed from the palace. The center of the road to the palace was sectioned off and a platform erected; the public, both male and female, filled in the roadway, thousands upon thousands of onlookers. Nadigh wore full Emperor's regalia: the ancient headpiece, gold suit, and white cape, crossed by a sickly green sash, the color of mourning on Kerasím. He gave a stern speech before the massive statue of Nághtas, Moragh and Rimas at his sides, proclaiming his investigation into the death of his father to be complete. He blamed a pact of obstruction, driven by fear, by factions of both Kerasím and the Union, funded by his brother Turwheg and several *bhísroti* who had already been dealt with. Turwheg seethed with blinding jealousy that it would come to pass a mere female would be in line to become Emperor, but he, a *bhísroti* of direct royal blood, could not, and placed that blame on his father. In Nadigh's view, this only underscored the need for a global change in the value of females, and furthered his resolve to broaden relationships with the Union.

Turwheg was brought out naked, bound by the wrists and neck and surrounded by a cordon of six guards, two of whom held chains connected to his neck bindings. No marks could be seen on him, he had not been beaten into confession, but his eyes held a blank panic no Kerasi in their right mind would ever show. His jaw had been stripped of his chin hank, the identity and pride of every Kerasi male. It was a deep and shameful insult. Nadigh read the charges aloud; Turwheg agreed to each. Nadigh pronounced sentence. Turwheg was dragged forward to a large block and made to bend. Nadigh drew his sword, the sword of his father, and his father before him, and his father before him. In one swing he severed his brother's head from his shoulders, then held the head high for all the onlookers and cameras to see. With his boot he kicked the body away from the cutting block and placed the head upon it, then reached for the front of his pants and before the crowd proceeded to urinate on the severed head. When finished, he said, "That is what happens to traitors of Kerasím, and to those who murder their father for gain, two crimes I will not tolerate. This is my word; this is my law." Nadigh and his entourage walked back into the palace.

Tokh watched Aila's reaction. "They will leave the body there until sunset, for anyone else to urinate on. It is not required, but it is considered a respect to the Emperor for those that do. It may follow tradition, but it will not win favor with the Union. You must think our practices extremely primitive."

Aila made a face, thinking. "Not necessarily. I was actually thinking how that practice will have to change. That's not something Rimas will be able to carry out as easily."

The comment brought a round of laughter to the morbid gathering, right down to prissy Zheníhda.

"The Union does not approve of capital punishment, although there is some leeway for individual planets to make specific cases for it. I don't know where I stand on that at the moment, I really don't," Aila said, "but I'll give Nadigh credit in that he had the nerve to carry out the execution himself. In the Union, one person passes the sentence, but he or she is completely removed from carrying out the punishment. It would make things much fairer if the judges themselves had to carry out the sentence. It keeps it more honest, I think. Our system makes us weak in that regard."

"That may be truth," Tokh agreed.

On the third day excitement rolled through the house. Kitras was granted leave and would be returning to the estate. Dalo screamed and jumped in place. She threw herself at Tokh's feet and kissed them, crying, before standing up again.

"When! When!"

"Sometime this morning." Tokh chucked her under her chin. He flapped his hands to dismiss her. "Go. Make yourself more colorful for him. Maybe wear a skirt? Or shoes?" Dalo sped up the stairs.

She made herself presentable in record time, running circles in her excitement. She hadn't seen Kitras in eight months. The children picked up her excitement until they were running and shouting as well.

"Go! Outside! All of you!" Zheníhda said, pushing them out the door. "Go watch for his transport. Don't go near the pool, and stay away from the landing pad."

The aircraft skipped over the hill an hour before lunch, a plain brown transport with no special markings. It crouched like an insect on the landing pad. The children's shouts brought the adults outside.

The door opened and a short set of steps unfolded. Kitras jumped down and put his hand out, but the second passenger refused help. The passenger's leg wore a sturdy plastic splint, he leaned on walking stick and a stripe of his hair was missing where his head wound had been repaired, but Masákh worked his way down the steps on his own, to the cheers of several in the yard. Dalo ran to Kitras, children following on invisible strings.

Tokh stepped forward and clapped his officer on the shoulder. "Masákh! It is good to see you up and about. You look fit for duty. I am assured from many sources the tales of your courage are not exaggerated."

Masákh dipped his head in gratitude. "I thank you, Lord General. I did no more than duty required."

"From what I heard and saw on the recordings, it was a battle for the history books."

"It was very brief." Masákh's eyes searched the courtyard until they located Aila, standing by Zheníhda. His face gave away nothing, but he raised his eyebrows as if to say, *No greeting?*

Aila stared as if seeing the dead. She remembered him falling, remembered him being covered in blood, remembered him being carried out, but nothing else. Seeing him alive, seeing him walking, seeing him wounded made her heart swell until it pressed against her ribs so hard she could feel them bending outward, and the pain that went with it.

No tears, you stupid female! They hate tears! She yelled inside her head, not noticing Dalo bawling her eyes out and Kitras kissing every inch of her he could reach. Aila ran to him, but one did not hug an unmarried Kerasi in public, especially an *aghát*, nor did she wish to hurt him by squeezing as hard as she needed. She wanted to kiss the living breath out of him, but never in front of the General, or Haghíde, or even the other ladies. She flapped her arms helplessly before him and blurted out, "I love you!" before collapsing to her knees before him, forehead in the dirt.

Masákh's face twitched with embarrassment. *"Get up,"* he whispered, but she didn't move. "Get up!" He couldn't kick her with his bad leg, and he couldn't lean on the bad leg long enough to kick her away with the good one. He tapped her unobtrusively with his walking stick, with no result. Mímihn darted forward and pulled her away.

Aila followed him like a puppy, never more than a hand's length away, trying her damnedest not to cry or touch him. No personal servant was more attentive as she plated and poured his meal while he spoke with the others. She said little, trying to play it cool before the other men.

"Wait five minutes, then follow me upstairs," he whispered to her after lunch. It took him almost that long to climb the stairs, using the handrail to take the pressure off his healing leg.

Dalo and Kitras disappeared while Zheníhda took the children outside. Haghíde followed Tokh to his office. Mímihn was in the lavatory. Aila dashed up the stairs. She tiptoed toward his room, but gasped when a hand reached out from the hall lavatory and grabbed her arm.

Masákh pulled her in and shut the door. He seized her in his arms and kissed her, a demanding kiss that took her breath away. Aila attacked him with twice the fervor, not letting up until she'd had her fill.

His hands squeezed her shoulders, her arms, touched the bruises on her cheek, picked up her hands to examine her wrists with anguish. The efficient detachment disappeared from his voice. "You are certain you are unharmed? Do not lie to me; I will know the truth. We had no idea who had taken you or where. Kitras was on the trail of Secretary Kel when he discovered you were also being held there. We moved as fast as possible. He told me much of your ordeal. It distresses me, the humiliation you suffered."

Aila's fingers ran through his hair, examined the healing wound on his head, the hair already growing back in the softest black sheen. She kissed him again. "Not half as much as my distress seeing you hurt. I would have killed Kel with my bare hands. I've been sick, not knowing how you were. You cut it to the wire. Ten more minutes and it would not have been pretty. Thank you! Thank you so much for rescuing me!"

"You hired me as a bodyguard. It was my duty. Haghíde said you saved my life, shot the secretary before he could kill me. I am in your debt."

Aila gave a coy twist of her head. "Only because of duty? Not because you wanted to save me? And no, we're even. You saved me from Sóghar back when, remember?"

Masákh bowed. "Then our debts are even. Yes, I would have traced you for personal reasons, without duty. My reaction when you were seized was less than disciplined, and I am grateful you did not see it. You proved the General wrong, and that is a very difficult thing to do. Although he felt your aim with a weapon was somewhat accurate, he did not think you would keep your head in battle, when many things are happening at once."

Aila laughed. She traced the sculpted edge of his goatee with her fingers. "Tokh underestimated my reaction to someone threatening you."

"The General should send you for *aghát* training. You are the same age I was. It would help you in your duties with the Union."

"No," Aila insisted. "I am quite happy not to get into the habit of executing my superiors. The Union doesn't approve of that." She squeezed the breath from him again. "As long as you're back."

Thirty-five

Aila had changed into her nightwear when the knock came at the door. Mímihn opened it. "Aila? I see the light under your door. Why are you not with him?"

"I left him reading. It's late. He is wounded. He needs rest to be strong again."

"He came back here for *you*. You belong with him. It is your presence that will heal his heart and his body. He will feel ashamed for being wounded. You must make him feel strong again. Tonight or never."

Aila had grown to hate her tendency to blush. It gave away far too much. To spend the night beside him, no danger, no distractions, no witnesses... Even though it might mean he'd want the sex she'd backed out on. Their mission was certainly over, but this was Tokh's house and walls had ears, not the least of which were Mímihn's. On the other hand, even if all they did was talk, or if he slept, she would be there to help him if he needed it.

Aila nodded. "Okay. I will." She grabbed her clothes and started to pull them on.

Mímihn squinted at her. "What are you doing?"

"Getting dressed?"

"Oh, young female! You have so much to learn! You do not go to him in street clothes." Mímihn took Aila by the hand and dragged her to her suite.

Mímihn tore through her wardrobe and found a short satiny gown of palest gold, clinging at breast and hips and held up by nothing but two bows tied at the shoulders. "Where is he from?"

Aila tapped her fingers on her forehead. "He told me once. Starts with a *Kha*."

Mímihn tapped her own forehead. "Half of Kerasím starts with *Kha*."

263

"Khin... Kinas ..."

"Kinas Dagh? Daghnahn?"

"Yes. I think that was it."

Mímihn smiled. "I know exactly what you need." She opened a drawer and squinted at the jars within, chose a perfumed cream and coated Aila everywhere with it. It smelled of heady dark nights filled with satin, pillows, and rich spices in bright colors, and bold powerful men with incredibly dark eyes. Mímihn fixed her hair, dabbed it with more perfume, and touched up her eyes and cheeks with cosmetics.

"Oh! Your necklace! You must wear your necklace. If he gave it to you, he will want to see it." Mímihn retrieved it and placed it around Aila's neck.

The stones shimmered and sparked, far too fancy for the simple gown. Aila's voice shivered with nerves. "I look like a consort,"

"Tonight you *are* a consort," Mímihn said with authority. "You will be his comfort from his troubles, his joy to forget them. That is your purpose."

"What if Tokh calls for him in the middle of, you know... ?"

"*I* will take care of Tokh," Mímihn said with a very unladylike grin, and pushed her out the door.

Aila's heart tried its very best to choke her, crawling up into her throat and cutting off her air. What if he laughed at Mímihn's excesses? What if he was sleeping? What if his leg hurt? What if he hurt her?

She tapped on his door, carrying a tray of delicacies and *lunahl* Mímihn had given her, hoping he was already asleep and she would be saved from monumental embarrassment. "Masákh?"

"Enter," he said, and her heart squeezed her throat even tighter.

He sat on a lounging sofa, resting his leg, reading or watching something on a lap screen. She placed the tray on his clothing drawers and shut the door.

Masákh looked up, then did a double take, eyes wide in disbelief. He shut off the screen and put it on the refreshment table next to him, and used his hands and good leg to push himself up higher on the lounge.

Aila wasn't aware she was speaking but she must have been, because she heard her voice saying the words. "I thought, with your injuries, maybe someone should stay with you tonight." She made herself sit by his knees on the lounge, even though he didn't give permission. "If you needed me to."

Masákh stared, taking in Mímihn's handiwork. He breathed fast, as if he'd raced her to the lounge, or maybe he'd caught the scent of the perfume. His eyebrows crept upward. "Do you realize what you are implying?" His tone suggested she was crazy.

Aila looked down at her hands tucked between her knees, feeling her damned cheeks burn. Either she was serious about this or she needed to leave and go back to her parents this very second.

Like hell! Thayer would never stop laughing at her. She was an adult. She needed to get this over with.

She lifted her head to meet his stare. "I can't imply it any stronger. There is nothing I want more than to stay here with you."

His expression hadn't changed, that *aghát* blankness, unreadable, not telling if she had pleased or offended him. "If you stay, it will mean you give me your consent. I will not stop this time, no matter what your custom."

She took a deep breath to steady herself. "I know. I don't care about custom anymore. I only know what I feel in my heart. I have just one condition: you can't hurt me. You can do what you want, but you cannot hurt me. Can you do that?"

He gave a soft snort of amusement and a pleased little smile appeared, shy and out of place.

Never confuse the duty with the man.

Even after four years, Aila had a feeling she didn't know the man at all, but what she glimpsed behind the duty was charming.

"I believe I can do that. Can you do what you want without hurting me?" Masákh gestured toward the brace.

"I believe I can do that." She leaned upward and kissed his lips.

Masákh didn't break away, holding her to the kiss as if he could consume her. His hands lifted her and drew her in until she sat on his lap, and the ferocity he'd shown a lifetime ago on the way to Kerasím emerged once more. Aila gave an involuntary shudder. His nose nuzzled her collarbone, breathing in the scented cream, his smile widening as he passed over the roughness of the necklace.

His lips burned their way to her shoulder, then up her neck. She tried to reciprocate, but never got farther than his ear before his head was moving again, searching for the best spot to tear into her. His hands slipped over the silky fabric, warm like a second skin over her breasts, down her back, under the edge of the gown and up to her hips. Mímihn had allowed her nothing under it. Her heart shivered under her ribs, leaving her weak.

"Is this what Kerasi do?" she mumbled. "Do you kiss like we do, or is there something else you like more?"

"Neck," Masákh gasped, leaving scarring kisses under her ear and into her hair. "To bare the neck is to put yourself at the other's mercy. To kiss a throat is to be trusted. Couples with desires place their lives in each other's trust. That is the difference between lovers and casual contact." To prove his point, he placed his mouth over her throat, scraping the skin lightly with his teeth.

Thank goodness he was *aghát* and his teeth had been filed flat. If Aila had felt electrocuted by his kisses, the brief shot of fear at the teeth at her throat intensified it. This was probably another of those all-important cross-cultural moments everything revolved around, so she let her head fall back, giving him her entire throat.

Her stalwart *aghát* groaned, ran his tongue up her windpipe and under her chin until he found her mouth again and kissed her as if trying to breathe for her. Aila broke free and returned the gesture, leaving kisses over the goatee, under his chin, until her lips tugged and chewed at the skin just above his collarbone.

Everything happened too fast. Aila never remembered his shirt coming off, but it did. His chest was smooth and almost hairless, just a little bit low on his belly. He pulled the ties to her dress. It collapsed, baring her pointy little breasts, the source of so much attention lately, and she covered them with her hands.

"*Ka*," Masákh said softly, and shook his head. He took her hands and held them outward. A strange light lit his face. "No. You are too beautiful to hide. You are the legend of Khéristal come to life, blinding me with your beauty."

Crippling nerves made her giggle. "Khéristal? Does that mean skinny little girl with funny pointy breasts?"

Masákh continued to hold her hands, his eyes dancing over every inch of her. "A thousand years ago, before Kerasím was united, Emperor Dihnar was at war."

"Dihnar, as in *Díhnarwharl*?"

Masákh nodded. "He had nine daughters and five sons. His oldest was Khéristal, a maid of fifteen. She was claimed to be the most beautiful female ever born. Men young and old asked to marry her, but Dihnar loved her and vowed he would not wed her to anyone who was not worthy of such beauty. Dihnar was caught in a fierce battle and his troops were decimated. Khéristal's mother was afraid the castle would fall, so she wrapped Khéristal in a robe of shining silver and sent her out to her father's side. Khéristal stood on a hill above the battle and opened her robe. The soldiers of both sides looked up and were blinded by her beauty, and the fighting ceased. A young *nhásarwharl* soldier named Fantoht looked away, too loyal to dishonor the Emperor's daughter by gazing on her. While everyone was blinded, Dihnar and Fantoht slew a thousand enemy soldiers before Khéristal closed her robes. Dihnar won the war and saved his palace. He gave Khéristal's hand to Fantoht and decreed a new caste, *díhnarwharl*, those who are more honorable than *nhásarwharl*.

"And you," Masákh let go and cupped her breasts in his hands, "are as beautiful as Khéristal. I cannot love you more." His lips touched her breasts and pulled them behind his teeth, tugging at her nipples until she jerked and shivered and stupid noises leaked from her throat. No wonder Thayer didn't see a problem sleeping with boys. If Aila'd felt electrocuted before, it was now taking her vision with it.

Masákh's lips never left her skin, down her throat, over her breasts. Those narrow claw-like fingernails tiptoed down her back, making her twitch and squeak with each light pointed touch until every inch of her writhed. He guided her leg until she straddled him, belly to belly, groin to groin. "What is your bloodprice, and who must I pay?"

Aila rubbed against him, breathless, while she gnawed his earlobe. She wanted him, wanted him so badly she hurt, wanted to crawl inside him until she disappeared. "It is my business alone, and I choose to give myself to you. Do it, Masákh. Do it soon."

Aila expected to stand up and help him to the bed, but he unfastened his pants with one hand, worked them down just far enough. His hands slipped under her, squeezing the undersides of her thighs, the curves of her backside, fingers exploring inside her until Aila wasn't sure if her heart was going to stop from fear or desire. She felt him pressing against her, hot, bare, rigid as stone. In one motion he lifted her bottom, opened her to him, and pulled her down over that impossible hardness. Aila gave a cry and stiffened up.

"*Shu, shu, falahndi arihl.*" He whispered the endearment in her ear, kissing it, the unyielding hands holding her down, pulling her to him, preventing escape. "There is less pain when it is quick."

"I'm okay. I just – wasn't expecting that. It's – really really good right now." Never had she felt so young next to him, so mortified at her inexperience she wanted to cry, but that would only make it worse. *Can I sound any stupider? What the hell am I supposed to say? Go home baby, this is Big Girl territory.* Her heart was pounding so hard she was sure he could feel it hitting him. He was inside her, filling places she didn't know she had, poking for room as he moved underneath her, her entire lower half tingling with the sensation. She was screwing a Kerasi, and she still had no idea what he even looked like down there.

You still don't know what to do, do you, baby.

"Move with me. Push when I push." He pressed her knees wider, pulled her hips to meet him, and the tingling turned to fire.

"Oh!"

Ohhhhh.

His lips continued to ravage her, hands guiding her as they moved together, until the fire started burning and something went nova through her middle and she cried out and lost all awareness of anything but his movement against her. He bit down on her shoulder and gave a very un-*aghát* wail, crushing her to him so hard she struggled to breathe.

Masákh gasped for air, as if he'd been drowning and just breached the surface. His arms released their squeeze, slid down until they rested exhausted on her backside. Aila collapsed against him, head on his shoulder.

"Don't move," he panted, holding her in place. "It does not apply to us, but two Kerasi cannot immediately uncouple. It requires a moment or two, unless the male wishes pain on the female."

"I don't want to move," Aila murmured against his neck. Her hips still ground slow against him, chasing the fading fire. "I want time to stop right now and make this moment last as long as possible. Just like this. Just like this forever."

Aila wasn't sure what she'd expected, if she'd expected anything at all. Build up her nerve to sleep with him, then actually sleep next to him, right? She hadn't thought a minute past that point. Maybe on Earth, but she was on Kerasím, with a Kerasi, and it seemed some of the rumors that circulated were based on fact.

After Masákh caught his breath and pulled free, he touched foreheads with her, eyes staring into hers, piercing and dark, and the shy little smile appeared once more, afraid to be seen on an *aghát* even in private. "You survived?"

Aila's insides still throbbed, alive as she'd never imagined. She gave a nervous little giggle. "I think so."

He rubbed at the toothmarks on her shoulder. "You are not hurt?"

She shook her head.

"Excellent." He stood up from the lounge, pulled the untied dress from her, lifted her naked in his arms, and carried her, limping, to the bed. He removed the rest of his clothing.

Aila frowned, seeing his back. Fading burns marked his arm, but five recently-healed brown stripes crossed his shoulders in a cluster, dark and obvious against his yellow-tan skin. Bleaching his skin changed the outward color, but couldn't change the color of his blood, or of scar tissue. She reached out to touch them. "What happened? Was that from the battle?"

Masákh sat and glanced over his shoulder. "That is a miracle. That is all I received for disobeying a direct order from my superior. I'm sure Tokh will call out that favor sometime in the future."

"*What!* Tokh beat you? Why? What did you do?"

Masákh smiled with discomfort, but it wasn't smarmy at all; the honesty in it made Aila's heart flutter. "I told you, my behavior following your abduction was less than exemplary. In the Union you would say I...," he searched for the correct idiom, "...'went crazy.' Tokh gave me an order to stay with the vehicle, I ignored it and began to trail your abductors immediately. When Tokh's retrieval crew caught up to me, I had come back to my senses and knew I had destroyed my career. I turned in my weapons, asked to be relieved of duty. Tokh could have had me striped twenty times, demoted me two ranks, imprisoned me, even humiliated me before his troops, if he was of that mindset. He did not. He striped me five times, berated me, and refused to accept my request for time off. I cannot imagine a lighter punishment. I am deeply ashamed of my behavior. I do not know if he put the incident in my file or not. It is a most serious offense."

Aila caressed his stripes and kissed the nearest one. "You threw your career away because of me?"

"I was not thinking clearly at the time."

The admission left Aila stunned. Masákh's career was everything to him. He lived and breathed it, ate it for breakfast, a hundred mind scanners and torture would never erase it from being the first thought of his day. He *was* the Kerasi diplomat program, engineered almost from birth to know nothing else. "That was incredibly stupid of you."

Masákh gave a faint smile of amusement. "It was." He bent down and removed the brace from his leg.

"You're supposed to leave that on. You'll injure it worse."

"I am not walking on the bed." Masákh lay next to her, his wounded leg over hers. It remained horribly bruised in a rainbow of browns and yellows. "We have gotten the urgency out of the way. Now we can take our time. First, like Humans. Then I will show you the Kerasi way, and you can decide which you prefer."

The nervous giggle trilled in the back of Aila's throat. She still felt like a naïve moron, just slightly less of one. She kissed the base of his throat. "Okay."

Aila caught a little sleep, spooned tight against him in his bed, his arms wrapped around her, leg over her to protect her, or perhaps to keep her from running away. His breath was so peaceful and soft on the top of her head she didn't want to disturb him, not for a second. Never had she suspected a romantic lay underneath the cold, hard shell of Tokh's most controlled and precision-driven *aghát*. The way his face lit up when he looked at her. The smile that grew bigger as the night progressed, daring to be released against his will. The way he shared a glass of *lunahl* with her, and showed her the proper way to eat the legendary aphrodisiac *patigha* fruit, cheek to cheek. The unexpected tenderness he showed, making love to her as a human male would, in complete opposition to the wild whirlwind he was as a Kerasi male unleashed, pounding at her with untamed fury from behind while she knelt, her face shoved into the sheets to bury her screams of ecstasy until he collapsed on top of her with a prolonged grunt. Not long before the suns rose, he took her once more without saying a word, lifting her thigh and entering her from behind as they lay there, so agonizingly slow and steady Aila could have died from the suspense.

She awoke to find him washed and dressing. Her eyes averted themselves from courtesy, but couldn't stop the curious little glances. Despite the intimacy of the night, she wrapped the bedsheet around her like a shield, while any shame of nudity had long been taken from him by training. "Where are you going?"

"We will be expected at breakfast. And I must confess to my commanding officer that I have bedded his 'daughter' under his own roof."

Aila turned gray. She hadn't thought about that part. What Kerasi taboos did she break? How angry would Tokh be? She slid forward on the bed. "Don't! Don't you dare tell him, Masákh! No! You can't tell anyone! On Earth, it is a private thing between partners only."

"He is supposed to know anything in my life that might compromise the performance of my duties. It is best if I volunteer the information before it affects me."

Aila grabbed his wrist. "Please! Don't volunteer it. If he asks you, tell him the truth, but don't tell him unless he does. Please."

He bent to kiss her lips, pulled the sheet away and kissed a dark pink nipple, so strangely different from Kerasi golden-brown. The timid smile broke out once more. "Very well. For now it is our secret. But hurry. Do not be late downstairs."

Aila threw on the abandoned night dress and ran back to her room as soon as he descended the stairs. Mímihn slipped in behind her. "Well?! Did you?"

Aila could not have blushed harder. One hand covered her mouth and the other gripped Mímihn's hand. *"Great Mother of the Emperor!"* She squealed and pulled Mímihn farther away from the door, fanning her chest. "We stayed awake most of the night. Four! Four times in the same night. I did not know that happened." Her cheeks felt two hundred degrees. Thayer was her best friend, but in many ways Mímihn was even closer. Both, Aila was sure, were good enough friends to help her hide a body, but where Thayer was tough as titanium and saw every rule as a personal challenge, Mímihn, whose life had given her every reason to knife it in the throat, could not have been more cheerful and girly if she tried. Mímihn lived for gory details because she wanted to make sure the other person was happy or didn't need help; Thayer got off on details just to prove she was better than other people.

Mímihn squealed and hugged her. "I told you, you would give him back his strength! Four is excellent. Their goal is always six – 'more than one hand can tell,' but most cannot do that without pills. Was he kind to you?"

Aila felt another wave of blood rush to her face. *"Sukh!* Very, very kind to me. I am too happy to speak!"

"I am so very happy for you!" Mímihn's thumb rubbed at a brown lovebite low on her throat. "Tokh had much strength, too."

Thirty-six

It was a strange breakfast. Aila knew she'd crossed the line from adulthood being a random number on a legal document to adulthood being a frame of mind and type of behavior, but this morning the line seemed to be tangible, another dimension she'd fallen into. Everything she did seemed to stand out for no reason: colors seemed brighter, sounds louder, the glint of innuendo seemed to taint the most innocent of statements, the actions of the others far different than any other morning. The harder Aila tried to pretend it was just another day, the more she felt there was a flashing sign above her head that said, "Had Sex All Night for First Time!" She noticed Dalo and Kitras, absorbed in each other to the point where they seemed to be in their own little world. Dalo sat so close she was nearly in his lap, Kitras poking her in the ear, in the nose, in the cheek, and Dalo blushing a deep bronze, pleased with the attention. Her neck was so covered in love-bites she looked as if she'd been strangled; Kitras didn't look much better. Haghíde watched them with amusement, perhaps not a small amount of jealousy as well. Mímihn darted around Tokh like a summerfly, giggling, teasing, whispering in his ear, until Zheníhda snapped, "Would you like us to clear space on the table?"

Tokh wrestled Mímihn's arms from his neck. "Only if you are offering to please me."

Masákh and Haghíde made mildly explicit banter, but it seemed as if only Aila, her cheeks feeling as if they were permanently on fire, paid attention to her meal. She wanted nothing more than to wrap herself around Masákh and never let go, but she dared not touch him even with a finger in front of the others.

Haghíde watched Masákh leave the breakfast table. "You look much stronger than you did yesterday."

It was true. Masákh stood straighter. He walked with less of a limp, barely leaned on his walking stick at all. Aila cleared his dishes for him.

"I slept quite well last night," Masákh said. "I'm sure it is being free of the hospital, and the good food."

Haghíde nodded. "And the company, I'm certain. I'm jealous, Masákh, but you earned it. Good as Kerasi?"

Masákh turned his head and gave an embarrassed snort. "More than I can say."

Haghíde's hand fell heavy on his shoulder. "Remember that, when you explain it to Tokh."

Masákh, Haghíde, and Kitras, all close in age, walked slowly around the courtyard, comparing stories of campaigns and politics, and the rescue that went down. Aila and Dalo followed behind, listening some but enjoying the company of the men more. They leaned on the cement wall overlooking the cliff, watching the water far below, bonds of friendship forging deeper as they spoke. Again the invisible line seemed to follow her; nothing had changed, the people, the words, the conversations, but for the first time Aila felt as if she belonged in the group as an equal, not just a tag-a-long mascot, the female Union *dáhneg*, that little experiment that went right.

A scream from inside the house made them jump. It repeated itself. Haghíde and Kitras raced ahead, Dalo close behind, worried for her baby, while Aila helped Masákh hobble faster than he should have.

In the great room, Tokh raged at Mímihn. "What are you screaming for, you fool! Do you want to bring the neighbors down on us, wondering what is going on? Haven't we given them enough cause for gossip, for the next hundred years? Stop your nonsense!" Mímihn's feet danced in place, and even Zheníhda had a glow about her, a loosening of the sour pucker until one could glimpse that she might have been quite pretty in her youth.

"We're going to the palace!" Mímihn shrieked to the room. She pulled the paper from Tokh's hand and squinted at it. "There! Right there! That is the word wife! Even Nihda can read that much! Read to them! Read to them what it says! I want to hear it again!"

"Please, Tokh," Zheníhda begged. "I want to hear it, too."

Tokh yanked the printout back. "It is an invitation to the palace, two days from now. 'Be it known General Tokh dar-Giláhn, his wives, son Kitras dar-Giláhn and wives, recognized daughter Aila Perrin daras-Giláhn; Aghát officers Mátokhan Mikhíristah, Masákh gha Lil, Haghíde Kitáhl, Tótoghar Randán, Ghírandar otta Paiéhr, Ráhnif Rihn; Command Officers, will make themselves present to the Emperor for a private honors ceremony and reception, and so forth. Transportation will be provided at midday."

Murmurs rebounded around the room. "Did you hear that?" Mímihn gushed to Aila, her arms flapping. "Wives! I am a wife, and I will go to the palace and see the Emperor! Me! Me! And now I can see him!" She squealed and spun in a circle until her ruffled skirts flared outward. The look on Zheníhda's face said she wanted to do that, too, but couldn't bring herself to break free of her dignity act. Wives were *never* included in imperial ceremonies.

"Ráhnif?" Aila said to Masákh. "From the palace? Why is he included in your crew?"

Masákh smiled his old smarmy smile at her, so superior for knowing information she didn't. "Did you think I would trust a random palace *aghát* with an unapproved and unscheduled tour of the city? Ráhnif has been our junior *aghát* for almost a year, replacing the opening Sóghar left."

"It took three years to replace him?"

"Few are chosen for *aghát*, fewer complete the program, then graduates must be screened. It is a lengthy process. He has strong potential."

Aila folded her arms. Her forehead wrinkled in distress. "I'm not sure I want to go back to the palace. I don't exactly trust the place."

"Security will be most tight," Tokh assured her. "It will be in private chambers and is limited to fifty honorees, families, and select Union dignitaries who have been cleared. No weapons are permitted. Nadigh will not be fooled twice."

"We will need clothing," Zheníhda realized. "Not one of us owns a thing worthy of wearing to the palace. We don't have much time. Tokh, find someone to accompany us to the city."

"You will all go, and leave me to my work," Tokh said. "I have much arranging to do."

As the crowd headed upstairs to ready themselves, Tokh's hand seized Aila's shoulder. He held it there, controlling her, and didn't allow her to turn around. "You are of my line but not of my blood. I warned you about bringing honor to my house. I wish to say you made a very good choice. It was long overdue. I approve."

Aila paused, but then his meaning hit her and she began to sputter. "General Tokh! How dare you speculate – Don't –"

He leaned in next to her. "I did not need his confession. You are like a new wife after a wedding night, shadowing and trying to please. You could not choose a better man anywhere on Kerasím, not even among *bhísroti*. He has long held deep affection for you; I know this as fact. Save your games of dishonor for the Union. You are on Kerasím; let him please you as only a Kerasi can."

Aila took a deep breath and blew it out slowly, eyeing the floor. And the stairs. And the wall, anywhere but at Tokh. "Thank you, Lord Tokh."

Aila made her second ground-to-orbit call of the day from Tokh's office. She dreaded each one more and more; each call put her one step closer to having to leave Kerasím and deal with her mother. The calls helped; Leila was much calmer than she had been four days ago, but Aila knew the biggest battle was yet to come. The ship itself might very well explode when Aila told her mother she and Masákh were now partnered. That battle would wait.

Leila answered the call without so much as a greeting. "Aila, what is this? What is this nonsense of them demanding we come down to the planet to some ceremony the Emperor is doing? Is this for real? Are they going to kidnap us or just kill us when we do? I'm not going. They will not get me off this ship, Aila. Don't you go there, either. Your father's trying to find out what he can, but they won't give any details. Bindai says it's important, but I'm not trusting anyone anymore."

"Mom! Will you stop? It's totally legit. If they're inviting you, it means I'm probably one of the honorees. This is momentous, Mom. They don't invite women to any event, and this time they are. This is history. You wouldn't come see me be honored in a ceremony? I'm a Union representative, Mom. Do you know how bad it will look if you don't show up? You will be snubbing the Grand Emperor of Kerasím, a man who worked hard and put up men to rescue me. Don't be that ungrateful."

Leila leaned into the video pickup. "If you weren't there in the first place, no one would have had to rescue you. And what the hell is this after your name? What does it mean, parents of Aila Perrin daras-Giláhn? Does that mean diplomat?"

Aila winced. She didn't realize the palace would jump on that so fast, but then again, Rimas herself approved it. "It's a legal thing, Mom. It means I'm under the direct protection of a General, so no one dares mess with me again. It's okay. I won't be using it anywhere but here."

Leila backed down. "Oh. That's good, I guess. I'm sure your father will want to go. You will be coming back to the ship afterwards, right?"

"That's the plan, according to Mr. Hhani." Aila formed the perfect noose and dropped it on her mother. "It's real easy, Mom. Either you come planetside and meet the people who put their lives on the line to rescue me, or I will refuse to come back. You're not allowed to sit up there in orbit and pass judgment on my friends until you've met them. It's the least you can do."

Leila's eyes narrowed. Her voice turned cold. "Is that Masákh going to be there?"

"Well, considering he's the one who pulled me out and kept me from being shot, and he almost died because of it, yes, you will have to greet him, and thank him, and be polite to him. That's my deal. You don't care enough to watch me be awarded, then I don't care to come home." Aila punctuated it with a single sharp nod.

Leila's mouth pinched up unhappily, emphasizing the stress lines that had formed in the last few years. "Don't make me call your bluff, Miss. And when your father drags you back aboard, we're going to have words."

Aila tried to keep her smile friendly. "I'm well aware of that, Mom."

Masákh hunted her down in her room that night. Aila was sorting through her clothing and repacking things. Everything she had left behind at the palace on their run had been returned to her. She'd bought a beaded dark green gown for this event, short and simple in design, with no ruffles or wide skirts to complicate emergencies, something that would match her necklace. She planned to wear the same gold and black shoes, and she'd bought a ruffled green veil to wear down her back, a decoration more than anything. She looked less like a dressed-up child and far more of a sophisticated adult in the new arrangement. That funny invisible line between childhood and adulthood seemed to run right down the middle of her packing case. She no longer liked most of the clothing she'd brought with her.

Masákh stood in her doorway. "I believe you are in the wrong room. This is no longer where you belong."

Aila blinked her eyes at him. "Am I? I was taught by my Kerasi teacher – you may know him, he's an *aghát* – that Kerasi females do not pursue Kerasi males. Males are the aggressors. It is the male that chooses the bride, the male that agrees to marry her, the male that beds her in the manner he chooses. So, being an unmarried female, I am bound by custom to be stuck here in this room, with this great big empty bed, wishing a male would choose me and bed me to his heart's content."

Masákh stepped into the room and shut the door. In a burst of motion as fast as his leg would allow, he rushed Aila, lifted her, and slammed her onto the bed with a violence that might have been play but could also have been frighteningly real. He loomed over her, dark, dangerous, powerful, his hands immobilizing hers, pinning her to the bed. "Is that what you expected?"

Aila gasped and lay back in surprise, insides quivering, not sure if she was frightened or thrilled. A brave smile broke across her face. "I think so."

She lay pressed against him, head on his arm, still unable to shake the stupid feeling, not knowing what to do or say. Either way he seemed pleased, staring down at her with a strange, almost dreamy expression. It just wasn't... Masákh.

"What are you staring at me for?" she said at last.

He gave his soft snort, his mouth nudged a little farther into a smile, but he didn't stop gazing at her. "You are so very young."

"I'm getting older every day. Is that good or bad?"

He sighed and broke the gaze, his finger teasing slow lines down her neck to the edge of the sheet she kept tight against her chest. "Neither. An observation. I cannot imagine having done this when you were younger. Perhaps it is right our limits should be raised."

Aila stared back, her insides more than a little queasy. "Well, neither can I, because I wouldn't have. It's still creepy. I'm still not sure I'm messed up, doing this. Were you thinking about me this way back then? Because that's really going to freak me out if you were."

Masákh gave a chuckle that wasn't quite successful at covering the truth. "You were the only unattached female in the building. We spoke with you daily. It is natural we entertained some fantasies."

"That's disgusting."

"You were a legal adult of marrying age on Kerasím. It was not wrong. We did not speak of it. We did not take liberties. We behaved most appropriately by Union standards."

One truth didn't erase the other. Aila changed the subject with a coy little smile. "When did you first decide you liked me, in the bedding kind of way?"

Masákh laughed outright. "I cannot tell you."

Aila poked him in the chest. "Tell me!"

"I should not tell you."

"But you will, or I'll pester you all night. And don't tell me it was the first time you saw me."

"We are on Kerasím. It is legal for me to strike you until you stop." It was a reminder, but there was no malice in his tone. "Very well. I could no longer deny my feelings when you escaped the embassy. I was far too distressed, both at losing you and knowing what you would face when we recaptured you. I feared being removed for allowing your disappearance. Even though I was angry, I was physically ill knowing you would face punishment, face it alone, and it would most certainly be terrifying for you. Nor would I be allowed to comfort you afterward; I had to continue to project anger. That is when I knew I was no longer being objective about the situation."

The creepiness fell away as he answered. Aila smiled with adoration and stretched up to kiss him. "You are so sweet! I would have let you comfort me, too. I would have done anything for a kind word at that point. What would you have done after the treaty was reached and I returned home?

Masákh smiled, but Aila knew the look. He knew something and he wasn't going to tell. "That never happened, so it is a situation I never faced."

"Of course it did. I escaped and went home. But you were captured and came back with me, so we never lost contact."

His silence as he searched for what to tell her became a lengthy pause. "No agreement was ever reached, so the thought is irrelevant."

Aila frowned. "It wasn't? I thought that's why you came to get me at Manning, because I could be released."

His eyes wouldn't look at her. "No. Mátokhan failed. The Union believed they could retrieve you on their own, so they ceased all communication with us."

Aila sat up. "So why did you come back for me? What was going to happen to me?"

"You could not be left in the past; we did not know what would happen to time if we did. We were leaving, and you had to be retrieved."

"*And?* Masákh, what was going to happen to me? I was going to be returned, wasn't I?"

Masákh turned his head. She could see him struggle to select only enough information as needed, not upset her. "No. You would have been turned over to a Kerasi as a gift."

Aila felt her insides turn cold. She stared at him with wide eyes. "Not Sóghar!"

"No. I would have made sure of that." He pulled her back down into his arms and kissed her. "Do not dwell on those ideas. They did not happen. The Fates made us wait until now. It is better this way, no? You are old enough to recognize your desires."

Masákh kissed her down the side of her neck, lingering kisses that should have fired up her heart. He pulled the sheet to her waist and continued his march lower, but Aila didn't respond. She had a terrible urge to run far away from him, too aware of who he was and what he'd been and what she was letting him do to her. She'd never realized, once again, just how close she'd come to total disaster. If Ross Halian hadn't been there the very second Masákh had tried to drag her from Manning Academy, she would have become the plaything of some hideous, stinking Kerasi, without any hope of rescue, just fourteen years old, like Mímihn. If not Sóghar, who? Would Tokh have taken her as another consort, alongside Mímihn? Would he have given her to one of his General friends? Or would she have become the prize of a *fáhganid* somewhere, maybe even Nághtas? The thought of Nághtas, so old and fat crushing her under his naked weight, with Nadigh helping hold back the great stomach to find his parts, made her want to vomit.

She pushed Masákh's head away. "Stop! Tell me, Masákh! Tell me you were at least a candidate to get me. Please! I might possibly have lived through that if you had gotten me. Nothing bad ever happened to me when you were around. Even Ghírandar would have been better than some ancient General."

A burst of laughter broke from him. "Surely Ghírandar would like to hear how attractive you find him." He pulled her up until they touched foreheads. "Yes, I... was in strong consideration. But it does not matter now, because none of it occurred. This is why I do not tell you information! You fear things that never happened, can no longer occur, and don't think about things that are happening now. Now I must *push* such thoughts from your head." His hand slid between her thighs as he kissed her lips.

The Kerasi word for *push* was also their common rude word for sex, *pushing* a female, *pushing* on her, putting a *push* to her, *pushing* her across the table. Aila wrestled him off her and sat up. "No, Masákh. You've *pushed* me twice; you won't die if you wait. You want to put those ideas out of my head? Then stop. Let me know I have a choice in the matter. Don't force me. I need to know I have the ability to walk out of here if I want without the threat of violence if I do. I need to know that you see me as a person with as much capability and intelligence as you, not just a female you can order about. I will follow you anywhere, do whatever you want me to, but I'll do it because it's what I want, not because of what I fear. I need to know I'm here because I want to be here, not because I'm a prize in a game I didn't know I was playing. If I'm only here as something you can *push* on and control, then I'm sorry, we're not going to be a pair very long, like it or not."

Masákh leaned back, silent but for a huffy snort every now and then. The confusion on his face was real, not just him trying to cover something up. He smiled, but it was the uncomfortable look he got when he was afraid his translation wasn't precise enough, apologizing for being misunderstood.

"I do not understand. I have already granted you that very opportunity. I have forced you into nothing, though I have every right. I have not made even a threat of violent behavior. Perhaps you are not aware where the law lies: you are claimed by Tokh to be his offspring. I have already bedded you, which he is aware of. He has the right to demand I marry you, or I can print a public contract from the computer, sign it that I take you as my wife. As your legal father on Kerasím, Tokh signs the document agreeing that you are now my wife and that fact becomes formal and legal. You have no word on the deed. You do not need to sign the paper. You would be mine to do with as I please, and the law would be with me. I could retain your paperwork, prevent you from leaving Kerasím, if I chose."

Aila's heart missed a beat and fell over with a thud inside her chest. "What?!"

"My words are truth; you may ask Tokh to confirm it." He gave a soft chuckle and caressed her cheek. "I would recommend you first put on clothing, however."

Aila still stared at him, so he continued. "I do not do those things because I know you are Union and that is not your way. I have been trained to walk the line between both worlds. Your way is as important to you as mine is to me; I understand that, and I wish to honor your desires. When we are legally paired by your laws, we will make it legal here as well, although we may find that if we spend much time here because of duty, it may be advantageous to declare our pairing here sooner, but I will wait for your agreement. Again, you worry about things that have already been resolved." He kissed the side of her head.

Aila stayed still in his arms, but her face held a melancholy sadness. "Thank you, I guess. That should make me feel so much better, but instead it makes me so confused my head hurts. You're always two steps ahead of me, and it makes me feel so blasted stupid. You're so incredibly smart, Masákh; how could you want to be around me when I'm this damned stupid?"

Masákh chuckled, and his face went back to radiating the admiration she loved to see on it. "I told you, you are very young. You do not have enough experience of Kerasím to know what to think, how to think, when to question and when to stay silent. You are just starting to learn that on your world. I wish we could spend a month here at Tokh's; Zheníhda and Mímihn could teach you much that I cannot. I will teach you to think like an *aghát*; then you will know how to conduct yourself when you are here. Then I will not worry about you as much."

The cloud lifted from Aila. "You worry about me?"

"Always. Look what happened when you left my side."

Aila smiled at last. "Yeah." She rolled him over onto his back and lay on top of him. "I can really walk out that door, and you won't stop me?"

"I would be most upset and angry, but no, I will not stop you. But I will demand reasons, and I will be quite vocal in my demands."

Aila nodded. "I believe you. I have no desire to leave, so we won't worry about that. Teach me. Tell me everything you know about your marriage rites. Everything. Even the things you don't know. Then I'll tell you mine."

His hands slid down her bare sides and back up. It was illegal for a Kerasi female to lie atop a male, but everyone did it and it was never enforced. Here was a law it did not bother him to bend. "I can do that."

Thirty-seven

Tokh's men trickled in all the day before: Tótoghar, Ghírandar, Mátokhan, Tokh's second in command Colonel Kaghán; three brownshirts and four *bhántanok* Chiefs in green, creating an impromptu party of old friends that started mid-morning and ran until the after-dinner drunken singing had been going on for at least an hour. Ráhnif and Kassán were already at the palace; they would join them there. The warm feeling of kinship washed over Aila once more. Even with the influx of officers she was not familiar with, she didn't feel the least bit in danger.

Aila tried to partake in the conversations, but Zheníhda pulled her aside. She was firm but not yet rude. "Do not pretend with me. I know where he was last night. If you are acting as his consort, then you will act like a consort and serve and clean the dishes. If you are acting as his wife, then you will join the wives to make sure the party is a success. If you are neither, Tokh claims you as daughter, and you will bring him honor by seeing that his guests lack nothing. Your place is with us."

"I am a political servant of the Planetary Union and I should be directly in the middle of those conversations," Aila said. "That is my job. But you and General Tokh have been the most patient of hosts, and I will be happy to assist you."

Aila filled and cleared dishes with the wives, enduring the hands patting her backside and the rude questions asked of Tokh.

"What did the notice mean, recognized daughter, General?" said Colonel Khagán. "Did you get caught dipping where you shouldn't have? I should think a General would know better. What did your battle-wife have to say about that one?" The room gave a rowdy howl and stomped their feet. Zheníhda did not miss the comment; Khagán's next plate of *vortag* legs seared with such spice he blistered his tongue on the first piece.

Tokh pulled Aila onto his lap as he would a child. "I have looked after her for years, put up with enough behavior to claim her as my own. It is by my order she was educated to the position she holds in the Union. She brings me honor and glory. I do not have to prove it; I say she is, and I will protect her as such. I'd better not see a single one of you trying to corner her somewhere! Your hands are not to touch her, or you will know my wrath." The finger that pointed to his men was two cups of *dhurwah* past its steady aim, but Aila was grateful for the threat just the same.

She put her arms around his neck and gave him a faint peck to the side of his head, in the safety zone of his thick hair. "*Soyavoh, Triskaris-Bo.*"

Thanks, General-Father.

With family and officers they numbered twenty-six, plus luggage, testing patience and plumbing as everyone tried to ready themselves at once. The private imperial shuttle was so large it couldn't fit on Tokh's landing pad. It settled itself in the main courtyard before the house, cracking paving stones with its weight. Mímihn held tight to Kesseh. She wore a sheer blue veil that trailed almost to her knees, flipped down her back. If she pulled it over her face, it would fuzz up her weak eyesight and she would be functionally blind, bringing dishonor to Tokh by announcing her previous position. Her fingers played with a corner of the veil.

"I feel so sick," she admitted to Aila. "I am so scared to go to the palace. What if we meet the Emperor? What if I do not have proper manners? What if he orders me out because I was a consort? What if he does something and I do not see it, and he thinks I insulted him? I will fail Tokh and he will look bad to the Emperor. Ai-la, I am too scared to do this! I am just a little *rhibáni* consort girl, not a *bhísroti.*"

Aila hugged her so as not to wrinkle either of them. "You are a high-*díhnarwharl* wife of a level-four General, and that is all you are. You live in a neighborhood filled with *dáhneg* and *fáhganid* females. You can do this. Keep your head high. I have been to the palace. I have met the Emperor. He is harsh but he is a good man who took great care of his father. I think he would forgive you. I will be your eyes if you need me."

Mímihn squeezed her hand in a death-defying grip. "Thank you, Ai-la."

Even Mímihn could make out the palace as they approached, the glowing white building larger and grander than anything else in sight. Aila pointed things out to Mímihn and Kesseh, describing the friezes on the sides of the building, the number of flags and towers, the way the grounds and gardens seemed to spread out forever, things Mímihn might not have been able to see. At least she would have enough information to fake it through conversation if necessary.

Landing at the palace had a different feel this time. Twelve heavily armed security officers met them on the roof, along with a colonel in charge of welcoming them. Aila and the *aghát* still had their palace identifications, but the rest were scanned, frisked, photographed, imprinted, and relieved of any weapons, right down to Dalo's toddler, Niboh. Nadigh wasn't playing.

It was only with great reluctance Tokh turned over his sword. "What if I promise to leave it in my quarters, search me if I leave the room?"

"I'm sorry, General," the Colonel explained. "*Tansohr Kheralin.* It is the order of the Emperor, and it is expressly written to include every last person, no matter what the weapon, no matter what the rank or caste. I guarantee your weapons will be safe and waiting for you any time you wish to leave the palace."

They were shown to a suite on the fourth floor, a huge open sitting area with a glass wall overlooking the gardens and a balcony to stand on for fresh air. Six bedrooms were attached, men in the rooms on one side of the center and women in rooms on the other. The greens were sent to dormitories at the end of the hall.

Aila clung to Masákh in the hallway after the others had gone in, picking imaginary lint off his impeccable clothing. "That's not fair. I don't want to be separated from you. Last time I was here, bad things happened. I don't want you that far away from me. Can't you come over to the female side? Tell them you're guarding us or something."

Masákh's eyes roamed the hall, noting the exits, the sitting areas, the monstrous paintings that could very well be hidden doors, the new surveillance cameras in the ceiling every so many strides. He wouldn't have been surprised in the least if they extended into the apartments as

286

well; Nadigh would be an Emperor who believed in the sanctity of spying. He bent his head and brushed her hair with his lips, keeping his back to the cameras. "We will be together all evening, and we will be together alone for the voyage back."

Aila stared at him in disbelief. "Are you kidding? My parents are on that ship! They're going to be here tonight. We're not going to be alone for a second from here on in."

He brushed his lips on her head again. "I will take care of alone time."

Getting ready for a major event with a roomful of women brought Aila a new wave of melancholy. The hours played out like a video entertainment that she was watching, detached and yet participating in it at the same time. Zheníhda had lost her perpetual disdain, as dumbfounded and excited as anyone else to be at the Emperor's palace. She raced around like a mother hen, helping everyone dress, fixing hair, even complimenting Mímihn, so afraid of not being perfect, of not showing Tokh at his best before the Emperor, that she upset her stomach. Dalo touched up Zheníhda's face with makeup, made her nose seem less pinched, her cheeks fuller, her eyes brighter. Zheníhda, the *hyrak* herself, smiled shyly at her reflection in the mirror, quite pleased. She wore a deep violet gown with black trims and a short silver veil off her dark hair, which she'd swirled up on the top of her head. Mímihn wore a dress of burgundy lace, younger and clinging and lower-cut than Zheníhda's, but for all her flightiness, she knew when to pull herself together and act like a wife bringing honor to her husband. Dalo had chosen a sparkling short black dress cut by diagonal bands of gold, and to Tokh's approval she wore strappy black heels on her otherwise bare feet. Dalo was not one for veils at all; Aila had yet to see her with anything larger than a ribbon hanging from her hair, but for the occasion she wore a glittered black demi-veil over her purple hair, so short it would not cover her chin if she flipped it forward. Dalo remained with Tokh's group, but Kitras rejoined General Rhigandir's unit, where he belonged.

The women whirled around Aila, laughing, chatting, being so *girly*, and Aila realized with mournful sadness that never in her life – whether due to the fact she spent too many months of her early teens in Embassy classrooms with various other displaced students, or a year of

287

isolation in Kerasi holding, or the following years of parental-enforced supervision and work among adults, not once, not even *once*, had she ever belonged to a clique of girls doing girly things together, talking girl talk, making dirty jokes, just bonding as women. Even among the Union delegates, they'd all gone about their business separately. She was still the youngest of the group: Zheníhda as old as her mother, Dalo twenty-eight, Mímihn twenty-three, but Aila had been accepted as part of them; she *belonged*. Thayer had been her best friend – only real friend – for the last few years, but Thayer was about as girly as engine grease. She loved Thayer, but this wasn't Thayer, and never would be.

Is a career worth leaving this?

The ceremony was scheduled in a private ballroom on the fifth floor, a fact even Tokh didn't know until the moment they left their suite. They were escorted upstairs by palace guards. Following another bodyscan in the hall, Tokh was announced to a fanfare and allowed to enter the ballroom, his entourage following. Aila caught sight of her parents sitting among the Union guests. Leila did make it, the significance of the act not lost on Aila, and for a second she felt bad for being rude. She wouldn't dream of embarrassing Tokh by breaking formation, but Aila did turn her head and wink at her mother, acknowledging her effort.

Nadigh's throne had been rescued from the Senate chamber and brought up here. It still bore his father's bloodstains, something Nadigh refused to have removed. His father passed the throne to him with his life; he would not let anyone forget. He sat on the throne at attention, back straight, chin high, dazzling in his ceremonial gold suit. His chin hank was thick and sculpted, clipped with a gold band bearing the great seal of his office. One hand held a long staff. Moragh and Rimas stood flanking him, looking no less official. Both wore gold cloth, but it didn't sparkle with metal filaments like Nadigh's. Rimas's dress hugged her form, both feminine and official at the same time. Her pink and brown hair was pulled back tight and rolled up to a knob on her head. A gold veil sprouted from it, too short to be anything but a decoration. Rimas was not one to hide behind anything, even tradition. Six more advisors sat to the side, two of them high-ranking Generals, by uniform.

Tokh dropped to his knees before the Emperor; they all followed his lead. When they were given permission to rise, Tokh stood to the side at his most formal, his dress uniform as immaculate as Masákh's, medals and ribbons and awards hanging off him like armored tiles, and presented each of them to the Emperor before they were shown to their seating sections. Aila didn't miss noting the drops of sweat above Tokh's brow, or the fact that on their way from paying respects to the Emperor, Zheníhda and Mímihn were gripping hands like two overwhelmed schoolgirls. Aila, known to the Emperor as a Union dignitary and now the claimed daughter of a Kerasi General, knelt and then walked over to the section reserved for females, to sit with her "family."

Two more teams entered and paid respects, including Kitras with General Rhigandir's unit, then Nadigh tapped his ceremonial staff on the floor. All doors were locked. No person, no signals, no information would leave the room. Nadigh stood, tall, fierce, commanding, and read a statement thanking everyone for their support and loyalty to him and to Kerasím through a most difficult time, explaining how it proved they were on the right course of history. Kerasím could change for the better, and it would happen under his rule. As an example, he declared the room caste-free for the night: all would sit together, eat together, share the same food and tables; if necessary, touch each other, all as one. Male would still separate from female, but female would be present, without threat.

"This is my word; this is my law," Nadigh ordered. "If anyone objects, you may leave the room now without reprisal. Stay, and you accept my vision. Should a difficulty arise later, it will be taken as an offense to me and dealt with harshly. This was to be my father's law had he lived; in time it will become my law, and we will practice it tonight." A low murmur broke out in the room. Nadigh waited, but not one person moved to leave.

He continued. "Our future begins *now*. You here: you are here tonight because you are my chosen to make that future happen. Every one of you will be my leaders of tomorrow. You will shape the futures of the generations to come. You have proven yourself through difficult times. You were loyal to my father, and you have chosen to extend that loyalty to me as well. For that, I am grateful. You are truly the best and bravest Kerasím has to offer. The past weeks have been trying ones not only for my family, but for all of Kerasím. Those of you here tonight have been elemental in keeping order, in working together, in solving crises of interstellar proportions. It is only right that I honor such loyalty."

Fifty people were being honored; eighteen of them belonged to Tokh's unit. Nadigh summoned men up unit by unit, calling each officer out and briefly recounting his part during the crisis. Medals and ribbons went out for bravery, heroism, loyalty, injuries; three officers were granted caste privilege. Tokh swelled with pride as Kitras received three awards, for heroism, loyalty, and service. Tokh's unit was called last.

Nadigh went into detail on the length of Tokh's service, how he was the first to declare loyalty after the assassination, how he had worked tirelessly toward Nághtas's goals of improving relations, right down to opening his home to Union citizens. Nadigh presented him with new citations for loyalty, service, diplomacy, foreign relations, and one for heroism for his stopping the assassination of four Union delegates.

"General Tokh dar-Giláhn: *díhnarwharl* is a noble caste that is supposed to be honorable above all the rest. You have proven yourself honorable beyond that of mere *díhnarwharl*. For that, I grant you the status of *díhnarwharl with dáhneg privilege*, to you and your offspring, from now until your line ends." Nadigh drew his ancient sword, the same one that raised Masákh's privilege, the same one that took Turwheg's head, and tapped Tokh on the back of his neck. "Rise, General Tokh, *dáhneg by privilege*."

He stood to a thundering of leg-slapping and foot stomping. In Aila's eyes Tokh was invincible; he was the strongest man alive, he cut off heads without throwing up, his reach extended to Emperors and satellites and countries half-way around the globe. He could do anything, and standing in front of a room of his peers, Aila could see the sweat on his face from where she sat. The man behind the duty looked about to faint.

Tokh thanked the Emperor and stood to the side as his men were honored in turn. All of Tokh's greens received two ribbons, for loyalty and service. His *aghát* all received one for loyalty to the Empire and one for special service. Masákh, Haghíde, Mátokhan, and Tótoghar received another for bravery, and Masákh for his injury in battle. What neither Masákh nor Tokh expected was Masákh being granted an Order of the Inner Circle, placing him with perhaps only twenty others – Mátokhan being one of them – who could be trusted to work directly on order from the Emperor, with no middle-man. It was a most prestigious award, and one that most certainly had political reasons behind it. Like Mátokhan, Masákh worked behind the lines and had made ties with those in places of power within the Union – besides sleeping with one of their dignitaries. The Emperor could request information or actions without anyone else knowing his moves. Aila knew what such a thing meant to him, a lowly little *whátaral* at heart, and she couldn't help but weep tears of pride for him. It was another honor to Tokh; not one other General could claim two officers inside the Inner Circle.

Nadigh made a bigger deal out of the last one called. "There is no precedent for this, not with my father, or his father, or his father before him. My last award is to a female. Not only a female, but a Human female, who has shown unending loyalty to the throne of Kerasím. Even when interrogated, even when threatened with assault, even when threatened by death, she would not withdraw her loyalty and faith in me. She was willing to protect Kerasi citizens at the expense of her own kind. Her courage and spirit are an example for Kerasi females. Her honor was such that she was accepted into the line of dar-Giláhn as one of its own. I have fifteen daughters; she is much like my own daughter Rimas: strong, proud, intelligent, and certain of her mind. She is an inspiration to all of Kerasím, both for what females are capable of and for our females to aspire to. My father, Emperor Nághtas, awarded her a medal for bravery at a very young age. I never expected to give this honor so early in my reign, and never to a female. Aila Perrin daras-Giláhn, for unwavering loyalty to the Empire of Kerasím, I award you the Star of the Empire, our highest honor."

The room broke out in confused knee-slapping, Kerasi applause, except for Tokh's cluster, where it pounded above all the rest. Aila stopped breathing. She had expected another token for bravery, maybe even an honorary little ribbon, like her *dáhneg* status or her protection of the Emperor, nothing remotely like real honor. Even Rimas didn't have such an award. She stood up from the women's cluster and knelt before the Emperor, head to the floor. Was she allowed to speak? Was that wrong? As a dignitary of the Union it wasn't, but as an honorary female Kerasi, it probably was.

She rose on command and allowed him to place the gold ribbon and silver star around her neck. Nadigh placed his hands on her head.

"Thank you, your Excellency," she said in her best Kherisi. "You honor me too well."

"You honor Kerasím," he replied. "You are returning to your homeland, but you will return to Kerasím, teach my daughters and our females about Union females. Rimas would like to converse with you."

"As soon as I am allowed," Aila swore. Rimas took her hands next and congratulated her. Aila turned to the room, found Masákh, and beamed at him. His face was perfectly neutral, but the pride in his eyes almost made her cry. It was only then, returning to her seat, that she remembered to look for her parents. Leila smiled, but it was a smile of distress more than anything, while Ramden Perrin, wearing his dress whites as a Union Fleet Admiral, grinned proudly and saluted her. Aila returned his salute. Tokh's women hugged her and fingered her medal in awe.

Nadigh went on to honor some of the Union officials who helped in the crisis – Ross Halian, Bindai Hhani, and others – but Aila never heard a word of it, staring at the star around her neck.

The banquet following was awkward. Aila wasn't sure where the hell she was supposed to sit – with the Union delegates or with Tokh's women, but in the end she stuck to the women. She would see Union delegates all the way home, though she did stop to hug her parents and the representatives and show off her medal. Several times Tokh was approached by fellow officers, inquiring about Aila's marriage status. The first time he relayed the message, Aila smiled, thanked the inquiring General, and insisted she had already accepted an offer. After that, he deflected the inquiries himself.

Mátokhan frowned down the table at her. "Are you actually spoken for, or is that something to make the old men go away?"

"No, it's real," Aila insisted.

"You didn't mention that before."

Aila tipped her head and gave him a sarcastic glare. "I shouldn't have needed to. If you don't know by now, you're a poor excuse for an *aghát*."

Mátokhan searched the back of his mind. Tokh was limited by caste to two wives. "Haghíde, do you know?"

"I believe so." Haghíde reached for his drink, preventing further comment.

"Masákh?"

Masákh remained composed. "I do."

"And?!" Mátokhan grew dark and testy. He caught Masákh glancing at Aila, and the pieces clicked. He jumped around in his seat and punched Masákh in his unburned shoulder. "You *trixahg*! You told me you weren't bedding her!"

"At the time it was truth. I was not." A cheer went up among the *aghát*, and they each reached to bang Masákh on the shoulder. Tótoghar and Ghírandar congratulated Aila as well. Aila bent her head and hid behind her hand, blushing, but Dalo and Mímihn soon teased her into accepting her fate with humor.

"Do you have a day yet?" Haghíde asked.

"It will be a while," Masákh said. "There are many difficulties to be worked out, but you will be at the celebration when it occurs, my friend. Be certain of it."

Union Secretary Bindai Hhani came up behind Aila and spoke softly to her ear. "If you're allowed to leave your table, your parents would like to speak with you."

Aila gulped her water. "Absolutely!" She caught Masákh's eye as she stood. *Ama*, she mouthed, and motioned with her head for him to follow.

Back in the connecting ballroom, several meeting tables had been set up for various family members to meet with sons they might not have seen in a while. Aila led her parents over to an empty one.

Leila hugged her all over again. "Oh my baby! They told us some of what you went through. I warned you! I warned you something like this would happen! We are so grateful it wasn't worse. No one could believe Kel was behind it, even after seeing the videos. Unbelievable."

Aila rolled her eyes. "Mom, the Kerasi never actually tried to kill me. The Union tried to kill me three times. You tell me who I should fear more. You're scared to be down here among my friends, but I'm scared wondering who's still out to get me at home. Seriously, I'm *afraid* to get on that ship. If Vanora was capable of sliding under your noses, who the hell else is still lurking there?"

"You've got me at your back now." Ramden Perrin got his turn to hug her. "I will know the background of every person on it, or they'll have to take a different ship. My little girl! My God, you look so grown up tonight! You have made me and your mother so proud, Aila. I can't tell you." He fingered the eight-pointed star.

She poked the rack of ribbons on her father's uniform. "Not bad, huh? If I keep this up, I'll have as many as you, without ever joining the military. It's looking kind of bad when the Kerasi keep honoring me, but the Union doesn't."

"That could very well change this time around," the Admiral said. "Bindai can't stop talking about you."

Leila glanced at Masákh several times. "Must he be here? We wanted to speak with you. Alone."

Aila took a deep breath. Standing up to Banukh the *fáhganid* was easier than standing up to her mother. Banukh never screamed. Her chest tightened up and she felt ill for a moment. In no way did she want to have this conversation with her parents, but it was now or in a few hours on the ship when she had to explain why she was not rooming with them.

Ever again.

And Mom didn't have the nerve to yell here.

I should have had a glass of gohr *or something first.*

"Yes, Mother. He does. You'd think you'd be a little more grateful to him for pulling me out of a locked shooting gallery. One hundred and sixty-eight people died, Mother. *Dead.* I lived because of Masákh. I was targeted in a plot partially masterminded by our very own Secretary of State, and Masákh is the one that led the team who rescued me. That's *twice* he saved me in the last two weeks." She motioned him to stand next to her.

Masákh bowed his head. "Good evening, Admiral. Good evening, Mrs. Perrin. It is an honor to have you visit Kerasím."

"Of course I'm grateful to you," Leila said with embarrassment. "Don't get me wrong. I'm extremely grateful for all you've done for Aila. I just – we haven't seen her in weeks, and I expected a private conversation."

Ramden Perrin shook Masákh's hand. "Truly, sir, we are in your debt for all you've done. You certainly did keep your word. Thank you."

"I've got something else to say," Aila said. The sick feeling worsened, like she'd swallowed a live fish and it was flopping inside her underneath all the Kerasi food. She took Masákh's hand in hers. "I hadn't planned on saying it here, but I don't see what difference a few hours are going to make. I will not be staying with you on the return trip. Masákh and I have agreed to a domestic partnership, to be formalized in a few years when I'm done with my degree."

Leila froze, then laughed. "You *what*? No. No. Absolutely not. Aila, don't get me started. Not here. That is *not* about to happen. I am not putting up with another of your wild whims. You can't go collecting people every time you go somewhere. People are not pets."

"Aila... Let's not get crazy," Admiral Perrin said. "Your mother's right, this isn't the place to discuss it. Let's save it for when we're back on board."

"I'm not listening to arguments. I'm not asking your permission. I'm telling you what's happening. If you don't like it, I accept that, but that's the way it's going to be. I am *this* close," Aila held up two pinching fingers, "to not coming back at all. I have found friendship here like I've never felt in my life – Hell, I've been given a family, a family that accepts me as I am, without constantly nagging me or questioning my motives – and you don't know how much it's hurting me to have to leave them."

"Oh Aila," Leila said with disgust. She turned away, holding her breath to keep herself contained.

Aila snapped. "*Oh Leila*! Here! Come with me." She grabbed her mother by the shoulders and bulldozed her clear across the ballroom and into the banquet room.

Thirty-eight

Aila shoved her mother straight to Tokh's table and bowed. He glanced up at her, giving permission for her to speak. "My apologies for the interruption, Lord General. I wish you to meet my parents, Leila Perrin, and Fleet Admiral Ramden Perrin, Undersecretary for the Union Defense Council. Mom, Dad, this is General Tokh, who has taken me in as a member of his family, sheltered me under his roof, cared for me when I couldn't function, and gone through great expense and great difficulty to keep me alive, both now and five years ago. If you want to thank anyone for my standing here beside you tonight, you thank *him*. I'm tired of you vilifying people you've never even met."

Tokh stood up, eyes blazing with delight. "*Gah!* The great Admiral Perrin of the Union Fleet! I am most honored to meet you, Admiral! Your power and strength caused us much grief. It is good that we may meet and come to understandings before trouble occurs."

Ramden Perrin shook his hand, the Union way. "I'm at a loss, sir. I don't understand how I've brought you grief when we've never met."

"For a year I listened to stories about the great Admiral Perrin and how he would blow my base from the planet, how large his fleet was, and how he would exact revenge should his daughter be harmed. We spent many man-hours searching for your fleet, monitoring for what move you would make. When my *aghát* made it behind lines, they met you and saw the words were truth. It has been a great asset for us to have your assistance instead of your hostility."

Perrin accepted the information with a raise of a silver eyebrow. "I see. Well, I would not dispute the claim of harm, but I'm not sure how much assistance I've given. You're the General Tokh Aila testified about, the one that held her hostage all those years ago? The one who damaged her speech and dumped her back in time? We spent many man-hours searching long and hard to capture you, but you slipped by us. You are still wanted for questioning. It puts me in a difficult place just talking to you."

Tokh hesitated only a moment. "I followed my orders and did my duty, no more, no less. If your daughter had stayed submissive like a proper female there would never have been a need for force. But I am sure you are aware, she is difficult to restrain. The fact I am misrepresented in the Union is the reason we must meet here."

"You above all people should know about duty, Daddy," Aila said. "Sit! Sit here with the General. You have much to discuss. He can tell you all about how he helped me, right down to stopping Vanora a split-second before she killed me." She pushed him into a chair and dragged Leila farther down the table to the female side.

"Aila! He's the one who held you hostage?" Leila whispered with terror in her eyes. "How can you…"

"And he's saved my life fifteen times in the last week alone," Aila replied. "Don't start."

"*Daran ama*, Leila," Aila said to the women. Mímihn stood up with a squeal to hug Leila, chattering at lightspeed. "Stand still, Mom. She can't see very well, she needs to get close to you. She might touch you, but it's okay. This is Mímihn. We would have been friends years ago, but I didn't speak enough Kerasi then. I can honestly say she's my best friend right now. If I could have a sister, I'd want her to be exactly like her."

"Hah! I fell for that once. She's not coming home with us, even if she's an orphan about to be executed," Leila warned. Aila had claimed Thayer was like a sister to her and begged to have her live with them. Leila had no charity left.

"You're safe, Mom. She's Tokh's second wife." Aila went down the line with introductions, translating as she went, but it was Zheníhda who seemed to take to Leila the most. Maybe it was the fact Leila was about the same age, or she was being a good hostess wife while Tokh spoke with the woman's husband, a man in decorated uniform, or the idea that Aila had a real mother and the burden of being responsible for someone Tokh randomly adopted would not fall on her after all, but her whole demeanor changed. She moved next to Leila, sent Dalo to get Leila some *lunahl*, and became a congenial hostess.

After a time, Masákh spoke to her ear and asked Aila to follow.

"Of course." Haghíde was off with his family, so she turned to Tótoghar. "Tótoghar, you've met my mother. Would you translate for her, please? I must meet someone else."

Leila's relationship with the *aghát* had been poor since the first time she laid eyes on them. It hadn't improved much, and none of them had forgotten. "I will do my best, as long as she does not hit me," he said, and came to sit with the women.

Masákh took her by the hand back to the ballroom. "Before they must leave, I wish you to meet my parents."

Aila stared at him in shock. "Your parents are here? You said they wouldn't be allowed at the palace."

"They would not have been allowed at a public ceremony under Nághtas," he clarified. "This is private and caste-neutral. They were invited, and I gave them the money to fly here in time so that they may meet you."

"That was very kind of you."

Masákh stopped at the doorway. "I must confess a secret before you meet them. It is a dark secret, not meant for other ears. Not even Tokh knows this, and he knows every event in my life for the last ten years. I hope it will not change your opinion of me, but I wish you to know before you make further plans. My parents are only *rhibáni*. I could not be accepted into an elite military academy as a *rhibáni*, therefore my sponsoring General had my birth papers changed to read *whátaral*. I have been *whátaral* only since the age of nine."

Aila kissed him on the cheek, right there in public. "You forget, we don't have castes in the Union. I don't care. I was not born *dáhneg*, either. I don't care if your parents are *ghinadín*, they still birthed a son who is the greatest man I've ever met."

He gave his soft snort of amusement. "You say that because you were not born here. Come."

Huddled in a corner of the grand ballroom, Masákh's family seemed frightened to be there, watching every person coming and going with just a touch of terror, waiting for the guard to appear who would beat them and throw them out for soiling the festivities. They could not bear to sit and shifted feet anxiously, pacing without going anywhere. The sight of Masákh brought a visible sense of relief. They

298

dressed well, but even Aila knew the clothing was not close to palace standards, and she realized the stress they must have felt. By Kerasi law they could not touch their own son, just one caste above them – with his added privilege, now two, and here they were at the royal palace, afraid of a reprimand just for stepping inside the grounds. Her heart went out to them.

Masákh motioned to her to come closer. "You have asked repeatedly when I will take a wife. The Union councilmember Aila has agreed to be my firstwife."

Masákh's mother lost her control. She'd seen the awards, spotted the *dáhneg* badge on Aila's chest, didn't dare touch her, so she wrung her hands, wailing with joy, and leaned on her daughter.

Damn convention! The Emperor declared the room caste-free. Aila stepped around the table and put her arms around Mrs. gha Lil. His mother cried harder, overwhelmed, and his sister joined in.

Masákh introduced her to his father, Masaruhn, a gentle-seeming man wrinkled and leathery from strong sun. His mother Namig was shy and reserved, with the same piercing dark eyes Aila had grown to adore. Namig had burst with pride over her son since he was first spotted by the military; being brought to the palace to see him honored by the Emperor himself was more than she could handle. She grasped Aila's hand and continued to weep in waves throughout the visit, thanking her over and over. Aila had heard of Masákh's older sister only once in passing. Tagani was bronze and slender, accompanied by her husband as a proper Kerasi woman would be. Her perceptive eyes took in everything around her, sorted it in her head and said little about it, so very much like her brother. Aila was now unsure how much of Masákh was just Masákh and how much she'd always chalked up to *aghát* training.

The surprise was his younger brother Narukh, someone Masákh had never mentioned. Of course, if Masákh was taken from home at the age of nine, and his brother was not more than four or five, he would never have grown up knowing him, a tragic side effect of being too exceptional too young. Narukh was more relaxed than his siblings, more easygoing, more talkative. He ran a second store for their father, making a decent *rhibáni* wage for his wife and two children. Aila realized with a shock he had Masákh's hair and jawbone, but looked like an average Kerasi, with a bronze skin tone. She'd grown accustomed to Masákh looking demi-Human, bleached and two-eyebrowed, with no chin hank. This, between his father and brother, was what he should have looked like. The difference shouldn't have mattered, but at the moment it did.

For the first time Aila sat down with non-military Kerasi, normal, ordinary middle-class people who did honest work for a living. They had no ties to the perks the upper echelons of the military complex enjoyed beyond Masákh sending them money for vacations and luxuries, their public meetings with their son strained by the difference in caste, but Aila liked them. They were just – normal people.

"Do you wish your parents to meet them?" Masákh offered.

Aila glanced at the gha Lils. "No," she decided. "Not here. Not now. This is too much for your mother. My mother is already half out an airlock. I don't want to make her worse. Perhaps there can be another time, more private." Masákh nodded.

Aila lingered with the gha Lils too long before slipping back to check on her parents. Dad and Tokh weren't bleeding, so they must be getting along. Mímihn squeezed her hand as she sat.

"You were gone so long!"

"I must meet Masákh's parents."

"Ah. Yes, you must."

Leila leaned around Mímihn. "Aila, our shuttle's leaving in an hour. You need to be ready."

"An *hour*?" Aila realized it would take her that long to say goodbye. She was nowhere near ready. The thought of leaving filled her with dread, and she wanted nothing more than to sneak off to one of the thousands of closets the palace had and be left behind. Aila started to make her way around the table with a heavy heart.

She made it down to her father and rubbed a hand down his back. "Find things to talk about?"

Ramden Perrin nodded. "Yes. I think we've cleared the air a bit on a few things. I don't think we see perfectly eye to eye, but it's a start."

"Mother says we're boarding soon."

"I suppose I better see to her." He stood up and bowed to the General.

Tokh stood as well. "We will see you to your ship, make sure you get there safely. Come, I will return you to your people."

300

He walked Aila over to Secretary Hhani, no longer a strange name on a list. "I return her to the Union as promised. I trust you will have removed any dangers to her. I have put her under the protection of my name; should your people harm her, it will create an incident between our worlds."

"Aila's a very valued member of our staff," Bindai Hhani said. "We regret the incident that took place at your home. We were unaware of how deep the deceit ran, a great mistake on our part, one that will not be repeated. The Union thanks you, General Tokh, for all you have done for us. We would encourage you to make a formal visit, be our guest, let us show you the best we have to offer, instead of some of the worst."

Tokh chuckled, the points of his teeth showing. "It is a gracious offer, Secretary Hhani, but I do not travel where there is a price on my head."

Hhani's face colored up. "I will personally see that you are cleared of any charges against you. I think you have earned that right."

"I've only been pleading that for the last four years," Aila said wryly. "They never should have been there to start with."

Tokh gave a nod. "You do that, and my sources confirm it, I would be willing to make the journey. My wife has become fond of your emissary, and would very much wish to visit her."

Hhani smiled, an honest gesture of good will. He gave a nod. "Very good. Contact Aila with possible dates, she will contact me, and we will see what can be arranged."

"I will wish to tour your military schools, compare them to ours, as well as your educational programs for females. I wish to see how you develop students like Aila. My daughter will be among the first to benefit from the Emperor's extended female programs; I wish her to learn to be as quick and tough as your females."

"None of that is classified; you may tour as many as you'd like."

Tokh gave a short bow. "Most excellent. Thank you."

Aila and Masákh reclaimed their luggage from the rooms on the fourth floor. "Where will you be staying?" Masákh asked her.

She turned and stared at him. "I thought I was staying with you? Aren't I?"

Masákh nodded. "Making certain your mother did not convince you otherwise. She will not be joining us, will she?"

"Hah! I'm not telling her the cabin number."

"Knowing your mother, she will beat on every door of the ship until she finds you."

Aila kissed him on the lips. "And if she does, we won't answer."

Tokh and the majority of his contingent, plus eight palace guards and three of the translation liaisons, followed them to the roof. The rest of the Union party boarded the shuttle ahead of them. Mímihn clung to Aila's arm, sobbing.

Aila stopped to hug her. "Please do not be sad. We can now send messages to each other, tell everything that is happening. I will return again, and bring you beautiful things from my world."

"I don't want you to go. Dalo will return home, and I will be left with no one but the *hyrak*."

Aila smoothed Mímihn's hair, done up so fancy for the celebration. "I don't think she will be as mean anymore. Maybe being here, learning things, will open her eyes. Be nice, and she will have to be nice in return."

Mímihn sniffed. "I will. I must be a good mother to Kesseh. Tokh promised me he will not make her marry at fourteen, like me."

Aila smiled. "He's a good man." She said goodbyes all around once more.

She saved Tokh for last. The engines on the shuttle began to rev up, making her raise her voice. "General, despite my fears and distrusts, you have been far too kind. I am deeply in your debt. I hope I can repay you some day."

"There is no debt, just repayment for wrongs earlier in the course of my duty. It took longer than expected, but everything did go by plan, just not the way we believed it would."

"I would like to come back and visit, if I may."

Tokh held his head high, and his eyes narrowed. "You are dar-Giláhn. I will be insulted if you do not. I will expect you for the New Year's celebrations. I will recall Masákh, and you will either follow him or be without."

"That's not going to happen," she said with a grin. "I will stay in communication, but do not trust the line. This is still all too new, with no working treaties yet."

"New to you, not to me," he said with a bow. "You will learn." He stepped forward and clapped a hand on her shoulder, the most he could do in public. Aila waited until he was done, then shook his hand in both of hers. She leaned in and gave him a peck above his eye. "Thank you again, General." She, Aila Perrin, former prisoner of war, kissed her fearsome captor, and meant every good wish behind it. Sometimes the world was too strange for words.

She had one foot on the shuttle step when Aila turned around and shouted, "*Hasak sim toh Haverowakh!*"

Tokh tipped his head to be sure he heard right, then let loose with a hard, braying laugh. He raised a fist high. "*Sukh! Sukh jihtya!*"

Aila entered the shuttle, followed by Masákh. She walked down the center corridor to the pod of recliners where her parents were and sat. The warning for liftoff came on, and they strapped down. The shuttle engines revved up to a monstrous noise, the ship shuddered, rocked, and lifted upward. She was going home.

"What did you say to him?" her mother asked.

"I reminded him I'm a pain in the ass, and he agreed."

"You realize we're going to have a long chat tomorrow, *in private*," Leila said, but her voice was civil.

Aila sighed. "I know."

"Your lady friends were very nice, though. That little one is something else. She reminds me of Mrs. Palmeter's daughter Jenna. Right down to that eyebrow."

Aila laughed softly. "Mímihn? I've never seen someone so determined to make the world a better place just by being happy. She's such a sweetheart. Tokh loves her very much."

"You know it's not going to be all fun and games when we get back," Ramden warned her. "The Kerasi may have thrown medals at you, but you still have to answer for the death of Secretary Kel on Union terms."

"What!" Aila's stomach tightened up to the point she felt ill. She leaned forward and glanced down the row to Bindai Hhani, speaking with his staff. Why hadn't he mentioned that to her earlier? What did he know? She'd speak with him as soon as they boarded the ship. Was it too late to turn the shuttle around and go back? "Daddy, he held a weapon to my head and threatened to kill me, among other things. What was I supposed to do?"

"The Emperor was very forthcoming with information, and I know he did it to clear you, but video works two ways, to clear and condemn," her father said. "Now, I can almost guarantee it will be just a formality, the evidence is overwhelmingly in your favor, but you can't take it as a joke, either."

Masákh's face had gone cold. Aila knew the look. He was not happy, and unhappy Masákh made her want to run. "As a representative of Emperor Nadigh of the Kerasi Coalition, I would caution your government to consider their proceedings carefully. The Emperor has made Aila a defender of the Kerasi people; to have her imprisoned by her own government could become an incident between us."

"You've always treated it as a joke, Aila. From the very start," Leila said. Her voice was wounded, and she stared out the port into the darkness, watching the lights of the cities disappear as they gained altitude. There was a brief, nauseating see-saw feeling as the artificial gravity kicked in. "You have no idea what you put us through."

"I could say the same, Mom."

Ramden held up a hand of peace. "As I said, it should be a formality. No one is going to dispute what happened or that the action wasn't justified – Bindai and Ross witnessed the last attack themselves. We just have to make a formal dismissal to close the books. Don't worry."

Aila slipped her hand into Masákh's. She leaned against his arm. "Are you really sure you want to get into this mess?"

His fingers tightened on hers, skin melding to skin and all the intimacy it implied. "For twenty-five years I have followed every order given to me without question, as precisely as possible. This may be the first time I have been able to choose a directive for my life by myself. I understand the difficulties I will face, but at the moment it is what I desire above all else."

Aila snuggled closer against him. She really wanted to kiss him for that statement, but visions of her mother screaming and slapping her for it flashed through her head. Masákh would grab Leila to stop her, Dad would grab Masákh, and there would be a major brawl before they ever made orbit. Kissing would have to wait for closed doors.

She gazed up at him, the stars in her eyes blinding in their sparkle. The world around them could blow up for all she cared, as long as he was with her. "Twenty-five years ago you set out to change a world. You and me? Together, we're going to change a universe."

When Tokh dar-Giláhn was young, he wanted just one thing: to walk around his town as one of the proud military cadets on Graduation Day, with a dashing uniform and sword. When he's snatched from the Academy by a perceptive General before he can graduate, Tokh's life begins an upward spiral toward power and glory that he never imagined.

Tokh is forced to balance his climbing military career against an explosive personal life that wants to hold him back: a wife he didn't want, sons who won't respect his will, a second wife he never intended, children younger than his grandchildren, and the accidental acquisition of his first true love, a blinded teenage consort, Mímihn; a combination of women that threatens to tear everything apart.

As Tokh's success on the Emperor's Emissary Project sends him ever deeper into palace politics and the tenuous diplomatic relations with the Planetary Union, he starts to believe in the Emperor's treasonous vision: why shouldn't a female take the throne of Kerasím? And why shouldn't his daughter be educated to be her first advisor?

Honor to the Emperor

Book three of the Prisoner of the Mind series

Susan Olesen began publishing her own magazine at the age of fifteen and hasn't stopped writing since. When away from the computer she has raised three children, three foster children, various unofficial adopted kids, and has started all over again with raising her granddaughter. If it's hungry or homeless, it will find her. Follow her on Facebook at Susan Olesen Author Page, or at cheshirelibraryblog.com. *Conflicts of Interest* is her seventh novel.